DREAM GIRL

INTO THE PARALLEL OMEGAVERSE
BOOK 1

JANE HANDLER

Dream Girl

Book One: Into the Parallel Omegaverse

Jane Handler

To everyone who wished they'd find a portal to another world or simply fall into one.

About This Story

Welcome to the parallel omegaverse! *Dream Girl* is a why-choose, non-shifting, omegaverse, fated-mate, portal romance and is book one of the *Into the Parallel Omegaverse* trilogy. *Dream Girl* ends on a cliffhanger, but I promise that Grace and her guys get a happily ever after in book three. This is a 'why-choose' romance, so Grace, the female main character, gets her HEA with multiple people, and ultimately, it's m/m/m/m/f/m. This trilogy is set in the same world as the HockeyVerse series, but you don't need to have read them to enjoy this series.

This is a portal romance–Grace is from our world and falls into another. Wes lives in a parallel world that's similar to ours. However, this world, being omegaverse, has evolved a bit differently, which affects everything from physical places to technology to laws. For example, the drinking age and driving age are both eighteen. The biggest difference is that alphas, betas, omegas, and many other designations exist. Each designation has specific characteristics.

In Wes' world, all love is legal and accepted, with same-sex and polyamorous relationships being common. Many people live in packs, and registered packs have all the legal rights of families, no matter what designation comprises them. There are also plenty of couples and throuples. Gender and racial equality are widespread. Birth control is freely available to all genders and designations.

While this story and world aren't particularly dark, some characters have darker pasts. As a teen, Grace suffered physical and mental abuse at the hands of her religious mother and church. Both she and another character have significant scars. Some characters have had mental health struggles, others have suffered the loss of family members or partners, and one has struggled with his designation. There is an attempted physical assault, as well as gun violence–though no one is injured. There's also some bullying/gaslighting outside the pack. Grace is bullied a little by someone in the pack. There's no cheating, no third-act breakup, and while there're some women causing drama, it's not to steal Grace's guys.

This is meant for adult readers. There are graphic spice scenes, some of which include multiple partners and crossing of swords. It also contains bonding, biting, knotting, praise, and other spicy things.

Enjoy your trip to the Parallel Omegaverse. Dreams aren't real–until they are.

If you're coming from the HockeyVerse: This is Grace/Rich Big Sister's story and this series comes *before* Finding the Forward. Part One of Finding the Forward starts a few weeks after this trilogy ends. You're not going to meet Verity until the next book. Yes, Grace's story is wild, but hang on, everything will explain itself in time.

Chapter One

Grace

Darkness swirled around me, chest pounding, sweat dripping down my back, as I fled as if my life depended on it.

Keep going, just keep going.

I tripped, hands stinging as I hit the ground. Every inch of me screamed to give up and just curl into a ball on the ground.

No. Stopping wasn't an option.

Picking myself up, I continued to run, pain clouding my head.

There's some light. Just a little further…

I looked around, a frown tugging at my lips. Where was I going again? None of this looked familiar.

Fatigue coated me. Each step was like running through quicksand. Did I have to keep moving?

No. No stopping. I had to keep going; I had to get…

But they were going to catch…

Who? What? Why? My head pounded, as my thoughts vanished like words off a dry-erase board. I paused, rubbing my head.

A lamppost illuminated a couple of benches through the trees. Maybe I could take a little break and compose my thoughts.

I ran to the park bench. My body collapsed onto it, exhausted. Something nagged in the darkest reaches of my memory. But I couldn't find it in myself to get up and keep moving.

Instead, I curled up on the bench. I'd rest for a moment, and that would make everything better.

"Hey there, why are you sleeping by yourself?" someone said, voice so loud I winced inwardly.

"Do you need a warm place to sleep? I'll give it to you," a different male voice jeered.

My eyes opened, head pounding. Four young guys that I'd never seen before crowded me. Where was I? I rubbed my head and hit a sore spot. *Ow.* Beyond the four guys were trees, green space, and playground toys. It wasn't quite daylight, though the lamp above me had gone out, and I shivered from the cold.

Why was I on a bench? Had my roommate kicked me out again so her boyfriend could stay over?

Wait, did I even have a roommate? I didn't recognize this park.

The blue maxi dress I wore had a tag, making me reach up and scratch it as I shivered again. Snow dusted the ground. No, I wasn't dressed for the weather.

Snow?

"Are you going to say anything?" The first one poked me with his finger. "Don't you want to come with us?"

"Leave me alone," I snapped, not in the mood for this, swatting away his hand. How dare he touch me?

"Guys, knock it off, something's wrong," another said. "Look at her bruises."

Bruises. Had I fallen? My memories felt sluggish. Maybe I was hungover. Adrenaline shot through me as I got a flicker of something. Running. Fear.

"Did you piss off your alpha, Sweetheart? I'll give you some place to go." One got into my space, leering.

"Get away from me." I fumbled for pepper spray or keys. But I had no purse, no pockets.

Alpha. What? I frowned. I ached. They all smelled weird; not like body odor, more like I was in a candle shop–or a middle school hallway.

"A pretty little thing like you shouldn't be out here alone." He grabbed me, trying to pull me off the bench.

"GET OFF!" I struck out with my fist as blood roared in my ears. "Don't touch me."

"Ooh, a fighter," one sneered, getting close to me.

"What do you think you're doing?" A large officer stormed over.

"Don't you dare run," another uniformed officer said to the others. "Freeze, all of you!"

"We found her on the bench," one said, putting his hands up. "It's not what it looks like. We were gonna call someone."

"Were you?" The officer's eyebrows rose.

My body shuddered as I shrank away from them, making myself small on the bench, hands up. I wanted them all to go away so I could figure out what the hell was going on.

"Miss, you can't sleep here. After I get your statement, do you want me to take you to a shelter? You can have a hot breakfast and, if you want to, maybe someone can try to help you out?" the first officer suggested, his look softening.

At least I thought they were police officers. So many things crashed around in my head, confusion overwhelming me.

"Where am I? What if they get me?" My chest heaved with anxiety. I was supposed to be running away from someone. The idea of being caught made a sob rise in my chest, mixing with my panic.

No, they can't catch me.

"Who?" the officer asked, voice kind. He looked at the other guys. "Them?"

"No." Squeezing my eyes shut, I tried to press the memories out. "Someone else. But I... I don't remember." My voice was a whisper as I opened my eyes. "I have no idea how I got here."

"You're hauling us in?" one man said, as the second officer cuffed them.

"You were trying to assault her," the second officer retorted, as the first called for backup.

The first officer studied me. "Do you remember who gave you those bruises?"

I frowned and looked at my arms, mottled purple peeked out from my sleeves. When I touched my face, it was tender, and I winced.

What happened? It was dark, I was scared, being chased...

"No. Not them. The people chasing me... I think." That seemed about right.

"Some people chased you, and you ended up sleeping here in the park?" His voice was soft and not accusing. "It's a little cold for that."

"Yeah." My teeth chattered. "Everything's a little foggy." I rubbed my head, willing myself to remember.

"What's your name?" he asked.

My mouth opened to answer, but nothing came out. I had a name. I could almost hear it. Looking around, my heart pounded with panic. "I don't know. Where am I? How did I get here?"

"You don't remember your name? Do you have an ID or your phone?" he asked.

"I... I don't have my purse." I frowned. It seemed like I had nothing with me—no phone, no wallet, and no ID. I looked up at him, confusion making my heart thump in my chest, my throat swelling. "I don't know what's going on." Tears pricked my eyes and dizziness washed over me.

"That's fine," he soothed. "We're going to get you checked out, and then I'll bring you to the station so we can figure out what happened. Come over to my car with me?"

"Am I in trouble?" Unease coursed through me. I *was* in trouble. Big trouble. I just couldn't remember why. Or what kind.

"No, you're not in trouble. You look cold. Let me get you a blanket." The officer led me to his police car.

Opening the car door, he had me get in. Taking a blanket out of a plastic wrapper, he draped it around me.

Much better.

"Can I get your thumbprint?" He held out a little box about the size of a cell phone.

I pressed my finger to the pad on the bottom half of the box. While I didn't know what it did, I didn't see any reason not to. The box beeped, and something flashed up on the screen at the top.

"Huh." The officer frowned at the box.

A cute little mini-ambulance drove up, and someone got out. The officer motioned her over.

"Can you give her a look-over? She's disoriented," the officer said to her, then turned to me. "Let the medic check you out, I'll be right back."

The medic took me to the little ambulance and looked me over, asking me questions, and running some tests using some unfamiliar instruments. I must be in a fancy county. Finally, the officer came back over to us.

The medic looked over at the officer when he came back. "The toxicology insta-screen came back negative, but that doesn't mean someone didn't slip her something harder than a recreational. Eazy-E, maybe? Pretty sure she's got a concussion, but she'll be okay until she can get to a doctor. No signs of exposure either. Thank goodness."

I had no idea what Eazy-E was, but I was hardly up on the latest street drugs.

"We're going to take her in and see if we can't figure out who she is," the officer said.

"Okay." No one could get me if I was in a police station. Right?

He helped me into the backseat, and he and his partner got into the front. Their cologne was overpowering, but I couldn't open the window.

I gazed out the window as we drove. None of the streets looked familiar. In the sunrise, I could see the outline of a city, and some mountains. It was quite beautiful here.

Mountains? Did I live near mountains?

Besides being unfamiliar, everything was a smidge different from what I was used to. Even the air felt different, clean and crisp, maybe a little thinner. *Eastside Station,* the sign said. *The eastside of what?* But I didn't want to ask too many questions until I knew what was going on.

Maybe one of my colleagues was playing a prank? They got me drunk, drove me into the next state, and left me there? I *had* done something... messed up their research, maybe? Why couldn't I remember?

Think, think.

That feeling of being chased, of heart-stopping *fear*, lingered. Also, I had bruises. My colleagues wouldn't hurt me. While the dress was pretty, it was itchy and had no pockets.

"Let's get you some tea," the first officer said as we entered the station. "Or would you rather have some coffee?"

"I'd like coffee, please." That sounded about right.

He led me down the hall and into a small room that looked more like a little living room than an interrogation room, but seemed to have a two-way mirror. The other officer brought me a coffee and a breakfast sandwich. I still had the blanket, which was fluffy and soft.

"Would you like another officer to sit in with us?" the first asked as the second left, leaving the door open.

I shook my head. "I'm okay."

"Let's go over everything you remember about your ending up on the bench, and the betas who tried to assault you," the first officer said, taking out a tablet.

Betas? I frowned.

I told him everything that I could remember as I gobbled the breakfast sandwich. While hot and filling, it didn't quite taste right; neither did the coffee.

The second officer came in with a little box again, and they had me put my thumb on it. Again.

Like before, it beeped, and he frowned. "That's odd. Let me try this."

We tried a different box that took a picture of my face.

It also beeped and flashed. The second officer's brow furrowed. "Huh."

"We'll try again later. A grid is down, so that's probably it." The officer waved him off, and we went back to the questions.

A little later, a woman in a lab coat strode in.

"I'm going to take a couple of blood tests. Quick and easy," she told me. Something about her was commanding. Like if she wasn't in charge, she was still someone.

"Um, okay." Blood tests? At a police station? But again, I didn't see any reason not to cooperate. If anything, I was glad everyone was going to so much trouble to help me, and I felt safe here.

She had two tiny pin prick things and stuck my finger with them. It didn't hurt, it wasn't even like being pricked on a thorn. I wasn't sure what she was doing, but it was simple, easy, and painless. My kind of medicine.

"You did such a great job." One, she put back into a vial, and the other one turned black. Her brow furrowed at the color. "Huh. It must be a bad test." She put it in a tiny medical waste bag and left.

"You're doing great. Let's talk about you a little. You don't remember your name, right, what about your birth date?" the officer asked, returning his attention to me after she left.

"Oh, I remember that." There it was. I gave it to him. Why I remembered that and not my name, I didn't know. The human mind was weird.

"You're sure?" His eyebrows rose.

"Of course. I'm twenty-seven." Ooh, I remembered something. "It seems like I haven't forgotten everything. Though what I can and can't remember is strange."

"The brain *is* funny like that." He asked me a bunch of other questions. My address, which I couldn't remember. Names of friends, some of which I could recall, employer, which I couldn't, occupation...

"I'm a..." I closed my eyes again. *Think, brain, think.* "I think I'm a mathematician." That sounded mostly right.

He asked me more questions. But it seemed like even when I could remember my answers weren't the ones he was looking for, which made my belly churn. Wrong answers led to bad places.

"What's your designation?" the officer asked. "Can you remember? That's going to help determine what resources we can use to help you."

Designation? "Um, I'm a heterosexual cisgender female."

He blinked. My belly sank. That wasn't the answer he wanted. My belly clenched in fear. What was he asking? Whatever it was, I didn't think I had one.

"Hey, it's okay," he soothed. "Can you remember anyone else we could call to get you? A roommate? Sibling? Friend? Significant other? Alpha?" He stared at my neck, then his gaze flickered to my hands.

I frowned. "Alpha?"

"Yes, or your pack? Your family?" he suggested. "Anyone?"

Pack? Pack of what?

He leaned forward. "If they're the ones that hurt you, you don't have to go back to them. I promise. We're just trying to figure out who you are so we can get you somewhere safe."

"I don't think I talk to my family. I..." I chewed on my lower lip. "Yeah. I think that my mother's gone." I could remember that much, but not specifics like her name or what she looked like. Or how she died. But I knew our relationship wasn't good.

"I'm sorry to hear that, but think—anything could be helpful," he prodded.

"I... I knew an alpha once. But he didn't hurt me. He'd never hurt me," I blurted as little bubbles in my brain burst with fleeting memories. A face. A laugh. Us sitting on the swings. Him holding me.

He'd been my best friend... and so much more.

"Do you remember his name?"

Another bubble popped, revealing a hint of memory. "His name's Fade. But..."

The next memory was like a punch in the stomach, and I flinched.

"He's not real." My chest shuddered at the memories of that painful lesson. "Alphas aren't real. He was just a dream." Tears pricked my eyes.

I wished he'd been real. Once I even thought he was.

But that was a very long time ago.

The look on the officer's face told me that wasn't what he wanted to hear, and my hands shook. This didn't make sense. It didn't help that it hurt to think.

But I also didn't want to end up in a psych ward. *Keep it together.* I took a deep breath. *3.1415926535,* I recited in my head to calm myself down. I exhaled and smiled.

"Sorry, sorry. I don't know what I'm saying, officer," I deflected, trying to smooth things over, wiping the tears from my eyes. "I'm pretty disoriented. Um, I know it's early, but did you get a hold of anyone? I know the ambulance checked me out, but I should probably go to the doctor."

"Let me check on that." With a nod, the officer stood and left the room, leaving the door a little open like before.

Hopefully, one of my friends would come and get me.

There was a knock on the open door, and a large officer walked in. He was older than the others and had a little gray in his beard, and dark skin, reminding me of the sergeant on a TV show I liked.

Wow, I could remember that but not my name. *Good job, brain. Not.*

"Hi, I'm Sergeant Hawthorne." He came over to the armchair where I was sitting. "Are you doing okay?"

"I..." Time to smooth everything over. Taking a deep breath, I blurted, "I'm so sorry for sleeping on the bench. Hopefully, I didn't break any laws. I'm so sorry that I don't remember much that's useful."

"It's okay. Please, may I sit?" He gestured to the other chair where the officer had been sitting.

"Sure. Am I almost done here?" Of course, I had no money, no ID, no phone, no insurance card. All that made me anxious since I still didn't understand what had happened. If they couldn't help me, maybe the hospital could?

"We can't find any of your friends. You probably have a concussion, and it's making it hard for you to remember, and you're scrambling their names," he explained, expression sympathetic.

There was something very relaxing about the way he smelled. I needed to get some of that to spray at work on stressful days.

Sergeant Hawthorne continued, "Did you want to press charges against those betas in the park?"

"No, sir." I shook my head. While it had been scary, I was pretty sure they weren't the ones I was running from.

What was going on? What I could and couldn't remember made no sense. I squeezed my eyes shut and tried to take another breath, but it came out like a shudder instead.

"Are you all right?" His voice was soft.

"I'm so confused. Why can't I remember anything useful?" I gasped.

"This must be scary. Can we talk about Fade?"

"He didn't hurt me." I shook my head, as more memory-bubbles popped, but they were older memories. No, often I'd felt like Fade was the only one who consistently showed me any genuine kindness. Which was why he was *imaginary*.

"He's your alpha?" the sergeant prodded.

I frowned, trying to remember more, then shook my head. "It was a long time ago, and I imagined him. He's not real–and neither are alphas."

"I'm an alpha, and I'm pretty sure I'm real. Who told you that?" He gave me a puzzled look.

"My mom, the doctors, the people at..." I took another deep breath at the onslaught of images and partial memories. Painful ones. "It doesn't matter. It was a long time ago."

No, I could do without remembering all of that. *A name would be nice, though.*

"I see." His look turned sympathetic. "Can you tell me again, what you remember about your injuries? Was there an argument? Did someone hit you? Were you in a car accident?"

For a moment I tried to remember what I needed. Useful things. Not fantasies or bad things.

Think, think, think.

"All I remember is running in the dark and being afraid. I can't even remember where I was running to and who from and why." My shoulders slumped as defeat coated me.

"Don't worry, we'll figure it out." He stood and left.

The woman in the lab coat came back in. She, too, was wearing some scent that smelled nice, spicy. "Sorry, this morning has been busy. Let's try this again." She had two more pricky things with her. Again, one went into the vial, the other turned black. "What's your designation, Hun? Am I giving you the wrong test?"

"I... I don't have one." My nose scrunched in confusion.

Her expression softened. "Hun, if they told you that because you haven't awakened, they're full of bullshit. It should show up on the test. Do you remember whether someone gave you any drugs? Maybe a guy handed you a drink that you didn't see being made? Are you taking any medication? Trevadol maybe?"

"I don't remember." I frowned as a few memories bubbled to the surface. Once I might have taken medicine. Yes, my mother made me and I didn't like them. While I could be taking things now, I had no idea what.

It seemed the further back the memories, the easier they came.

But there were things I didn't want to remember.

"That's okay, you sit tight now." She left, the door still open.

"What do you think, Doctor?" Sergeant Hawthorne's voice drifted through the open door, though I couldn't see anyone.

"I think you're right. My guess would be an omega in hiding, using heavy-duty blockers and suppressants. Or she hasn't fully awakened. At her age she'd get some bullshit about being a late-bloomer. She could also be a petite beta on Trevadol or one of the other medications that can make the prick-test glitch. She should get a scan. And those bruises, I want to hurt whoever did that to her," the lab coat lady said.

"What do you think, Detective Lawson?" the sergeant added. "Thanks again for making the trek from Mid. No one handles these cases like you."

"Thanks, Sarge. I miss this place," a new female voice said.

"She mentioned alphas not existing. Maybe we're dealing with someone escaping from an extreme equalist cult?" he said.

"That's frightening. I'd like to talk to her, but first I want to make a call," the unfamiliar voice said. That must be Detective Lawson. Their voices faded as they walked away.

Was this a dream? This didn't feel like a dream. It was almost...

Another memory-bubble popped, and I squashed it down as fast as I could.

No. I didn't even dare to think such a dangerous thing.

I wasn't in another world any more than the guy from my dreams was real.

This was all just some weird, concussion-induced dream. I curled up in the chair and covered myself with the blanket. Maybe when I woke up everything would make sense.

Chapter Two

Wes

My cell phone rang, as I sat at my desk in my office, trying to work, head pounding. I winced, answering, "What?"

I felt like shit all morning. Even a breakfast burrito and three cups of coffee hadn't fixed it. But I had work to do—even if it hurt to stare at all my monitors.

"Hello to you, too," my older sister chuckled.

"What do you want?" I growled, not appreciating the interruption.

"I need you to come down to the Eastside station."

"Eastside?" I frowned at my phone. Lexi usually worked at the Midtown station. My sister was a detective with the Special Victims Unit.

Her voice grew soft. "Some betas tried to assault a young woman sleeping on a park bench. She's fine but shaken—and clearly suffered some trauma *before* the betas bothered her. She doesn't remember her name or where she's from and has no ID. We contacted every hospital, shelter, and in-patient facility in a hundred-mile radius, and no one matches her description. We even checked local universities and missing person reports."

"Wow, that's awful. Why are you calling me?" My pack was powerful–and rich—and my sister wasn't afraid to use our resources. But her pack had plenty of their own.

"When we ran her prints and facial recognition, since she has no ID and can't remember her name, they came up blank. It's as if there's no record of her. When we asked for her designation, she said she was a woman. We can't tell exactly what her designation is from her scent, so we did the prick-test, and it came up as *unknown*. She also seems to think alphas aren't real–"

My heart stopped, and my free hand clenched. I'd heard that before. My stomach churned. "Maybe she's been raised equalist."

As in those who thought designations shouldn't exist and were just fabrications to help keep the masses down.

"Maybe. However, she said that once she knew an alpha, but everyone told her that she imagined him," she told me. "Wes, she said his name was *Fade*. She smells of *peaches*."

"Don't fuck with me, Lexi." I hit my desk with my fist, stomach churning. No one had called me that in a very long time.

"I'm not. She looks an awful lot like the girl in your sketchbooks. Your dream girl from when we were kids," she breathed.

My jaw gritted. "Grace Ellington doesn't exist. Neither did where she said she came from. We looked and looked and never found her."

We'd looked for her *hard*. I'd hacked databases. Lexi had poked around. Nothing.

"Just come down–"

"No." It was so sharp it was almost an alpha bark. "While I feel sorry for this young woman, she's not my Grace, because *she doesn't exist*. I have to go." I hung up and put my head in my hands.

Grace Ellington had nearly destroyed me. Only Evan and the military saved me. There was no way my heart could take that again.

Because the girl I'd been in love with, my soulmate, was only a dream.

Chapter Three

Grace

The idea that I'd somehow wound up physically in another world, was ludicrous. It was something from fantasy novels and theoretical equations.

Yet what other explanation was there, other than my brain was so scrambled by the concussion that I was hearing and seeing things not quite right?

They also couldn't find me. Even if I were in another state, or Canada, shouldn't someone be able to find me in some database without me having an ID?

So many things here weren't quite right. It was as if I were in one of those movies where they'd shifted into another, slightly different version of their world.

"I'll take her to the Center in Midtown, considering I know everyone there and they have the most resources," Detective Lawson said, voice drifting through the open door.

"Hopefully, they can help her," the sergeant agreed.

At least, I thought it was him.

Detective Lawson came in, highlighted dark blonde hair in a smart bob, face kind and *almost* familiar. She wore a blue suit, not a uniform, and had a cute red tote-purse. Her scent was light, and crisp. She wasn't large like the other officers, however, she was much taller than me.

Okay, pretty much everyone was.

She smiled. "Are you ready to get out of here?"

"Please. You found my home? I want my bed." I stood, my very soul weary and ready for this to be over.

"We're going to get you looked over. They'll take care of you and figure out who you are so we can get you home. I'll go back to the station and try to find out who's chasing you," she replied.

"Thanks." At least they all believed me. This could have been *bad.*

I followed her through the station to an unmarked car. We started driving, and again, I looked out the window hoping I'd see something familiar. Anything.

We went to an unfamiliar drive-thru and got burgers and fries that still didn't taste right. Wherever I was, it was pretty, and clean--modern, but not so built up that there was no space.

Finally, we approached a building that looked like a hospital, one surrounded by other buildings–and a giant fence.

My chest seized. Of course they would. How could I have been so naïve?

"3.1415926535," I whispered, eyes closing. "8979323846."

"Are you all right?" Detective Lawson asked.

"You're placing me on a 5150?" I took another breath and muttered. "2643383279."

"A what?" Her face scrunched up in confusion.

"A psych hold?" One more breath. "5028841971."

"Of course not. We're going to the Omega Center Clinic. They'll check out your concussion and injuries and run some more tests. They may do a mental health evaluation, but that's standard. You'll probably meet with an advocate, which is also standard," she explained. "Are you reciting *Pi*?"

Yes. Yes, I was. *Good job, brain. Can you remember my name and how I got here now?*

I opened my eyes. "Why is there a fence?"

"It's the Omega Center. They want everyone to feel safe. The one where you live probably isn't this big. There's not just a clinic and a matching center here, there's also a full hospital, rec center, and housing. It's nice and safe–no one's going to bother you. The staff is almost entirely beta and omega. Alphas are restricted to very specific areas, and the security is all delta," she explained.

Nothing, this all meant *nothing*.

"There's also a high level of confidentiality, so if someone is looking for you, they shouldn't be able to find out that you're here," Detective Lawson added.

Well, that's a relief.

We drove to the gate. She flashed her badge, and the guard let her in. The door we went through, guarded by a guy in a security uniform, said *Clinic Entrance–No Alphas.*

The lobby was cute, with plush chairs, and a cart with tea and snacks, and cheerful art on the walls.

"Detective Lawson," the receptionist behind the desk greeted. She looked at me. "Hey, Hun."

"Jane Doe. Twenty-seven, concussion, and possible assault," Detective Lawson told her. "We'll need one of Claire's team," she told them.

"Jane Doe?" the receptionist blinked.

Detective Lawson leaned in and said some things I couldn't hear. Someone in scrubs, possibly a nurse, joined them.

I kept myself busy by getting some tea from the cart. Maybe that would taste better. There were pictures and colorful brochures. *Know your rights and options,* one said. *Rockland Regional Omega Center Services and Programs,* another stated.

Rockland. Where was that? I needed a map.

The nurse came over to me, expression kind—and she didn't reek of perfume. "Let's get started while they talk, okay, Hun?"

She took me back to a room where I stood on a machine. They did more pinpricks and the box thing. They, of course, didn't work, and no one really explained what they were for—and I didn't ask.

"We'll get some blood and do a full workup." The nurse brought me into another room and took a vial of blood. It was small and painless. After she finished, she took me to a cute exam room—like it actually felt inviting and comfortable, not sterile and impersonal. She asked me a bunch of questions, some quite personal, then left, assuring me she'd be back soon.

Detective Lawson came back in. "They're going to get you checked out. Hopefully, they can help you with what happened. You can trust them, they'll take care of you, and I'll be in touch."

While I didn't want her to leave, I'm sure she had work to do. She left, and another woman came in. Cute, petite, and curvy, she had dark hair, and wore a badge with her photo and the word *Advocate* on it and a polo shirt that said *Rockland Regional Omega Center.*

"Hi, I'm Carly. I'm an advocate here at the Center, and I'm going to stay with you while you get checked out. While we have a lot to talk about, the nurse is going to do some exams, and then we'll get some scans. A few other people might want to talk to you, too. Are you hungry?" she asked.

I shook my head. "I'm fine. Thanks."

"It's okay to be scared. We can get you some clean, comfortable clothes, too. Your dress is torn and dirty." She smiled and squeezed my hand.

I started to cry. "I don't know what's going on."

"Oh, Hun. No one's going to hurt you here. It's going to be okay," she assured, hugging me. Her body spray smelled of cookies, though it wasn't overwhelming.

It's going to be okay.

How I hoped that was true. Or that I at least remembered *something* useful. Soon.

Chapter Four

Evan

*B**eat with a stand mixer until stiff peaks appear.* I frowned at the recipe Wes' sister had sent me. Not only was I a terrible cook, but I had no idea what a stand mixer was. Could I just mix it with a spoon? We probably had one of those handheld mixers somewhere...

"What are you doing, Love?" One of my alphas, Brennan, came up behind me, the scent of pine trees enveloping me right before his muscular arms wrapped around my waist.

"Hi, Handsome. Just failing to make Wes a cake. Proving, yet again, that I'm a shit omega." I grinned. The stereotypical omega was a soft, tiny female that loved to cook and craft and stay home. I was a big dude, held down a job, and couldn't cook worth a damn.

Brennan trailed kisses down my neck. "You're kidding, right? Otherwise, I'm going to have to punish you for talking badly about yourself again."

"I'm kidding." I hummed as I felt his cock press into my backside. For a while, I'd lived in fear that some perfect little omega would steal my alphas from me. But it wasn't like that anymore.

"Why are you making a cake, it's not his birthday yet?" The kisses intensified, as Brennan focused on his bond mark at the base of my neck, making me shiver.

Brennan was the tallest in the pack–even taller than me. He was muscular and fit, but not broad. His black hair was neatly trimmed, pale face cleanly shaved, and those blue eyes always made me swoon.

"Wes has been having a bad day. I thought it would be nice to make his favorite. But, considering I have no idea what I'm doing, I might just cheer him up some other way instead." I squirmed as Brennan's hands roamed, threatening to distract me from my task. My cell phone on the counter rang.

"Leave it," Brennan breathed in my ear, pressing harder into me.

I glanced over. "I'm on call, and it's the Center. Which means I've got to take it. I'm sorry." Pushing down the desire to let him take me to bed, I grabbed it. "This is Evan."

"Hey, Evan, it's Claire, I need an advocate," she said.

I switched into work mode. "I'll be right there, what do we have?"

"Sixteen-year-old omega that's just awakened. Mom's insistent she gets matched immediately even though she isn't of age–or anywhere near her first heat. She won't listen to the doctors. The girl's agreeing with her mom, but I'm not sure that I believe her. We're a little overwhelmed here today, so I need you to come in and do your thing," Claire said.

Matching a newly awakened sixteen-year-old? Yeah, not in this century.

"I'll be right there." I gave Brennan an apologetic kiss and straightened his tie. "It's the usual. I'll be back. You look handsome."

Brennan sighed. "If you weren't doing something important, I'd order you to stay home so I could take this suit off and miss my dinner."

"Sure, you would." I washed my hands and shoved my phone in my pocket, giving him a wink.

My guys respected me. They also understood my work. While there were plenty of laws to protect omegas, someone had to speak up for the ones too afraid, young, or naïve to do it themselves.

"Don't you have a party to attend with your parents tonight?" I added, given he was in a tux, feet bare.

He went to a lot of fancy events with his family. Often, Jett or I went with him. One thing about Brennan was that he looked good in everything.

Or nothing.

"Unfortunately. I can take you on my way there?" Brennan offered. "I know you can fend for yourself, but my Alpha instincts hate that you go off alone so much."

Alphas had a thing about protecting people—especially their mates. However, unlike most omegas, I was alpha-sized and ex-military. I could take care of myself. But I understood their worry, and it made me feel loved, not suffocated.

"I'd like a ride. Thank you." I started to clean up. "If Jett wants to stop by the Center after his shift with a caffeinated beverage and a ride home, I wouldn't mind."

Jett, being a beta and a police officer, could go places at the Center that Brennan couldn't. I had a feeling I was going to need a pick-me-up after this case.

Traffic made it take longer than usual to get to Midtown. The entire Center was surrounded by a large fence with a guard gate. We primarily used delta security. Deltas were one of the rarer designations but made for great protectors since they were physically strong enough to stand up to alphas and weren't going to be swayed by their bark, their alpha compulsion.

The best-known Center function was its matching program. Omegas could safely meet vetted packs and alphas, both for permanent bonding and to ease them through their heats if they weren't ready to mate–or simply didn't wish to.

Omegas were encouraged to register with their local Center after they awakened so that they could receive the healthcare they needed and get educated about their choices. Identified omegas that hadn't awakened were welcome, and we had plenty of classes and activities for them, too.

When we pulled up on his motorcycle to the guard station, I flashed my badge and Brennan showed his ID. He drove me up to the staff entrance, which said *Staff Only–No Alphas Allowed.*

I took off my helmet and gave my well-appointed alpha a kiss. "Thank you for the ride. Have fun."

Waving at the delta guard, I used my badge to get in and went to the main area the advocates used.

Claire was waiting for me and handed me a tablet. "Rose has gotten her checkup and bloodwork and is ready for you. I've separated her from her mother, but Mom's getting impatient."

"Suspicions?" I looked over the file.

"I'll let you do your magic; she's in room one." Claire was middle-aged, her long braids swinging as she moved. Like me, she wore a pink Omega Center polo and a badge.

Every omega who came to the Center was eligible for an advocate, who regularly met with them and acted as a guide and educator. Those under eighteen were legally required to have one. They could also be legally appointed. Mostly, I worked with teenagers and young adults. All our advocates were omegas or betas with omega family members. We had degrees in social work and extensive training. I might not be the advocate that stayed with her, but considering her age, I might.

The room Rose was in was cozy, like a little living room. Most of our spaces were designed to put omegas at ease. I watched through the window as the tiny, pretty, teenage redhead played a game on her phone.

I knocked and then opened the door. Immediately, the girl tensed, and I made note of her body language, and how she relaxed as soon as she scented that I was an omega and not the giant alpha I resembled.

"Hi Rose, I'm Evan Wilson, and I'm an advocate. How are you?" I smiled, trying to put her at ease.

"You're an omega? You're so big." She had braces, her hair in a French braid, omega scent reminiscent of bubblegum.

While bloodwork could detect an omega during early puberty, an omega wasn't considered mature until they awakened or 'blossomed,' which meant that special tinge to their scent that marked them as an omega came in, indicating that they were ready for their heat, their fertile cycles, to start. Usually this happened during their late teens or early twenties. Sixteen was pretty early, though not unheard of.

"I am. May I sit?" I asked.

Rose nodded. "I've never met a male omega. Is your alpha a man or a woman? Sorry, is that rude?"

"Not at all. Where are you from, Rose?" I asked. Male omegas weren't nearly as rare as they used to be.

"A small town you've never heard of. It's a pretty long drive. Mama said the alphas would be better here."

While there was no law that said you couldn't go to another Center, and people came to us from all over since we were a regional center, something about her words made warning bells go off in my head.

"My pack's all guys. Want to see?" I pulled up a picture on my phone. A client's reaction to them always offered me insights.

"Ooh, they're so big. I can have more than one alpha?" She giggled as if the idea was scandalous. "They're so cute."

Huh. Packs were pretty common, especially in cities. My guess was that she was from farm country. Probably to the east of us, where the beta populations were thick and alphas and omegas were rarer. North was ranch country, which tended to have more packs.

"You can absolutely have more than one. Which one do you like best? I won't get jealous or tell." I grinned back. That, too, offered insight.

Of course, she could be from the west of us, where there were a lot of fundies. They thought packs were a way to control the population, and every alpha having an omega of their own was divine right.

"Him." She pointed to Wes, with his dimples.

"Good choice. Tell me about you, you're sixteen? What's your favorite subject in school?" I asked, trying to get the conversation going.

Rose told me all about school, her friends, and her hopes and dreams–like wanting to be a surgeon.

"You know, omega doctors are really needed, and not just in the Centers," I told her.

She frowned, salty sadness in her scent, as her shoulders slumped. "My mom says I can't be a doctor now."

"No? Why?" I frowned. There were no laws stopping her.

"She..." Rose sighed. "She pulled me out of high school. Said my omega scent was a distraction to the other students. But if I don't graduate, I can't go to a university, and if I don't do that, I can't go to medical school. She said that once I have babies, I won't have time for school or a serious job. We were going to cheer nationals." She wilted, her scent going sour.

So much to unpack there. Between science and laws, the days of omegas having to stay home were long gone. Not to mention legally, she *had* to be in school until she was eighteen.

"I know plenty of omegas with kids *and* careers. If you want to stay home, go for it. But there's no reason not to work if you're cautious," I told her. "Why doesn't your mom enroll you in an omega school?"

While nowadays most schools handled all designations, some omegas thrived in all-omega environments. These schools usually had competitive academic programs and classes about omega physiology and psychology. Some even facilitated job placements and pack matches.

"We can't afford it. I..." She chewed on her lower lip. "I'm hoping I'll get an indulgent alpha who will let me finish school and attend a university. My sister thinks that's dumb."

"It's not dumb at all. But you don't have to get matched right away. You're *sixteen.* We can put you on suppressants so you don't go into heat, get you scent and pheromone blockers, educate you on everything happening to your body, and outline all of your choices. Most importantly, you can finish school–and attend a university. Plenty of omegas do just that. You know, my packmate

has a foundation with scholarships for young omegas at one of the
local omega schools. With all those advanced classes you take, I
bet your grades would qualify you for it. I'm not sure if they have
cheer, but they have some sort of competitive dance team. Do you
want me to push it through?" I asked, hating the idea that she'd
been pulled out of school.

"Could you really?" Excitement danced in her eyes.

"I can and will." I disliked seeing omegas' options taken away
from them for non-reasons.

Her head bowed, as her scent continued to have a salty tinge.
"My mom would be mad. It's my duty to get matched as soon as
possible."

More warning bells. Hmm. Why would she want that?

An old practice was where alphas paid the omega's family a fee.
Now, packs gave their omegas money or assets of their own so
that they would have security and independence if they needed or
wanted it.

"I'm not your mom's advocate, I'm yours. Think about it. Now,
how do you feel? Was there anything that you think might have
brought it on?" Sometimes omegas awakened early during trau-
matic events because they hoped an alpha would save them.

She shook her head. "No, I was at cheer practice; I'm a flyer. I
felt fine. The day before I'd even had a physical. Coach got me into
the locker room and called my mom. I was surprised, because the
prick-test I had in middle school said that I was a beta. My mom
says she wasn't surprised given how small I am."

The scenario she described was perfectly reasonable because the
basic blood test, the prick-test, that most kids had in middle school
wasn't always accurate.

Something still didn't sit right with me.

"Do you have a significant other?" I asked her, looking for answers. Maybe she was getting romantic with an alpha partner, and her body got overexcited. I saw that a lot.

She shook her head. Okay, not that then.

I asked a few more questions about her life, then I stood. "How about if I get us a snack?"

Rose grinned. "I'd like that, thank you."

I left, noting that she didn't ask about her mom.

Claire watched us through the window. I left the room and joined her.

"Have another workup done–and keep her mom away for the time being. I want to make sure she didn't drug her teenager," I told Claire.

There were some drugs, both legal and illegal, that could push a beta on the edge of being an omega over–or make an unblossomed omega awaken.

"Really? Shit." Claire grimaced.

"There's just too many things that make it feel similar to what happened outside Rock Springs a couple of years ago. We should probably alert some local Centers in case this isn't isolated," I added.

"Good catch. That's why I called you. I am curious why they came all the way here," Claire added.

"Me, too. Given her school can't handle her, I recommend that she be sent to Finchley and can start considering matches no sooner than *after* graduation." I made notes in her file. Even that was early.

"Brennan just loves you offering scholarships to Finchley," Claire told me.

My alpha wouldn't argue with a teenager getting an education–and away from a potentially harmful family. There weren't many good reasons to match your teenager.

"After my talk with her mom, and speaking with the doctor and the intake counselor, I was getting the idea that Rose should be made a ward of the Center and sent to school so mom doesn't take her elsewhere, so I agree with your recommendation. Sixteen and they want her to be matched. Not in her dreams." Claire shook her head.

I nodded, glad my boss agreed. "Okay, let's get this rolling. I'm going to get her a snack."

Chapter Five

Evan

Leaning against the wall, I sighed, looking at my phone.

What I truly needed today couldn't be bought at a coffee shop.

We'd figured out that Rose's mom had bribed a doctor to use drugs on her teenager, hoping to snag a rich pack and leech off their assets, because their family was having money issues. The police were here and taking statements.

He didn't even illegally obtain the legal version of the drug, which was highly controlled. No, he used the street drug version, mega-push, that traffickers used. At least this seemed to be an isolated incident. Not that it made things any easier.

For now, Rose would stay in Center housing while she had more tests and went through some basic classes. Eventually she'd go to Finchley, one of the local omega schools, which had a high school program and dorms, so that she could finish her education.

"Some people suck." Carly joined me, her sugar cookie scent, with a hint of oak, preceding her.

"How's your day going?" I asked. Carly and I had first met in advocate training. She was also a mated omega.

"I could use a consult for my Jane Doe," Carly told me.

"Sure. I have some time. Jane Doe? Fundie?" Wow. Most people were in the database. One of the few groups that refused were the fundies. Sometimes we got young omegas who ran away to escape that life, usually ones who didn't want to be force-bonded to alphas twice their age.

"Something about her doesn't scream *fundie*. She also has a concussion and can't remember her name or address. The police thought she might be an omega, so Detective Lawson brought her here. But the designation tests all came up as *unknown*. Since she's gotten basic care, they want us to dump her in a shelter. I understand that we can't keep her if we're not sure she's an omega, but she's injured and scared." Carly frowned.

"Unknown? Even after the rare test?" Huh. There were three major designations—alpha, beta, and omega. There were also a handful of rarer, minor designations, like deltas and thetas, which were separate tests.

"Not yet, but we did the full blood workup and not just the prick-test. The lab is having issues because of the earlier grid out-age," Carly said as we walked toward the clinic wing.

Something felt *off*.

"Hey, it's Carly." She knocked on the open door of the exam room. "I brought my friend Evan."

All I could see was the back of a Center sweatshirt and short blonde hair.

"I want to go home. The doctors said I'm going to be fine with a bit of rest. I'm just disoriented from the concussion," the unnamed woman demanded.

"I know you want to go home, Hun. The moment you can remember your name and address, or the name of someone, your alpha, a friend, your pack, your neighbor, anyone we can find—we will get you there," Carly soothed.

"I gave you every name I remember, and I told you, the only alpha I know is Fade, and they took me from him." She turned on the bed, hugging herself, eyes teary, as the scent of peach pie with a hint of vanilla ice cream hit me right in the face, along with the tang of burnt sugar fear.

"Who took you from your alpha, Peaches?" My hands fisted. The time I'd spent in the military, and having younger sisters, left me with strong protective instincts, despite being an omega.

Was he the one who hurt her? She was probably in her mid-twenties. Freckles dotted her snub nose. Grey-blue eyes were framed with long lashes. Tiny and wearing center-issued sweats, her peachy aroma was so intense that I wanted to lick her. Bruises covered her face and neck.

"He wasn't real, anyway. Why do you keep asking me this? It's all in the past, promise. A childish fantasy. If I'm not on a 5150, then you need to let me go. I have work tomorrow. God, I feel awful." She curled up on the bed, putting her head on her knees.

Before I could go to her, Carly hauled me into the hall.

"Domestic violence?" I whispered. "Those bruises…"

"She says it wasn't this Fade, who of course had no hits in the system. Dr. Davidson found a mate bite though; an older one that looks odd. I can't smell a mate on her, but we know I don't have the best nose. Doc's running a test to see if there's a bond. Our girl here also has a lot of scars–old, scary scars. She has a concussion, which explains the disorientation. Still, I've never seen anything quite like this." Carly looked like she wanted to cry.

I didn't see a mate bite, which would indicate that she'd bonded with an alpha. But just because the neck was the favorite place to put it didn't mean it was the only one.

"Pack tattoo?" I asked. Not that all packs had them. We had rings. Mine was on my right pinky, right next to the ring Brennan gave me, when he, Jett, and I mated.

Carly shook her head. "I didn't see a wedding ring or anything either."

Wes and I didn't have rings, just matching tattoos.

"What does she remember? Anything?" I tried to put the pieces together.

"Her memory is really spotty. She said some guys were chasing her. She woke up in the park, unable to remember her name. Then, she got into a scuffle with some betas and ended up at the police station. None of this makes sense. Even the park cameras didn't tell the police how she got there. It's like she just... appeared?" Carly's nose scrunched.

"Maybe she escaped an illegal omega trafficking ring?" I asked. One had been busted last week, she could be part of the remnants. They could have scrubbed her record in preparation, which could explain why we couldn't find her.

"It could be that the massive power outage caused a glitch in the system when it went back up," Carly said.

"That makes much more sense." I went back inside the room, and before I could help myself, I was at the bed, wrapping the unknown young woman in a giant hug. "It's okay, Peaches. Cry all you need." I held her to me as she cried and cried, each sob shattering me into a million pieces.

This job did me in every single day. But we were saving lives.

She didn't have that special extra undertone that indicated an omega. I didn't get beta or alpha from her scent either. Given her size and how good she smelled, I could understand why they brought her here for more testing.

While omegas came in all shapes and sizes, including industrial-sized ones like me, they tended to be short and pretty–like Peaches here. She was *tiny*. Like way under five feet small. She looked underfed and was probably touch-starved. I could see it in her face and the haunted look in her eyes.

Where did you come from, Peaches?

"Evan, Rose is ready to get settled," Claire called from the doorway.

"Don't go," Peaches said, chin stubborn, tone pleading. "Please?"

"I'll come right back," I assured her.

I went over to the residential wing and got Rose settled, bringing her extra presents from the care closet, such as a giant stuffed animal, some big pillows, a cozy blanket, and some fuzzy slippers with a matching robe. All things that would help an omega feel safe.

"I don't understand. Why would she do that to me?" Rose said softly, but didn't cry, her bubblegum scent salty with sadness.

"I don't know. But we're going to keep you safe. You have such a bright future ahead of you, and we'll be with you every step of the way. Now, let's go over the agenda for the next few days," I promised.

After we finished, I stood. "I'll check in tomorrow. Call me anytime."

I snagged some ice cream from the dorm freezer, then went back over to the hospital wing to find Peaches.

"I didn't think you'd come back." Peaches had a blanket wrapped around her. Carly was still with her.

"Jett can wait." I grinned and held up three individual containers of ice cream. "I came with reinforcements. Which flavor do you want?"

"Jett's your significant other?" She took the cookie dough one and dug into the ice cream with the little spoon that came with it.

"One of them." I nodded, taking a seat next to the bed. I held out the other two to Carly, and she took the mint chip.

"How many do you have?" There was no judgment in Peaches' voice, only curiosity.

"There's five of us in my pack. Three alphas, one beta, and me. But I'm not with them all, if that makes any sense." I started to eat my chocolate ice cream.

We talked for a little bit as we ate our ice cream. Claire came to the door and motioned for Carly and I. We joined her in the hall.

"Boss says to discharge her and drive her to a shelter. The good one's full, but 4th Street has room," Claire told us, looking glum.

"4th Street? What about the hospital?" I frowned. 4th Street wasn't a domestic violence shelter, just a homeless shelter.

"She has no ID, and we can't find her in the system, so the hospital can't access her insurance or records. Given the tests can't confirm she's an omega, we can't claim she's under our jurisdiction. Which means we have to let her go. If I could keep her here longer, I would." Claire sighed, then left.

"Fine." Carly's scent went sour with unhappiness as she ran off toward the nurse's station.

"A shelter? What if they find me there? I could put other people in danger." Peaches stood there, blanket and all. Fear swam in her eyes, and the scent of burnt pie touched my nose.

"Who?" I stood closer to her.

She closed her eyes. "I can't quite remember who. But I think I remember why. They probably wanted my work. Government? Rival company?" Her shoulders slumped. "The police didn't find me with anything, not even a purse, so they must have gotten it. Not that I can remember what it was." She rubbed her head with a hand.

That didn't sound good. I was also good at reading people, and her fear was real. Why wasn't anyone taking her seriously?

"Come home with me. We'll keep you safe." The words came out of my mouth before my brain caught up.

The protective part of me wanted to bring her home where I'd cuddle her as we watched movies and ate takeout, using the guys as pillows.

"I don't know you, and for all I know..." She shuddered as I held her tight.

"I know. But we're good dudes. We can use our connections to find out who you are and who is after you. You'll be safe," I assured. That's what she needed right now.

"But why would you help me?" She frowned, looking up at me.

Why *was* I bringing a complete stranger to my house? Other than that she smelled good, and I wanted to? She could be dangerous to *us* in so many ways.

"I have three sisters, and if one of them couldn't remember who she was and feared for her life, I'd hope that some good people would keep her safe until I found her," I replied honestly. "Tell you what, Jett should be here any moment. Meet him and then decide. Anyway, our place would be better than a shelter. You can leave at any time if you find it too weird."

She thought for a moment. "Okay."

"I'll be right back." I joined Carly at the nurses' station. Dr. Davidson was arguing against sending her to a shelter.

"At least give me until I can finish running all her tests," Dr. Davidson muttered. "With that concussion, she should be under observation until morning. Her disorientation worries me."

"Talk to Claire, this isn't my call," Carly replied, expression sour.

"I'll bring her home with me," I told them.

"Oh, good." Dr. Davidson looked relieved. "When Detective Lawson comes looking for her, I don't want to explain why she's not here."

Very few people won against Detective Lawson. The detective might not be an alpha, but you crossed her at your own risk.

"There you are." Jett stood there holding my iced coffee, his light amber scent carrying a hint of pine. His black hair was pulled back for work, a couple wisps escaping, brushing a golden cheek. He wasn't as tall as me, or nearly as broad. But the beta was the fittest–and fastest–in the pack.

"I'll discharge her, and I'll let the detective know that she's with you," Dr. Davidson told me. "Take her to the hospital if things get worse, yes, she's not in the system, but they can't legally deny her if it's urgent. Also, she needs to follow up with her doctor. Not that it looks from her file like she has one. Maybe there's a clinic that you can recommend her to?"

"We'll watch her." I took a sip of iced coffee and hummed. "Thanks, Jett. This has been a day."

Jett pulled me aside. "Please tell me that you didn't adopt a stray. Bren will be livid if you bring a stranger into the house. That's a bad idea on so many levels. Why *would* you bring a strange omega into the house?"

His look went serious, and the scent of amber flared slightly, as we walked toward Peaches' room.

Omegas could get a little territorial of their alphas, especially when it came to those who were unbonded. But packs with multiple omegas existed–and I felt nothing but the continued urge to lick her.

"Not an omega. It's just for the night. I'm hoping you and Wes can use your skills to figure out who she is. She has amnesia, no ID on her, and we can't get a hit in the system," I told him, taking another sip.

"How can she *not* be in the system?" His eyebrows rose.

"I don't want to cause any problems." Peaches stood there in the hall, still wearing the blanket and some fuzzy slippers. "I just want to go home. Hmm, I can almost see the address in my mind. I'm near the research plaza. Maybe we can go for a drive? I'm sure I'll know it when I see it. Of course, I don't have keys, but at least we'd know?"

"Okay, which research plaza? Redstone?" I asked. It could be the Spaceplex. Jett could probably break into her place.

She frowned, then sighed, rubbing her head. "Why can't I remember anything useful?"

The look on Jett's face said it all. Yeah, there was something about her.

"This is Jett." I grinned. "Jett, this is, well, I've been calling her *Peaches.*"

A haunted look crossed her face, and her scent grew a tad salty. "Fade used to call me that."

"Is that okay if I call you that?"

She shrugged. "It's better than *hey you.*"

"You're okay with coming home with me for now?" I added. Something in me needed her to come home with us.

Part of me would be sad if she didn't come with us, because I felt an instant connection with her. Hopefully, one of my alphas felt the same way...

...and she didn't have a decent alpha who was looking for her. Okay, I should hope she had a decent alpha looking for her. Selfishly I wanted to keep her even though I knew nothing about her.

"I'm worried that they'll come after me. I can't even see their faces." She rubbed her temples. Her nails were sport-length and painted pale pink.

I held out my hand, desperate to touch her. "Come on, a movie and some food will make you feel better."

Chapter Six

Wes

"Anyone home?" I called from the empty kitchen as I entered from the garage, putting my shoes on the rack. Jett and Brennan didn't like shoes in the house. We had another rack by the front door, too.

My phone rang, and I ignored it. I didn't want to talk to my sister. Whatever girl she found wasn't my Grace. My Grace didn't exist.

If she did, somehow, somewhere, my heart simply couldn't take it.

"In here," Evan called from the living room. "We have company."

Company? We didn't entertain much. Hopefully, it wasn't my sister.

I stopped in my tracks as the scent of peaches hit me like a brick wall. My dick hardened instantly as my brain froze. A little blonde sat curled into Evan on the couch, with Jett on Evan's other side. The remains of dinner lay on the coffee table.

Evan looked over at me. I ducked back into the kitchen. Emotions bombarded me as I put a hand on the wall trying to settle myself.

"Babe, are you okay?" Evan came up behind me.

Fucking shit, my sister was right.

Grace was here.

And real.

"Why is Grace Ellington in the living room?" I shook. Turning, I held onto my omega so I wouldn't run to her.

What the fuck did I even do?

While I wasn't a small alpha, Evan was bigger than me, and a little taller. Closing my eyes, I grounded myself in his lemonade scent, as my headache grew worse.

"Didn't you see the group chat? Jane Doe ended up at the Center with amnesia and a concussion so I brought her home. Is your headache any better?" He rubbed the back of my skull. "Um, did you say that her name is *Grace?*"

"Yeah. Lexi called me about her, but I didn't know it was actually her–or that Lexi dropped her off at your Center. Fuck. I need a drink." Stepping away from him, I walked straight to the bar cart, ignoring the confusion coming through our bond. Grabbing a bottle of Brennan's good bourbon, I poured myself a glass. "Wait, why did you bring her *home?* Did my sister put you up to it?"

"No. The Center couldn't keep her and she needed help. I thought we could help her. So, you know her? That's great. I'll take one of those. Shit afternoon at the Center," he sighed. "Who is she?" He eyed the tent-pole in my pants. "Um, if Lexi knows who she is, why is Peaches still a Jane Doe?"

"Peaches?" I used to call her that. I downed my glass and poured another. "Lexi never actually met Grace."

Hunching over the counter, I tried to block out the fear and hopelessness I'd had knowing that Grace was being hurt and I couldn't do anything about it. I was an alpha. Her alpha.

I failed to protect her. Failed to find her.

I *failed* her as her alpha.

"Babe, what's wrong? I feel that." Evan wrapped his arms around me.

"Remember me telling you once that I dropped out of university and joined the military because a girl fucked me up? That's her." After I couldn't find her, I wondered if perhaps Grace wasn't even real, and I'd spent all those years invested in nothing. A dream.

"Really? That's the girl? Wow. You never told me what actually happened. Will you tell me now? Please?" He held me tight, comforting me with his scent, his touch, and some alpha-calming pheromones.

"I was in love with her. Well, I thought I was. I was twelve when we first met. The last time that I saw her I was nineteen." How did I say that for seven years I dreamt of her? That I'd never met her unless asleep. The only pictures I had of her were sketches. She was the love of my literal dreams.

"I don't care that she finally found me after all these years. I have you." Turning my head, I stole a kiss from him.

Lies. I cared a lot. Why now? Was she okay? Who'd hurt her? Who was after her?

How the fuck did she even get here?

"Of course, you have me. Wow, she found you," he breathed.

I looked into the eyes of the man who saved me. "That was a long time ago. Now I have you and a pack, and *nothing* will ever take me from you. I'm sorry I never talked much about her. The story is weird. I'm surprised Lexi even believed me."

"Evan, do you have any more of that tea, I still feel awful," a feminine voice said as someone entered the kitchen.

My body instantly went on edge at her scent, which wasn't quite right, not that I'd ever smelled her outside my dreams. I looked over at her, hoping that it wasn't actually my Grace.

I was happy. Successful. There was no room for a ghost.

"Fade." Her grey-blue eyes went wide.

The pain in my head exploded. It actually was her.

My Grace.

She looked a lot like I remembered. Her hair was short, and Grace was older now. But so was I.

Had she always been so small? The bruises on her face and her neck made me want to hurt someone. My hands fisted as I stared at her. Her peachy scent went sour as she stood there, conflict raging on her face.

She wasn't real. Otherwise, I would have found her and saved her from her awful mother. I would have been the alpha she need-ed—and deserved.

Grace looked awfully real despite being a dream. Despite her claims that we both existed, just in different worlds.

The alpha in me wanted to hold her, soothe her fears, protect her—and bury myself inside her.

But the man in me had been deeply hurt by her disappearance. I couldn't do this again.

"No. No. It can't be." Tears streamed down her freckled face. "I…"

"Hey. Come here, Peaches. This is my mate, Wes. He isn't going to hurt you. I promise." Evan let go of me and bundled her into his arms with a gentle tenderness.

She buried her face in his chest. "I know. He'd *never* hurt me. Fade, they said you weren't real. You don't understand, they said *you weren't real.*"

Every cry was a knife in the heart.

They'd told her that, repeatedly when they'd hurt her and tried to make her forget me. It had broken me to know she was being harmed and there was nothing that I could do about it.

After I stopped dreaming of her, I thought that meant she was *dead*. That she had died and I'd let them take her from me because I couldn't get to her and save her like a good alpha.

"She told me that the only alpha she knew was named *Fade*. When were you Fade?" Evan's voice grew quiet as he rubbed the base of my skull with one hand, the other still around her.

"Middle school. I was trying to be fierce after we moved here. It doesn't matter. I have you," I assured him. We'd only just gotten Evan *over* his insecurities. Grace was exactly the type of girl he'd always feared would take his place.

But I was over Grace. Way over her.

No. That was a big fat lie as I ached to hold the crying girl in my omega's arms as she muttered *Pi* under her breath.

No doubt about it, that was my Grace.

But if she was actually from another world, like she told me in our dreams, how did she get here?

No. I knew that answer.

"This concussion is messing with me. All this talk of alphas and omegas and now you're here? Why are you here, Fade? Why am I here? What's going on?" She looked up at me, eyes tearing and pleading just like they had in those last few dreams.

Grace had been struggling to hang on, to keep coming to me in sleep, despite everything they were doing to take her from me.

"You have a concussion, Peaches, and now you can't remember anything?" That, too, made sense. Somehow, coming here messed up her memories.

"You're real, aren't you?" Grace reached out from Evan's arms and cupped my face with her soft, tiny hand. "You feel real."

Fuck. I sent all my love through our bond, hoping her appearance didn't make him slide back into a dark place like it had after Caroline.

At the same time, he was *holding* her. All I got back from my omega was love.

Shit, she was thin.

"I remember you. Why can't I remember my name, but I remember you? I'm not dreaming. No. I always knew they were dreams, before. Of course, I also thought they were real." Her voice went wistful. "How silly of me. Dreams aren't real. I don't feel well. But it's so nice to see you again. I... I missed you so much. It was like they took part of me away when I stopped seeing you in my dreams." Grace just stared at me, her lower lip quivering.

While she didn't come to me in my dreams every night, she visited a few times a week, for seven years. We shared our hopes, had adventures, and fell in love. We had an entire life together in our dreams that was just us.

She was my Dream Girl. My peaches. My love. My soulmate. *Mine.*

Until her mom got concerned about the boy in her teenage daughter's dreams and sent her away to a place where they could make her forget me.

"It's been a long time," I told her, biting off *It's nice to see you, too, who did this to you, stay with me forever.* "I see you've met my mate, Evan. My husband." I added that last part because I wasn't sure if she remembered what *mate* meant. They didn't have that where she lived.

Closing my eyes, I breathed in Evan's scent, trying to avoid the smell of peaches. But all I got was a cocktail of the two of them that made me even harder.

You can have them both.

True. But could I do that to Evan? Not to mention, you didn't just bring someone into a pack. I had the others to consider.

"I don't even remember my name. I'm exhausted and achy, and my thoughts feel like sludge. Why am I here, Fade? Why? I'm so confused." Her voice was pleading.

"Your name is Grace Cassidy Ellington," I said, her words tugging at my soul.

"My name, oh. That *is* my name. But something's not quite right," she whispered, frowning.

"No?" Evan rubbed her back. "Is your last name different now?"

Maybe she was married. That would make this easier. Another growl ripped from my lips, the alpha in me not liking the thought of my Grace having another mate.

"Hey, I've got to go. Will whatever this is here be okay? Do I need to call someone?" Jett came into the kitchen and gave us a worried look.

"We'll be fine," Evan assured, letting go of her. Jett kissed him, put his shoes on, and went into the garage.

The look of longing on Grace's face as she wrapped her arms around herself broke my heart.

I was fucked.

Evan turned to Grace. "You said someone took Fade away? How?"

How was he coping with this? I wasn't. My soulmate from another world was here. In person. In my kitchen. Hurt and with amnesia.

All I wanted to do was hold her tight and kiss away her tears.

"Drugs—among other things," I said softly.

"It was my own fault. All I had to do was admit that Fade wasn't real, and everything was a dream, and then it would stop." Her tone went mocking, and she winced, as if the memory hurt her.

It probably did. The shit they put her through...

"I don't blame you for not finding me, Fade. I mean, if I couldn't find *you*, then why should you find me? Anyway, I always came to *you*." She peered up at me.

Grace was right. In our dreams, we were always in the park by my house, my room, my favorite places. She could come to my world in our dreams, but I couldn't go to hers.

"Are you saying that your parents used drugs to make you forget him?" Evan went into social worker mode.

"It makes more sense than the boy in my dreams being *real*." She looked away, still hugging herself.

It was worse than that. So much worse.

"But the boy in your dreams can be real, Peaches. People do dream of their scent matches. I helped someone track down their dream alpha a few months ago. Why didn't your parents take you to a Center?" He looked at me, silently asking me the same thing.

Her world didn't have Omega Centers.

People only dreamt of their scent matches, their soulmates. Not that everyone with a soulmate dreamed of them.

Evan hugged me to him, clearly feeling my conflict through our mate bond. "Easy, Babe. It's okay."

It wasn't okay on so many levels.

Her head cocked. "Doctor. I'm Doctor Grace Ellington. I re-membered something useful. Finally."

Doctor. She did it. She got her PhD.

And came to me.

She finally figured it out. My sweet, brilliant, Grace used her theorems to find me, keeping that childish promise to get to me, just like we'd talked about over and over.

I'll find you. Promise. What did I even do?

Evan was in full-blown work mode, probably the only reason he was functioning, and not the hot mess he was when Brennan's ex tried to force her way into the pack.

"You said you were researching something, and the men that attacked you were after your research, do you remember what it was? You're a research scientist? That sort of doctor?" Evan prodded.

"I remember how you wanted to become a string theorist and prove your parallel world research." I studied her. "You did it. That's all that makes sense. You did it and made it here like you promised, and somehow scrambled your brain in the process."

"How... how do you know about that?" Her face scrunched up. "It's just something I do for fun. I know, it's ridiculous, but I think trying to prove it has been driving me since I remembered how fun math was." Her head cocked. "Wow, I just remembered something else."

"What are you talking about?" I stared at her.

She thought? Something wasn't right. Even if her memories were messed up from coming here, shouldn't she at least remember that?

"Your entire theory about why we were both real, and how we could travel to each other in our dreams, was based on math. You were going to prove it so you could visit me in real life using the string cheese theorem. That's how you were going to find me. But your mom didn't like how focused you were on math. Hearing you tell me about what they were doing to you undid me. I tried to find you. I really did." My voice broke, and my hands fisted as I wrapped my arms around Evan to keep myself from going to her. "So did Lexi. We tried so hard. One day you never came back to my dreams."

It crushed me.

"I think it's just string theory? But it's just that, a *theory*. It wasn't even a good theory; it was a hobby." She grabbed my drink off the counter and drained it. "I mean, I think I do work with string theory, but..." She turned to Evan. "Why can I remember that and not how I ended up here? What is wrong with me?"

"Brains are weird," Evan soothed.

"It was your life's work, well, it was going to be. Don't you remember?" I frowned, even more confused. It wasn't some *silly thing* to her.

"No." She chewed on her lower lip and made herself small. "In case you haven't noticed, I'm in this predicament because I don't know how I got here." Her chest shook as her big, blue-grey eyes seared my soul. "But I remember you."

Those words were bullets in my chest.

"I... I miss you." She hugged herself again. "There's a lot I don't remember about you—and us. It makes sense now, why I always had this drive to pursue that research even though that wasn't my actual field, so I could get to you. But it was all theoretical. So how did I physically travel here? How would I dream-travel? None of this makes any sense. Just like what I do and don't remember. It's nice to see you, but I'm so confused that it hurts." Frowning, she muttered numbers and walked out of the room, like she did when she needed to puzzle things out.

"I'm so sorry. Um, I'll make her go." I pulled Evan tighter to me so I wouldn't run after her. "Somehow, I'll make this up to you."

"Are you saying Grace dreamt of you, then traveled from a parallel world to get to you?" Evan's eyebrows rose. "Parallel worlds, like something out of a movie?"

"Yeah. Her world's kinda like ours, but doesn't have designations. I know it sounds weird, existing in other worlds, but that's all we could think of when we couldn't find each other in real life," I told him.

"No designations? Is everyone a beta?" Evan checked his phone again.

"Um, I guess? Wait, you believe all this?" I blinked. Sure, I had, once. But it had been over the course of the seven years I dreamed of her.

Evan shrugged. "While it could be disorientation from her concussion, the theories she's talking about are *real*, well, as real as any theory. Spencer was obsessed with parallel worlds for a while when we were younger. That would explain why there's no record of her–she's not from here."

The fact that Evan just *accepted* the possibility of her being from another world took me aback. But then again, he'd grown up with our packmate Spencer–and him talking about the possible existence of parallel worlds didn't surprise me. That man was a mad genius.

"You're not angry about her?" My brow furrowed.

Evan shrugged, sending reassurance through our bond. "Why would I be? She *dreamt* of you across the universe. It's quite romantic."

"She's exactly the type of person you feared would take us from you." I took a swig directly from the bottle, even though Brennan would have a fit if he knew.

Part of me wanted to go to her. I wanted to fix it, like the alpha I was.

What I wanted was her.

Whatever we'd had was still there, and I felt the tug.

But I had Evan now.

Evan pressed his forehead to mine. "Babe, I'm a little more secure now. I'm pretty sure that she's not going to steal you from me. In fact, I'm downright drawn to her. I'm curious, does her pussy taste like peaches? It was so hard not to lick her when she was using me as a pillow. I didn't know how she'd react."

"What?" I kept rubbing my head. "It was a dream, yeah, but her pussy tasted like peaches, and when we fucked–" I stopped myself. "I'm so sorry."

"Stop." He wrapped his arms around me. "It's okay to be attracted to her. You loved her, right? I'm actually surprised you didn't pull her in your arms and kiss her–and that she didn't do the same to you. That wasn't how I'd expect a lovers' reunion to go."

Me neither.

"I bit her," I blurted. I might as well lay it all out.

"During dream sex?" His eyebrows rose.

My horny teenage-self had lots of dream sex with Grace. Especially after I went full-blown alpha at seventeen and my knot came in.

"They used drugs to keep her from coming to me in her dreams, and because she was good at math. Which was always so weird. When they sent her to that awful place, I tried to bond with her so that I could track her and get her out. They *shocked* and *beat* her to get her to admit that I wasn't real. Who *does that* to their kid? I could feel her slipping away." I looked at him, hoping that he understood.

She'd been my everything.

Then they ripped her from me.

"It was all I could think of. I loved her, Evan. But I couldn't feel the bond when I was awake, and I couldn't track her in my dreams. Then... she stopped coming. I was so desperate that I confided in Lexi. That's why my sister became a detective; she helped me look for Grace and liked it. Please don't hate me. I should have told you, but then I had to explain Grace and it sounds weird when I say it outloud. We were kids, and it was a dream and..." My head bowed as guilt ate at me. "I'm sorry."

"I think she's hot as fuck. I'm not threatened by her. Also, it's not illegal to be bonded to both of us." He grinned and looked toward the living room.

"Why are you being so reasonable?" I hadn't expected that with everything he'd been through.

"I felt something the moment I met her. That's why I brought her home. I can see her fitting in with this pack. Fitting under you. Oh, yeah." He waggled his eyebrows, a little lust shooting through our bond.

"*Evan.*" Though she would. No, no, *no*. I wasn't going to have thoughts of how she'd look between us.

"Actually, I want to watch her take your knot as she sucks my dick." He put an arm around my waist. "I read her file. There's a bond mark under her right breast."

I sucked in a breath. "I don't know what to do about her. If she doesn't remember she had theories, how can she use them to get home?"

She had to go home, right?

"Do we need to send her home? If the only reason you want her to leave is that you're worried about my feelings, then I say we go in there and comfort her and help her figure out what happened," he told me. "Obviously, she's been through it."

"You've got to be kidding me." No, I didn't want to hold her.

A growl emitted from my chest as my fists clenched. Okay, I wanted to cuddle her, stroke her hair, and make everything okay the way I couldn't when we were teenagers.

"Why are you being a dumbass? Okay, she broke your heart, but it doesn't sound like that was her fault. Look, she's here now, and alone, scared, and confused. I won't be your excuse to be an asshole." Annoyance made his lemonade scent sour as he scowled at me.

"She undid me." It would be so easy to let her back into my life. Not to mention, something in me was stuck on the idea of having both of them in bed together.

"She's scared, Wes. Someone's *after her*. There are vast gaps in her memory. She has no record, so she doesn't exist here—and it's pretty clear she needs help." He walked toward the doorway. "You fucking dreamt of her. That means she's your scent match and not just your mate. You should be greeting her like you've just been reunited with the love of your life. Do you know how many people would love a second chance with their lost love? If you're going to be a fuckwad and deny her the comfort she desperately needs, then I'll do it for you. That little body fits so well in my arms." He left the kitchen. "Grace, Peaches, come here," he said from the other room.

Another growl rumbled in my chest.

Evan liked her. Fuck. I'd never known him to be like this. My phone buzzed.

Lexi

The center said my Jane Doe was discharged to your omega. She's at your house? That's Grace, right?

Me

Yeah.

Lexi

I'll be by in the morning.

For a moment I sat there, looking through the group chat–including Evan's latest additions.

Evan

We figured out who Jane Doe is. Her name is Dr. Grace Ellington. She's a research scientist or something, and I'm keeping her.

Brennan

We can help her, but she's not a puppy.

Spencer

What sort of scientist?

Evan

String Cheese.

Brennan

???

I found myself adding to the chat.

Me

Theoretical mathematician with a specialization in string theory or something.

My phone beeped with a response.

Spencer

Quantum mechanic? I could use one of those. Do you know what field specifically?

Me

I don't think she brought her wrenches.

I couldn't help but remember her math jokes.

Brennan

What does quantum mechanics have to do with biotech?

Jett

Do I even want to know?

With Spencer? No. That man would either save the world or explode it.

With a sigh, I walked into the living room. This wasn't her world. It would break me to lose her again–and unlike last time, I don't know if I could come back from it.

At the same time, my childhood love was here and upset. My omega was welcoming, not jealous.

I had another chance with the woman I thought was dead.

My alpha screamed at me to stop being a knothead. To go to her and make it all better.

Hugging her sounded nice. After all, she was scared–and *here*.

Whatever I'd been through had been so much worse for her–and not her fault. Evan was right, I needed to get over my hurt and comfort her.

After all, what harm could come from a few cuddles?

Chapter Seven

Grace

"3.1415926535," I muttered as I walked out of the kitchen. "8979323846." The guy I'd been told repeatedly that I'd imagined was *real*.

Not only was he real, but I was here with him and his husband. His sweet, kind, sexy, giant husband, who smelled like lemonade.

Which meant that my hypothesis was correct and I was in another world. But *how?* Even if I had proved those theorems, how had I actually *brought* myself here?

I curled up on the couch, the movie still playing, the food abandoned, nausea washing over me, as I tried not to hyperventilate at my world being upended. "2643383279."

All I could think of was that it had to do with whoever was chasing me.

"5028841971."

My breathing slowed. Closing my eyes made it better, though the nausea remained. I hurt all over, and my head ached.

In some ways, seeing him was reassuring. He was real. I tried to wade through my sleepy brain to recall if Fade was correct about me having those theories as a little girl.

"6939937510."

Those memories I wished I didn't have reminded me that some harsh methods had been used to convince me that it was all a fantasy. It had taken a whole lot of therapy to get me where I was now. That made it difficult to just accept everything.

Part of me wanted to. Wanted him.

"Grace, Peaches, come here." Evan came into the living room and launched his giant frame onto the massively oversized couch, hauling me into his arms and covering us with a fuzzy blanket.

While Fade hadn't been small, Evan was *big*. Fade had a fierceness to him, under his church-boy good looks. Evan was a giant teddy bear. An exquisite, muscular teddy bear, with light brown skin, giant brown eyes, and short, very curly, dark hair.

I shouldn't let him hold me. But I felt miserable.

Also, I shouldn't have come home with a strange guy and his boyfriend. But there was something about him that was comforting. Like Fade had been so compelling all those years ago.

"I... I used to date your husband," my voice went soft. "I didn't know, I..."

"You can have him, but you get me, too," he laughed. "I'm sure this is confusing for you. We'll figure all this out, okay? Spencer will help. You're going to love him. Hey, if I get to be too much, tell me to fuck off. I'm touchy feely and our pack makes a whole lot of sex jokes. But we're all about consent here. So please, speak up."

"I appreciate it." Why did he smell so good? Why did Fade smell so good? I'd never been with two people before. How come I liked the idea of having him, too?

Fade walked into the living room, smelling of fresh laundry and sunshine. Tall and muscular, he drew your attention. His dark blond hair hung in his hazel eyes, and he had dimples when he smiled, and freckles.

Hot damn.

"I know, right?" Evan whispered. "Wes is hot."

"Wes?" I blinked.

"That's my actual name. I guess you don't remember. For a while I tried to be cool and go by Fade, but it didn't stick. Come here, Peaches. I... I didn't mean to be a dick back there. I'm sorry. It's just a little shocking that you're here after all this time." Fade, no, Wes, squeezed in with us, pulling me into his arms. "I'm so happy you're here."

"I don't know how I got here. But I don't think I brought myself here. Sorry. As romantic as it is that I might have crossed the universe for you, I think I was chased." I sobbed, hurt at the thought of disappointing him.

"Peaches, it's okay. It doesn't matter how you got here. You're with me and Evan now," he soothed.

I felt cozy and safe with them. The day had been so confusing.

"There's so much I can't remember." I melted under the muscles I could feel beneath his button-down. He whispered into Evan's ear, and Evan kissed him.

All I could do was stare. That was *hot*.

"I think she likes what she sees, don't you, Peaches," Evan teased.

"How did you snag such a cute husband?" I deflected.

Wes looked away, hurt clouding his eyes. "Your disappearance fucked me up. I went into the military. There I met Evan."

"I'm so sorry. In the end, I just couldn't hang on anymore. I tried. I'm so sorry that I was weak." My chest shook. I'd felt so bad about hurting him by giving up, but in the end—and moving forward—I had to focus on myself so I wouldn't go under. Or die.

Shit. I'd rather not recall how that place nearly killed me.

"No. Don't apologize, Grace. None of this was your fault. I'm the alpha, and I should have protected you. Yeah, okay, I saw you in my dreams. But I also know what that means. You were mine to love. You trusted me, and I couldn't save you." His muscular arms wrapped around me.

The raw sadness hit me right in the chest as tears ran down my face.

"Easy, both of you," Evan scolded, running his large hand through my hair. "None of this is either of your faults. You're together now."

"I didn't mean to implode your life," I continued to cry. Had I ruined everything?

"I know, Peaches. You're not wrecking anything. I'm just feeling too many things all at once. It'll be okay. You're here, and that's all that matters." Wes held me close.

Heat built between us. But it also didn't stop my analytical mind. "If I'm from another world, and I'm the one with the theories, how were you supposed to save me?"

Evan snorted. "She's got you there."

"I'm the alpha. It's my job." Hurt crossed his face.

"You didn't abandon me." If I forgot him, that was different. Clearly, he didn't forget me and it hurt him a lot, which made me feel *awful*.

"I... I didn't mean to hurt you." I cupped his face with my hands, feeling that pull again.

Being here with him felt right in a way I hadn't felt in a long time.

"I know, Peaches." His eyes closed as if savoring my touch.

"We will figure this out." Evan leaned in and kissed him again.

For a moment I wanted to lean in and kiss Wes, too. I could practically feel that stubble on my face, his hands on my body.

"You're so cute together. Evan, you're going to have to finish explaining your four men to me," I said, shaking myself out of my thirsty daydream. Like did Wes have four husbands, too? I was so curious.

Evan and Jett had tried to explain their *pack* to me, which seemed to be their all-dude polyamorous family that lived in what smelled like a frat house and looked straight out of a show about fancy homes.

"I only have three husbands. Spencer is my platonic life partner. He's my best friend, and I'd walk through fire for that man, I just don't want to fuck him. Jett is with me and Brennan. Wes has only me. There's so much room for you, Peaches." Evan touched his light brown nose to mine.

"You, sir, are getting a little ahead of yourself." I laughed to cover the fact that the idea of having both of them made me clench.

Why was I so thirsty? I didn't even really know them. While Evan seemed into multiple partners, I wasn't sure if Wes was.

"Oh, I'm not *sir*." Evan grinned, snuggling into me. "Unless you want me to be."

That banter. I'd never had a truly serious partner that wasn't my dream boyfriend. Was it normal to want them both so badly so soon?

"Will you stop? You're going to make her uncomfortable," Wes play-scolded, rolling his eyes.

"It's fine." I leaned into Wes, putting my legs over Evan. Then I realized what I was doing and tried to sit up.

"Stay." Wes pulled me back onto him. "You're so fucking small. And thin."

"I've always been small." I shrugged. After all, I was four-foot-ten. Wes and Evan were well over six feet, with Evan being a little taller.

"Who hurt you? Did someone check you out?" Wes frowned as he looked at my face and examined my bruises with care that reminded me of better times.

"At the clinic, they did scans, exams, bloodwork, and stuff. Today I talked to a lot of people. I'll be fine. I'm just tired." Laying my head back down, I got cozy, letting the sense of rightness and the yearning for it, override my common sense.

His nose went to my head, and he sniffed me. "You still smell like peaches, but something's not right."

"The doctor said that someone drugged me. Would that change it? Sorry, I don't quite understand why scents are so pronounced here." No one said I smelled of peaches back home–and no guy I knew ever smelled like them, well outside of Wes. This entire world smelled like a candle shop.

I closed my eyes and inhaled, getting a hit of his clean laundry scent. There was a chuckle, and my eyes flew open as I realized my face was buried in Wes' shirt. My cheeks burned.

"Sorry." But I didn't move my face as I sucked in the scent of him. I remembered that smell. Oh, how I loved that smell.

"He smells good, right? You can lick him. I might want a turn being licked, though," Evan teased, dark eyes sparkling. "Well, if you like how I smell."

Oh, I did. *Down girl. We don't lick people we've just met.*

"It's chemical. I have a video on it that gets pretty deep into the science that you might like when you feel up to it," Evan replied. "Different people are attracted to different scents. My dick stood up when I met Wes. It also signifies designation. One sniff of him and I knew he was an alpha. Just like I smell like omega."

"And I smell like peaches and nothing. I still don't truly understand," I replied. I mostly thought when Fade, Wes, had spoken of alphas, that he meant it colloquially, like the *alpha male* bullshit some men at my parents' church spouted.

Until Wes got his magic alpha dick. Now *that* I remembered as another memory bubble popped.

"Carly showed me a video at the Center to try to get me to remember what I was. Still sounds like bullshit. You're ex-military and giant," I replied, still not fully understanding all this alpha and omega nonsense.

Wes' dick was biologically different from anything in my world. That was why I called it *magic*. When we slept together, it felt... *Hey, stop that.*

"Stereotypes *are* bullshit. We've worked hard, both with laws and science, so they're not limiting. For example, while alphas are leaders, not all leaders have to be alphas. Alphas like to get their way, but we no longer allow that to be at the expense of others. Sure, omegas and alphas are biologically drawn to each other, but that doesn't make omegas property," Evan explained.

"There are fewer omegas than alphas, right?" I tried to remember everything Wes had told me.

"More than half the world is beta, about a quarter are alphas, omegas are maybe ten percent, and the rest are some of the rarer designations, but we can get into all that later," Evan assured. "Traditionally, omegas are valued by alphas. Packs are often formed because there are fewer omegas than alphas, and well, the more people to protect and love them, the better. Betas and other designations are in packs, too. Jett's a beta, and just as valued as anyone else."

"Oh. I see." My eyes closed, as warmth and safety encompassed me. "Wes, are you an engineer now? That's what you were studying, right?"

"I was. However, the military realized that I was a very good hacker. I might have hacked a few government databases trying to find you. While I know you said that you were from another world, I scoured this one just in case." His voice went low and rough. "I met Evan there. After we both got out, Evan and I mated. I began working for Spencer's biotech company in cybersecurity while Evan finished up becoming a social worker. We formed a pack with Jett, Brennan, and Spencer. I still work for Spencer. I never finished university."

I wasn't sure what all that meant–except for the part where he didn't become an engineer.

"It's my fault." Tears streamed down my face. Going to college to be an engineer had been so important to him.

"No. I could have finished. Still could. But Spence pays me a shit-ton, and I like my job." He wiped my face with his hand. "Don't cry, Peaches. None of this is your fault. Honestly, I like what I do so much better. I thought I wanted to study engineering, but as it turns out, I really just wanted to please my dad. But my dad didn't care, he just wanted me to be happy–and he likes Evan and my pack."

"Oh, that's good." I felt nauseous again–and sleepy. "I shouldn't have had that alcohol."

"Yeah, booze and concussions probably don't play well together. I'm glad you're real, Peaches. Evan, is there any more food? Who cooked? Jett?" Wes stroked my hair lightly like he used to when we'd lie on his bed or sit in the park and talk for hours.

"Yep. What's left is only what's on the table. Peaches, you barely ate. Was Jett's cooking not your style? Too spicy?" Evan asked.

"It smelled delicious, and I like spicy food. But only ice cream and tea taste right. Why does nothing taste right?" I sighed.

"It could be the concussion. I'll order something. Do you want anything?" Wes's body shifted under me, but I didn't want to move.

"I'm fine." The nausea increased.

"Ooh, I'll share some of that. Maybe we should get some soup for her for later?" Evan said, looking at Wes' phone.

"Tell me about your day? Who got in trouble?" I asked, wanting simply to hear his voice.

"Who got in trouble?" Evan chuckled.

"When we were little, that's how I'd get him to actually give me answers longer than a word," I replied, moving so I was more comfortable between the two large men. "I was ten when we first met."

I drifted in and out of sleep as they both told me about their day. Suddenly, bile rose in my throat, and I shot up, almost tripping as I sprung off the couch. I nearly fell over the coffee table as I tried to get to the bathroom off the living room before I vomited. Everything swam, my equilibrium off. I made it just in time.

"Should we take her to the hospital?" Wes asked as I greeted the porcelain god.

Evan sighed. "We'll monitor things. Given, you know."

Everything swam as I stood, then washed my hands. I stumbled and fell right into Wes.

"I've got you." Wes pressed me to his muscular chest.

"I don't feel well." It was almost a sob as my knees sagged.

His chest rumbled, and a warm feeling washed over me, like a hot bath. Suddenly, it stopped.

"I... I'm sorry, Evan," he whispered.

"Stop it. Don't apologize for doing what you're meant to do. Purr for our girl. Shit, both of you need therapy, a good railing, and ice cream," Evan replied, wrapping his arms around both of us.

"You think therapy, a good railing, and ice cream cures everything," Wes retorted.

My eyes closed. "Can you do that rumbly thing again? Please?"

"I'm going to make you some more tea and find some medicine. Food should be here soon," Evan said. "Go comfort her, dammit. Or I'll take her to my room, purr for her, and not let you in."

Wes picked me up and hauled me onto the couch with him. "You like that? I always used to purr for you. It's something an alpha only does for very special people."

I'd been special to him once? That hurt my heart. I was pretty sure that for much of my life I hadn't been special to anyone.

"I've got you. You're here and I've got you," he told me. Covering me with a blanket, his chest rumbled again, sweeping away all of the pain and nausea. I was content. Loved. Like I'd been once, a very long time ago.

Chapter Eight

Evan

"I'm going to take her upstairs," Wes told me, our food finished. We hadn't gotten Grace to eat, but she'd had some tea and now slept on top of him.

"Should I come up or do you want some alone time with her? I'm fine with either." I cleared off the coffee table. She did better when sleeping on his bare chest.

As she should. I slept better with one of my alphas, too.

"If it's all right with you, I'd like you to stay with me. But I'm sure Brennan would be more fun." Wes scooped her up in his arms, careful of all her bruises. "I'm worried. Shouldn't she be at the hospital?"

"We should take her in the morning if she keeps vomiting. But we're going to have to be careful, get our story straight, and hope that anything she says that's out of the ordinary is taken for disorientation," I replied. We didn't need her institutionalized, or worse, becoming a government science project.

Wes nodded. "Her not having a record is going to be a problem. Not just if she has to go to the hospital, but if she stays for any length of time."

She couldn't get a job, have a bank account, go to the doctor, or do any number of things if she didn't exist. That... now that I could fix. I kicked myself for not thinking of it hours ago as a preventative measure, even if she didn't stay for long–assuming she could even get back.

Or wanted to.

Parallel world. Shit. If I hadn't been friends with Spencer my entire life, I wouldn't believe it. She somehow crossed the universe to be with my mate. So fucking romantic.

Wes *was* pretty special. Hopefully, she'd think I was too.

"I'll be up soon." I gave him a kiss, then stroked Grace's soft, blonde hair, and took the dishes and garbage into the kitchen. After I cleaned up, I headed upstairs.

The two upper floors were a series of suites, with a few shared spaces. On the second floor, Brennan and Jett shared a suite. Spencer also had one. There was a library and an open space with a piano where I often found Brennan when he had a bad day.

Up on the third floor, I walked past a big open area with a sunken living room and the sunroom with a giant bay window where sometimes Wes liked to sketch. Usually I slept in Wes' room, which was on the other side of the sunroom–or with Brennan and Jett. But I had my very own suite, with a lounge where Jett and I often retreated to watch the movies *we* liked and a desk where I could do some work, and my bedroom, and my nest, where out of respect, no one entered without my permission, and a giant bathroom and closet.

In my suite, I booted up my work laptop and got my headset, checking the time on my phone. She should still be up. I sent her a text.

"While I get your overwhelming omega need to help people, I don't fucking do that anymore, you doofus," a tart voice answered over my headset.

I rolled my eyes as I got into the clinic files and found Grace's records. "Um, yes, you do, Ri. This isn't for the Center, so you can charge your full rate."

"Oh. What have we got? The usual?" Interest tinged her voice.

"We might have to take her to the hospital in the morning, so I'll need at least the bare bones by then. Maybe we can blame it on a glitch or the downed grid or something when more info appears?" I started sending Riley the files she'd need.

Sometimes omegas needed new identities, and the Center would facilitate that. Riley had created more than one for me. She was supposed to be on the straight and narrow now. But I knew she wasn't, which was why I felt no guilt in asking. She was good, and I could trust her implicitly.

"By morning? Fuck you. How much extra can I charge? Wait, if this isn't for the Center why are you sending me Center records?"

I ran her through the barest basics of Grace's case, leaving out the parallel world travel. "Since there's no record to delete or work from, you'll have to build one from scratch."

She whistled. "That costs extra if you want it done right. Who the fuck has no record?"

"Someone from a country that doesn't keep a database? A person coming from a fundie community?" Fundies generally didn't believe in being part of the government, because they felt that it was the government's fault every alpha didn't get their own omega–even though it was mathematically impossible without unethical actions like omega breeding programs.

"All I need by morning is the ability to get her into the hospital and well, anything with the police since she's got an open case. Eventually, I'd like her set up with a basic past so that she can be employable." I continued looking over the tests and notes from the doctors.

She whistled. "How big are the pockets I'm fleecing? This is looking to be an expensive job."

"They're my pockets, not the pack's. While I'll pay you what's fair, please don't fuck me too badly, I don't make very much. Let's put her down as a beta, maybe alter a tox screen to show Trevadol in order to explain why she came up undesignated?" It was a common anxiety medication that fucked with the basic prick-test. Sometimes omegas in hiding took it for that specific reason.

For a moment I only heard typing.

"Can't. Bloodwork shows some variant of Oxotipoline," she retorted.

"Oh. Well, that could explain her memory loss." My belly dropped. It was a sedative commonly used in human trafficking. The designer version, Eazy-E, was sometimes used by sexual predators.

There was more typing. "Okay, they only ran the common designation blood test on her. Since we can't make her pass as a beta, should we use a rare for now? You've seen her, I haven't. What would be plausible?"

I ran through the rare designations. Someone of her size wasn't going to be a delta. Theta? Maybe. Her reaction to scents–and her scent–would make it too difficult for her to be an Iota. Hmmm. Maybe with her size we could try to pass her off as a gamma?

Gammas were more of a genetic anomaly that was given its own term than an actual designation, and sometimes didn't come up on tests. They were *almost* an omega, but for some reason their body halted the process. Sometimes a genetic switch was thrown, other times it was environmental. Usually, they had some of the general physical and psychological attributes associated with omegas, but lacked an omega's scent, pheromones, and perfume. They were often resistant to alpha barks. Each gamma was a little different.

"Let's put her down as a gamma. I also need her to have a PhD in theoretical mathematics or something equivalent. In case you need it, she likes romance novels, action movies, and can recite *Pi* to way more places than most people. She smells of peaches. The only pictures I have of her are not very pleasing." I sent the photos they took to document her injuries.

"Creating a PhD? Are you serious?" she huffed.

"Fine, I'll have Wes help me," I replied, not up to her attitude tonight.

"I'm a better hacker than Wes. Fine." She drew the last word out dramatically. "Her birth year is fucked up and doesn't correspond with her age. Her city of birth doesn't exist."

"She has a concussion and is suffering from memory loss and disorientation. Oh, her birthday is right after Wes'." At the Center she said she was twenty-seven. Wes was twenty-nine. Which meant that if he bit her when he was nineteen, she was only seventeen.

Ooh. That naughty, law-breaking, cradle-robber. I gave a birth year for Grace that would make her legal then, to head off any problems.

Had the bond test come back? Because of the legalities an alpha-omega bond implied, it was a government test. Wes and I never got married, but because we were bonded and had registered it, we had the same rights as spouses and were accepted as such.

Nope. Not yet.

We went over more things as I made note of what I needed to do on my end. I had other connections to reach out to that could help make Grace's record complete and real.

"Okay, I think we're good," she finally said. "I'll let you know if I need anything else. Night fucker."

"Love you too, Ri. Night." I logged out of the Center files, making it look like I'd never been there. Then, I checked a few tasks off my list and sent the first part of the payment.

Closing up, I went to find Wes and Grace, hoping that this was a precaution, and that we wouldn't need it soon.

Chapter Nine

Grace

At some point, we'd moved to Wes' room, which was done in blues and greens, and had a big, soft bed. I'd been sick a few more times, but felt better curled together between Wes and Evan like a Grace sandwich. It was delicious. So far, I liked this world.

I lay there with my eyes closed, enjoying the warmth, coziness, and safety. It was morning.

"Are you sure this is okay? The moment it's not, this stops," Wes said quietly to Evan.

"I'm *fine*. Are *you* okay? You still care for her, don't you? I'm fine if you do," Evan replied.

Wes sighed. "I do. I never stopped caring about her. What's going to happen when she goes home?"

Eventually, I'd have to get home. Right? I had a job. An apartment. A plant. *I think.*

The problem was, I still cared for Wes, too. Barfing aside, last night was pleasant. He'd grown up, but was still the strong, caring person that I remembered.

One thing that I could recall was an intense feeling of loneliness back home. Of not fitting. Certainly, I didn't have *this*. Growing up, no one had listened to me the way Wes had. I felt seen when I was with him.

Loved. Wanted.

With Wes I felt like I belonged.

When I was young, every night when I went to sleep, I hoped it would be a night that I'd go to him.

"How about we nurse her through her concussion and, you know, figure out who chased her, before we fuck with the multiverse?" Evan suggested.

"*Multiverse* implies variations of ourselves. There's no Grace Ellington here. Believe me, I looked," Wes replied. "What? I listened to her. In school, I did so well in math and science because of that."

"Hey, I'm going to take a shower and make some coffee. I've got to go into work later, but I think we can leave her here for a bit by herself. She'll sleep a lot in the next few days, and that's for the best," Evan said.

"I already told Spencer that I'm coming in late today," Wes added.

"I love you. You also could use a shower," Evan said, the bed shifting.

For a moment after I heard him leave, I continued to lie there, eyes closed.

"Are you awake, Peaches? You could use a shower, too," Wes replied, stroking my hair.

My eyes didn't open. "I like it when you do that."

"Can you manage on your own?"

"Yeah." I may have unabashedly snuggled with someone I'd only ever been with in my dreams, but I *wasn't* ready to shower with him.

I let him help me out of the enormous bed and into his fancy bathroom, with a spacious shower with clear glass doors.

"What, no whirlpool tub?" I joked, still a little wobbly. My head continued to pound, and my brain was still sluggish. A fancy house like this needed a fancy bathtub.

"That's in Evan's room. Um, I'll get you a towel and some clothes." His chest was bare, with a military-ish looking tattoo on his shoulder. A black infinity heart tattoo was on his left pectoral–Evan had a matching one.

He left, and I turned the shower on, letting it warm up as I stripped out of his T-shirt I'd slept in. I washed my hair and body and rinsed out my mouth. Closing my eyes, I let the warm water wash over me.

"Shit," Wes whispered.

My eyes opened. Wes stood there, towel and clothes in hand, staring at me through the clear glass door.

"Oh, my scars, yeah, they freaked the doctor out, too." Turning off the water, I grabbed the towel and wrapped it around myself.

"At that last place your mom sent you to, they did that to you?" He growled a little.

"Yeah." My voice went rough. My memories of Wes were getting stronger.

"I'm sorry." He wrapped his arms around me.

It felt safe and comfortable as heat built between us once again.

"It's not your fault. Or mine." I looked up into his eyes.

"It still hurts to see you hurt, Peaches. It tears me up inside that they did that to you."

His lips pressed to mine, and for a moment it was like in our dreams—the later ones when we'd been more than friends. He tasted of toothpaste, his lips soft, yet demanding, as he pulled me closer.

It felt so good, both familiar and comforting as my hands moved up his back.

Yes, this I remembered. Kissing him. Loving him. Being loved by him.

Hungry for more, I pulled him close, continuing our kiss. I felt him harden through his boxers, and heat seared me. All I had to do was drop the–

What was I thinking? He had a husband. We weren't teenagers. I pulled away, guilt filling me.

"Um, thanks for the clothes. Shower's all yours." Grabbing the clothes out of his hand, my heart pounded as I walked into his room, putting the clothes on as I moved.

My face burned with mortification. What had I done? The last thing I wanted to do was hurt Evan. He'd taken me into *his home* and not minded that I was his husband's ex. If anything, that made him even kinder. I also didn't know him well enough to tell what was banter and what was serious.

"Grace, wait." Wes followed me.

My heart continued to thud. "It's fine. I won't read into it. Um, I'm going to get some coffee."

Oh, how I wanted to read into it. In some ways this felt so right, and I just wanted to accept it all. Accept him.

He wasn't mine anymore. This wasn't my world.

Before he could say anything else, I left. Eventually, I *would* have to go home–and that would break us both all over again.

Chapter Ten

Evan

Jett and Brennan sat at the kitchen table, talking quietly, drinking coffee, and having a moment.

"Hey, Love." Brennan stood when he saw me. His arms wrapped around my waist when I came over to him.

"Hey yourself, Handsome." I leaned into him and stole a kiss. "How'd last night go?"

"Yet another stupid party." He shrugged, still holding me. "I got the scholarship for Rose set up. I'm happy to help, but please go easy for the rest of the month." His family had a big foundation, and I made good use of it educating my baby omegas.

"I'll try. Hey, Hot Stuff." I gave Jett a kiss.

"Good morning. How's Peaches?" Jett asked as I got myself a cup of coffee.

Brennan looked around. "Where is she?"

"It was a little rough last night; concussions are a bitch. She's upstairs with Wes." I added milk and sugar to my cup.

Brennan's eyebrows rose. "You left her with Wes?"

"Yeah." I took a long drink of coffee. That was exactly what she needed right now. It was evident in the way she reacted to him. She was *his*. I had no urge to fight that; there was enough of Wes to go around.

Jett looked at his phone, sighed, and stood. "Work. Sorry."

"Will you tell me *why* you brought home a stray? I'd like to understand." Brennan opened the fridge as Jett left the kitchen. "Eggs?"

How much did I tell him? He wasn't familiar with parallel world theories. He didn't even like multiverse movies or read fantasy novels.

"Eggs would be great. I'm starving. Honestly, there's something about her. I looked at her bruises and wanted to punch someone. She smelled *right*. Also, I didn't want her to go to a homeless shelter when she couldn't remember her name." I sighed, trying to articulate my feelings in a way that didn't reveal things that weren't mine to tell.

Maybe I was getting it through my bond with Wes. Maybe I was attracted to her all on my own.

"But she does now, which is good. Her being brought to your Center, meeting you, all of this is very suspicious." Brennan got out some vegetables and cheese.

I got out a pan and rolled my eyes. "It's Lexi's case. You know why she brought her to the Center."

"Given Grace now knows her name, I want her gone. We'll still help her. But I don't like people here." Brennan was a territorial introvert. Our home was a castle. A private castle. We didn't even have a housekeeper—we rotated chores.

No. Her leaving wasn't going to work for me.

"Are you afraid that this will be like Caroline? Wes asked me if I was okay last night so many times I was ready to smack him. Grace isn't trying to worm her way into the pack or use us. She's scared and needs help. I'm sorry for bringing her home without running it by everyone, but the circumstances were extenuating, and this is where she needs to be," I replied.

"We don't know her—or anything about her. I want her gone from the house." Brennan sighed as he cooked.

"Just meet her." I knew she'd fit right in with us if they gave her a chance.

"He's right, I should go." Grace tumbled into the kitchen, hair soaking wet, feet bare, wearing some too-big shorts and a shirt that smelled of Wes.

"Peaches, where are you going to go?" I poured her some coffee while watching Brennan's reaction, as he took in the bruises on her face and arms.

"There's a domestic violence shelter on the other side of town that owes me a favor, I'll call them. Do you remember who hurt you? Was it your husband? Wife? Alpha? Parents?" Brennan continued to cook.

Grace looked up at me, lower lip quivering. "I kissed him. I'm so sorry, Evan. You've been nothing but kind to me and..." She sobbed. "I'm going to wreck everything. He's not mine anymore. I don't belong here."

"Hey, it's okay." I brought her to my chest, comforting her. Mmmm, she used Wes' body wash.

"What?" Turning off the stove, Brennan spun around, eyes flashing. "How dare you walk into *my* pack and pull something like that? Evan was kind enough to *bring you home with him,* and you act like this? We're not looking for members, and you can't whore your way into our money," he growled.

She burst out of my arms and marched over to him, looking fierce, not scared. Grace's hand flew out as she smacked him across the face. "You have no right to speak to me like that. I'm not a whore. Or a slut."

Wow, there was a lot to unpack there. I enjoyed seeing this fierceness in her. Her scent flared with anger, filling the kitchen with spicy peaches.

It was a stark contrast to her crying a moment ago.

Brennan growled. I stepped between the two of them, because if she came from a world with no alphas, like Wes said, she had no idea what she'd done.

Either that or she *was* a gamma. Part of what made being a gamma dangerous is that they didn't always respond like omegas or betas–like an alpha would expect–and in a volatile situation that could end badly.

Wes had said that her world didn't have designations, but maybe they just used different words. If someone hurt her so badly that she *forgot her mate,* it could halt the genetic process of becoming an omega and make her a gamma. I could absolutely believe her being an omega. Most scent matches were alpha and omega, but not all.

"Brennan, stop. There's a lot going on here that you don't understand," I told him.

"She came into our home and kissed your alpha, and you're okay with it? Because I'm not." His pine scent went spicy with anger, as I caught his frustration through our bond.

"She's not Caroline, so stop projecting. I'm okay with it," I fired back. "She fucking needs him right now, not a shelter, *him.*"

Her head bowed. "Whatever Wes and I had was a long time ago. He loves you, Evan. I can see it. The last thing I want is to come between you or to hurt you. You're so kind. I'll leave."

"Good," Brennan growled.

I was torn between whom to comfort. While I could feel his anger, his conflict, I could smell how scared and confused she was. "Bren–"

"Oh. Hello." Spencer entered the kitchen, dressed for work in his favorite suit, barefoot, and smelling like well-oiled leather. His eyes fell on Grace. "You must be Dr. Ellington. I'm Spencer Thanukos, it's a pleasure to meet you."

"Um, hi. I'm Grace." Grace's expression was priceless as she took him in.

Spencer was handsome in a distinguished, Mediterranean, alpha gentleman billionaire sort of way, complete with olive skin, a little bit of grey in his dark hair, striking grey-brown eyes, and hint of a Greek accent. He was a few years older than me, and I'd known him my entire life.

His head cocked. "You don't belong here."

What the fuck? He didn't say it meanly, but I still gave Spencer a sharp look as he put the kettle on.

Grace drooped. "You're right. I don't. I'll go."

"Grace, you and Wes have a lot to figure out. Maybe you're still a thing, maybe not. I'm here for both of you, either way." I wanted, no, needed, for her to stay.

"Grace and Wes are *exes*? I'm not okay with this. Neither is Spence. She goes, now, Evan," Brennan demanded.

His tone and the anger in our bond made me bristle.

"Just because she doesn't belong here doesn't mean she has to leave." Spencer walked around her in a predatory manner, like she was a tasty little morsel.

Okay, she was. A tiny little snack-sized candy bar.

"I should. Eventually, I'll have to go home. I already messed everything up for him once, I don't want to do it again. I'm not a home-wrecker." She winced, her scent going bitter.

I brought her to my chest, protecting her from the alphas in the kitchen. "Grace, Peaches, stop worrying about me. I'll say something if you cross a line. Like I said before, you and Wes have a lot to work out–and I'm *okay* with that and aware it will include kissing and then some."

Wes' knot would make it all better.

"How did you get here, my good doctor?" Spencer took tea down from the cupboard, and a cup, and poured hot water into it.

"She came from the Center, Spence, remember?" Brennan snapped.

Grace met his gaze, and it was almost like an unspoken conversation passed between them.

"I... I don't know. The memories are blurry beyond being chased and waking up in the park." She flinched.

I hadn't mentioned Grace's potential interdimensional traveler status to Spencer yet. But if anyone could take one look at her and tell, it would be him.

"I see. There are ramifications if you can successfully accomplish this at will," Spencer replied.

"How did you know?" She looked at me. I shook my head.

"You still smell a bit like neutrons." He handed the cup to Grace. "Drink this. Eat what you can, then go back to sleep–or at least rest."

"Yes, sir." Her chest trembled a little.

"Someone should see to those bruises. I'm off to work. I'll be late tonight." Spencer gave her a pleased, almost smug, look, slipped on his shoes, then left through the garage.

Now Spencer, oh, she could call him *sir*. He actually preferred *Daddy*. Hmm, I could be okay with that. He was a good guy. Spencer wasn't with anyone in the pack and hadn't had a partner in ages.

"What the fuck was that? I'm so confused. If that man wasn't a fucking genius..." Brennan glared, pheromones pouring out as he tried to overwhelm Grace with his alphaness without actually posturing. "Who sent you? We don't negotiate with exes."

"I don't negotiate with assholes." With a scowl, she plopped down at the table and gingerly sipped her tea.

"What's going on here?" Wes joined us, in jeans and a T-shirt, feet bare, fresh laundry scent flaring with concern.

"Grace is your ex, and you didn't think to mention it?" Brennan growled.

"Don't growl at me." Wes flipped him off and picked up the cup of coffee on the counter I'd poured for Grace. "I feel like shit."

"Wow, you're all rays of sunshine today. I need coffee and some of whatever Brennan's making." Lexi sailed in, wearing a red blouse, black slacks, and carrying the oversized work bag I'd gotten her for her birthday.

I hadn't heard the front door, but she had the code to get in.

"This is pack business, Lexi. You're not part of this pack, so go away." Brennan went back to cooking.

Lexi was a beta and had a pack. I should introduce Grace to them. They were fun–and drove my growly alphas crazy.

"Detective, do you have an update? I didn't expect you to come by." Grace looked a little uncomfortable.

"Oh, right? Um, Grace, this is my older sister, Lexi. I've talked about her to you before." Wes downed his coffee.

"Oh?" Grace looked uncomfortable, her scent growing anxious, and I put a hand on her shoulder to help settle her.

I got the feeling last night that she was touch-starved. My cuddles would help, but Wes' would be better.

"I was wondering if that was you," Lexi said. "It's so nice to finally meet you."

"Fuck me," Brennan muttered.

"Later, Handsome." I wrapped my arms around him as he cooked. My other alpha needed some reassurance, too. He did *not* like change.

"I... I'll be right back. I think–" Grace ran out of the room, making a puke-face.

"Wes, we need to talk." Lexi looked at me, then at Wes. They looked so much alike, though Wes was taller and broader. But Lexi was tall for a beta.

Wes sighed. "You can talk in front of them. I want to be open about this."

"Fine. The doctors at the center did some tests, which went through government labs, per protocol. The results have some legal ramifications." Lexi helped herself to some coffee and then leaned against the counter, red nails tapping on the ceramic cup.

"She's some sort of illegal designation, isn't she?" Brennan made a face.

"The Center doesn't even give that test." Lexi frowned. "Weird that your mind even goes there."

Illegal designations were just that, *illegal*–and their fate wasn't kind, even though it wasn't their fault they were born that way. Many of them tried to pretend to be something common. Usually, those tests were given at special government facilities with court orders.

"What does Grace remember about your relationship?" Lexi added.

"You *knew* they were together, and you let my omega take her home?" Brennan growled at her.

"I've never met Grace. However, I had suspicions. That knot-head wouldn't come to the station to see if it was her. I took her to the Center because the growly alphas at Eastside think she's an omega who hasn't awakened yet or is on some heavy-duty suppressants and blockers and dunks herself in scent-neutralizer every day," Lexi retorted.

That was a perfectly reasonable thought. Laws aside, many un-bonded omegas erred on the side of extreme caution, especially if they were independent and career-minded. That's how I got through the last part of my military contract. Just because laws existed didn't mean there weren't knotheads out there.

"I don't know exactly what she remembers. There are huge gaps in her memory still." Wes drooped as sadness and regret pierced our bond.

I left Brennan and went to Wes.

"Will someone explain what is going on?" Brennan demanded.

"Basic version? Grace and I were together when we were young. Her mom didn't like it—and sent her to a terrible place to make her forget me. I tried to find her and wasn't successful. Eventually, I gave up, thinking she was dead. I haven't seen or heard from her since I was at university." Defeat crossed his face and I squeezed his hand.

"Oh, fuck. Who does that? Wait, I knew you then—and in high school. You had a serious girlfriend?" Brennan put eggs on plates.

Brennan and Wes had known each other since high school, because of their sisters, though Brennan was older. I was older than Brennan and Jett, but not as old as Spencer.

"It was sort of long distance, and I didn't talk about her much since it was a little weird and people would tease me that she was imaginary. Including you." His gaze shifted to his sister. "They did a bond test?"

"Yep." Lexi grabbed a plate and helped herself to a fork from the drawer. "It came back positive."

Brennan exploded with anger, spicy pine filling the kitchen. "What the fuck, Wes? You have a *mate* and never disclosed it when we formed this pack? Or after Caroline? Do you know what sort of legal ramifications this has? I mean, I get it, she was missing, but you didn't tell us."

A pack was a legal entity, and not everyone in a pack had to be bonded to someone–or each other. It was a contract that gave us the legal rights of spouses and made us a family.

"How could you do this to us–to Evan?" Brennan yelled.

If a bond was found, Wes would be responsible for her, given he was the one to administer the bite. Since Wes was part of a pack, the pack could be liable for her care. Usually, there were protocols and legalities when bringing a person into an existing pack.

Brennan *really* liked protocols.

I got between my alphas. "Will you stop? I'm fine with this."

"Why?" Brennan asked. "One of your alphas bonded with someone without your permission."

They'd put a clause in the pack charter after Caroline that gave me veto power.

"He bonded with her before he ever met me, which makes this something very different. Grace isn't going to steal Wes. She's not going to ruin the pack. She's a mathematician who smells like peach pie with a hint of vanilla ice cream. I wonder if she bakes." Maybe she knew what a stand mixer was. I could ask Lexi, but she'd make fun of me.

I purred, using my omega ability to calm my alphas and diffuse the situation before someone threw a punch.

"She does, well, she used to," Wes whispered. "I don't feel the bond. Ugh, I still have this fucking headache."

"You don't feel it? Good. It could be considered an abandoned bond given she disappeared and how long it's been since you last saw her. I'll call the pack lawyer." Brennan relaxed slightly.

"That might not negate anything in this situation. Does she feel it?" Lexi asked.

Wes shrugged.

"Seeing them interact, I can tell something's there," I told her.

"Evan, I *will* file the paperwork if you want me to." Wes looked away, remorse flowing off him.

A mate bond could be broken, but it required drugs to dissolve them—and a legal reason to use them. Since the process could be misused, it was lengthy. But it was important that a method for un-bonding existed, since occasionally the ability to create bonds was abused. Alphas could bond with designations beyond omegas. Omegas also could also create bonds, they just didn't leave a physical mark.

"Let's not go there until you two figure your shit out and we can have a conversation like grownups. We have to consider her needs and wants, too," I replied, grabbing a plate. To mitigate the power imbalance, Grace's desires would carry more legal weight.

I wasn't sure she'd survive breaking a bond with her *soulmate* in her current state. Not everyone did. Not to mention the long-term effects it would have on both of them.

Why were my guys being stupid?

"If you bonded her, why isn't she in a database? It's like she doesn't exist," Brennan added, taking a plate to the table. "Jett, food," he yelled.

"Well, there was that power outage that brought the northeast grid down yesterday, which could have affected the database." Lexi held my gaze. "Maybe they'll find her once everything has been reset."

Copy that. Lexi knew that sometimes the Center created new identities for omegas in danger. Good thing I started the process. I'd text Riley and see where we were.

"It's complicated." Wes sighed, ignoring his plate. "I bonded with her because I was thinking of her safety. Things with her mom were *bad,* and I wanted to find her. Obviously, it didn't work." His head hung. "We'd even talked about marriage. Sorry, Evan."

"Why do you keep apologizing? I didn't even know you then. You can marry her. Shit, I'll marry her if you don't." I grinned, only partially teasing. "She'd make a beautiful bride. She's a rose garden girl, too, isn't she? With harp music—no, a string quartet. Ooh, and a chocolate fountain."

I could see it. Because of my work at the Center, I'd helped plan many weddings and bonding parties. Plenty of alphas married their omegas in addition to mating. Jett and Brennan were both bonded and married, because Jett was a beta and their mate bond didn't have the same legal weight as me and Bren—or me and Wes. It was at their wedding when the four of us realized that we might make a good pack.

"Not this one, please?" Lexi put down her plate and withdrew a small book from her bag and opened it. "I got this from Dad's last night."

There was a pencil sketch of Grace, surrounded by flowers, wearing the most horrific wedding dress ever.

Wes snatched it from her. "Invasion of privacy much?"

"Stuff at Dad's is fair game. Also, I have more." She handed Brennan and me each one. "It's interesting to see how he's improved over the years."

These sketches in the book I had weren't as good. But I could still tell it was Grace. A little Grace with ponytails and freckles on a swing.

"I remember those charcoal sketches you did for that art show—they were her." Brennan handed the book to Lexi. "Fuck."

"He looked for her, and so did I," Lexi said softly.

A bolt of concern shot through my bond with Wes. I looked over, and he stood there, frozen, with a stricken look on his face.

"Something's not right." Wes set the sketchbook down and yelled, "Grace!"

"What else could go wrong?" Brennan muttered as Wes took off for the living room.

"Guys," Jett yelled at about the same time. "Get in here."

Still holding the sketchbook, I ran into the living room, Lexi following.

Jett was on his phone. "I'd like to report a medical emergency."

Wes knelt on the floor, panic coursing through our bond, fear flooding the room, as Grace lay on the living room carpet, convulsing, the room reeking of rotten peaches.

Chapter Eleven

Wes

My gut twisted as I saw Grace on her side, seizing in the living room. I knelt beside her, not knowing what else to do but hold her hand. Fuck. Fuck. Fuck.

"I'd like to report a medical emergency," Jett said on the phone. "Seizure. Don't know if she has a history, but she got a concussion yesterday." He gave them our address.

"Fuck," Lexi whispered, standing behind me.

All I could do was kneel there as Grace *kept* seizing. How long did they last?

"I'll be right back," Evan said softly, sending reassurance through our bond.

"I was talking to her, and she started shaking and fell. She's in a safe place, and on her side. It's still happening, I set a timer," Jett added to the person on the phone.

My chest shook. "It's okay, Grace. I'm right here."

She had to be okay. She just had to.

The shaking slowed. Good. "Come back to me. I'm right here. It's going to be okay."

Grace stopped shaking and whined a little, calling to my alpha instincts.

"I'm right here," I told her, squeezing her hand.

"Seizure ended." Jett read the time off to the emergency dispatcher. "Great, I'll stay on the line until they get here." He looked at me. "They'll be here soon."

"Grace, are you okay?" I hated this feeling of helplessness. I'd felt it over and over when we were teenagers.

She whined again, met my gaze, and then her eyes closed.

Lexi crouched next to me, voice soft. "Wes, they're going to take her to the hospital, and you're going to go with her and you're going to be very careful about what you say."

I nodded. "Right. I don't want her to end up on a psych hold."

Like her mom had done to her more than once.

"That, *and* I don't want you to end up being investigated for *abuse or neglect*," she whispered. "This is going to look bad. When I show up because she's part of an open case, and was found yesterday bruised, afraid, with amnesia, and possibly on the run? Yeah, that's not a good look."

Her words were a punch in the stomach. "Shit."

I'd never hurt her. But the law would think otherwise.

"You're bonded to her, but it's not registered. She's not part of your pack. You're not married, and you don't have a legal agreement. Sure, she was missing, but you never filed a missing person report. Not to mention, the Center documented all those old scars on her body—and her current bruises." Her tone and look were warnings.

I nodded. "I can see what doctors—and the law—might think. But she'll set them straight."

"The law will take more than her word into consideration, since she could be coerced, or barked, into saying that it wasn't you. I handle these sorts of cases all the time. You'll be considered guilty until proven innocent," Lexi warned. "With *facts.*"

I gulped, as her words hit me. "Brennan's probably calling the pack lawyer."

"Not sure that's going to help; at least not the way you'd want it to. Brennan's *pissed*. At least it's early enough in the morning that you can pass off what she's wearing as PJs instead of the fact that she has no clothes. Which will be seen as neglect," she added.

Fuck.

"Here's your shoes, phone and wallet." Evan joined us, dressed, holding my things.

"Regardless of whatever you feel, whatever might happen in the future, *in this moment* you've got to good alpha the ever-loving shit out of this," Lexi continued. "Evan, will you please help him because you know how this is going to look."

"Of course. Wes, put on your shoes." Evan knelt down with us and stroked her hair. "I'm right here, Peaches."

I took them from him and put my phone and wallet in my pockets and shoved my feet in the shoes, right as Jett opened the door and two beta paramedics came in with a bag and a board.

"She had a seizure. Is she going to be okay?" I asked the female paramedic, voice shaking. I'd just gotten her, I couldn't lose her already.

She nodded. "We'll get her to the hospital, and then they'll check her out. Are you her..." She looked at Grace's neck and hand, though she frowned at all of Grace's bruises. "Significant other?"

"Yeah." I gulped, still clutching her hand. It was the quickest explanation. "We were about to have breakfast. Why isn't she waking up?"

"It's common after a seizure this long," she assured.

"Where are we taking her? The Center? Somewhere else?" the male paramedic asked as he bent down to shine a flashlight in her eyes.

Evan elbowed me. Oh, he was talking to me? Jett was talking to Lexi.

"Mercy Hospital?" I replied. Brennan's family had their name on the wall. "I'm coming with her."

"Of course," he assured. "There's room for the both of you." He took a little box and pressed her finger to it to access her record.

Oh shit. Right.

"The grid her record was on was glitching yesterday, so if you get nothing we'll try again at the hospital," Evan told him. "We're good for it, promise."

"There she is," the male paramedic confirmed. "Gamma. Wow."

She had a record? Gamma? What? Confusion shot through me.

Evan came up behind me and whispered in my ear, "I'll explain later."

"Grace is pretty special," I sputtered. What? How? When? So many thoughts and questions were running through my head.

They got her onto a board, and I held her hand as we went outside to the ambulance. Jett and Evan came outside with us, deep in conversation.

I got in the back with Grace, Evan went up front.

The woman asked me questions as she got Grace hooked up to monitors. Terror shot through me as I fumbled through them. Lexi was right, this was going to look bad, and with Brennan not on my side...

We got to the hospital, and as they wheeled Grace into the hallway and spoke to the doctors, she seized again. One doctor shouted, and she was wheeled off. I trotted to keep up, still holding her hand. What had happened? Was it the concussion? Something else?

They'd done a lot of things to her when she was a teenager. It could have left her with health issues.

"I'm going with her," I demanded, not letting go of her hand. I needed her to be okay.

"It's okay, let them do their jobs," Evan said, prying my hand from hers.

"But–" I stood there as they continued moving, *with my Grace.* No, they couldn't take her from me. Not again.

"Why don't we go do the paperwork," an alpha nurse said firmly. She sat me down in a waiting area with a tablet.

I wanted to stay with Grace. The form on the tablet was partially populated with all sorts of things. An address I didn't recognize. A blood type. A partially incorrect birthdate. Me.

Mate: Wesley Lawson, Alpha

"Evan..."

My omega put an arm around me and leaned in close, lips brushing my ear. "So, I got a record going for her last night. It's nowhere near done, but hopefully it'll hold for now."

"How do you even..." While I'd taught Evan a lot, he couldn't create a government identity for someone.

Evan chewed on his lower lip. "Sometimes the Center gives omegas new identities. I used someone I trust implicitly."

"Oh. That makes sense." Not that the idea of an illegal record seemed any better than no record. "Gamma?" I didn't know much about them.

"You didn't see her slap Brennan. That was a total gamma move. I had to put her down as something, and that made the most sense with the information I have. I know it won't hold up on a major scan, but we'll build that in somehow," he whispered. "We have to protect our Grace."

Grace had slapped Brennan? No wonder he was in a mood. I wasn't sure what slapping alphas had to do with designations, though.

"Let's go over this together. Then, I need to call Spencer. I told Jett the same story you told Brennan. We're going to need to brief Grace when she wakes. Lexi is right, this could get serious, quickly," Evan said.

"You keep saying *our*." I looked at him, part of me pleased he liked her so much.

"Do you not like it?" His look went amused.

Oh, I did. Too much. All night I kept thinking about what Evan said about him watching her take my knot while she sucked his cock.

"Right now, you have to think like her mate, because in the eyes of the law you *are*," Evan told me. "I don't know the staff here like I do at General or the hospital at my Center."

Think like a mate. I nodded. "Grace likes pink and cookies."

Evan chuckled. "She told me green. She's older now. Her favorite ice cream *is* cookie dough."

We went through the forms, then Evan left to make some calls. There were so many things I knew about Evan that I didn't know about Grace, things a mate would know. Not to mention, I didn't actually feel her like I did Evan.

I felt something though–little flickers through my still-raging headache.

Finally, the doctor came over to me. "Wes Lawson?"

I stood. "Can I see her?"

"Grace has had a couple of seizures. We're getting some scans and running her bloodwork. Does she have a history of seizures? Her medical records are not very robust. We do have her records from the Center." His tone dripped with judgment.

"I don't think so." I shook my head, not remembering her ever mentioning that. Of course, they did *shock* her when she was teenager.

"I see." He asked me a few more questions.

"Can I see her? Will she be okay? When can I take her home?" I pressed, worry burrowing within me.

"We want to admit her and monitor her for a day or two to make sure there isn't any permanent damage. Is she going to be okay here in the Omega Ward or should we have her transferred?" he asked.

"Here's fine." Mercy Hospital was the best, where else would they take her?

Omega Ward?

"Go wait on the second floor. The nurse will let you know when she's ready for visitors. Someone should bring her things so that she'll be more comfortable," he added.

Things? I nodded. "Of course, Doctor. Thank you."

He left, and I texted Evan, hoping he'd know.

Me

> She's being admitted, and might be here a few days. Doc says to bring her things.

Evan

On it.

Not knowing what else to do, I went up to the second floor to an area outside a guarded set of doors that said *Omega Ward.*

I sat there in the waiting room, letting Spencer know what was going on, and checking my emails from my phone. Unable to do much work from here, I started looking up seizures and concussions. Also, gammas.

Oh, gammas fell under omega law? Was that good or bad?

"Excuse me, Mr. Lawson? I'm Sharice, one of the hospital case-workers. I'd like to chat with you about Grace." Sharice was a no-nonsense middle-aged beta.

My belly sank. "Of course."

"While I understand that she was attacked yesterday, she also has a lot of old injuries." She gave me a look, as if I'd caused it.

Fuck. *Stick as close to the truth as possible.*

"Her parents were horrible. I know this looks bad, but *I didn't hurt her*. Not yesterday, not ever," I told her, hoping she believed me.

She asked me a bunch of questions, unimpressed by my answers. Where was Evan? I could use his help since he knew how to navigate all of this.

A large, imposing, man in a suit with a badge and a hard expression strode over to us, and my belly twisted.

"Sorry to interrupt, you are Mr. Lawson?" he asked.

"Yes." My heart lodged in my throat.

"I'm Detective Orson. I'm taking over for Detective Lawson regarding Miss Ellington's case," he growled.

While that made sense, I'd rather deal with my sister.

"Doctor. She's *Doctor Ellington,*" I corrected. I wanted to bristle at him, challenge him for even thinking I'd hurt my Grace. But that wouldn't help.

"I'm going to take him down to the station for a little chat," he told the social worker.

What did I do? Immediately asking for a lawyer would make me seem guilty. *Think like a mate.* If this were Evan, or one of my packmates, I'd cooperate.

I stood, trying to project innocence and confidence. "Of course. Whatever you need, Detective. Is it okay if I let my omega know? He went to get Grace's things, and I want someone to be here when she's allowed visitors."

"Go ahead." He started walking.

I followed, texting the group chat an update about Grace and that I was going to the station. Hopefully, this wouldn't end with me being detained.

Chapter Twelve

Brennan

I walked into the living room and saw Jett on the phone, Grace on the floor, and Wes looking like the world was ending, Lexi crouched next to him. Evan was nowhere to be seen. Probably upset by all this.

We didn't need this right now. We'd barely recovered from Caroline. How dare Wes keep this from us? We were a family, and families didn't hide things. Families also protected each other. Clearly, Wes needed to be protected from himself.

I stalked back into the kitchen, grabbed my phone, and dialed Morty, our pack lawyer.

"Brennan, it's a little early, is everything okay?" Morty asked.

"Apparently, Wes has a mate no one knew about, and she showed up yesterday," I growled, anger bubbling inside me. How dare he?

"Wes? Not who I'd expect," he replied. "I always thought Spencer would have a secret mate or baby. What does she want? Money? A place in the pack?"

"Of course she wants mo–" I paused. Grace hadn't asked for anything. She also seemed willing to leave. But everything still felt suspicious. "She wants something. I just don't know what."

"Are you looking to buy her off or dissolve the bond legally? I'm assuming there is a bond? Is it consensual?" he asked.

"No money. We don't negotiate with exes. They were young when they bonded, apparently. It could be considered abandoned. Wes said he'd file the paperwork. I need this handled quickly and quietly. My pack, my omega, can't handle another Caroline." I looked out the window and saw an ambulance pull up.

Evan wanting to keep her worried me. He had such a big heart, and I didn't want to see him get hurt.

"I can't believe Wes kept this from me," I added, the betrayal still stinging.

"Did he say *why?*"

"He thought she was dead. Wes doesn't feel the bond, but the test was positive." I understood that her parents didn't want her mating Wes back then. But they weren't teenagers anymore. If someone was keeping me from my mate, I certainly wouldn't wait *years.*

"Yes, I can work with that," he replied. "Did she seem... agreeable?"

"Yes." After all, she said she'd leave.

Lexi marched into the kitchen with her annoying bossy face on.

"I've got to handle a few things here. I'll talk to you later." I hung up before he could respond.

Her arms crossed over her chest. "I hope you didn't do anything stupid."

"I'm trying to protect my pack, Lexi," I growled. "Also, no shoes in the house."

"I didn't expect to stay. I was going to take her to the station. Of course, you're trying to protect your pack. I get it. Just please, don't do anything before you talk to Wes and Evan and get the full story. Grace is... complicated, but yesterday I didn't get that she was a danger to your pack, but she probably is *in* danger," Lexi replied. "And she's *terrified.*"

"All the more reason to get her out of my life." I rubbed the bridge of my nose with my thumb and forefinger. "Are you taking her to the station?"

"She's going to the hospital. I think Wes and Evan are going with her."

Jett came in. "Wes and Grace are *mated?* I'm so confused."

"I'll be in touch." She left.

"I've already called the lawyer," I huffed, looking at all the abandoned dishes. "Do you want me to warm up your food, Honey?"

"Please, Dear? Huh. While Grace seems sweet, her memory loss and no records feel off," Jett replied. "Hopefully, she's okay. That was a serious seizure."

"I'm sure she's fine." I put his eggs in the microwave.

"Do you think Wes still cares for her?"

"I'm worried more about what this means for the pack—and Evan." I took out his plate and put it on the table, then began cleaning up.

Jett refilled his coffee and sat down. "I'm worried more about Wes. But I know you have our best interests at heart, Honey."

I kissed Jett. I'd do anything to protect my family. Right now, I needed to do for Wes what I refused to do for myself when Caroline showed up.

Chapter Thirteen

Grace

"Can I see Wes *now?*" I asked, as the nurse wheeled me from the strange MRI I'd had. Exhaustion pressed down on me. I still wasn't entirely sure what had happened other than I'd had a couple of seizures and was in the hospital.

Part of me really wanted Wes, though so far I hadn't seen Wes–or Evan. However, I *had* briefly talked to a detective and a hospital social worker. Knowing I wouldn't get put on a psych hold for mentioning Fade or alphas was a relief. But I was still afraid, not that I'd slip and mention parallel worlds, but that my lack of records or knowledge of their world might make the doctors suspicious. If everything seemed a little off to me, I might seem a little off to them.

"You need to rest. I think someone went to get your things," the stern nurse told me as she brought me to a room upstairs.

Things? I nodded. I'd been trying to say as little as possible. Except when that male detective and the hospital social worker tried to imply that Wes hurt me. That I shut down.

Fortunately, the nurse hadn't let either of them talk to me for long. The detective had no updates. What if they found nothing?

What if they did?

Not to mention, I was here in Wes' world, with the man I'd dreamed of for seven years. I felt so many things about this.

Too bad my brain wasn't cooperating. My fingers itched to write equations I couldn't quite remember and figure all this out.

We arrived in a private room that felt more like a hotel than a hospital. She hooked me up to some monitors as I sat on the rather large hospital bed.

I wouldn't blame Wes if he left me here. After all, I wasn't his problem, and I didn't want to mess up the life he'd built.

If this was weird for me, what was it like for him?

Brennan's reaction worried me. That guy had some issues. He also reeked of privileged asshole–the kind that could cause problems.

There was a knock on the door. "Peaches?"

Evan came in with a duffle bag and some balloons attached to a little bear.

"Evan." It was nice to see *someone*–and he looked happy to see me.

The nurse gave him a look. "Excuse me, you are?"

"I'm Evan, her omega." Evan showed her the sticker on his shirt and gave me a kiss on the cheek. "Roll with it," he whispered, putting the balloon bear on the nightstand.

"Those are so pretty. Thank you." The gesture overwhelmed me. I looked around. "Where's Wes?"

"Hopefully, he'll be here soon. I brought your things." Evan took stuff out of the duffle bag. "We were so worried, we even forgot to put shoes on you." He bent down and put fuzzy sage-green slippers with little pom-poms on my feet.

They'd been bare, but someone had given me socks.

"Thanks." They were so soft and plush.

Evan added a couple of chenille pillows to the bed and wrapped a matching blanket around me–all the same shade of green.

The nurse finished up and gave us a look. "You can stay, but let her rest."

"Promise." He kicked off his shoes and got on the bed with me, covering us with another soft and fluffy blanket.

I snuggled into him, desperately needing that reassurance. "Hi."

"Hi. Cuddle right in there." His voice got soft. "Okay, Wes is still at the police station. Did you talk to anyone?"

I nodded. "A detective that wasn't Lexi and a social worker. But I didn't say much other than that Wes didn't hurt me and what I remembered from yesterday. It's so hard to think, and I'm so tired. He's at the station?"

"Yes. They're still looking for who hurt you. Let me tell you what's going on." Evan filled me in as we snuggled on the rather comfortable hospital bed.

"Nothing, so much of this means *nothing*." I frowned. "But having a record is good, right? Why would Wes get slapped with a neglect case? I don't understand."

"I know, Peaches. Oh, I had to change your birthday year so you were a year older, just to head off... things." Evan looked anxious.

"Why?" I frowned.

"Did Wes ever mention anything about bonds and mates?"

"Maybe?" I thought for a moment and another memory bubble popped. "It's like marriage, right? Only you can feel each other. You said there's a concern that he's not taking care of me, but what about me taking care of him? It's a partnership; mates take care of each other."

"They do." He stroked my hair. "Did Wes ever bond with you? Bite you, but not just a nibble, like a special bite."

Again, I thought for a moment, trying to find everything in my brain. There it was. "Oh. So we could find each other. But I only felt him when we were together in our dreams."

"Do you feel him now?" he asked.

My nose scrunched. "I wouldn't even know what to feel. Should I?"

Evan kissed my temple, soft and light like a butterfly. "Concussions can mess with bonds. You won't be able to read his mind, but you should be able to sense him and his feelings. You... you should also be able to feel me."

"I should? How?" I blinked. All I felt was fatigue and pain.

"Since I'm bonded to him, we should technically feel each other through our bond with him."

"Oh." I got comfortable on his chest. "So what does that have to do with my birthday?"

"First, your world uses a different year system. Second, Wes said that he bonded with you when he was nineteen. Considering how your birthdays fall, there was never a point where you were eighteen with him being nineteen. So, I changed it so you were legal when he bit you. Just to head off any other issues," he told me.

"Oh. Okay. That makes sense." Honestly, it didn't matter to me. Wes getting in trouble, did. "Um, you have two marks, right? One for each alpha? Did I get that right?" I saw them last night when he had his shirt off.

"Yeah." He took off his polo shirt, and I saw two bite marks, one on each side of his neck. "The one on the left is Wes, the one on the right is Bren. Jett has a bite from Brennan, too, same place. Only alpha bites leave physical imprints, but believe me, I've marked all three." He gave me a lusty wink.

Oh, was that why I liked to bite Wes? He'd never complained; if anything, he told me to bite harder.

"Is that why I want to snuggle you and why you smell good?" I buried my head in his neck and inhaled his lemonade scent.

"Could be. Or because you think I'm sexy. But go ahead. We need to convince the hospital that while we might have things to figure out, no one's being neglected." His arms wrapped around me.

"We're going to pretend?" I winced. Lying made everything worse.

"No. We're going to act on these genuine feelings we have. All three of us. Responsibly and consensually. We're going to work all this out, including some hot sex, ice cream, and therapy."

"I... I'm going to have to go home, eventually. Spencer's right, I don't belong here." If I played house with these two and then had to leave...

"He also said that doesn't mean you have to go. Part of working through this and not just acting on it, is so that if you go home, no one goes to pieces. Not that I want you to go home. No one's going to make you have sex, but I'm all for that." He nuzzled me and gave a little sexy growl.

I laughed. "I'm here for the banter."

This place made me *thirsty*–especially for Wes and Evan.

And Spencer? Oh, yeah. All of Evan's guys were so sexy. Even Brennan-the-grump.

Still, what was I thinking? I barely knew them. But it felt so right.

"Good. I know you're still trying to work through everything, but people are going to expect us to act a certain way," he told me. "I'm your omega. Us cuddling in your hospital bed–perfectly normal. My bringing you fluffy blankets and pillows, very normal."

"These blankets are like clouds." This world seemed full of soft blankets, and I was all for it.

"Did I get the right shade of green?" he asked.

"It's a pretty shade of green," I said, petting the soft blanket.

His eyebrows rose. "Forest or spring?"

"Emerald. But sage green is nice, too, I like it." I cuddled into him. "I like snuggles."

"Me too. Still like pink and cookies?"

"Mauve and chocolate chip." I nodded. "What else is normal?"

"You sleeping in Wes' or my shirts. Someone from the pack always being here with you. Wes and I touching you. Oh, and lots of little normal couple things." He started playing with my hair, which was comforting and made me sleepy.

Normal couple things? Yeah, I wasn't sure I knew what those were.

I leaned into his touch, because it felt nice. "I'm pretty sure that I wasn't very good at relationships. After my mom cut me off, I was in my PhD program and too busy trying not to starve. Also, going through massive and expensive therapy to get over what my mom put me through. Not to mention I have issues."

"They cut you off?" He frowned. "Oh, you remembered something else?"

"You're right. I did." My brows furrowed as I tried to think. There really was no rhyme or reason to what I remembered other than older memories were a little easier.

"Take your time, Peaches." He kissed my forehead.

I winced as a particularly painful memory surfaced. "After I was *rehabilitated,* I went to the local state university to study to be a teacher," I said slowly as I shoved the memories together.

"She literally had the love of math beaten out of me. When I found it again and decided to pursue my childhood dreams of getting my PhD in math instead of coming home, teaching and marrying some church boy, yeah, she cut me off. My dad and I eventually reconnected when he divorced my mom. Still, I didn't even know my mom had died until one of my brothers accosted me right before I graduated to inform me she left me nothing and everyone hated me. Once that would have devastated me, but I no longer cared, I was living my dream. And now... now I'm here. I still don't know why or where *here* is." My *actual* dream.

While Wes had told me he lived in *Rockland*, I never did specifically figure out what mountain range he lived by. His world had been strange, because while some cities and states were called the same things, other things were different. Not that we'd really dug into the geographical, historical, or political differences of our worlds. Mostly we just talked about *life*–school, our families, hobbies, our hopes and dreams. I never asked him to draw me a map.

"Wow, you remembered a lot, good job." Evan stroked my hair.

"That one hurt," I whimpered.

"I'm sure it did. You can still achieve your dreams here. I think Spence would hire you." Evan kept stroking my hair. "But that's good to know. While your mom keeping you from him will help Wes from being deemed a neglectful bond mate, you've been an adult for a while."

"I didn't think he was real. I'm struggling with that, Evan. They hurt me, drugged me, told me over and over I was imagining things, and now..." I shook a little. It was so much to take in.

"Sorry, Peaches." He nuzzled me again. "I'm sure this is so much for you. Don't stress too much about keeping things straight right now. I've got you."

"Because I'm the disoriented one with the head injury? None of this is Wes' fault. You can't neglect someone who doesn't exist. But it's not like I can tell the whole truth. I should never have come here." I sniffed, feeling awful for causing problems.

"Did you come here? Like, did you flee the men chasing you and you came here so Wes could keep you safe? Were you dumped here?" he prodded.

Squeezing my eyes shut, I tried to picture it. I was running, there was shouting, and then... black. Park bench. Those guys. Nothing else came. "I don't know."

"That's okay. We'll get to know each other a little. You should know things about us and the rest of the pack," he added.

"True. I know what you, Jett, and Wes do for a living, but what about Spencer and Brennan?" I was curious, especially after Spencer just *knew* I wasn't from here.

"Brennan's in real estate. He's loaded—and so is his family. His mom owns half the city. He's also grumpy, likes privacy because he grew up in such a public family, and is overprotective, which explains, but doesn't excuse, him this morning. Spencer's a genius who made a shit-ton of money in pharmaceuticals, then shifted into biotech. He's always had an interest in quantum physics, but I'm not sure how he figured out so fast that you weren't from here—I didn't tell him," Evan told me.

"He said that I smelled of neutrons. I didn't know they had smells, but it makes sense that some sort of particle might cling to you during inter-world travel. Do you think he can help me get back?" Oh my god, Spencer was hot in a sexy silver fox way. I'd make some science with him.

Whoa, girl. What about Wes and Evan? There I went with the thirsty thoughts.

But multiple husbands seemed to be a thing here.

"Do you want to go back?" Evan asked.

I thought about it for a moment. My gut instinct was to say *no*, despite my brain insisting that I had to. "Won't my being out of sync mess things up? I don't want to cause an incursion."

"I'll leave that to you and Spence. His offer of a lab is sincere. But you should let your brain heal first."

"That sounds good. Will you explain what a gamma is? I've never heard of it. Only alphas and omegas." Being here in his arms felt so good, so right, even though I'd just met him.

"I'll do you one better. I brought those videos." He got up and took the laptop out of his bag. "I have to go to work soon, but we've got enough time to watch some."

Chapter Fourteen

Grace

I woke to the sound of tapping.

"Hey, don't you have to go to work?" My stomach rumbled as I awoke from my nap. The clock said it was well after lunch. Evan was squished with me on the hospital bed working on his laptop.

"Wes isn't back yet. The nurse said to press the call button, and they'll bring you food." He looked worried.

"Okay, I'm going to use the restroom first. You said that you brought me some clothes?" I was in a hospital gown, which was much cuter but not really any better than in my world.

"I brought you a shirt of mine and a shirt of Wes' and some PJ pants and stuff." He went bashful. "I guessed your size. But I should know them since you need clothes–not that you aren't adorable in Wes' stuff. Carly from the Center stopped by. Gammas are technically under omega laws, so you're being assigned an advocate."

"Oh, okay. This is bad or good?" I frowned, not really understanding, though Carly had been nice.

"While you legally can decline an advocate, I'd rather you have a Center advocate than a city case worker. The social worker that you met with earlier works for the hospital, and makes referrals," he explained. "I also told Carly that it might be better for you to have an advocate that wasn't her, because of me."

"Okay." Grabbing the clothes, I dragged the monitor with me into the bathroom. When I came out, Evan was speaking with an older woman in a pantsuit who was holding a tablet and wearing a badge. She smelled a bit like old books.

"Grace, this is Mrs. Beekman, from the Center. I'm going to step out and make some calls. I'll be right back, okay?" Evan gave me a hug and left.

"Hi, Grace. I've been legally appointed to you." Mrs. Beekman looked kind. "I'm here to make sure *you* are okay and that your rights and wishes are advocated for. We're going to have lots of talks, and I know you're exhausted and recovering, so we'll keep this one short, okay?"

"Okay. My memories are still so scrambled, and it's hard to think." I got back on the bed and curled up in the blankets.

I thought she'd walk me through everything, but instead we just talked, which was nice.

"How do you feel about Wes having an omega?" she finally asked.

"I love Evan and want to keep him forever." My head ducked. The idea of multiple husbands seemed both scandalous and practical.

"He seems like a dear. I don't know him well; they had me brought from another Center. It's a lot, coming into an established pack when you don't know most of them—and you have rights," she told me. "Do you mind if I use the restroom? My bladder isn't as young as it used to be."

She stood and went to the restroom. Where was Evan? I hope he brought me food. I didn't want to bother the nurses.

Evan had left the door open, and a man strode in without knocking. He wore a suit, but seemed a little shady, and smelled like string cheese that had been in your lunchbox all day.

"Who are you?" I demanded. He didn't look like a detective or a doctor. Fear hit me. Had they found me? I went to call out, and it stuck in my throat.

"That doesn't matter. What matters is who are you and why are you here?" he prodded.

I swallowed my scream and blinked. "I'm Grace and I had a seizure?"

Confusion shot through me. Not the people chasing me then?

"You haven't seen Wes in years, and now, right as Compass BioTek is doing very well, here you are. What, him being some working-class boy wasn't attractive, but then you saw some gossip write-up on his rich pack and thought you'd cash in?" he pressed, getting very close to me, his scent of string cheese cloying.

Oh. *Asshole alert. Ding ding ding.*

"I don't care about power or money." I frowned, anger bubbling up inside me. "How dare you even think that?"

"So, it's Wes? You thought you'd take Wes from his family–and omega?" he growled.

"I didn't come to mess anything up. Please leave." I made my voice tart.

"Then why did you come? You're *not* getting any money from them. Is that clear?" he sneered. "Little whores get nothing from this pack. They don't negotiate with exes."

"Loving someone doesn't make me a whore." My voice rose as I inched closer to the side of the bed, looking for something I could use to defend myself. Maybe I could hit him with the lamp.

"You need to leave. Now. Or you're not going to like what happens." He took a threatening step toward me.

A toilet flushed, and the bathroom door opened. Mrs. Beekman. For a moment I'd forgotten about her.

"Did you just threaten her, young man?" Mrs. Beekman demanded, looking fierce.

The man looked flustered. "Who the fuck are you?"

"Grace's advocate from the Omega Center." She flashed the badge around her neck.

"Look, the pack doesn't want her, so—"

"The pack doesn't want her? Really, Eli? Because Wes and I want her here." Evan strode in, angry. The air had turned spicy.

"Evan. I thought you were at work. I was just trying to find out the truth so we don't have a situation," Eli backpedaled, scooting back toward the door.

"This is bullshit. Get the fuck out of here," Evan demanded. "Grace, Peaches, are you okay?" He cuddled me to him as I sobbed. "Mrs. Beekman, I swear, Wes and I had no part in this."

I pressed my face into Evan's shirt. "Someone tried to threaten me. How dare he. I... I'm allowed to love Wes." My chest shuddered. "Right?"

"You absolutely can love Wes." He planted a kiss on my head.

"Who was he?" Mrs. Beekman asked. "This doesn't bode well for your pack or your alpha."

"Eli works for one of the pack lawyers." Evan sighed. "All I can think of is that our head alpha is afraid this is going to end up like when his ex reappeared. Which it's not. This is very different. He's trying to protect—"

"So, you're defending him?" she countered.

"Not at all, just trying to explain. I'm sure this is all a misunder-standing," Evan soothed. "Even if it's not, I don't condone this. Understood, Peaches? This isn't me or Wes. *We want you here.*"

My head went mushy. "I don't even understand what's going on. I should but..."

One of my monitors screamed, and everything went black.

Chapter Fifteen

Wes

I texted Evan as I sat in the hospital waiting room on the second floor.

They won't let me in. Are you still with her?

She'd had another seizure, been *threatened,* and they *still* wouldn't let me see her.

I am. She's sleeping again, but she asked for you.

While I understood Brennan calling Morty to find out where we stood legally, I didn't get *sending someone to threaten Grace at the hospital.* We didn't even know what was going on—not that anyone was telling me anything. Sure, I had so many questions. But

Grace was here. *My* Grace. Something I'd imagined happening for so long.

That old excitement bubbled to the surface. As well as that ingrained alpha need to be by her side. She was *mine.*

"You okay?" My sister stood there with a concerned look on her face.

"Why are you here, Lexi?" I sighed.

"I said I'd stop by." She dropped into the chair next to me.

"They won't let me see her." My shoulders drooped. Grace and Evan needed me, and *the nurses wouldn't let me in.*

I *could* try to alpha my way in. But that would make it worse.

"She's not alone, is she?" Lexi frowned.

"Evan's been with her all day." I rubbed my temples. "Do you have anything? I've had a headache since yesterday."

"Sure." She fished a bottle of pain reliever out of her bag.

I took two tablets dry. "Thanks. I'm so pissed at Bren. Sure, he said he didn't specifically ask Morty to send Eli, but still..."

That dumbass move could hurt us. A lot.

"I told him not to be stupid." Lexi rolled her eyes.

"I understand him being mad because I kept something huge from them, not that I ever thought it was huge until today. But for a moment there, I thought I'd end up in a cell." The detectives did a great job of making me feel like a bad alpha.

She patted my shoulder. "Me too. You're not out of danger. Detective Orson is a hardass."

"I know, and I understand Bren being worried about Evan. *I* worry about Evan. Look." I showed her a picture of Grace sleeping on him, covered in blankets. "He's attached."

"It's better than them hating each other," Lexi replied.

"Yeah." It made it easier to accept all this, accept Grace. Part of me still wasn't sure I should–or could–go back to what we had. If it was even real. But it felt like it was real.

So real.

"Do you want me to see if the nurses will let me check on her? Maybe Evan can come out and give you a kiss. I think you need one," she offered.

"Thank you." That's exactly what I needed right now.

She left, and I went through my emails on my phone. I never had made it into work. One more thing I'd failed at today. I texted Evan.

Me

> **What kind of takeout does Grace like?**

That seemed like something a mate would know. When we were kids, she liked pizza, cookies, and ice cream.

Evan

> **Grace says she likes carbs. Especially potato-based ones.**

Brennan had also sent a string of texts about needing to talk to me. *Nope. Not interested.*

A few moments later, Evan entered the waiting area. "Hey, Babe."

"Hey, Babe." I pulled him to me, relishing in the comfort, the warmth, of the person I loved most. "This has been a shit day."

"I know. Bren can be such a dick sometimes." Evan sighed, nuzzling me, giving me a hit of lemonade and calming omega pheromones, peaches clinging to him. "This is going to be shitty. I hope they don't remove Grace from us because of his fuckery. That's not what she needs right now."

"She needs to nap on your chest in a pile of blankets?" My head tilted.

"Preferably with you in it. She needs *you*." He held me tighter. "I'm fucking serious. She needs you. Your cuddles. Your care. Your love. She probably could use your knot."

I frowned.

"If you're not ready, fine. But please believe me when I say that I don't care if you fuck her. I want to fuck her when she's ready for me."

There was no lie in his statement.

"I believe you. Thank you." Leaning in, I gave him a kiss. "I don't feel her. That's bad, right? The detectives made me feel like shit over it."

What I needed was to drag him into my bed.

"She has a concussion. Maybe that's why you've had a headache." He rubbed the back of my neck.

Oh. That made sense. "When her concussion's better, I'll feel her?"

Did I want to feel her? Maybe. I was so confused about all of this. I knew in theory that you could love more than one person. After all, Brennan loved Jett *and* Evan. Evan loved Jett, Brennan, *and* me. But I hadn't grown up with multiple parents. Could I? Should I?

"Probably. You should buy her a big fluffy blanket in emerald green and bring it to her along with a container of cookie dough ice cream," Evan suggested.

"Why?" It seemed like there were a million other things I should be doing right now. Presents could wait.

"Your mate's in the hospital, Babe. I got her balloons and brought her things, but you should bring her something," he told me.

"Right. But I don't even have a car here." Ice cream would be nice, but there had to be something she'd like more than a blanket.

I'd just brought Evan his favorite snacks and some books when he was in the hospital.

Brennan strode into the hospital waiting room like he owned the place, still dressed for work in an expensive suit.

Wait, he sort of did own the place, given his family's name was on the wall.

I scowled. "What do you want?"

"We need to go. Jett's waiting in the car." His look was all business as his arms crossed over his chest.

"I'm not going anywhere with you, asshole," I retorted.

"I'm trying to protect the pack and Evan," Brennan parried.

"I can speak for myself," Evan interjected. "This is a mess, Bren. The entire pack can be investigated for this."

Brennan winced. "I know." He drew Evan to him. "I'm sorry, Love."

Evan leaned his head on Brennan's shoulder. "I know. But I'm tired of being used as an excuse for you two to be assholes."

At first, when Brennan was interested in Evan, I'd thought I'd be jealous of *my* omega being with someone else. But now it was a comfort knowing that someone was always there for him–and we were all there for each other. It's not like I hadn't known Brennan since high school, and Jett and I had a lot of common interests.

I was still pissed at Brennan.

"Don't I get an apology? I'm the one who could go to *jail*." My arms crossed over my chest, and I scowled at him.

"Fine. I'm sorry I caused all this. But I'm not giving you a kiss," Brennan told me. "Now get in the car."

"We can't leave Grace alone," I retorted, not wanting to go anywhere with him–or leave.

"Maybe Lexi will stay longer?" Evan asked.

"We've been summoned by my mother. Spencer will meet us there." A glum look crossed Brennan's face.

"Oh, fuck," I muttered. I texted Lexi, and she agreed.

Brennan was an adult, with his own pack. Mostly, as long as we handled our shit so that it didn't reflect badly on her, his mom left us to our own business. Her bringing us in like this meant we were in a lot of trouble that could reflect badly on her and her position in the community.

We squished into Jett's sports car, and we drove in silence.

"I hope you fired Morty," Evan finally said.

"I did. We're going to need a new lawyer," Brennan replied. "I'll punch anyone who suggests Katie."

Katie was his twin sister, the golden child—and Lexi's best friend and packmate. I'd met Brennan through them, we'd all gone to the same high school.

"How bad will things get?" Evan asked. "I didn't meet with the police, just the social worker and Grace's advocate."

"I could be placed on leave for this. Is Grace okay?" Jett asked as he drove.

"She was awake when I left. But yeah, the doctor's worried about the seizures and the head injury—and the memory loss being permanent," Evan said.

We pulled into the parking garage of his mother's company. If we were meeting her at her office and not at a restaurant or her home, then this was serious.

Spencer waited for us in the lobby. We got into the elevator that would take us to Brennan's mom's office on the top floor. The doors opened onto a sumptuous lobby. The door to his mother's office stood open.

"Time to gird your loins, gentlemen," Spencer told us.

The five of us filed in like children in trouble. Siobhan Morris was one of the most respected alphas in the city—and the most formidable. Which was why we called her the *queen mum*; but never to her face.

"Sit, boys." Her red hair was up in a bun, the green of her silk blouse accenting her eyes perfectly. Every inch of her, impeccable and pulled together, just like her empire and family.

We all sat, except for Spencer, who leaned against the wall.

Brennan took a deep breath. "Mother, I can explain–"

She held up a hand, her cedar scent spicy with anger. "The time for explaining has passed," she snapped. "Do you know what I had to do to keep this from exploding? No. You don't. Now, let me tell you how this is going to go."

No one did anything but nod. We didn't even ask how she knew.

Taking a deep breath of an annoyed parent trying to keep their temper, she continued, "Grace will be in the hospital for a couple of days. While she's there, you'll care for her just like you would if Evan were in the hospital. When she's discharged, you're going to bring her home and wait on her like she's a princess. You'll cooperate fully with the doctors, advocates, and police. This will continue not only until the investigation has been closed in your favor, but until it is beyond any doubt that all five of you are caring gentlemen, and not a bunch of assholes who don't have their shit together. Am I clear?"

"Yes, ma'am." I didn't have any problems with any of this. Grace needed someone to take care of her until she was better, and we knew who was chasing her, and how she got here. At the very least, I could do that.

I *wanted* to do that.

"So, we're not being investigated?" Brennan's head cocked.

"Of course you are," Siobhan retorted. "Because you had to be a knothead and take this from Wes being investigated to your entire pack on the verge of being *charged.*" Her voice stayed low, manicured hands folded neatly on her desk, which was more unnerving than if she yelled.

"Thank you, Mother, but you can't expect me to bring a stranger into my home and make her part of my pack. We have no idea who she is and what she wants," Brennan argued through gritted teeth, frustration rolling off him.

Jett put a hand on his shoulder, and Evan squeezed his hand.

"Do *not* bring her into your pack or do anything rash without going through proper legal channels—and certainly not until the investigations are over," she ordered. "While Grace isn't part of your pack, she is legally Wes' mate. Wes' *injured* mate, who is *part of a police investigation*. I'm not asking you all to court her, but you certainly need to care for her appropriately."

Brennan growled. "I don't like people in my house."

"Wes and I will take her to mine then," Evan said.

As part of our pack agreement, Evan had his own cabin in the mountains. Grace would love it there.

"You will not hide her away—or do anything that makes you look guilty," she snapped.

"I don't pay off exes," Brennan pushed, unwilling to submit.

His mom gave him a hard look. "Please don't pay her off."

"She wants something," Brennan retorted, face flushing with anger. "I protect my pack."

"Of course she wants something. Everyone wants something. But that doesn't mean what she wants is dangerous to you. She has a concussion and barely remembers her name. I'm pretty sure she doesn't have an elaborate plan to steal your money, trash your reputation, and tear apart your pack. Poor timing? Yes. Is there a possibility that whoever's after her is a threat to you? Absolutely. But at this point we have no reason to believe she's dangerous," Siobhan lectured.

"What if she is?" Brennan continued. "What if after we've cared for her and let her worm her way into our home and pack we find out her intentions are disingenuous?"

"Grace isn't like that," I interjected, annoyed he'd even think that.

"Then we will deal with it *appropriately* at the *right time* and not act like impulsive toddlers. Bren, I know Caroline affected you, but I thought you were in therapy for that." Her look went hard again.

"Well, if we would've known that Wes had a *mate*, then perhaps we could have planned for this. I found a way to legally dissolve the bond. We'll have a new lawyer draw up the paperwork. Grace seems agreeable. She'll sign, Wes will sign, they'll disolve the bond and we'll go back to our lives." Brennan looked pleased with himself.

"What if I don't want to?" I'd just gotten her back–and there was still so much we didn't know. Not to mention she was in the hospital, in a strange place, alone.

And dissolving our bond was permanent.

"She doesn't understand what that all entails. Also, with how fragile she is, I don't think she'll survive that," Evan said softly.

That made my belly drop. "What do you mean?"

"You'll do no such thing, Bren. Was I not clear that rash actions will make this worse?" Siobhan snapped.

"She's right," Evan agreed. "What your mom is suggesting is the right way to go from a legal standpoint–and that of decent people. Grace needs our help, and originally we agreed to help her. I stand by continuing to do that. Also, I like Grace, a lot. Maybe she'll end up fitting in with us."

"Evan, I'm so happy that you like her, but let's not get ahead of ourselves. Your pack's goal is to help Grace get better and to get past all three investigations without causing a scandal or anyone going to jail." She gave Evan a smile–she had a soft spot for him.

"Of course, Siobhan." Spencer gave her a dashing look. "We'll care for her so well that there will be no doubt that she's adored. If she'd like to stay and be employed in my Special Projects Division, I'd like that very much. I'm sure there's so much she could contribute."

"That's so kind of you, Spencer. She's a scientist?" Siobhan *adored* Spencer.

"Theoretical mathematician. Personally, I think she's out of Wes' league." Spencer grinned at me.

I flipped him off. "Damn right she is. What if she doesn't want to stay with us? She had a life before this."

"If that's what Grace wants, we'll help her with that. *After* she's better, the investigations are closed, and I can sleep knowing none of you will go to jail," Siobhan said.

"This is assuming she can go home." Spencer looked at me.

Had Evan told him?

Jett nodded. "I've been thinking about why now? She's been an adult for years."

"Her mom died," Evan blurted.

"She did? That could do it," I breathed. I still wondered how a parent could do to their child what Grace's mom did to her. "Also, I think she graduated recently."

"I have things to do, boys." Siobhan's voice went stern.

"We're supposed to act like she's one of us? What do we even tell people?" Brennan frowned.

She gave him a hard look. "What's there to tell? Wes' mate has come to stay with you. It's only scandalous if you let it be. Act like it's normal, and people will accept it as such."

Brennan sighed. "Are we done?"

"No. You will fire all your pack legal representation and hire off a list I approve. However, Katie will personally handle anything regarding Grace, which will include working with the police and her advocate," she told us. "You *will* cooperate."

"Katie? Are you serious?" Brennan grimaced.

"Do you know what sort of scandal this could be? The charity gala is coming up. Not to mention the State Street project is high-profile and right now is giving me a headache. Now, *do we have an understanding?*" She met every single one of our gazes, demanding our agreement.

We all nodded. There was no other answer.

"Good." She stood. So did we.

"Thank you, Siobhan, for assisting us," Spencer added.

"Yes, thank you," Jett said, squeezing Brennan's hand as we went to leave.

"Of course. Wes, when I mentioned not needing to court her, I was talking to them, not you," she added. "Woo her, care for her, learn about her. As her mate, you'll be watched closest. If you have any fond feelings for her at all, you'll act on those–and if you don't, you will find some, since they can spot fakes."

"Absolutely. Evan and I are going to get her favorite ice cream and bring it to her," I replied. Buy her little gifts, take her to the actual places we'd been to in our dreams, care for her? Okay, I could handle that.

"Excellent." She nodded.

"Suck up," Brennan muttered.

"Evan, will you be engaging an advocate?" she inquired. "It is your right. No one will blame or begrudge you. But it will need to be planned for."

Brennan and I froze. What?

"No. I'm not angry that Wes has an undisclosed mate. I don't see her as a threat. I'm not going to challenge her. However, I *will* be wooing the shit out of her." He grinned. "Oh, Siobhan, you're going to love her."

"Don't make Wes look too bad." She patted him on the shoulder.

We got in the elevator. Jett and Evan both had their arms around Brennan. We all reeked of alpha dominance.

"Fuck." Brennan hit the elevator wall with his fist, the sour pine filling the small space. "I can't believe she's asking us to do this."

"I know she can be overbearing. She's not the head alpha of our pack—you are. But right now, she's just trying to keep our asses out of jail," Jett soothed.

"Yeah, but..." Brennan's head bowed.

"We need to tread carefully, but I don't think this is a bad thing at all," Spencer told us.

When we got into the main lobby, I pulled Evan aside. "Did you tell Spence?"

Evan shook his head. "No, but I think he figured it out. This *is* Spence."

I nodded. "True. Why do I have the feeling that if we let them talk science, they're going to end up changing the world and making billions?"

"He might also make a move on her. Oh, you should have seen how she looked at him this morning," he laughed. "*Daddy*."

I growled at the thought of someone besides Evan wanting *my* Grace.

Evan laughed more. "That's my Wes. But would that be bad? I mean, it's *Spence*."

Spencer was a good man and while I enjoyed talking science with her, she'd probably like someone on her intellectual level.

Assuming she stayed.

"Are you sure you're okay with this?" I tipped my forehead to his. "If not—"

"Will you *stop?*" Evan smashed his lips to mine, reassurance searing our bond.

"Are you coming with us?" Brennan called.

Evan went over to Brennan and Jett and gave each of them a kiss. "I love you, but I'm going to go help Wes stay out of jail. We'll call a car. But if one of you could drop off my car and some stuff for us in the morning, I'd be grateful."

I looked at the pictures Lexi had sent me. "Shit. Lexi brought some of her packmates over to the hospital."

Evan came over to me, looked at the pictures, and slid an arm around my waist. "Grace making friends with the sister pack isn't the worst. It's not like we don't know them."

"What did you mean about her not surviving being un-bonded? I know it hurts, but I didn't know it killed people," I said quietly as we called a car.

"Losing your mate, whether it's drugs, death, or otherwise does kill people sometimes," Evan said softly. "After Spencer's mate died, I fucking worried about him to the point I took a leave of absence from the military–and they weren't soulmates. They don't call people who'd lost their bonded scent matches *soulbroke* for nothing, Wes."

Spencer's mate had died a long time ago. They'd started dating at university and I'd never met her.

"Oh shit." I sucked in a breath. "I don't want to un-bond her. Even if it didn't break her soul." That sounded awful. My phone alerted me that the car was almost here.

"Good." Evan squeezed my arm. "Now, let's go buy her some ice cream."

Chapter Sixteen

Grace

I woke up feeling like a cozy cinnamon roll. Apparently, I'd slept *on top* of Wes and Evan, covered in a mountain of soft and fluffy blankets.

Finally, they'd allowed Wes to come join me, and I loved the cuddles. I needed reassurance from more than Evan that things would be okay–especially after the last seizure when that awful man had been here.

At least Evan had been with me–and well, Lexi and her pack when Evan had to go.

But I had them *both* now. Being close to Wes like this made all those old feelings come bubbling to the surface. How right it felt to be in his arms. How good he smelled. How kind he was. I still didn't know how I had gotten here or why. But if I had to be in another world, at least Wes was here. Before we were a thing in our dreams, we were friends.

Hopefully, we still were. I could use a friend.

There were parts of me that wanted him to be much more. Would actual sex with him be as good as it had been in my dreams?

The door opened, and the nurse checked on me and the monitors. My cheeks warmed as she eyed the guys sleeping in the bed with me.

She just grinned, whispered that she'd send in breakfast soon, and left.

I carefully extracted myself, put on my slippers and matching robe, and went to the bathroom.

When I came back in, a handsome man with olive skin, salt and pepper hair, and a nice suit, was setting things out on the table.

"Spencer. Hi." My voice caught in my throat. Wes was handsome. Evan was beautiful. Spencer was *mesmerizing*. Polished, put together, elegant, and probably in his mid-to-late thirties. He smelled like a freshly oiled baseball glove, and it was fantastic.

"My good doctor." Spencer turned and smiled. "I come bearing breakfast and requested items."

"Oh, thank you. That coffee smells wonderful." On the table was a box of fancy pastries along with a drink holder filled with cups.

"Try this." He handed me a cup.

That accent. If Greek gods were people, they'd look like Spencer. His brown-grey eyes were beautiful, very different from Wes' brown-green or Evan's deep brown.

I sat down and took a sip. It wasn't coffee. Maybe some sort of tea latte? Also *delicious*. "Ooh."

Things finally tasted right. And this? *Yum.*

Spencer nodded. "Indeed." He sat down and took one of the beverage containers. "Do you recall what equipment you need for your research?"

Equipment? It was nice that he wanted to give me a lab at his company, but what exactly did he think I was doing? But then Evan said he was a mad scientist with a biotech company. I had no idea what sort of scientific advancements they had here. Many, if I were just going by my medical care.

I took another sip of the frothy, milky tea. "It was just a hobby I was passionate about. I... I don't think I got here myself by using that research."

"There's a lot to consider when working on theories such as that," he agreed. "Also, as I said before, there could be ramifications not just to proving them, but making them work."

"True." That was the biggest reason I didn't think I brought myself here. It was one thing to prove parallel worlds existed. It was another to configure the theories to actually get from one to the other.

And to actually build a reliable way to travel between parallel worlds? It wasn't just a scientific marvel, it was a big bullseye. If one person could figure it out, who else had?

"It doesn't faze you? Where I'm from? I'm from elsewhere. I've come to that conclusion. Not that I'd admit that to many," I said quietly, hoping that I could trust him.

I needed to trust them. Someone. But I wasn't always good at picking the right people.

"That's shrewd. No, it doesn't. I've always had an interest in those theories, though my personal research doesn't lie therein. What specifically were you working on, do you recall?" His voice was so silky.

I'd been thinking about that since last night. One of Lexi's pack-mates, Rami, was an engineer working on the lunar program, and our conversation had set some things loose in my murky brain. "Qubits."

He nodded. "Like mapping the six dimensions?"

Something loosened in my mind and another memory bubble popped. "No, I didn't get on that project," I breathed. "Mine was much more fundable. I don't remember. I'm so sorry."

But I got flickers. Fences. Badges. Guys with guns.

"Something more practical? Excellent. Not remembering is *fine,* my good doctor. You don't have to be sorry. I also understand if it's proprietary and you can't tell me." He opened the box. "Try."

"Oh, I will. Evan says you have a biotech company? What do you do?" I took one of the beautiful little pastries that had yellow cream and berries.

"Mainly, we focus on painless ways to give medical care. Non-invasive scans, entire batteries of tests with a single drop of blood, vaccinations without needles."

"Oh, I had the most curious MRI. Back home you had to be in a tube and lie still for ages, this took a few minutes, and I sat in a chair." I took a bite, and flavor exploded across my tongue. "Mmmm."

"It's the fine yet simple things that make life worth living," he told me.

"Mmmm, do I smell coffee?" Evan mumbled, sitting up. "Hi, Spence."

"A bag with things for you and Wes is on the chair. I brought your favorite," Spencer added.

Evan poked Wes. "Food." He got up, came over, gave me a kiss on the cheek, then lifted me up and sat in my chair and put me on his lap.

I leaned into Evan. It should be weird. But it felt so deliciously right.

He looked at the logo on the cups. "Aren't we fancy?"

"While you two will eat anything, I figured our good doctor would appreciate them." Spencer handed Evan a cup.

Wes sat up. He wasn't wearing a shirt. "Spence. Hi."

"Katie was over at the house this morning. She gave me a bag and said that Lexi wanted this given to you. It's in the duffel," he added.

"Oh." Wes practically leapt out of bed, went to the duffel, and found a plastic sack. He opened it, and a silly grin crossed his freckled face as his hazel eyes danced.

A silly, gleeful grin.

"Grace, someone wants to see you." His voice went singsong.

"Who?" I couldn't help but grin back. *This* was the Wes I remembered. Playful, boyish Wes.

"Mr. Hippo." Wes withdrew a plush blue hippo from the bag. One that used to be on his bed when we'd hang out in his bedroom in our dreams.

"Mr. Hippo." My hand went to my heart. The fact that Wes had brought me his most treasured possession to comfort me, was everything.

Wes put him in my arms. "When he heard that you were here, he was thrilled. He missed you so much."

I hugged the well-loved stuffie, which smelled of Wes. "Of all Wes' things, I loved Mr. Hippo most." Mr. Hippo was large, soft, and silly. "Thank you for remembering."

"I know how much you loved him, so I thought a visit from him would cheer you up." He squeezed my hand.

"Mr. Hippo? I'm going to learn so many things about you, aren't I?" Evan laughed as he snagged a pastry, and Wes gave him a kiss.

A thought hit me. If Mr. Hippo were real, other things were.

"This is perfect. Um, can we go to the park? Our park?" I asked Wes. The place where we'd first met in a dream. It was near his house, and we'd often met there.

"Of course. Ooh, we can take a paddle boat out on the lake. We'll see my room, too." He beamed. "That would be so much fun. I'm so happy you're remembering things."

"Yes! I want to see everything." All of the places that we'd been to in our dreams actually existed here. I'd absolutely like to swing on our swings, ride in a paddle boat, and make out in his childhood bedroom.

"I'll show them all to you. Promise." He squeezed my hand and then disappeared into the bathroom.

"Katie came over this morning? I'm sure Brennan's in a mood," Evan replied to Spencer.

"Yes. She sent you action items," Spencer added.

"Oh, I met her last night," I nodded. They'd all been so nice.

Wes came back out. "Katie came over last night, too?"

"Yes, she brought the food. She didn't stay long. Katie's Brennan's sister?" I asked. She was part of Lexi's pack. I'd also met a couple of others. Their pack seemed larger than Wes'.

"Yep. Katie is Bren's twin and a lawyer." Wes picked me up as if I were a doll and put me on *his* lap. "Mine."

Um, okay. It wasn't unpleasant, but no one had done this to me before.

At least my tea was within reach. I looked at Evan. "Is this one of those things I have to put up with?"

"You love it." Evan grinned.

I sort of did. There was a sense of comfort in it. Of *rightness.*

"Is this for me?" Wes picked up the last cup. "Sorry if I'm going to leave you shorthanded, Spence."

"I'll be okay alone, Wes. The doctor says I'm going to sleep a lot because of the concussion." I felt bad keeping him from his work.

"There are things that he can do from here–and at home. But I need you in the office for that meeting next week," Spencer added.

"Perhaps by then, Grace will be feeling well enough that she can have a tour."

We finished breakfast, and Spencer stood. "I will see you all later." Coming over to me, he kissed my hand. "Until later, my good doctor."

All the breath left my body. He winked and left.

"Told you," Evan laughed.

"I... I'm sorry. He's..."

"A flirt," Wes agreed. "And a showoff. Honestly, I'm glad he likes you. Spence is a good guy. Hand me my phone?"

Evan got his and Wes' phones.

"Spence wasn't kidding about Katie and the action items." Evan scrolled on his phone. "I've got to go to work this afternoon. I'll bring dinner, but I should spend the night at the house."

"Is that how you do it, switching off every other night or something? Curious," I asked.

"Not scheduled, but we try to be respectful. But I'll schedule you, Peaches. Every weekend I'm not working, you're mine. We should visit my cabin soon," Evan said.

"You can't have her all the time." Wes nuzzled my neck. "But a weekend at the cabin sounds nice."

"That tickles." I batted my hand at him. "What if I want Evan all the time? I'll fight Brennan for him. Jett, too."

"Go easy on Bren? He has redeeming qualities. This is just bringing up memories of his ex, Caroline," Evan told me.

"I suppose." I sighed dramatically. I was actually confused and a little angry about what Brennan had done. "Caroline was a bitch?"

"They went to the same university here in Rockland. They knew each other longer, but she didn't go to high school with Bren and Wes. Anyway, Bren was ready to marry her," Evan said. "But she wanted to travel the world after graduation. They stayed friends, sort of, after they broke up. She was at Bren and Jett's wedding.

Then, she started working at his company because she was done traveling. At some point, she made herself indispensable to us to the point where we were considering bringing her into the pack. Except that she tried to *replace* me."

She *what?*

"What? No one could replace you," I reassured.

"It was awful." His look went pained. "She went to great lengths to turn us against each other. She kept telling me that I wasn't omega enough for them because I'm not the stereotype. It got nasty. Finally, we realized what was happening, and Bren kicked her out. As revenge, she did some shitty things, like release a sex-tape they made when they were young and stupid. We weren't certain that we'd get through everything, especially the emotional damage, because we hadn't been a pack that long."

"Oh, Evan." I got off Wes' lap, stuffed hippo in hand, and hugged Evan. *How dare she?*

"I'm over it. Bren, obviously, isn't. He cared about her. While he never mated her, they have a long history." Evan held me tight. "When you walked in, it was a gut instinct for him. Protect us, and me, before you annihilate us."

"I have no sex-tapes, promise. I will punch her in the tits if she bothers you again," I promised. Still, I wasn't sure how I felt about Brennan's actions, even if I could understand where he was coming from.

If I had someone like Evan, I'd protect him fiercely too.

"You have an epic slap, use that," Evan agreed.

"Can we not?" Wes asked.

Evan made a dramatic face. "Fine."

"I'll defend you," I promised. Deep in my heart, I knew that to be true. I'd only been here a few days, and already I'd do anything for them.

Chapter Seventeen

Evan

"**O**h, hey, Evan." Carly waved me down as I went to leave the Center with Rose to take her shopping for some things. I'd grab a couple of things for Grace, too.

Inwardly, I groaned at Carly's expression. *No more. Please.* If one more person asked me if I was okay, I'd scream. Every omega here was sad and angry for me that Wes had a mate I didn't know about. Carly even offered to be *my* advocate.

It wasn't like that–and I was *fine.* I was also glad that I wasn't being put on leave, given everything with the investigation into the pack.

"Give Grace a hug from me." Carly gave me a huge hug. "Home visit. Soon. Be ready," she whispered in my ear. "See you tomorrow." She waved and left.

Home visit? Shit. I should've expected it. Getting ready for that would be harder than just buying Grace some basics at the mall.

A muscular, full-figured, beta teenage girl in fishnets, a plaid skirt, boots, a punk band shirt, and a studded jacket, stood in the lobby's corner, backpack over her shoulder. Her made-up cat-eyes narrowed at me as she scratched her face with a black-polished middle finger, right by her tiny nose ring. Green clip-ins accented her dark, dark hair, which wasn't nearly as curly as mine. She had our mom's hair; I had our dad's. Like him, we were both tall for our designations.

"Ri, hey." While she came by sometimes, I was a little surprised she was here today and not at school.

"Today is the day you feed me, did you forget?" my baby sister asked, eyeing Rose.

It was Thursday? I'd spent all day thinking it was Wednesday. *Whoops.*

My little sister preferred the independence of living in her high school dorms to staying with us. However, every Thursday was early release, so she met me here and we'd get food. We also did fun things on weekends, and sometimes I'd randomly find her in the house, which annoyed Brennan sometimes, but sisters *were* allowed.

Of course, I'd hate to see what would happen if we tried to ban them.

"Not at all. You said you needed shoes. Rose needs some clothes. I thought we could go shopping together and get some food after." I actually didn't know if Riley needed shoes or not, but she wouldn't turn them down.

"Rose, this is my little sister, Riley," I introduced. "She's a freshman. Rose is a junior."

Riley eyed Rose in her pink dress, which complemented her red French braids. "She's going to my school?"

"She's starting at Finchley on Monday," I replied as we went outside to the parking lot.

Riley went to Hadley Hall, a very exclusive prep school here in Rockland, which Spencer paid for. It was the same school that Wes and Lexi had gone to on scholarship, where they'd met Brennan and Katie.

Rose glanced at Riley's shirt. "I love that band. I've always wanted to see them live."

"They're amazing. I saw them last summer at a festival with my sisters," Riley told her, looking a little wistful as she climbed into the back of my 4x4. "You can sit up front as long as you pick good music."

Riley had been four when our parents died. I'd been in the military, so my sisters and grandparents had done the bulk of actually raising her, though Spencer had helped a lot. Now, my baby sis was here with me for high school, as one of my sisters finished her degree, the other worked her dream job, and my grandparents got to travel and enjoy retirement.

"I need gym shoes, shoes for the school dance, a dress to go with the shoes, the *good* sports bras, and markers. Are we going to the big mall or the fancy mall?" she asked.

"The big mall," I told her as I drove.

"Great. We'll start with the food court for a snack, then after power-shopping we'll go to the burger place with the unlimited fries," Riley said.

The girls' discussion immediately turned to stores and bands. As soon as we parked, Riley led us to the food court. While they ate hot pretzels and made their shopping plan, I mentally went through the home visit checklist and started ordering things for rush delivery. My phone buzzed.

Wes

How was work?

Swoop was a big discount store where you could get pretty much everything you needed for yourself and home *in one swoop.* I'd probably take Rose there soon to get school supplies.

There was also a text from Jett.

We all tracked each other's phones, for safety. Grace still needed a phone.

Riley and Rose brought me to a store popular with teens.

"Would Grace like anything here?" Rose looked around at the racks of colorful clothes.

"Grace?" Riley gave me a look as she held up a black crop top with a rose on it. "Rose, this is you."

"So cute. We're getting some things for Grace, too." Rose did a happy dance and took the crop top from her.

"Maybe a cute math-themed shirt? Some comfortable dresses? Basics?" I worked on a home store delivery on my phone. I had no idea what Grace liked to wear.

Riley stood at my elbow. "Doctor Grace?"

"Yep." I put *stand mixer* in the search for funsies. Oh, that's what it was. Some of them were cute. I ordered one. Jett made a bunch of complicated things, he'd probably use it, too.

"Wanna tell me who she actually is?" My sister went through a rack of dresses.

"She's nunya." I grinned, as I added a blanket in the living room colors, some throw pillows to add to Wes' room, and curtains and cushions for the window seat in the room we'd make into hers.

If we were getting a home inspection, Grace needed a room of her own.

Riley flipped me off. "Fuck you very much."

"You rarely want to know much about them." I shrugged. It was safer that way.

She held up a strappy dress. "This could be cute for the dance. You didn't add Wes as her mate right. I fixed it for you. You're getting reinforcements?"

Usually, she made the base, and the Omega Protection Program made it real.

"Yes." I'd need to pull in all the favors to make sure Grace's record was perfect. I wanted to keep her safe. Keep her here.

"Is she actually Wes' mate?" She added a sparkly dress to her pile.

"She is. Not telling you the story because it's not mine to tell." I wasn't sure if my sister would believe that Grace traveled from a parallel world.

"Wow. Okay. Are you good with him having another mate?" she asked me. "Will I like her? Do you like her? Does she have a cool job?"

"I like her a lot. She's a theoretical mathematician." I kept close to Rose, whose pile was very floral. Yeah, I hoped Grace stayed with us. Sure, this wasn't her world, but she belonged with her mate.

Riley whistled as she looked through another rack. "Smarticle. What does Spencer think?"

"He wants to hire her." I added more towels and another robe to my online cart. I was glad he was on our side.

Riley started laughing. Then she stopped. "You *are* okay with it though? If you're not, I'm happy to fuck some shit up."

I loved her protectiveness.

"I'm good. Grace is very sweet. But I do need everyone to stop asking me if I'm okay," I huffed. "Can you come over tonight and help me do some stuff around the house? I'll pay you?"

Her eyes rolled. "The chore rate? Do you know what my savings look like?"

I did. Her overseas bank account, too. I wasn't her only client. Now that she was at a fancy high school her racket now was more fake IDs for clubs and altering grades for the rich kids at school. She'd promised my sisters that when she moved to Rockland she'd stop hacking for money–which hadn't happened, the projects had just changed.

"I'm supposed to spend the night; we have a day off tomorrow. We're going to the movies. Did you forget again?" She held up jeans that were more hole than fabric. "For the doctor?"

"Maybe this?" I pointed to a T-shirt dress, as I added paint, hardware, and some stick-on wallpaper border to my online cart. "Did I really? It's not on my calendar." Today had been, but I'd lost track of the days of the week.

She grinned. "I do have the day off tomorrow. I was supposed to go to the movies with Marcos, but he's being a little bitch. You can keep me, pay me, and take me to the movies."

"I have to work tomorrow, but we'll go to a movie on Saturday afternoon. We can even go to the dine-in theater," I promised, looking over at Rose thoughtfully going through some racks.

"Deal." Riley peered at my phone. "That wallpaper is stupid. Get the other."

"Okay." I sent the order off. Going to another shop, I ordered Grace a phone, then focused on those two as we made our way through the store and paid for our purchases.

"Where next?" I asked.

"Shoe store." Riley took my hand and dragged me across the mall.

Taking a seat, I watched as the girls tried on athletic shoes.

Jett walked in and came over and gave me a kiss. "Hey, Baby."

"Hey, Hot Stuff. They didn't put you on leave, did they?" I asked, worry pooling in my belly.

"No, but I'm on desk duty and I'm done for the day. Thought I'd work on Katie's action items she made to help keep our pack out of trouble." He rolled his eyes. "*You* are one of them."

"Me?" I picked up a pair of sneakers that might work for Grace.

"She wants us to stay close to you in public." He grinned and got very close, nuzzling me.

"Get a room, motherfucker." Riley grinned.

"Ri." Jett fist-bumped her.

My sister held up combat boots. "For Grace?"

Jett nodded. "I think she needs a leather jacket. Like the one she liked in the movie we were watching the night she arrived."

"Why not." Mmmm, she'd look cute in it. I couldn't wait.

Jett brought a bunch of things to my car, and we continued our shopping. The accounts were getting a workout today.

While the girls tried on ridiculous dresses in an upscale department store, I got a couple of nicer things for Grace, as well as a messenger bag with equations on it. It was professional enough for work but cute enough for every day, and probably more than I should be spending on her. She did have a birthday coming...

"Hey, sorry, I stopped and got her a leather jacket and boots." Jett looked around the store. "Where are the girls?"

"In dresses," I replied as we went across the aisle to that department.

"That's perfect. But my alpha is right, you girls shouldn't be here alone," a voice I couldn't see stated as Riley swished in front of the mirror in a long black gown.

"We're not alone. Like I said, my brother is over there buying shit," Riley said. "Evan, where the fuck are you?"

"Right here," I called. The scent of tulips hit me as I wove through the racks of designer dresses and froze. So did Jett, his amber scent going bitter.

"Still, if they really cared, they'd keep a closer eye on you," she prodded. That voice. That silky, judgmental voice.

"Evan, please? For the dance?" Riley ran over to me and posed.

"You look amazing." I couldn't catch my breath. No. It couldn't be. She'd left the city and found a wealthy pack in the South.

A voluptuous, perfectly coiffed brunette turned and smirked at us, cleavage nearly spilling out of her designer blouse. "Why, hello, boys. I didn't expect to see you in a place like this. After all, this is a store for people with *taste.*"

"Uncalled for." Riley made a face. She turned to me, "Evan, *please* can I have it?"

Forcing myself to take a deep calming breath, I focused on my sister. "Of course you can. It's perfect for the dance. Why don't you change, and we'll buy it and get dinner?"

"You're ignoring me?" Caroline smirked, holding onto her alpha like he was a trophy. "But you've always been a clueless oaf, haven't you?" She tossed her hair.

While she looked the same, the feelings of insecurity didn't come. Neither did anger. I didn't even feel pity.

"I have nothing to say to you." All the things I'd wanted to say to her evaporated. She wasn't worth the words.

"Hey, bitch, leave my brother alone." Riley scowled.

"Ri, get changed, take Rose with you." Jett got between me and the other omega. He turned to her. "Go away, Caroline."

Caroline? Riley mouthed as she left.

Unfortunately.

An alpha in a suit got between us and glared, copper scent flaring, then turned to her. "Is there a problem?" he drawled.

Caroline's red lips smirked. "I've changed my mind. Let's go someplace more... discriminating." Taking her alpha's arm, she waved, her small hand festooned in large rings. "See you around, boys. Give Bren my love."

Jett put his arm around me, sending comfort through the bond. "Are you okay?"

"I am." But while I might not feel like being angry at her anymore, Brennan certainly did.

Chapter Eighteen

Brennan

"What do you mean nothing can be done?" I exploded as I paced my office. "She's *here*. She shouldn't be here."

"You can't ban Caroline from the city. The alpha she's with is here on legitimate business. Also, she's *from* here," Katie replied over the phone.

"She *spoke to Evan*." How dare she? That bitch exploited my feelings for her, emotionally damaged my omega, and then tried to ruin my pack, business, and reputation.

No. After everything she did to Evan, I didn't want her near him. The audacity!

"It's not like she showed up at your house. They were at the mall. They're leaving tomorrow. Legally you can't do anything," she added. "She's allowed to exist."

Not here. I took a deep breath. Sometimes I regretted taking the moral high road.

"She ruined my life," I retorted. I was over her, but not the damage that she caused.

The pack group chat lit up on my phone.

Evan

Not making it to the hospital tonight. Can someone please make sure Wes and Grace get food?

Me

The hospital will give her food. Wes can get his own.

Wes sent an emoji of the bird.

Spencer

I can stop by with dinner.

I also got an alert from the door cam. A photo of a woman with a bunch of sacks popped up. *Another* delivery?

"Caroline's a bitch, and releasing a sex-tape was shitty," my sister lectured, still on the phone with me. "So was draining your accounts. But it's been nearly three years. You got some of the money back. Your career and reputation recovered. Evan is fine. Your pack is fine. Well, except for you, apparently. Maybe you should think about all the good things that are in your life instead of what's bad."

Ugh. I took another deep breath. "The timing is off with this Grace nonsense."

"I'm not sure there ever is a right time for something like this, not that I'd call it *nonsense*. Mrs. Beekman really doesn't like you. Mom won't be happy if the Center decides you're an unfit pack. Oh, you didn't complete your action items," she added.

"Fuck your action items, Katie." I ended the call. While I did care for my twin, she also infuriated me. This was my pack, and I knew what was best. Not Katie. Not my mother. Me.

It was getting late. I might as well head home.

I texted Jett.

Me

> **Do you want me to pick up anything for dinner?**

Jett

> **I'm full from burgers–so are Evan and Ri. But I can make something for you if you don't want takeout.**

Ri? Oh, it was Thursday.

Me

> **If I pick up a steak, will you share it with me?**

Jett

> **Sure. Get some fancy beer? Love you.**

Me

> **Love you, too.**

I finished up my emails, and drove home on my motorcycle, stopping off at the store to get something to make for my dinner.

Bag in hand, I walked into the kitchen and took off my shoes. "I'm home."

No answer. But Jett and Evan were here–I could feel them through the bond. Riley's boots were by the rack, ones that weren't there this morning.

I went up to the second floor, but it was empty. As I went up to the third floor, I heard voices and smelled peaches and vanilla.

Riley's voice floated down the stairs. "While I get taking off all the tags and washing everything, why do I have to wash some things a bunch of times? Why am I using scenty things in the dryer?"

She sat on the floor of the sunken living room, surrounded by piles of stuff. "Also, what's with the incense? I feel like you're teaching me something, but I don't know what."

"Hey, Handsome." Evan's face broke out into a silly grin as he stood, ran over to me, and gave me a kiss.

That greeting made me feel so much better.

For a moment I just hugged him, needing some rightness in this awful day. His usual lemonade was tinged with the scents of anise, bubble gum, amber, fresh laundry, and peach pie that clung to his clothes. Part of me didn't like him smelling of Grace.

"Hi, Love. Hi, Ri." My eyebrows rose. Usually, she didn't come over on Thursdays, she just did something with Evan.

"Tomorrow's a day off. She's helping me get things ready for Grace." Evan had paint on his face.

"Saturday we're going to the movies, and Jett said we could go hiking on Sunday." She picked up an armful of clothes and scampered down the stairs.

Hiking. Okay. Sure. Hopefully the weather would be good. It was the end of February, so you never really knew.

I surveyed all the clothes and things on the floor. There were new pillows and chairs in the living room. Plants and boxes littered the hall.

My nose wrinkled. "Do I smell paint? Where's Jett?"

"In here," Jett called from another room.

Evan took my hand, excitement and pride coming through the bond. "Come see."

He led me past some assembled furniture and a mattress in the hallway. We went through the glass doors to the sunroom, which had been cleared out. Not that there was much in there. One wall had been painted dark green. Some sort of printed mauve and green border ran along the top of the other three walls. Jett sat on the floor, building something as incense burned.

Annoyance rose in me. "I thought you were getting her some clothes and a hairbrush."

Evan wrapped his arms around me, trying to soothe me. "Everything beyond Katie's budget, Wes and I paid for."

Katie gave him a *budget?*

"You shouldn't have to." I made a face, disliking how much he'd spent, given Grace's presence was temporary.

"It was mostly Wes. But I got her a birthday present," Evan added, looking pleased with himself.

Jett looked up to Evan. "When's her birthday? Should I save the jacket for then? Hand me that wrench over there, would you?" He turned to me, all smiles, holding two pieces of wood together. "Hey, Honey. How was your day?"

"Stressful. You bought her birthday presents?" My hand went to my face. This was how it started. Next thing she'd be under me, keening for my bite.

"It's a week after Wes'. Do you think she'll like the usual places?" Evan handed something to Jett.

"She'll need a dress. We didn't buy her anything that fancy," Jett replied.

Evan thought for a moment. "Maybe something poufy? Or strapless?"

"Strapless." Jett nodded.

"No dinners, no dresses." I rubbed my forehead, overwhelmed by all these plans.

No plans. Plans meant that she was staying. I needed the stranger in my house to leave as soon as possible.

"She's Wes' mate. We should do *something* for her," Jett countered.

"Backyard birthday barbecue? She might not feel up to a fancy dinner, anyway." Evan ignored what I said as he crouched down to help Jett by holding something still.

Seeing my two guys shirtless assembling furniture should be sexy, but all I could feel was annoyance. "Why does she need a bed? I figured she'd just sleep in Wes' room."

"Probably. But she needs her own space, too." Evan took out his phone, nodded, and put it away.

"Why?" There were bags and piles *everywhere.*

"So I have a place to fuck her." Evan grinned at me. "I like her a lot. I want to fuck her eventually."

I sighed. "What does Wes think of that?"

"He's all for it. I think she is too."

Of course she was.

The doorbell rang. I made a face. "More?"

"That's stuff Ri ordered for herself." Evan stood, looked out the door, and partially closed it. He cupped my face with his hand and lowered his voice. "We have to plan for a home visit. I'm working my way through the visit checklist so that we don't fail. Mrs. Beekman isn't playing games."

Jett tipped up what he was building, and Evan helped him.

"On the phone she was brutal, more than the other lady. Where did they find her? I don't remember ever meeting her at your workplace," Jett said.

"She's a supervisor at another Center. She's going to look for things such as, *Does Grace have her own space? Is it clear she's not restricted to her own space? Are her needs being met?* So yes, we're making her a room and going to do something for her birthday since it's so soon. I think we're doing a great job here." Evan beamed, proud.

What they'd done was impressive. But making her a space would let her think that she could stay.

"We are," Jett agreed as they continued to assemble what looked like a canopy daybed.

"Jett, you're playing along? I thought you felt something was off." I figured if anyone would side with logic, it would be him. Unfortunately, Spencer was enamored with her.

"It is. But I like my job and I like everyone not being in jail. I know these detectives, and I know how home visits work. If the Center finds something wrong with us, they *will* act. These things can snowball fast. Let's follow the checklist and prepare for the home visit. She's Wes' mate, and that accounts for something," Jett replied.

I frowned as they screwed the mirror onto the dresser, because I hadn't known all that. "What if we fail the inspection? The Center's not actually going to take her from us, are they?"

While I didn't want her to stay, the Center *removing* her from us meant we were unfit.

We were fit. She just didn't fit.

"They could," Evan replied. "I took a girl from her home the same day Grace arrived, no visit needed. With everything going on, we don't want to fail this or any other home visit."

"There could be more?" I stepped back as they moved to another part of the bed.

"Well, yeah, we follow our omegas for some time. Gotta make sure they're okay," Evan told me.

Something caught my eye, and Riley had her face pressed up against the glass doors of the room.

She slipped in. "You know the doors are glass, right, Doofus? Should I add curtains to my next order?"

"Or something?" Evan agreed. "Thanks for your help."

"That's what you pay me for. I'm going to do shit to my room while the clothes wash." She flipped us off and left.

"I let her get some new stuff for her room. Um, Caroline made a comment about Riley being alone in the store, and it bothered me. She wasn't alone, I was at another register," he told me. "We don't need Dependent Services getting involved."

"She's fifteen, so why can't she be alone in a store? Caroline would call Dependent Services." That bitch. Ruining everything, as usual.

"I wish we had more time. There's no closet or bathroom." Jett looked around. "What will Grace use?"

Evan thought for a moment. "Right, I forgot to order a wardrobe. I'm putting stuff for her in Wes' bathroom. Maybe I should add a desk for her in Wes' room? Or a corner of the library?"

"I don't want her on my floor. In fact, I want her away from me as much as possible. When is she coming?" I scowled, not liking all these changes. I didn't like change. It wasn't orderly or predictable.

"Saturday or Sunday, I think," Evan told me, conferring with his phone.

I huffed, done with all this Grace talk. "I'm going to go cook some steak. Do either of you want some?"

Jett reached out and squeezed my hand. "I'll be right there, Honey."

"I'm good. Thanks, Handsome." Evan shook his head and went back to helping Jett.

I went down to the living room. Riley was in her room blaring music. I went into the kitchen. Taking my bottle of good bourbon, which someone had been in, I poured myself a glass and got out what I needed to make dinner.

As I cooked, I realized the kitchen had stuff in it we didn't have before, such as a fancy stand mixer. Ugh. Why? I hated counter clutter.

"I know you don't like people in the house, but we have to play the game, Honey. Thank goodness Evan knows how. But we all have to be on board." Jett came up behind me and slid his arms around my waist, which reassured my alpha that everyone still cared for me.

I flipped the steak over to get a sear on both sides. "Fine. The faster this is over, the faster she can be gone."

"What if Grace stays? She's Wes' *mate*." Jett let go of me and got a beer out of the fridge. "Ooh, you got the really fancy beer. Thanks."

"How did I not know that he had a mate? Or a serious girlfriend? I knew him then." I frowned. "There was someone, but I also think he was also dating other girls..."

"Maybe they had an open relationship? Perhaps they took a break because her mom sounds like an asshole. That's what's really bugging you, isn't it? That you knew him then and didn't know about Grace?"

"Of course not." Yeah, it rankled. "Why didn't he disclose it when we formed the pack—or when we locked everything down after Caroline? I don't want Grace to stay. We're not supporting her." I took a sip of my drink and sighed.

"Legally, we have to keep her if she and Wes want to continue to be mates—unless we cut Wes from the pack. That would get messy since he's mated to Evan. Spencer's trying to hire her, so I don't think money will be an issue. Are you jealous that Evan likes her so much?" he teased, an arm around me as he sipped his beer.

Maybe. I could share Evan with Wes since Wes was first—and the reason I'd even met him. I could share Evan with Jett because Jett was my husband, and we shared everything. But I didn't want to share Evan with Grace.

However, I looked like an asshole saying he couldn't be with her; especially since she was with Wes and Wes didn't mind.

"Evan was good to Caroline, and look what happened." I glared at the steak.

"I know." He patted my shoulder. "But not everyone's like her."

"But lots of people *are*. Wes and Grace are scent matches, aren't they? It's the only thing that makes any sense." I took the steak off the heat and put it on a plate to rest.

There were also a bunch of stupid stories about scent matches, like dreaming of them and shit. Whatever. That was for movies. Plenty of people didn't have a scent match with their omega–since an omega could smell mouth-wateringly delightful and be *the one* without being your soulmate.

Also, I hadn't missed Evan's comment in my mother's office about him not thinking Grace would survive an un-bonding.

"Scent match. Huh. I was wondering about that." Jett nodded. "I've never heard of a scent match with a gamma, but given they're usually failed omegas, that seems plausible?"

Evan wasn't my scent match. But I loved him with my entire being.

For a time, I'd thought Caroline was mine.

When we started dating during university, things got intense, fast, as they often were between alphas and omegas. I could see us mating, forming a pack, having kids, and sharing a life together.

When she wanted to travel after graduation instead of being with me, it broke my heart. But I loved her, so I let her go and moved on. When she returned, I welcomed her into the life I'd built without her. Brought her into my business. My home. We'd talked about making her part of our pack.

Then she nearly destroyed us. Me. I'd loved her, and she'd wiped the floor with my very soul.

The worst part was, I didn't even know why she did it.

Chapter Nineteen

Grace

"TV or books?" I asked as we sat at the table in my hospital room, playing a game using a board and marbles that he'd gotten off the hospital game cart.

"TV." Wes moved his marbles over mine and took them.

"Books," I replied. He'd taught me this marble game in our dreams. Usually we'd play it at the park, sitting at one of the picnic tables.

"Favorite animal?" Wes asked.

"Horse." I moved one of my marbles to another space. After Evan had left, when I wasn't napping, we'd been catching up. We used to know everything about each other.

I loved learning about adult Wes and his life. However, spending time with Wes only cemented how lonely I'd felt since I'd stopped dreaming about him.

He nodded. "Wolf."

"Mountains or beaches?" While we'd grown and changed in many ways, I didn't think we were all that different deep down. That ease between us was still there.

"Mountains," he told me. "Did you ever get to the beach?"

I nodded. "The PhD program I went to was only a few hours from, well, according to your maps, Bayside. We sometimes went to the beach."

Or as I called it, San Francisco, but the region was still referred to here as *the Bay Area*.

"In college, I was a cheerleader for the football team. We played teams near the ocean," I added. Football didn't exist here, well not American football. *Fútbol*, as they called it here, was soccer. Rugby was very popular—hockey and lacrosse, too. Wes had played rugby in high school.

"Was that the university you wanted?" he asked.

"No. I went to the big local state college for undergrad, then for my PhD program, I went to work with a professor I'd met in college," I told him, as I captured one of his marbles.

I'd studied maps, trying to figure out where I was. There *would* be similarities between some worlds because there were only so many original ideas in the universe. Somehow, I'd found a world that overlapped a lot, yet still had so many differences. It was *fascinating*.

It was interesting, because some cities and states were nearly the same. There was New York City, Boston, Philadelphia, even Portland, and Vancouver. Some were similar, like Motor City was Detroit, and Rockland was essentially Denver. Las Vegas was called Glitter City of all things. But a whole lot of the country also looked *much* different.

In this world, the migration to this continent wasn't fueled by religious freedom, but freedom from strict designation laws. Betas flocked here *en masse* to be free of stringent laws that were almost feudal in some places. They didn't want to be conscripted to fight alpha wars, work alpha land, or be forced into specific positions solely because of their designations. They just wanted their own land, their own laws, representation, and the ability to achieve on merit, not birth. This caused everything to develop much differently.

"Something you've taken up since we last talked?" I asked.

"Boxing. Jett's into boxing, too, so I have someone to spar with." He took three of my marbles, landing one of his in the safe zone.

I leaned my head on his shoulder. I'd missed *this*. Him. He'd been such a big part of my life for so long. I hadn't realized until now how big of a hole he'd left. "I finally learned to ride a bike."

"I'm proud of you." Wes beamed at me. "Evening showers or morning showers?" He moved another marble into the safe zone.

"Evening bath with bubbles and a beer." I laughed, moving one marble into the safe zone.

"She drinks. I think I even heard you swear." He grinned and took one of my marbles. "Scandalous."

"I know, right?" I moved another across the board. Growing up, I'd been such a good girl, in my small, conservative, religious Midwestern town. Well, except for my dream boyfriend.

"I take morning showers, mostly so I don't smell like sex when I go to work in the morning."

"Do you have lots of sex?" I bit my lower lip. The more time I spent with him, the more specifics I remembered about our time together.

"It's part of the territory when it comes to alphas and omegas." He pulled me close, his nose almost brushing mine. "I remember us... do you?"

"Yeah." My voice went breathy. Would it be like that in person? "Do you actually have a magic alpha dick?"

One of the big biological differences he explained was that an alpha cock had a knot on it, like a wolf, and it could lock into someone. He'd shown me in our dreams once he'd awakened as an alpha.

Oh, he had shown me.

"When I bring you home, if you'd like, I'll show it to you and see if I can jog your memory." He gave me a smoldering look.

Part of me warmed at the thought, remembering some of the extra-special fun we'd had together.

Frowning, I looked into his eyes. "Will Evan mind? I don't know how this works."

"No, Evan won't mind. But we don't have to do anything you don't want to, Grace," he assured me.

"Why do I want to let both of you have me? Talk about *scandalous*." I focused back on the board, trying to ignore the feelings he ignited inside me.

"It is okay here, and we're consenting adults." He captured my last piece. "There's a lot of reasons. I mean... I always thought what we had was real. Maybe it is. Or maybe it's that we're both incredibly sexy." Wes shimmied his shoulders. "Where were you living when you left, you'd graduated, right?"

I busied myself putting the pieces away so I wouldn't kiss him. It might lead to other things—and I wasn't sure I wanted to do that in a hospital. I frowned as I searched for the memory. "Not that far from where I'd gotten my PhD. I... I think I'd worked there even before graduation."

Maybe.

"What's your favorite smell?" I added, going back to our little *get-reacquainted* game.

"You." He nuzzled my side with his nose, making me laugh, as the door opened

"I haven't heard you laugh in a while." Spencer stood there with a bag. "I brought dinner. Wes, I don't want to interrupt, but did you sign all the documents HR sent you?"

Wes nodded. "Yep."

"Hi, Spencer." I waved, face warm, given he interrupted us being silly. But he didn't seem fazed.

"Hello, my good doctor." He smiled at me.

We chatted for a few moments.

"I've got to go, but good night." Spencer left.

"No Evan?" I tried to hide my disappointment as I cleared off the game so Wes could set the food on the table. "I know he was staying at the house tonight, but he said he was going to drop by."

"I know. We forgot it was Thursday." He kissed my temple.

"What's on Thursday?" I asked. Wes was constantly touching me, which didn't help my thirsty thoughts.

"He does something with his baby sister every Thursday. She lives at her high school but sometimes spends weekends with us." He took containers out of the bag.

"Evan was telling me about his sisters this morning when you were troubleshooting work stuff. I can't wait to meet her." I liked teenagers. Back when I was supposed to become a teacher per my mother's demands, I'd wanted to teach high school, not kindergarten.

"We can tell him we miss him." Wes whipped out his phone, took a picture, and sent it to him.

Wes

Miss you.

Evan

Miss you both. Peaches, kiss him for me, okay?

While Wes and I had cuddled a lot today, we hadn't kissed since yesterday morning after my shower.

I took Wes' phone.

Wes

Are you sure it's okay? ~ Grace.

Evan

It's okay. Kiss him more than once and have a sexy cuddle–or more.

"It's really okay, isn't it?" I chewed on my lower lip. I watched a couple of videos today that helped me to understand more about how packs and relationships worked in this world.

"It is, Peaches." He cupped my face with his hands. "As long as you're not out to break our hearts or break us up, we're all yours. All you have to do is wrap your head around it."

It would be so easy to do that. I still felt so much for him. Leaning in, I kissed him slowly, reacquainting our lips. My heart sped, and before he could wrap his arms around me, I broke it off, brain screaming for more. Like whatever a sexy cuddle was.

Giving him a coy smile, I opened a container.

I got a better look at the food, which was not only artfully arranged, but garnished, and had little containers of sauces. "Spencer went to a fancy restaurant, didn't he?"

Wes held up the bag. "Yep. He's a showoff. You said your favorite carb was potatoes, these are some of the best mashed potatoes in the city. After this, we can cuddle some more."

My insides melted. I was getting myself into trouble. But I'd think about it later. Right now, I'd eat dinner with the person who had once been more important to me than anyone in all the worlds. Someone who was very much real despite everything they'd told me.

Someone I might still be in love with.

Chapter Twenty

Spencer

"I find it curious how a successful alpha like you didn't have a pack until so recently. After all, you are so much older than everyone else, Mr. Thanukos." Mrs. Beekman stared at me across my desk as we sat in my office.

So much older. Ow. I was less than three years older than Evan. I'd started graying very early–after Elaris died.

"Time," I brushed off. "Not all alphas have packs, you know."

Also, the fact I'd lost my mate should be on record.

"True, even so, you also don't have personal relationships in or outside the pack. Don't you want children, a connection?" Her tone turned judgmental.

Ow. I shrugged. "I'm fine with the arrangement."

Not that long before Evan lost his parents, I lost my mate, Elaris. It had devastated me and for a moment I hadn't been sure I'd recover. Selling our company that we'd created together, back when we were still students, because I couldn't run it without her, and focusing on Evan and his sisters, had been exactly what I'd needed.

I'd started this company, and then we'd formed our pack. Sure, I got a little lonely sometimes, but I was fine. They were good people, and I cared for them all so much.

"Do you have any other questions for me?" My calendar sent me a reminder. *Leave work early and spend time with Ri so she doesn't feel neglected.* I shot off an email to IT to find and close whatever loophole Riley had exploited. It was a game she and Wes played.

"That's all for now. Thank you for your time." Mrs. Beekman stood and left.

Brennan texted the pack group chat with a screenshot of two women entering the house.

Brennan

Who's at the house?

I had no idea who they were, but one of them wore an Omega Center polo.

My executive assistant, Mrs. Katsopolis, came into my office. Her wife and my father had been research partners back in Greece, and she was like a second mother to me. She'd been my assistant from the very beginning of Compass BioTek, though it had taken a lot to lure her out here.

"I'm a little concerned about what Special Projects is actually getting up to. Especially with the lab you're making for this mysterious Dr. Ellington," Mrs. K told me.

"I don't know what you're talking about. You know exactly what they're up to." I kept my expression neutral. She was convinced that I was continuing my father's research in secret.

Her eyebrows rose. "Did you see that Riley hacked your calendar again?"

"At least this time she rescheduled my meetings." Personally, I didn't mind moving today's meetings. Usually, Riley and I met on Tuesdays, but sometimes she came to eat ice cream in the cafeteria on other days. Mrs. Katsopolis adored her.

As did I. I was counting down the time until she was old enough for a work permit so I could hire her. She was incredibly talented and needed some direction before she ended up in jail for hacking into the wrong things.

"This was dropped off. You're seeing someone?" She set a bag from my preferred jeweler on my desk.

"They're for Grace." Hopefully, she'd like everything. I tucked the bag away in my briefcase.

Her lips curved into a smile. "You're courting her?"

This was my contribution to getting her set up before the home inspection.

"Did you find out about the new portable particle accelerators?" I changed the subject.

I was considering courting Grace once she settled in with Wes and Evan. The moment I met her in the kitchen, I felt something that I hadn't in a long time. Not to mention she was extraordinary—and very different from my Elaris.

"A particle accelerator isn't a good courting gift," she laughed.

"It depends on who it's for." The particle accelerator was actually for all of Special Projects. We'd still need to use the large one at Rock Tech, one of the local universities, occasionally.

Her look softened. "You're right. Though back in my day they were the size of rooms, not refrigerators. Having one in the building makes me nervous, given how dangerous they can be... and what happened."

Same.

"Grace reminds me of your wife," I whispered, remembering how often they'd come over to our house for dinner when I was growing up.

"That's what concerns me. When will Grace be out of the hospital?" Her brow furrowed in concern.

"Hopefully tomorrow," I replied.

Evan replied to the group chat.

Evan

Department of Dependent Services and the Omega Center are doing a home visit.

I frowned. That didn't bode well.

"I understand your concerns about the particle accelerator. They're safer than they used to be, and we have more mandatory security protocols now." The lab my father and Dr. K had at their university in Greece had been destroyed in a supercollider accident, taking most of their research and staff with them. I'd been there that day, helping out as I so often did.

I'd only just left when the accident happened, and luckily hadn't been seriously hurt. Unfortunately, so many others had.

At least it didn't cause a black hole, or worse. A supercollider explosion was no joke. Not to mention, they were researching the fifth and sixth dimensions. I loved to help him, not necessarily because I wanted to follow in his footsteps, but because I enjoyed learning new things.

"I see." She nodded and left my office.

Another text came through the chat.

Jett

Headed home.

I finished a few emails, then packed up my laptop in my briefcase, and grabbed my phone and the bag.

"Heading out? Have a good weekend. Give Riley my love." Mrs. K waved as I passed her desk.

I waved back. This wasn't the first time Mrs. K had warned me about the dangers of following my father's research. I understood that far more than she knew.

But I wasn't a physicist like my father. Like many people in the Thanukos family, I was an entrepreneur. While they'd taught me about business, my father taught me how to recognize brilliance. Also, I understood enough about science to know what truly had potential.

Instead of following in my father's—or family's—footsteps, I built an empire of my own.

When I got home, Jett sat at the table, texting frantically, his amber scent a touch burnt with fear.

"Everything okay?" I looked around the empty kitchen as I took off my shoes.

"No. I caught the tail end of it." Jett shook his head. "I'm glad you're here. I need to go, but I didn't want to leave them."

"Dependent Services came? Caroline called and reported Evan?" I frowned.

"They don't work that fast. Usually, if there are kids in the house and someone is being investigated for domestic abuse or neglect, it would make sense for Dependent Services to swing by for a welfare check. However, if Caroline calls, it's not going to help our situation," Jett explained.

"Did the home visit go well? You all worked hard," I said. We'd been up half the night.

My phone lit up.

Evan

> **Can you come home for lunch? Ri could really use you.**

Oh, he thought I was still at work.

"It wasn't a visit for Grace. It was a welfare check for *Evan*. He said it was routine and that it went fine. I think he even knew the person doing it. It was the Dependent Services officer who came with her that was the issue. Shit, she was hard on Riley. I think she upset Evan, too. Why are you home so early?" Jett asked.

"Riley hacked my calendar again. I'll take care of them. Go to work." I headed upstairs and texted Evan.

The sunken sitting area on the third floor now had a gaming chair with a pillow that said *fuck off*. Evan sat on the couch holding Riley, who had her face pressed into his chest.

Riley was crying, her anise scent salty with sadness, which made me want to hurt someone for her. She was essentially our pack's child. I'd known her all of her life.

"Hi." I put my stuff on the chair and joined them on the over-sized couch.

"Fuck of the morning to you, too," Riley mumbled.

"I got your meeting request. Is the fancy pizza arcade sufficient, or does this warrant something else?" I asked softly, holding them both. They were my family, and we'd been taking care of each other for a very long time.

After my father had died, my mother and I moved to Rock Springs, a little over an hour away from Rockland. She wanted to be close to her university best friend–Evan's mom. My mother had since returned to Greece. But moving there had been just what we needed.

"Meeting request?" Evan's eyebrows rose, and glanced from me to her and back again.

"I worked hard last night and today. You and Jett have to work. I deserve some fun on my day off. Your IT department sucks, hire me," Riley said.

"As soon as you're sixteen. That's when you're old enough for a work permit–and as long as your grades don't suffer," I told her. Her birthday was in November.

"Really?" She sat up, brightening. "The fancy pizza arcade can cure anything." Her look went sly. "We need to play the dance game."

"I suppose." I gave her a fond look. She thought I hated the dance game, but I actually enjoyed it.

I turned to Evan. "Is everyone all right? What did Dependent Services want?"

If everyone was this upset, it didn't feel routine.

"I know we were waiting for Riley's next physical, but I think we should have her officially tested today," Evan said softly.

"Oh. I see." I got out my phone to make an appointment for her at the private clinic we went to.

"Tested for what?" Riley's head cocked. "Brilliance?"

"Rare designations. We could swing by on the way to the fancy pizza arcade, then have ice cream after. Since doctor visits get ice cream." I found an appointment on my phone and booked it.

Riley thought for a moment. "Am I that chaotic, adventurous one?"

"A kappa? No." I shook my head. They were nearly extinct, mainly because they were impulsive thrill seekers that chaosed themselves right out of existence with their fun-loving, but not usually well thought out ways.

Evan pulled her to him. "I suspect you're a theta. Thought that for years. Your doctor said that since you showed up as a beta on the test they did in middle school, that I should wait until high school to test you again. That's usually when the rare designations appear."

"What's a theta?" Her look became curious as she leaned into him.

"Hyper-independent, smart, misanthropes who like to collect wealth." Evan grinned.

She pushed him away and flipped him off. "You're shitting my dick. Don't call me out like that."

"It's an actual designation. My mother was pretty sure I was going to be a theta," I replied, pocketing my phone. "They're closer to alphas than betas." My father had been an alpha, my mother a beta, but there were thetas on my father's side.

Evan's parents had been betas, and him being an omega was a surprise. But genetics could be funny like that.

"They must not have gotten into all that in health classes." Evan frowned.

"We only got the basics in biology–more than last year, but nothing interesting. We have the big health class next year. Wait, so I'm not broken?" Tears welled up in her eyes.

Evan brushed away her tears. "Never. Even if you don't designate as a theta, you're still not broken."

My heart ached, and I squeezed her hand. "I'm so sorry you think that."

"I... lately..." She wriggled out of Evan's arms and hugged her knees to her chest. "One of my teachers gives me shit about not having lots of friends and my activity choices. Then this asshole Dependent Services lady is like, '*Don't you feel abandoned being on the first floor? Don't you feel excluded living at school? Don't you miss your sisters? You do all these chores for money, like you're a maid?*' No, you fuckwad. I *like* the independence of being at school."

She did–and she needed her independence fostered.

Riley glared at us. "Living up here with you assholes all the time? Fuck that shit. I'd live in the guesthouse if you'd let me."

"Yeah, you legally can't live there on your own," Evan said.

"Can I live in the basement? There's that locked room down there."

"Not right now," Evan told her. "But you have a nice room, away from everyone."

The locked room in the basement was the nest that came with the house. Evan hardly used it, preferring the cabin.

"It doesn't hurt to ask." She shrugged. "I enjoy living here. My sisters are fun to do things with, but it sucks ass living with them because they're bossy bitches. I like doing chores for money because then I can explain where my money came from to my nosy sisters because they're not cool like you."

"Where is your money coming from? We talked about this." My eyebrows rose. While she was an incredible hacker, her overconfidence would end up with her getting caught.

She made a face. "Be cool, Spence."

"The Dependent Services officer clearly didn't understand how to raise a teenage theta. If we could get an actual test, that would help us if she chooses to make our parenting methods an issue," Evan said quietly. "She also didn't like that we're all guys."

"Um, antiquated. Again, not a problem. If I want estrogen, there's plenty at school." Riley rolled her eyes. "No, I don't miss having a mom. Fuck, I shouldn't have let her get under my skin like that."

Oh. Yes. That would be the tears. Evan's family gave *everything* for Riley. But they'd never be her parents. There was a tiny part of her that wanted what her siblings had, and she barely remembered. A part she tried never to show.

"Do you want to talk about it?" I asked, not suppressing my alpha urge to make it better for those in my care.

"No. Before you bring up Grace as a mom-substitute, she probably can't even bake cupcakes and hates rom-coms—and don't even go there." She glared at me.

I knew Riley secretly liked rom-coms. But I'd never tell.

"Grace," Evan breathed. "She's not a replacement mom for you. I promise. No one can replace our mom."

"I know. But that asshole brought it up. Anyhow, I'm going to get changed." She stood and then hugged me. "Thanks for not ignoring my meeting request. Love you too, fucker. Have fun at work, Doofus." Riley went downstairs.

"Are you okay?" I scooted closer to Evan and put an arm around him.

He sighed, snuggling into me. "The Dependent Services officer got nasty with me about sending her to boarding school and taking her from my sisters. But it'll be fine. My sisters will back me up in that Riley *chose* all of this. This was best for her—and them. They get to live their lives, my grandparents too. High school seemed like a good time for a change of location. Though I probably should have done this sooner for my other sisters' sake."

"The school is an excellent place for Riley, and you're right, a theta designation will help explain our choices. I'm here and I'll back you, as always." I smiled. Before my mother and I had moved here, we'd visited them often—and they'd visit us. Even though he was a little younger than me, I loved spending time with him and his family.

"I'm so glad," Evan told me. "She also complained about Riley's vocabulary."

I shook my head. "We got her that way."

"Yep. And well, we swear a lot, so it would be hypocritical to get on her for swearing without us cleaning up our own language." Evan sighed. "I should get to work. You'll be fine with her for the afternoon?"

"I'd much rather have pizza than deal with spreadsheets. The Omega Center visit went well?" I prodded, curious because it was a visit for him.

"It was just Carly. Given the situation, it's routine to check on the other omega in the house. Bren's going to be pissed since she had to go into *every* room. But it was fine. I answered the questions truthfully, and I have nothing to hide. This was to make sure *I* was okay," he said.

"Are you okay?"

"Yes." He rolled his eyes. "I don't have any issues with Grace being here."

"You're half in love with her, aren't you?" I asked. I saw the way he looked at her, was with her.

"Half?" He laughed. "Spence, I didn't fall for Wes this quickly or hard. I'd like to think it's not only the bond talking."

"Of course not," I assured. "I like her, too. She's fascinating." I looked forward to getting to know her better.

His eyebrows rose. "You're not fazed by Grace being from another world?"

"No. I'm intrigued, especially since she can't remember how she got here. Not to change the subject, but Mrs. Beekman might still come by for an inspection?" I asked.

"My guess would be tomorrow. The integration team will start calling, too," he added.

"What if she has to leave?" I was a little worried about the prospect, given how close Evan was getting to her.

"All the more reason for Wes and Grace to work through their shit—so no one gets hurt if that happens. Am I selfish for wanting her to stay?" Evan's brow furrowed.

"No. I think she should stay." I wasn't going to stop Grace from getting back to where she came from. But if that's what she wanted, we needed to discuss what dangers it could bring her–or me.

She might not know the rules. I barely did.

My father hadn't known the rules. He and Dr. K had paid the price, as had so many others who had needlessly died in the explosion.

I just hoped Evan and Wes' hearts weren't broken in the process.

Evan's phone buzzed, and he looked at it and sighed. "See you tonight?"

"See you tonight." I went down to my suite and changed into something more appropriate for the pizza arcade.

One worry of mine was that someone might come after Grace. She'd also *come here*. Those means may not have been sanctioned. I had so many questions.

However, we needed to be cautious. The reason I knew that Grace had traveled from another dimension was because she had that same smell clinging to her that those men had. The ones who'd come from nowhere and arrested my father and Dr. Katsopolis, then took them away for breaking this world's interdimensional travel ban.

Right before the men had blown up the supercollider in order to hide what my father and Dr. K had found.

Chapter Twenty-One

Grace

I sat on the hospital bed watching another video from the Omega Center's library as I struggled to understand the social complexities of this world–and my own emotions. Meeting with someone from the *integration team* validated my feelings, but also brought up some of the challenges I might face.

However, he didn't address the biggest issue–this wasn't my world and I didn't belong here.

Wes came back into the room and slid into bed. He pulled me to him, his scent enveloping me, soothing me. My brain still felt like sludge, and I wanted another nap.

"Is everything okay with work? HR's not putting you on leave because of the investigation, are they?" I still felt bad about him missing work.

"Nope. Just getting you added to all my stuff, like my health insurance. While we set up a record for you, so you'd have the basic coverage everyone has, Spencer generously provides additional private insurance to employees."

"Oh, I've been wondering how this would get paid for. This is a nice hospital," I replied. "Thank you."

"You're my mate, you should be on all these things–and yes, you and Evan can both be on everything. So, I've been getting it all done," he assured.

"Right, another one of Katie's action items so you don't go to jail." I deflated a little. We'd already signed some sort of agreement between us that Katie had sent over.

"Hey, what's wrong? Something's been bugging you. What did Mrs. Beekman say?" He stroked my hair, concern etched on his face.

"Nothing." My shoulders slumped. She had assured me that I *deserved* to be with someone who loved and cared for me–and that I loved and cared for in return.

It left me even more confused.

Tomorrow morning, once I was cleared by the hospital, I'd go home with Wes, where he'd take care of me until I recovered and the investigation finished. I wasn't even hooked up to the big monitors anymore; just a small wrist one, which I'd take home with me.

Then what? What would happen when I remembered? Brennan didn't want me there, and Jett was doing everything for appearances, since his own career could be in jeopardy.

"Was it the integration team person who said something to you?" Wes prodded, brow furrowing.

"Not specifically. I understand Jett coming by with cookies and Spencer bringing food and giving you time off work. I'm okay with being an action item to them. They don't know me. I'm an interloper. Bringing me home with you is a big deal." At least according to what I'd been told.

"They're going to love you once they get to know you," Wes soothed. "And you're going to love them. Even Brennan."

I wasn't so sure about that.

"How much of everything you're doing is because it's what's expected of you as an alpha, and how much of it is because you actually care for me?" I blurted as I looked away, pain blooming inside me. "I don't want you to go to jail. But I need to know where I stand." Given that I was falling in love with him.

If I'd ever fallen *out* of love with him.

It was all of the silly things. Him feeding me ice cream. Bringing me Mr. Hippo. Playing games. Talking.

"Grace, Peaches?" He tilted my head toward him and ran a thumb down my face in a way that made my insides shiver.

"I'm not doing all these things *just* to keep me out of jail, promise." He pressed my back against his chest. "It's not for appearances. Granted, some things are getting done faster because of Katie's lists. But they'd all get done eventually, because I *want* to do these things for you. I want to bring you home with me—not because I've been told to, but because *that's where you belong. That's where you've belonged from the very first time I saw you in my dreams and you told me that you were going to marry me."

"I did tell you that." It was the very first thing I'd said to him when I'd seen him in my dreams that very first night.

"You know, I still don't understand how wedding cake gave you interdimensional dream travel abilities. But I'm so glad it did." He buried his face in my neck.

I remembered that too. When I was ten, I'd gone to a wedding and someone had given me a piece of cake in a tiny box. They told me that if I slept with it under my pillow, I'd dream of my future husband.

And there he was. So, I walked over to him and told him that one day I'd marry him. Then, I'd seen him in my dreams again and again.

"I'm so glad that you're here. I want you to be a part of my life. Evan does, too. I'm sure there will be bumps and squabbles, but we can make this work. You're not an action item, you never have been. You're the love of my life. Yes, I have Evan, and a pack, and I love them. But there's enough love in me for all of you. I promise." He leaned in and kissed me, soft and sweet, the first time tentative. The second was more assured.

My very soul absorbed all his words, making them part of me as their warmth trickled through my system, my heart happy. On this level, I knew what he said was true. That he wanted me here–and I wanted this.

Wes pulled away and pressed his forehead to mine. "I'm right here, and I don't want you to doubt for one second that as long as you're here, you belong with me and Evan."

My brain wasn't as convinced.

"But *why?* Why do you and Evan want me? Why do I want to go home with you and let you have your way with me? Why does my heart pound when you touch me? Why am I sad that Evan hasn't been by today? Your biological imperatives don't apply to *me*. I'm not from here. It's only a matter of time before they figure it out. Then what?" Tears pricked my eyes. I didn't want this all to end.

Wes hauled me into his lap, and pressed my head to his chest, arms tight around me. "How do we know the biological imperatives *don't* apply to you? Just because your world doesn't have definitive designations doesn't mean that they don't exist on some fundamental level, even if they don't manifest biologically the same way."

"True. Have we had this argument before?" I calmed a little under his touch.

"We have."

"Mrs. Beekman asked if we were scent matches. She said it's like soulmates. Are we?" I buried my head in his chest, getting lungs full of his delicious scent.

"We are. It was something we figured out a long time ago." He pressed his lips to the top of my head.

"But why? Why would I be your match when I don't even live in the same world? That's so mean. What if I never got to you?" I started to cry.

He covered us with the blanket and planted little kisses on my face.

"Why does that affect me? Why do you smell so good?" I sobbed. Everything crashed down on me. "3.14159265." I sucked in a breath. "3589793238." I closed my eyes and willed my body to relax. "462643383279."

"That's it, Peaches, relax," he soothed, purring as he put another blanket over us.

"502884197169399375..." It came out raspy, as my chest shook.

"I have you, and you're going to be okay."

My breath slowed. "1058209749." I inhaled another lungful of Wes. "44592307816406."

For a moment, we lay there in the fuzzy blankets; him holding me and purring.

Finally, the purring stopped, and he turned us so we faced each other, noses touching. "The obvious is that your theory that we exist in a universe of simple parallel worlds and not a multiverse is erroneous. For some reason, your Wes never appeared in your world, just like my Grace never appeared here, and our biological imperatives were so strong that it pulled us to each other through the dream realm in an effort to unite us."

I clenched. "Why is it so sexy when you talk science? Even if I stand correct at us not existing in the multiverse. But back to scent matches. I can get behind that. But when I watched a video to explain it, the video stated that it only happens between alphas and omegas. I'm not an omega. I'm not even a real gamma."

"But I think you sort of are. Even before my test came back as alpha, I felt all those things toward you that alphas feel toward their omegas. You don't have to be mature to recognize a scent match. After I awakened, there were so many signs that your omega was in there waiting to blossom, especially in those last months. My guess would be that because of the differences in your world, it never happened since some of those specific biologics don't exist. Still, there was no doubt in my mind that you truly were *my omega*. You still are. Even if you're not genetically, you are where it counts." Wes pressed my hands to his heart. Heat flooded my body.

"If you're trying to get into my pants, it's working." I leaned into him and stole a kiss, contemplating letting him have me in the hospital after all.

"About time. Want me to put up the door sign? I still need to determine if your pussy tastes like peaches." Evan stood there, holding a bag, with a look of desire on his face.

I should be mortified. I should apologize, make sure he was okay with what Wes said. Instead, I popped out of bed and launched into his arms. The warmth of his giant body cocooned me, and his lemonade scent wrapped around me, going straight to my needy core.

"Evan." I buried my face in the crook of his neck. As I wrapped my legs around him, my entire being, soul to brain, gave a satisfied shudder. Because I needed him too.

"Peaches." Evan pulled me down on the bed, covering me with his body, smothering me with lemonade satisfaction.

"Evan, how much did you hear, I–" Wes' voice shook.

"Stop." Evan sandwiched me between him and Wes as he kissed Wes. "I'm going to have to start a fund where every time someone apologizes needlessly we put money in it, and at the end of the year we go on vacation."

"To the beach." I melted between the two of them, my insides going gooey. Oh yes, I'd love to spend a week lying on a beautiful beach with them all day and fucking them all night long.

"Absolutely." Evan's lips captured mine as he pinned me to Wes's chest with his body.

"Evan–" Wes started.

"No. Don't you even dare undermine that breakthrough by apologizing to me. She belongs with us." Evan kissed me again, punctuating his statement.

"Why? Wes is my alpha. But are you getting it through the bond? I mean, it would be statistically improbable for both of you to be scent matches with me *and* be together, and could we even?" I frowned, still trying to understand it logically.

Evan rubbed his fingers across my forehead, smoothing out my worried brow. "I don't care. You sniffed me and practically had a fucking orgasm. Can we take her home now? I need to be the filling in a Wes and Peaches sandwich."

"Is this a thing we're going to do?" My heart pounded with anticipation, my legs rubbing together.

"Yes." Wes buried his face in both our necks. "You two smell delicious together."

"Filling?" I wasn't exactly sure what he meant.

"Yep." Evan rolled us away from Wes, then rolled back, so his back was to Wes' chest, and I was facing Evan, so he was in the middle. "Like this. I'm the filling."

"Ooh." Sure, it might be scandalous compared to what I grew up with, but the idea of being between both, to be loved on all sides, delighted me—and I trusted Wes.

"Do you want to see him knot me? I want to see him knot you. Just like I want my dick deep inside your sweet peachy pussy as you come around me," Evan added. "Wait, do you know what knotting is?"

"Yes, teenage dream Wes showed me." I gave Wes a bashful look.

Wes leaned over and kissed me. "We'll go at your pace, but here, all these things are normal. All love is normal. There's so much we want to show you."

My panties got wet at his words. "I want to try." I looked at Evan. "It's okay if I sleep with your husband?"

Something I shouldn't want so much, but did.

"Yep, because I'm going to fuck yours–and you. Is that okay?" Evan ran his body up and down mine, setting every one of my nerves on fire.

"Yes. Can I be the filling sometimes?" I tilted up my head so I could see them.

"Yes. Also, yes, I've mentioned to Bren and Jett more than once that I planned on being with you if that was something you wanted and no one objected. Oh, I can't wait to see you take us." Evan put his hand on my ass, rubbing it. "Do you like ass-play or do we need to work you up to it?"

"Never tried it. This guy in high school tried to tell me that ass sex didn't count, but he just sort of wanted to shove it in there. A lot of my friends back then believed that you were still a virgin if you did only butt stuff." I chewed on my lower lip, enjoying the sensation of his touch, this closeness.

"That's hysterical–and wrong. We'll start nice and easy." His lips grazed my ear. "I can't wait. Anything you don't like?"

"Mean words, or being too rough, is that still right?" Wes said, positioning us so we were both lying on him. "Anything else?"

I nodded as he stroked us. "Um, I don't think I can handle being tied up, blindfolded, or spanked."

"Well, you can do that to me, Peaches," Evan breathed. "I'm not very experienced with girls, but I will eat that pussy. Do you suck dicks?"

"I wasn't very good at it." I gave Wes a coy look, remembering the few things we'd tried in our dreams.

Neither one of us had any experience, and I couldn't look things up since my parents would know, and I was terrified of asking my friends. Wes, on the other hand, got sex classes in school.

"Evan can teach you." Wes kissed him on the cheek. "Our safe word is *trampoline.* The moment someone says it, *we all stop.* Any of us could say it the moment something isn't okay–that includes me, okay?"

"Anytime? Any of us? Okay." I liked that idea, because while I'd like to try everything, I wanted to be able to stop if it was too much.

Wes nodded. "Anytime. Anyone."

"We have to communicate, right? So all our needs are met?" I added. That's what the integration person said.

"Yep. Communication, boundaries, we'll get there. Toys?" Evan asked, hand still on my ass. "That's how I'm going to get that ass ready for my dick. There are some others I want to try with you, too, at some point."

"I think so? I'm willing to try." I nodded as Wes' hands trailed over my body. "Can I use them on you?" That could be fun.

"Yes." Evan grinned.

I moaned as Wes' hands brushed under my right breast and my body bucked. *Touch me more.*

"That's it," Wes whispered. "Come at my touch."

"Why do we still have our clothes on?" Evan mumbled, his hand stroking my leg.

There was a knock on the door. "Grace?"

"Fuck." Wes threw a blanket over us.

I squirmed, but he held me tightly.

"Stay. There is nothing wrong with this," Wes growled.

"Not at all," Evan replied.

"Come in," I called, a little breathless, not wanting this to stop.

The nurse came in, but she didn't seem fazed one bit that all three of us were piled on the bed. "Grace, Hun, we have to get one more scan and some more bloodwork so your sexy men can take you home tomorrow."

"Oh." Right. Disappointment shot through me. I was enjoying myself so much.

I flopped on top of Evan and gazed into his brown eyes. "Will you be here when I return?"

So that we could continue where we'd stopped.

"Probably not. I'll be here tomorrow morning to bring you home, promise." Evan leaned in and gave me a soft kiss.

"Oh." I drooped a little at the thought of him leaving. I'd like more of this.

"I'll be here." Wes helped me off the bed and gave me a snuggle. "Mr. Hippo will be here too." He made Mr. Hippo dance.

I laughed and put on my slippers. "Let's go."

So I could come right back to Wes.

Chapter Twenty-Two

Grace

The door of my hospital room burst open. A tall and curvy teenage girl with a nose ring, winged eyeliner, a black dress, and platform shoes sauntered in. "Fuck of the morning, bitches."

"Hi, Ri, I wasn't expecting you." Wes zipped up the bag.

Me neither, but I was excited to meet Evan's littlest sister.

"Spence had an outdoor business meeting, and Bren and Jett are busy doing married-people things, so you fuckers get to hang with me." She grinned and held out her light brown hands in a pose. Her nails had tiny bats on them.

"Bren and Jett are on a bike ride," Evan corrected, coming in. "Spence is golfing. Sorry we're late. Mrs. Beekman showed up bright and early and threw everything off."

"Did we pass?" I asked. Evan had mentioned that she might visit to make sure their house was acceptable.

"She loved the way *I* decorated your room," Riley told me. She looked me up and down. "You're Grace? Fucking shit, Wes."

I'd put on actual clothes today. I'd been wearing Wes' shirts and yoga pants most of the time. But today I had on a green shirtdress and slip-ons with peaches on them. The dress was so soft and flowy with no tags. It wasn't itchy and had pockets.

Wes grinned and waggled his eyebrows at me. "I know, right?"

I couldn't help but giggle. "You must be Evan's little sister?"

"What if I'm not?" She gave me a sly look.

"We could pretend. Or leave them and get iced coffees?" I offered.

"Boys are stupid." She nodded.

"Peaches." Evan gave me a kiss and a bear hug.

"Evan." I buried my face in his shirt.

"Get a room, ew," Riley said.

Was the appropriate response to apologize or kiss him harder? Evan tipped up my face and kissed me. Riley scratched her nose with her middle finger.

"Got you." Wes scooped me in his arms and planted a kiss on my forehead. "Let's go home."

Evan took my things from me, and Wes carried me out the door and down the hall.

I leaned into him. "Shouldn't I be in a wheelchair?"

"Why, when you have a perfectly good alpha to carry you?" Wes grinned.

"You're impossible." I felt ridiculous. The nurses grinned and waved as we left.

"You know you love it," Evan replied.

I sort of did. After years of caring for others, or trying to be on my own, it felt nice to have someone take care of me.

"Front," Riley called as we got to a black 4x4.

She climbed into the front with Evan. Wes and I got in the back. We drove, and I leaned into Wes.

"Um, where are we going?" Riley's face pressed against the window.

"Nunya." Evan grinned at her.

Riley flipped him off. "Fine, be an asshole, you doofus."

The car stopped, and we got out. Rather, Wes scooped me up and carried me. The four of us walked across the grass and a play area came into view.

"Cute, but you don't need to take me to the park to play," Riley snorted, looking around.

It had snowed a bit this past week, and there was snow on the ground, and in the trees, but the sun was out, and I wore a jacket.

"It's the park, it's real." Tears pricked my eyes as he carried me to the swing set, the weather a little cool but pleasant. "A little different, but it's real."

I was here. This was our park. My chest shuddered.

"They redid it a few years back, but here it is." Wes got on the swing, me on his lap, and held me, soothing me with his touch. "Yes, this is our park."

"It's for them. This is where they first met," Evan said. "But I'll push you on the swings."

"If it'll make you happy." With a huff, she sat on the swing, and Evan pushed her.

Riley turned to us. "You met at the park? When?"

"I was ten." I closed my eyes and felt a little hum in my chest that hadn't been there in a long time.

"My dad's house isn't far from here. I used to come here all the time to sketch or play rugby with my friends," Wes explained. "I was actually sketching on that bench when I saw her on the swing. She was wearing a ruffly pink dress." He kissed the tip of my nose.

I sat on his lap as we swung, kids playing around us. In our dreams, we were always alone.

Evan and Riley went climbing on one of the structures. We went back to the car a different way, passing some benches and a lamppost that we didn't pass by the first time.

My heart jumped. "Wes, walk backward."

He did.

"Stop." My breath caught in my throat as I could see myself stumbling in the park through the trees in the dark, then crawling onto the bench.

"This is where they found me. I... I didn't realize that it was our park. I came to our park." My heart sped a little, and I recalled something from our dreams.

"*What if I can't find you?*" *I asked Wes as we gazed up at the stars.* "*Sometimes you're not where I am, and it's scary.*"

"*Go to the park and wait for me on the bench. I'll always find you at the park.*"

"I'll always find you at the park," Wes whispered, pulling me to him.

How had I come to our park when I didn't know how I got here? When I hadn't thought Wes was real?

"What's happening?" My chest shook. *If only I could remember everything.*

"Lexi didn't say it was our park you were found at. Just that you were at the Eastside station. Hey, you're here with me, now. That's all that matters." His breath was warm on my ear. "Let's go home."

I was here with him—and I'd come to our park.

We returned to the car. Evan drove us through a fancy, forested subdivision with large lots and came to their massive three-story house. He pulled into the garage, which had several motorcycles, and we got out, Wes continuing to carry me.

"Shoes off." Evan tugged off my slip-ons and put them on a large wooden shelf that had a bunch of shoes on it. Everyone else did the same.

"You can put me down," I told Wes as we crossed the kitchen.

"I will, in my bed." He grinned as we walked up the backstairs.

"We have to show her to her room, you asshole." Riley made a face, following us.

We went up to the third floor and stopped at the sunken sitting area I vaguely remembered.

"This is my chair." She pointed to a low chair with a pillow that said *fuck off.* "And yours." It was an overstuffed chair with a pillow with a peach on it. "I got all your favorite video games for us to play together."

"Thank you." I didn't know much about video games.

"I made you a room." Riley tugged on my hand. "Evan and Jett put shit together, but I made it pretty. Okay, Spence helped, too."

We stopped in front of double glass doors that had an intricate vine design on the glass.

"How beautiful," I breathed.

"Ri, did you paint this? It's fantastic," Wes said.

"Better than curtains." Riley preened as she opened the door. "I know you'll probably sleep with them. Fuck, that sounds wrong. I know you'll probably spend your nights with the human pillows, but this is where you can escape from them and keep your shit. Doors even lock."

"It's amazing." The room was long, like the length of two rooms, but the width of one generous one. There was a giant bay window with a seat the size of my childhood bed. It was covered with pillows and cushions. A beautiful potted plant stood in one corner. There was a wooden wardrobe and a dresser with a mirror on top. On one side was a canopy daybed, also festooned with pillows. Everything was done in greens, with hints of peach and mauve. It was very soothing and garden-princess like.

"The bench in the window opens, and there are more blankets in it," Riley told me.

"It's beautiful. Thank you. This wasn't your room, right? I don't want to turn anyone out," I said as Wes gently set me in the window seat like a delicate doll.

"Fuck no." She rolled her eyes. "But I'll show you mine later. It's cute. It would be cuter if I could stay in the guesthouse out back."

"Nope." Evan shook his head. "Not my rules."

"Laws suck ass." She made a face.

I tugged Evan to me. "Thank you."

They made me a room. My insides went squishy. I'd never had a room so pretty, that had been made for me with such care.

"I'm glad you like it, Peaches. The only downside is that you'll have to use Wes' bathroom." Evan kissed me, and I unabashedly kissed him back, even though Riley was there with us.

I noticed that there were no doors other than the glass one Riley had painted.

"I need help with my homework before we go to the movies." Riley grabbed Evan's hand and pulled him out of the room.

"You like it? They worked hard to make it nice." Wes pulled me to him.

"This is amazing. I love this window seat." I wanted to curl up and read here.

"Do you need anything? Food? Shower? Nap?" He trailed kisses down my neck, each one sending shivers down my spine. His eyebrows waggled. "Something else."

I laughed, going gooey inside.

He scooped me up and went down the hall to his rooms. *Rooms.* Wes had an entire suite of rooms all to himself. Such a luxury. As was my big, beautiful room, which was so much larger than my tiny apartment.

Wes kicked the bedroom door closed, and we flopped onto his gigantic bed. For a moment we lay there among the soft covers that smelled of him and Evan. Pressing my face against his chest, I let all the comforting scents wash over me.

He stroked up and down my back in a languid but maddening rhythm as he pressed light and soft butterfly kisses on my face, which made my nipples pebble.

"Evan... Evan won't mind, right? Like really and truly?" I murmured as his kisses trailed down my neck. While the thought of both of them made me hot and bothered, I wanted to start with Wes. Reacquaint myself with his body, with being loved.

Then I'd be ready for more.

"He won't mind at all. Evan can join us tonight—or tomorrow when Ri goes back to school." Wes kissed my collarbone, making my body tingle with anticipation.

Maybe I'd only had Wes in my dreams, but my body still remembered what it felt like. I wanted him. I'd wanted him for days. Would it be as good in real life as it had been in my dreams?

"I'm not much more experienced than the last time we had sex. I remember trying a couple of times to date, mostly because of parental pressure, but nothing felt right. Not to mention, well, some people don't think I'm beautiful when I'm naked and I'm not sure if I can be with someone that isn't okay with all of me," I admitted, my voice breathy as my back arched, hoping he got the hint and touched my aching breasts.

Wes' kisses moved down my back. "All of you is beautiful."

That was exactly what I needed to hear.

"I'm so curious what it would be like to be with both of you. Talking about everything last night, oh boy," I sighed in memory, heat rising inside me, making me wet.

"I'm so glad." He touched his forehead to mine. "After you, I tried, but... no one was you. Until Evan, who is most definitely not you. He sort of lacks some things you have and has things you don't." Wes buried his face in my breasts.

"I'm glad you have him," I gasped as he bit my breast through my clothes.

"I need you naked." Taking my dress, he pulled it over my head, revealing my cute and sporty bra and panties. Wes attacked my lips as I fumbled with his shirt, like we were horny teenagers.

The last time we had sex, we'd been exactly that—horny teenagers, desperate for reassurance and each other. I threw his shirt some place, our kisses growing frantic as he slid his fingers under the back of my bra to undo it as I unzipped his pants, his cock hard against his boxers.

His scent became stronger, swirling around me in a cocktail of passion and familiarity, as he nipped at the bottom of my lip, hands caressing my breasts. Wes' fingers hit that sensitive spot under my right breast and my breath hitched, heat flaring through me as my panties grew damp.

"Pants off," I demanded, not able to remove them fully with the way we were positioned on the bed.

"Bossy," he teased, wriggling out of them, but staying in his boxers, then diving at me on the bed, attacking my breasts with his lips.

"Right there." A moan escaped my lips as he teased my nipples with his tongue. His hands traveled down my body, removing my panties, then running up my leg.

"I missed these breasts," he groaned, taking another mouthful. "And that pretty cunt of yours. Did your pussy miss me, Peaches?"

"Yes." I arched my pelvis as he took my nipple in his teeth and bit gently, as his fingers rubbed my clit. "Right there, right there." Pleasure burst through me.

"Right there, what?" He looked at me, eyes a glimmer, then vanished. "Sorry, we... we don't have to play that game."

"Right there, Alpha, please." I grabbed his hand, pushing it right where I needed it, the old phrase coming naturally to my tongue. In this moment, it felt so right.

"Oh, the sound of that. I need to taste you. Open." He pushed my knees open and buried his face between my legs, nuzzling my thighs, my curls, my damp folds. His tongue darted out, licking the length of me, then settling on my clit, sucking, and licking me like I was his favorite ice cream on a hot day. "Mmmm, sweet and delicious." Wes teased and tasted me as I moaned again. "That's my perfect peach."

The first time he'd gone down on me, I'd been scandalized. I had no idea that was something people did.

Then I begged him to do it again.

Two fingers slipped inside me, and I gasped as they created a maddening rhythm.

"So wet," he whispered into my clit, pulling me closer, practically growling into me.

"Yes," I moaned as his fingers found all the sweet spots, his mouth unrelenting as he continued to feast on me.

"I want you to come all over my face," he murmured as he nibbled.

Don't need to ask me twice. He thrust an additional finger inside me, my body shaking as waves of pleasure washed over me as I inhaled lungfuls of his intoxicating scent.

Wes continued working me with his lips, his fingers, making my body shudder in a way it only had in my dreams, working me back up to my peak, making me see stars over and over.

"Oh yes, yes, *yes*." This. I'd missed this so much. I'd missed *him*. "Wes, I want you inside me," I breathed.

"Are you ready to see my magic dick?" He sat up, eyes bright. "I've been waiting for days to show it to you—and I came very close to doing so last night."

"Gimme." I grinned back, reaching for his boxers, helping him pull them off. "Please, Alpha." I smirked.

For a moment, I stared at it. It was long and thick, even more so than I recalled. The fleshy part at the base was already partially inflated–a part that the boys back home didn't have. The alpha knot. It got bigger as he got aroused, then when he pushed it inside me, it would lock, sealing us together until it deflated.

"Is it everything you remember?" His look got heated, as he fisted it, giving it a couple of strokes.

"More." I licked my lower lip in anticipation and reached out, running the tips of my fingers up his hard length, as he gasped, closing his eyes.

"That's it, touch it, remember it. This is all for you and Evan. What do you want to do with it? Do you want me to fuck your pussy with it? Do you want me to take you slow or fast? But either way, I'm going to make you remember how much you loved my dick, as you scream my name," he growled, gasping again, as my fingers traced his knot.

Wes had talked to me during sex. I'd often called him *alpha* in bed. But it had never been quite so graphic.

More, please.

"I'm going to taste it." Crawling forward on the bed, I ran my tongue up it and around his knot. I tried to take the tip in my mouth, but I started laughing. The first time I'd tried to give him head, we'd been in the paddle boats, and it had been so awkward we'd fallen into the lake.

"I'm glad my dick makes you laugh." He pulled me down onto the bed, grinning.

Wes leaned in and sucked on one nipple, flicking it with his tongue and nibbling on it until I gasped.

"Are you on birth control, or do I need a condom? Evan bought some in case you wanted them," he asked. "Evan and I aren't on birth control. We should fix that."

Men could and did go on birth control here. Nice.

"I got a shot back home, but the doctor here put something in my arm, said it was standard and I could get it removed. Um, I think enough time has passed." I moaned again as he lavished attention on the other breast.

"May I please have you, Alpha? I need to feel you. This is all for you." I widened my thighs to make room for him. As fun as this was, I wanted him inside me, to fill the emptiness I'd had in my soul for so long.

Emptiness that might just be him.

"Absolutely." Covering my mouth with his, he slid his length inside me, in one smooth motion.

A sigh escaped my lips as his hard cock filled me, making me gasp. "Yes."

He settled himself inside me and swiped back a piece of my hair with his hand as his gaze met mine. "Are you okay? You feel so good. So warm and wet and ready for me."

"Full. I need you to move." *Fill me. Claim me.*

Love me.

"As you wish." Wes pumped up and down, in firm, hard strokes, sending waves of delight through every inch of me.

A heady feeling embraced me as I bucked against the sensation.

"That's it, Peaches. I'm not going to last long. I... I don't have to knot you if you're not ready." He sucked on my neck as he continued to thrust in and out of me, pace unrelenting.

A memory struck me as our bodies continued to meet, pushing, and grinding with a fervor I hadn't felt in so long, something halfway between a prayer and desperation.

My body continued its urgent rocking as another orgasm threatened to crash down on me. "I want you."

"You have me." He kissed me hard, as if trying to push all his feelings into a single kiss.

Bracing for the crash, I lifted my pelvis, trying to pull him into me, my body knowing I didn't quite have all of him. "I want your knot, please, Wes, Alpha, please."

"Are you sure?" he whispered, pulling out almost all the way.

"With all my heart. Knot me," I pleaded, needing to be joined with him.

Needing to be whole.

He growled, and thrust his entire length in, pushing his knot inside me, stretching me until it popped in place, locking us together.

The wave of release crashed down on me, and my teeth clamped down on his shoulder, right where I always used to bite him during sex as I came on his knot. Our bodies moved as he continued to rock, his knot sending delicious sparks through me as he brought me to another peak. Another growl came from his throat as his hot release filled me, him adjusting me slightly against his knot, then kissing me hard. I climaxed again, and my body continued to tremble as he pulsed inside me.

Claiming me. Filling me. Making my soul complete.

"That was perfect," he murmured, nibbling my neck, kissing and licking me in a way that sent little sparks of delight through me. "You were perfect. Are you okay?"

I looked into his eyes, falling into them. "That was incredible." Tears pricked my eyes, and I buried my head in the crook of his neck, inhaling his scent. "I missed you so much."

"I missed you, too," he breathed, wrapping his arms around me and shifting our locked bodies into a more comfortable cuddling position. "I'm here. I'm here and I've got you."

He started to purr for me, wrapping my body in warmth.

"I know." For the first time in a long time, I felt happy. Truly soul-busting, joyously happy. Like a puzzle I didn't know I'd had was finally finished.

I was treasured. I was loved.

I was complete.

Chapter Twenty-Three

Wes

My face buried in her hair as I held her close. The scent of our lovemaking clung to her, to me, as she dozed in my arms.

Grace. I had my Grace back. I didn't want to give her up. Whatever she had in that other world, it would be better here. Not just because I was here. We'd love and appreciate her far more than her world ever did.

A soft rap on the door broke through my musings. "Wes?"

"Evan, why are you knocking? Get in here," I called.

The door cracked open, and his face appeared. "I wanted to give you privacy."

"You don't need to knock. Seriously. If Grace has a problem with it, we'll tickle her until she relents." I nuzzled her with my nose.

"Gimme." Eyes still closed, she reached out for Evan.

Evan slipped in and closed the door. His eyes brushed over our naked bodies. We were no longer joined, just cuddling, as I contemplated another round.

I grabbed his hand and squeezed it, sending all my love through the bond. *You okay?* I mouthed.

He nodded. Then he gave me a saucy wink. *Felt that,* he mouthed back.

"We'll make it up to you." Her voice went soft. "I..."

"Oh, Peaches." Evan dive-bombed the bed, wiggling in between us. "It's okay to need some alone time. Was it magic?"

"It was." She snuggled into him, making satisfied little noises that made me want to fuck her again. Fuck both of them.

He pressed his lips to her forehead, then leaned in for a kiss from me.

I captured his lips and kissed him like I'd missed him, my hands traveling over his clothed body. "You're leaving for the movies?"

"Turns out, we're all going to the movies." He leaned into me.

"Grace *just* got out of the hospital." While the movies weren't strenuous, with Riley there, I couldn't exactly make out with him. With them. Cover them with a blanket and tease them, playing *don't make a noise* as I made them come over and over in the darkness, hoping the air filters in the theater were good enough that we didn't get kicked out.

"I know, but it's a movie, not a hike. Katie's action items." Evan's eyes rolled.

Grace frowned. "Are omegas not allowed out without alphas? Because that's bullshit."

"No. It's more of a social construct," Evan explained. "We're a pack. A family. Why *wouldn't* we do things together? Omegas tend to *want* to stay close to their alphas; it makes them feel safe and happy. I drive myself to work a lot. I do things with just me and Riley. It's more like my being overly independent looks weird.

While it works for us, Katie thinks they need to be extra doting right now."

"Alphas need to protect. It's easier to protect your family if you're there with them," I added, giving each of them a kiss. "It stems from the days when you stuck close to your omega because they might get kidnapped."

Grace's look went horrified. "That doesn't still happen, does it?"

"Not like it did. But there are still assholes and criminals. Also, Evan can defend himself against an alpha. But most omegas can't, so there's that safety factor. It's like how your dad made you keep pepper spray in your pocket," I explained. Her dad had seemed to genuinely care about her, but he wouldn't stand up to her mom.

"The movie theater has big reclining seats, so you can curl up and sleep," Evan added, stroking her hair. "We've got to leave soon. Oh, and Ri picked out your outfit. But you don't have to wear it."

"I feel like I sort of do. She's testing me, making sure I'm worthy of your time." Grace sat up on her elbows, the blankets slipping off to reveal her pale breasts, the shell pink nipples teasing me as if to say *Come play with us.*

"Sounds about right." Evan gave her another kiss, then nuzzled her neck. "I love the smell of him on you."

"I can't wait to smell you on her, but Ri will get pissed if I have my way with you and we're late," I said. "Want to join us in the shower?"

"Fuckers, we need to go in thirty," Riley yelled from my sitting room.

Evan looked at the door and grinned. "I'll make it until we get home. Grace might have to entertain Ri, though."

"I'll take one for the team. I like teenagers." Grace grinned back and got out of bed, the blankets dropping completely. Her bruises were a lot better–especially the ones on her face, but that's not where Evan's gaze went.

Evan sucked in a breath at the sight of her back, which was covered in ugly scars in the center. Those strokes had been carefully placed so they'd never be seen if your clothing was modest. *Modest is hottest* was one of the many bullshit things she'd been taught.

The sight of them made me want to hurt someone. It was a good thing that the people who did that to her were in another world. How could they do that to *children?*

"Sorry, I... I can wear a shirt when we're in bed if it makes you uncomfortable." Grace's head bowed as she fumbled for a blanket, scent going both sour and salty.

Evan wrapped his arms around her, taking the blanket from her hands and tossing it on the bed. "Please tell me that your partners didn't make you wear shirts to bed or make you feel uncomfortable about your body."

She turned away. "What partners? I'm okay with the fact that others are bothered by my scars."

That was a lie. It hurt her. I could tell.

"Your scars are beautiful." He pulled her to him and kissed her.

I stood and embraced them both, covering them with my scent, comforting them, with my touch, letting them know I loved them, imperfections and all.

"Ri wants to bake cupcakes and watch rom-coms with you. But I didn't tell you that," Evan said.

"We're having a welcome-home barbecue for you tonight, so maybe you can make cupcakes together. I mean, if you know how to make cupcakes?" I added. Cupcakes would be nice.

"Evan!" Riley yelled.

I sighed, wishing we could stay like this a little longer. "Ri's favorite sport is cockblocking."

Grace giggled. "Well yeah. She's fifteen. I know how to make cupcakes. That sounds fun. I'm going to take a quick shower."

I seized Evan and gave him a deep kiss, a promise that I'd see to his needs later.

Evan gave Grace a little kiss and smoothed her hair. "I'll make sure you make it up to me tonight, okay?"

"Yes, sir." Grace smirked, swinging that little ass of hers.

"*Fuck.*" Evan's eyes stayed on her as she disappeared into my bathroom. "If she keeps calling me *sir...*"

"She was raised to call people that out of politeness." I shook my head at his expression.

"I'm familiar with the concept. Also, I was in the military with you, but *fuck*. Love you."

"Love you, too. Are you sure this is okay? I want to check in now that it's happened." I pressed my forehead to his. Not that I sensed any resentment or hesitation through the bond, but I wanted to ask, anyway.

"Yep. Did you knot her? I half expected to feel her bond with you after you did that." Evan leaned into me, resting his head on my shoulder.

"I did. I should've waited. But she begged, and well, I couldn't deny that." I grinned at the memory, her cute little pleas echoing over and over in my head. "I thought that it might happen, too. However, the doctor said it could be awhile because of the concussion. What if... what if I never feel a bond with her?"

"Do you want to?" he asked.

"More than anything." My voice went growly.

"Well, maybe you should bite her again. It's been a while anyway," he added.

"True." While the bond mark an alpha left was permanent, it wasn't uncommon to bite it over and over. Maybe it needed a little boost.

His fingers traced Grace's little bite on my shoulder. "She didn't bite you hard enough."

While it felt good when she bit me, no, she hadn't. She never did.

He kissed it and left. I slipped into the shower with Grace. Part of me didn't want her to wash off the scent of our lovemaking because we were going out. That primal part wanted everyone to know that she was well-fucked. But I also hadn't had a good shower in days. Well, there were more ways to make her smell like me than fucking.

Showers were also fun.

Chapter Twenty-Four

Evan

"**C**an we talk about Grace? If she and Wes have known each other since they were kids, and played at the park, why does she have no record? If Wes and Grace are mates, why are we just hearing about her now?" Riley asked me while we waited for Grace and Wes on the couch of the third-floor living room.

"It's a weird story—and not mine to tell. I don't even know all of it. Grace's mom was a big part of it and she went to great lengths to keep Wes and Grace from each other. I know Wes loves her—and I'm pretty sure she loves Wes," I replied.

She rolled her eyes. "That's obvious. It's just weird."

"Yep. But I like her. What do you think?" It would be easier if my sister liked her.

"The verdict's still out." Riley shrugged.

Wes joined us, holding two hoodies. "Grace, are you ready?"

The door opened, and Grace came out of her room. She wore the black math crop top with a long-sleeved shirt under it, and frayed denim jeans. In her hand were the motorcycle boots Jett had bought. She wore makeup and had covered all her bruises.

Hot damn. It was clearly a Riley outfit. I gave my sister a look. She flipped me off.

Wes gave Grace a kiss. "You look hot. Who bought the boots?"

"Jett," I replied, coming over to them. Pulling her to me, I ran my hand over her covered stomach.

"I don't do crop tops," Grace said softly, eyes downcast, her scent taking on a hint of sadness.

My hands fisted at the thought of her scars. Wes came up behind me and pressed his body to mine and ran his hands over me, nuzzling my neck.

"Your eyeliner. Fuck. How did you do your makeup like that?" Riley checked her phone. "We need to move, fuckers."

"Here, I have this for you." Wes slipped a thick zip-up hoodie over her arms. "Do you need one too?" Wes also had my favorite of his hoodies in his hands.

While I had a jacket, that wasn't why I wanted to wear it–or why he asked me to.

"Thank you." I snagged a kiss as I took it from him.

"If you want to know how to do eyeliner like this, I can teach you. I figured it was what you wanted me to do when you left the liquid eyeliner with the clothes," Grace said as we walked down the backstairs. "Back when I did roller derby, that's how I did my makeup."

"Roller derby?" Riley asked.

"Um, yeah. Maybe you don't have that here? Women on skates play a game where they skate around the rink in a circle, trying to keep each other from getting all the way around. It's a little rough," Grace said. "It was with my department when I was getting my PhD. We all had math names. I was *Peach Pi*. We played other departments, it was fun."

"Skate smash, you did skate smash at your university. That's hot," I breathed, holding Wes' hand as we went into the garage. It was rough and tumble, even more than hockey.

"Respect." Riley fist-bumped her. "I like watching the pro leagues on TV. Before I moved in with these assholes, I used to play. I'm going to try out for my school team. Tryouts for next year are after spring break so we can train all summer. I want to do the summer camp the Rockland Raiders run, too."

"That sounds fun." Grace nodded. Yeah, we should probably catch Grace up on sports, movies, and other things most people knew here.

We drove to the movies and crossed the lobby. Grace held Wes' hand, looking around at all the people and movie posters.

"No popcorn?" she asked as we went to our theater.

"Inside. You've never been to the fancy movie theater? You need to go on better dates." Riley found our seats, which were all in a row together.

Riley sat on one side of me, Wes on the other, Grace next to him. I should let her sit between us, but I was feeling a little selfish. The chairs were giant recliners that had movable armrests, tray tables, blankets, and pillows.

"What are we getting, fuckers?" Riley had out her phone.

"Popcorn," Grace piped up, settling into her chair, her feet not even touching the floor.

"They have actual food here. You never had lunch and should eat," Wes told her. "You should eat food, too." He kissed my cheek.

Riley rolled her eyes. "I plan on eating food, Wes. Happy?"

"Very. Everyone should eat food." Wes looked like the smug fuck he was.

We placed our food order. Grace moved up her armrest and curled into Wes' side, covering herself with a blanket. He tucked her in, giving her a fond pat.

I felt bad dragging her out so soon, but we couldn't leave her home alone. She might even like it. It was a spy comedy.

Better dates. Where could we take her? Usually, Wes and I kept our dates low-key.

Wes grabbed my hand over the armrest and squeezed it.

"Oh, fuck." Riley made herself small in her chair.

"What?" I followed her gaze and saw a lanky teen guy in a leather jacket, eyeliner, and boots enter the theater with a couple of men.

"Marcos." She ducked her head.

"I thought he was your friend. What happened?" Frowning, I watched him look at his phone, then his head whipped around and he headed straight for us.

"He is. I don't like people flaking." She made a face.

While thetas were independent, they were also insecure and wanted to feel like they were needed and belonged without being smothered. It was a rough balance.

"Riley." Marcos' entire goth face lit up. "Hey, I texted you, a couple of times. Is everything okay?"

"Yeah. Went home for the weekend. Pack stuff." Her voice went flat.

"I get that. Thanks for being cool about yesterday. I found out why they wanted me to change my plans. Papi and Dado came home to surprise me for my birthday! They didn't want to tell me in case they couldn't make it. But they're here!" Marcos beamed, clearly oblivious to her posture and expression.

Her arms uncrossed, and she sat forward, mood instantly changing. "Wait, your papi came home? Dado, too? Shit. That's great."

"*I know.* Yesterday, I got to spend the *entire day* with *just* him and Dado. I miss them so much when they're away."

"Just you? Fantastic. Your birthday's this weekend?" Riley leaned forward even more.

He grinned and leaned in. "Don't tell. It's tomorrow."

Well, this was super amusing. I was pretty sure Marcos was a young alpha. An alpha and a theta. That could get interesting, considering alphas needed to protect and be needed, and thetas liked to pretend they didn't need anyone.

"Marcos, our seats are over here, Mijo," a man called.

"Papi, come here. I want you to meet someone." Marcos waved him over.

"You want me to meet your papi?" Her grin went nervous.

"I do." Marcos looked over at me and suddenly realized that Riley wasn't alone. "Is this your pack? I'm so sorry to interrupt."

"Part of them, and no, it's fine." Her head ducked a little as she grinned.

"It's so nice to meet you." Marcos turned to me as four guys joined him.

"This is my brother Evan and his mate, Wes. The blanket potato on the end is Grace," Riley introduced.

"Evan and Wes." Marcos nodded. "Ri talks about you. No Spence?" He looked around.

"He had an outdoor business meeting. But maybe we can go visit him this week? The cafeteria at his work has good ice cream; they change flavors on Wednesdays," Riley replied.

She wanted to take him to visit Spencer? Oh boy.

"Outdoor business meetings last forever, don't they? Pops always has them. I've tried to take it up, but it's *so boring*." Marcos looked over at a rather imposing alpha, who was older than Spencer, grey in his dark hair.

That dad of Marcos' reminded me a bit of my old drill sergeant and looked a tad familiar–he might be law enforcement. The man messed up Marcos' hair.

"Anyway, Ri, meet my four dads. Papi, Dad, Pops, and Dado, meet my friend Ri, from school–and her family," Marcos said.

"It's so nice to finally meet you. He talks about you all the time," the one he indicated as *Papi*, said to Riley.

"He does?" Riley smiled and ducked her head. "He... he talks about you, too."

Wes leaned in, voice barely audible, "Is that?"

I nodded. *Papi,* the shortest and slightest of the four, was a lithe and handsome man, with dark wavy hair and tan skin, *come-hither* eyes. He was an omega, and also a *very* famous actor, named Antonio Caruso. He played heartthrobs who could ballroom dance, had perfect aim, and drove fast cars.

We met the others. Dado was clearly an ex-military alpha. Dad had a more easygoing nature about him and could be a beta, it was hard to tell with all the scents flying around. Pops, the one who might be law-enforcement, seemed like he was head alpha.

"I'm so glad to meet you all as well," Antonio told us.

"It's always nice to meet Marcos' friends." Pops kept an arm around Antonio's waist. He kept glancing over at Grace, who'd sat up, but was still huddled against Wes.

She was pretty, with her delicate features and grey-blue eyes. They could also be trying to figure out where she fit, since *blanket potato* wasn't one of the usual descriptors used in families and packs. Wes kept one arm around her as he held my hand. His look clearly said *mine.*

"We should take our seats," Pops said. "The movie will start soon, and we haven't ordered yet."

"I'll be right there," Marcos said as his dads went to their seats.

A few people gave Antonio appreciative looks as he walked by, Pops' arm around him the entire time.

"I know things are busy, but if you could at least answer the text about math, I'd appreciate it," Marcos told Riley.

"Marcos," Antonio called.

"I should go. I'll see you Monday?" he said.

She smiled. "Yeah, fuck you later."

"Fuck *you* later." He grinned and ran off.

"You should probably choose a different parting phrase," I laughed. "Unless, you're..." They were at that age, and we had those talks.

"Oh, my fuck, no." Her look went aghast. "We're just friends."

"Sure," Wes teased.

Riley flipped him off. "Shut the fuck up."

"He seems nice," Grace whispered.

"He does. You have a lot of classes together, right?" I prodded.

"We're both freshmen." She rolled her eyes.

The young server came by with our food. "Aww, you have such a cute family."

"When did we start looking old enough to be Ri's dads?" Wes asked, after she left.

"Four dads. I've never seen that," Grace murmured.

"His pack is massive," Riley replied. "He's a day student. It's not that uncommon. You grew up fundie or someplace where there are no packs?"

Grace blinked. "My parents were pretty conservative."

Right, at some point we'd need a backstory for Grace.

The lights dimmed, and we watched our movie and ate our food. Grace got her popcorn, and Wes decided to feed it to both of us.

Partway through the movie, my phone kept vibrating. I peeked at it.

Work

> **I know it's your day off, but there's stuff going on with Rose. Can you come in?**

Me

> **At the movies. Is it an emergency?**

It can wait.

I'll come by soon.

"Everything okay?" Wes whispered, leaning into me as I put my phone away.

"Work, I need to swing by after the movie," I whispered back.

We finished the movie, and I stood in the lobby texting, waiting for Riley and Grace to return from the bathroom.

Wes wrapped his arms around me. "Ri has a *boyfriend*?"

"She's fifteen." I nodded. "I should have another talk with her about healthy relationships."

Her test had come back confirming she was a theta, so things were going to be different for her–especially relationships.

"Have fun with that," Wes snorted. "One of the dads is famous."

I shrugged. "We have Spence and Bren."

"Which is still weird." He grinned.

Wes and I were from working-class families. I hadn't realized that Spence's family was ultra-rich, and slightly famous, until I was an adult. While Spencer liked nice things, Brennan's upbringing and family were way flashier, and it took a little getting used to. Jett's family was more upper-middle class–not Brennan and Spencer rich, but better off than Wes and me.

Riley and Grace joined us. Grace looked at Wes holding me, and ducked under my arm, so she was with us. She smelled like Wes and felt so very right in my arms.

"Is this okay? We're in public," Grace murmured.

"Always," Wes assured. "Look."

We looked at other families in the lobby. A woman between two men, a baby on one man's chest. Two men holding the hands of several kids. Three women with their arms around each other, one visibly pregnant. A group of teenagers jockeying for hand-holding positions. Two young Goths gazing into each other's eyes.

"You're cute, but I'd like ice cream," Riley demanded.

"I have to handle something at work. Drop me off, get them ice cream, go to the store, then call me and we'll see where I'm at." Since I was only just getting to know Rose, it would be better to see her face-to-face.

I drove us to the Center, and they dropped me off. Checking in at the desk, I went to find Rose.

She was in her room, making a beaded bracelet. "Evan!"

"Hey. Sorry, we were across town. What's up?" I took a seat.

She sighed, focusing on her bracelet, not me. "Am I making the wrong choice by not getting mated straight away?" Her head bowed, and she pushed her phone to me. "Should I drop the charges against my mom? I mean, she was just looking out for us."

"You're sixteen. In this class of crime, and given your age, charges will be pressed even if you don't want them to," I told her. "Also, there is *nothing wrong* with wanting to wait. In fact, considering you're sixteen, if you wanted to take a mate, we'd have to get a judge involved. May I?"

Rose nodded, sniffing a little.

I looked at her texts. Oof. The one from her sister was pragmatic, and along the lines of *If Mom's in jail, and you're not mated, how are the rest of us going to survive? I can't pay all the bills with the job I have.*

Her brother was more like *I miss Mom, why did you take her?*

It was the vile texts from other family members, especially her uncle, about her being ungrateful, calling her names, and other mean and even strange things.

The only supportive one was from her stepdad. *Stay in the city and go to school on the scholarship. I'll figure it out.*

But this wasn't Teatime-Era Britain. Some young omega didn't have to put aside her own dreams and marry someone she didn't like in order to save her family.

"I can send a social worker to see what sort of aid your family qualifies for." I didn't want Rose to think for one moment that she had to trade her life for theirs.

"Oh, that sounds good. I just worry. I don't want my siblings to starve because I was selfish." Her head bowed.

"Of course. But you're not selfish. I'll do what I can. How is everything else going?"

She told me about what she'd been learning. I got a text from Riley asking if I was done. There were also messages in the group chat about tonight.

"Do you need anything else from me? Sorry, my packmates are having a cookout tonight," I said.

"I'm okay, see you tomorrow." She smiled.

I left, making the social worker and aid requests through the system, then met Wes in the parking lot. Climbing into the back seat with Grace, since Riley was in the front, as usual, I leaned over the seat to give Wes a kiss, which tasted chocolaty.

"Here, we got you some ice cream. We went there last. It's only a little melted." Grace held up a small paper sack.

"Thank you." I gave her a kiss, too.

"Ugh." Riley made a face.

"Do I apologize or flip you off? I don't have it sorted." Grace giggled.

"Scratch your nose with your middle finger; maybe kiss him harder," Riley replied.

Grace kissed me harder. She tasted of cookies.

"Wowza." Wes laughed as he drove off.

"We'll make it up to you later." Grace kissed me again.

"Let's go home." I opened the bag, took out the lidded container, and ate my ice cream while Wes and Riley debated hacker things and Grace snuggled into me.

You have such a cute family. Yes, I did.

Chapter Twenty-Five

Grace

I lay on the big loveseat in the living room, the same room where I'd watched a movie with Jett and Evan that first night. Only Wes was my shirtless pillow. Evan was on the giant couch with Jett and Brennan. Evan and Jett were also shirtless. Spencer and Riley sat on beanbags.

Full of grilled steak, we were watching an action movie with the same actress we'd watched the other night, and the man we'd met in the theater, Antonio, one of Marcos' dads.

Four dads. That was a whole lot of dad jokes.

I remembered that my dad used to tell me dad jokes. Usually to cheer me up after a fight with my mom. Once I reached puberty, it felt like we fought about everything. Why did I wear that dress to church? Why did I have to take so many advanced classes? Why wouldn't I go out with so-and-so's son?

The movie ended. Spencer frowned at me. "Should you be watching so many movies? You should rest your eyes."

"Probably." I shrugged.

Riley sprung to her feet, giving a stretch. "I should get some homework done. I put aside a cupcake to bring to Marcos for his birthday. It's clearly labeled. If anyone eats it, I will cut you."

She was probably going to text Marcos some more. They texted mostly by sending pictures. Like when he needed help with homework, he didn't ask—he sent a picture of the math problem with a question mark drawn directly on it.

Earlier, Riley had shown me her room, and we made cupcakes.

"We're still going hiking tomorrow?" Riley asked Jett.

"Yep. Who's going?" Jett asked.

"Not me." I yawned.

Brennan gave me a look. "Not outdoorsy?"

"I don't think I could handle a hike tomorrow. I do enjoy hiking and camping–"

"And skate smash," Riley chimed in.

She'd shown me a video of her favorite team. Skate smash was roller derby meets professional wrestling set at a rave–on *ice skates*. It looked fun–and kinda dangerous.

"Skate smash is hot." Jett shrugged.

"Wes, if you want to go hiking, I'll stay with Grace. I have work to catch up on," Evan said.

"I can stay, too," Wes offered, arms still tight around me.

"Good, this trail's too hard for you two anyway." Jett grinned. "Bren, coming?"

"I think I will. Spence?" Brennan looked at Spencer.

Spencer gave him a look that clearly said what he thought of the idea. "I've got to get some work done. Good night, Ri." He gave her a hug. "Good night, everyone. I hope you had a nice evening, my good doctor." With a wave, he went up the stairs.

Riley was grinning at her phone. "Yep, homework time. Good night, fuckers."

Wes stroked my hair. "Let's head upstairs?"

"Sure." Before I could get up, he scooped me up. "Seriously?" I laughed.

He play-growled and twirled me around. "Yes."

"Hey, don't break anything," Brennan grumbled.

"Evan?" Wes leaned in to give Evan a kiss, which brought me *very* close to Jett and Brennan. I couldn't quite identify what Jett smelled like, just that it was warm and a little musky, but Brennan smelled like Christmas trees.

"I'll be up in a bit," Evan said, staying in his spot with Jett and Brennan. They were sweet together.

Wes carried me upstairs, right to his suite of rooms. He plopped me onto the couch of his little sitting room, which had a couch, a TV, and some bookshelves and an alcove with a beanbag that smelled a lot like Evan.

"Are you doing okay?" he asked, joining me and pulling me onto his lap. "What do you think of my family? I know they're different from what you're used to. But they're good guys, and I care about every single one of them."

"I can see that. I like that all love is normal here and families come in all flavors. It wasn't that common back home." Tonight made me understand that they were a family, and Brennan took his job as head alpha seriously.

Wes snuggled me. "I like how you roll with that. Bren wasn't mean to you?"

"No." I shook my head. He didn't make me feel unwelcome, or completely ignore me. But he didn't make a point to talk to me like the others.

"Good. We've been friends for a long time. I even talked about him to you. He'll come around," he assured me.

"Okay." The part that always sought approval *did* want him to like me. If anything, to prevent any fights. I just didn't like it when people didn't like me or were mad at me.

"Do you miss home? Is any of this too weird for you?" His head tipped to mine.

"It could be the concussion, but I'm just rolling with it," I told him. "Is it awful that I don't miss home?"

"No." He shook his head. "But it would be okay if you did. Are you sore from earlier?" His hands roamed to my clit.

"A little," I admitted. "But that doesn't mean I don't want more."

It had been easy to fall back into his arms, into our old ways. Everything was so comfortable, like we'd never been apart.

"Good. While I loved our dream sexy-times, you in real life..." He gave me a smoldering look, "incredible."

Oh, that it was. My chest shook a little as the space between us practically shimmered with desire. I leaned in and kissed him.

I heard a door and footsteps. A moment later, Evan entered.

"Now that... mmmm. My turn. But who first?" His grin went sly. "Is that okay?"

I nodded. "It is."

"We can stop anytime," Evan told me.

Wes pulled him between us. Capturing his face in his hands, Wes devoured Evan's lips. When he stopped, his look was almost feral.

"Mine." Wes pulled me across Evan's lap and kissed me as well. "Also mine."

"Of course, Alpha." Evan's eyebrows waggled, as he put a hand on my ass. "Mine, too." He leaned in and brushed his lips across mine, soft and sweet.

I looked up at them. Never had I thought that I needed two guys, but here I was. Evan kept rubbing my ass, and I could feel his hard-on under me. Wes' tent-pole was *right there.* All I had to do...

My panties got wet at all the scenarios open to me. Mmmm.

"Do you like that, Peaches? Do you want me to touch you?" Evan's hand slid under my waistband.

"Yes." My body shivered with anticipation as his hand moved over my panties.

"Wes never took you there?" Evan said as he rubbed my ass through my panties, my head resting on Wes' dick.

"We were just starting to get adventurous." Could I just nom on Wes' dick through his pants?

"Did you start fucking before he got his knot or after?" Evan kissed Wes, who stroked my back.

"Before. We'd been friends for years and years at this point–and well, we may have kissed a bit. I was studying reproduction in biology, and I had questions. Growing up, I... I never had much sex education other than *good girls don't let men plant seeds in their lady gardens until after marriage.* I also didn't have anyone else who I trusted enough to go to. I knew Wes wouldn't laugh or get mad." My eyes closed, as I remembered that particular homework help session.

"So much to unpack there, Peaches. Wes helped you with your homework?" Evan waggled his eyebrows, his hand still rubbing me.

"I did. We had a couple of talks and... demonstrations. By then I'd had all the sex education and some of the alpha classes." Wes' hand caressed my breast. "So sweet."

"Mmmm, I can imagine. Wes, when you officially awakened, were you like, *hey, got my knot, want to try?*" Evan kissed the back of my neck, his breath warm.

"Pretty much," Wes replied.

I sighed in memory, as Evan's hand moved down to my pussy, the tension building inside me, and I moaned.

"That's it. Relax. Let us take care of you," Wes whispered.

Oh, I wanted him to. It felt good. It felt right.

Evan's caresses grew urgent, and my need increased. I ground myself against his dick.

"What do you need, Omega?" Wes asked Evan.

"I need to taste our Grace, then I need to fuck her as you knot me," he breathed.

Oh, yes. I wanted Evan's cock—and to see Wes knot Evan.

"Yeah?" Wes rumbled. "You still want her to suck your cock as I knot her?"

"Please, Alpha," he moaned.

Oh, yes please. I hummed at the thought.

Wes' dick was right there. I moved my face and gave it a nibble through his pants. Wes jumped, and I giggled.

"Clearly, you need my cock, too. Both of you need to be fucked so hard, don't you? Licked and touched and knotted until there's no doubt who you belong to." Wes growled, nipping my nose gently with his teeth.

"Please, Alpha," I panted. I was so close.

"She called you *Alpha.* So hot, Peaches." Evan ground into me, and I moaned again.

"You don't get to come with your clothes on." Wes gave each of us a kiss, then scooped me up. "Peaches, I'll try to go slow, but this might get a little more... intense than when we were kids. Do you remember the safe word?"

I nodded, leaning against his bare chest, his scent intoxicating. "Trampoline."

"That's my sweet peach," he praised, kissing my temple. "Don't be afraid to use it if we get to be too much."

Wes put me on the end of his bed, which reeked of him and Evan–and him and me.

"Clothes off, both of you, now," he ordered.

He didn't have to ask twice. Sitting on the end of the bed, I came face to face with Evan's cock. It wasn't quite as long as Wes', and didn't have a knot, but it was *wide*.

"You'll get that soon." Evan tugged off my shorts and panties. Wes set things on his nightstand.

Yes, please.

"Peaches, get on all fours so Evan can taste you," Wes instructed. "Other way, yeah, just like that."

He rubbed my bare ass as I faced the headboard, knees sinking into the soft comforter.

"So beautiful. All of you is beautiful. Especially this pussy, which I'm going to taste," Evan said, getting on the bed so he was kneeling behind me, at the end of the bed. He stroked my back.

Evan licked me from clit to asshole, as lightning shot through my body, and something warm and slick coated my ass. The room filled with the most delightful smell, a smell that made me want to fuck–and be fucked.

"How does she taste, Omega?" Wes growled.

"Delicious," Evan breathed, as he licked and nibbled my clit. "Oh, yes, Alpha, right there. Peaches, I'm going to fuck you with my fingers, then put something in there to get that cute little ass ready for the day both of us can fuck you at the same time."

Heat spiked through my core at the thought of both of them at once as someone's fingers circled my ass. Both of them at the same time? I gushed at the thought.

"Mmmm, I smell that." Evan feasted on my pussy as a slick finger entered my tight hole, which stung slightly as it stretched.

"I smell *you*, Omega," Wes growled. "Relax, Peaches." Wes leaned in to suck on my nipple.

I gasped as Evan's finger slipped past the muscles and began to move as I tried to hold off the heat building inside me like an inferno.

"Oh, Peaches," Evan sighed, as a finger also entered my pussy.

My knees shook. "I..."

"That's it," Evan said.

"I..." The muscles in my ass clenched.

"Put the little one in, but don't switch it on," Wes said. "You're doing great, Peaches."

Evan removed his fingers. Emptiness washed over me as I whimpered, aching to be full again.

"I know, soon," Wes soothed, his chest covering my back.

Evan put something warm and slick on my ass again. "I'm going to slide this in."

Something poked at my hole. It slid in, and I gasped as it popped past the ring of muscles as Wes nipped one of my breasts.

"You did that so well," Wes praised, kissing me, then getting up and kissing Evan, who groaned. "You're both perfect."

Evan licked me again, his tongue lolling over my clit like I was a tasty treat.

"I need some dick," I groaned as a maelstrom of passion brewed inside me. "Please, please..."

"Whose dick do you need," Wes asked.

"Evan, I need Evan's cock," I muttered.

"I need your knot, Alpha," Evan groaned. "Please."

"Fuck our pretty peach, Omega," Wes growled.

Evan put his hands on my hips, brushing his thick length against my opening.

"Peaches, look at the mirror on the wall." He gently turned my head.

I watched as Evan entered me, his thick cock thrusting inside me as my inner walls quivered. He was big, and thick, and I felt so full between his hot dick and the toy in my ass. So full. So loved. My body threatened to explode with sensation as pleasure crashed over me in a way I never knew I needed.

"How does her pussy feel, Omega?"

"Perfect. She's so nice and wet for me." Evan moved. "Alpha, please. I need your knot."

"Almost," he growled.

In the mirror, I saw Wes behind Evan, stroking his ass as he sucked on the bite mark on his neck.

"Peaches, do you like being fucked by my mate?" Wes asked.

My head flew back as Evan grabbed my hair, kissing me fiercely as his thrusts intensified.

"Yes, yes," I cried between kisses.

"Alpha, please knot me," Evan keened.

"Watch me take him as he fucks you," Wes told me. His knot was mostly inflated, his cock hard as he thrust it inside Evan, who moaned.

Evan's hand played with my clit as his thrusts intensified, matching Wes stroke for stroke as he pounded his ass, knot inflating as I watched in the mirror. Wes' hand tangled in my hair. I whimpered, needing to come.

"That's it. Come all over Evan's dick," he breathed. "Omega, come on my knot."

Wes thrust his knot into Evan. I saw Wes' jaw bite down on Evan's neck and my whole body shuddered in release. As another scream ripped from my lips and warmth spurted inside me. My orgasm took me hard and fast, rippling through my body like whiplash.

Evan's hands didn't stop as I came, and came, him *still spurting* his warm cum inside me, as our alpha crooned to the both of us.

"I come a lot," Evan breathed in my ear, as he bit down gently on it.

We collapsed in a heap on the bed, me underneath the both of them, Wes' knot locked in Evan, Evan still inside me. It didn't feel suffocating, being under two large and muscular men. It felt safe, comfortable.

Wes purred, filling me with warmth. "I loved seeing my mates fuck each other. Beautiful," he murmured. "Is everyone okay? Evan? Grace?"

"I like it." I was so boneless that was all the words I could get out. It hadn't been a week, and I wanted to stay. Sure, there was my work, but I could get a job here.

Wes was here–the love of my life that I had dreamed of across worlds.

So was Evan. My big teddy bear with the thick cock.

I was theirs. I wanted them to be mine, too.

# Chapter Twenty-Six

Wes

The two people under me were mine. Their bodies, their souls. All mine. Mine to please. Mine to delight. Mine to protect.

Mine to fuck.

Any doubt I still had about Grace fitting with me and Evan, about not being able to do right by my omega by adding Grace, had disappeared the moment Evan took her as I knotted him.

Mine.

Contentedness hummed through the bond. I couldn't quite feel Grace, other than a few happy sparks, but there was no doubt how she felt by the blissful expression on her face. It was the face of someone happy and well-fucked.

Sex, arousal, pheromones, and Evan's perfume, which he gave off when aroused and ready to entice alphas into fucking him, filled the room, creating a heady cocktail that made me ache to have them again. Peach lemonade was becoming my favorite fragrance.

My knot softened enough to release myself from Evan, but we still laid there as I stroked them and purred for them, assuring them that they were loved.

Finally, I sat up and got the water bottle off the nightstand and handed it to Evan.

He sat up and took a couple of gulps, then brought Grace up to his chest. "Here."

Without a second thought, she drank from the bottle and leaned into him, humming. I took the bottle back, took a few sips, set it back on the nightstand, grabbed a wipe, and cleaned off my semi-hard cock.

Evan reached for the canister; I shook my head.

"Up, Peaches. I want to taste Evan on you—and I want you to taste you on Evan." I patted her cute little ass.

I positioned her on the bed on her knees, much like she had before with Evan. Only this time she was facing the foot of the bed, with her hands right near the end.

"Wider." I opened her legs further and brought her ass up higher, so she was showing off her pretty pussy, the plug in her ass winking at me.

I ran a hand down her creamy ass, trying not to let my anger at the scars on her back—or how I could see her ribs—come to the surface.

"Beautiful. Look how lovely you are presenting for your alpha. Now taste your omega, Peaches," I encouraged. "Arms on the bed. Guide her, Evan, but be gentle."

"There you go," he crooned, as he brought his cock up to her mouth and she lapped at it like it was a lollipop.

"Do you taste yourself on him?" I switched the plug in her ass on.

She gasped as it vibrated. "Yes, Alpha."

"Good. Now, I'm going to taste you." Moving her legs out even wider, I devoured her, tasting my Omega's sweet and tangy cum mixed with her peachiness.

"That's it," Evan cooed to her, sheer pleasure shooting through our bond. "Put it in your mouth. That's it. I've got you. Take what you can."

"Fuck," I snarled, burying my face in her wet pussy, needing more of this cocktail.

I continued to nibble on her as she squirmed against me, seeking more. Grace rode my face, thighs shaking, as my cock throbbed. She really tasted like peaches, earthy, musky peaches, and I fucked her with my tongue, rubbing her clit with my fingers.

Grace mumbled something, but her mouth was full of our omega's dick. But in the mirror I could see her eyes dancing with delight, her face awash with pleasure. I might not feel her like I could Evan, but she was *enjoying* herself. The intense scents in the room attested to that.

So was Evan.

"She wants your cock, alpha," Evan translated. "Oh, yes, right there."

"Do you want your alpha's knot, Grace?" I asked, ready to sink myself in her pussy.

Grace nodded, whimpering, as she squirmed and wriggled.

"Keep that ass up." My knot pulsed, ready to please my Princess Peaches and make her scream. I thrust inside her, and she came immediately, her wet heat squeezing me, teasing me.

"Oh, fuck." My knot fully inflated as I felt the plug vibrating through her thin walls. I thrust in and out of her in long, firm strokes, over and over, keeping an eye on her and Evan. I pulled back and thrust again. And again.

I teased her clit with my fingers as I continued to ride her sweet pussy, working her back up to her peak. My teeth nipped at her neck, her jaw. *Mine.*

She writhed and moaned, her muscles fluttering around my cock. The air was thick with pheromones–mine and his–the smell of all three of us, and sex. Every breath made me high, as I got ready to fill her completely.

"Alpha, I'm going to come," Evan groaned. "Yes, that's it, Peaches. Can I come in your mouth?"

She made a noise that sounded affirmative.

"Try to swallow as much of your omega's cum as you can, but it's fine if you can't. There's plenty of time for that," I told her.

She swallowed it down.

"Show Evan how well you take my knot." I pulled all the way out. As much as I loved taking her from behind, I wanted to look into her eyes as I knotted her.

Grace whimpered, and I rolled her over so that her back was to the bed and smothered her with a kiss. I thrust in, fast and hard, pushing my knot into her, seating itself inside her, my heart pounding as waves of pleasure washed over me.

Her pussy spasmed as my cock pulsed, filling her, as I rocked gently, making sure I was buried and locked deep inside her.

"I love the way it feels through the bond when you knot her," Evan moaned.

"So good," I praised, riding the high that came with knotting someone I loved, as I found my rhythm, one hand playing with her clit, the other with her nipple.

She grabbed my hand and moved it to that spot under her right breast.

I stroked it, and she came again. "That's it."

Holding her tight, I clamped my teeth down on the underside, right where I'd marked her years before, biting until I felt the metallic tang of blood in my mouth. By breaking the skin, my saliva introduced proteins to her system, which in turn produced a chemical that bonded us to each other.

Hopefully, it would reignite the bond between us—the bond that was either weak because of the concussion or because we'd bonded with each other in our dreams. I needed it to snap into place, to make her smell like me. Smell *claimed*. Make me smell claimed. Connect me with her more deeply.

Her body spasmed under me, hard, as more little sparks of her pleasure flitted through the bond. It wasn't anywhere near what I got from Evan. But there she was. Finally. Right in my heart, my soul, where she belonged.

"It's okay, Peaches, I've got you." Evan laid down beside us and kissed her. "Delicious."

My cum pumped into her sweet pussy, which continued to spasm around my knot. I lavished nibbles and attention on that bite, sending shivers through her with every lick.

Grace and Evan made out like horny teenagers, which made my cock twitch inside her. I wasn't sure what she could feel, but I sent all my love, all my pleasure, to both of them.

"Oh, I feel that," Evan moaned.

I turned up the speed on the little plug in her ass and continued nibbling the bite under her breast as I rubbed her clit. "Come for me."

Her responsive little body trembled as I watched–and felt–the orgasm wash over her. My rocks and thrusts gentled as Evan moaned and wrapped his arms around her, holding her, and her entire body relaxed, flecks of contentment and satisfaction fluttering through the bond.

"There you are," I breathed. Our bond wasn't broken, it was just the concussion, and relief washed over me. She was there.

"Your turn," she moaned.

"Your greedy pussy needs another orgasm? I can do that." I toyed with the plug in her ass.

"Wes, I... I'm going to come," she screamed.

I spasmed as her teeth broke my skin, making my knot pulse harder as I came again inside her. "Harder—you have to draw blood, Peaches."

"You're not going to hurt him, promise," Evan told her. "Bite hard."

"Peaches," I cried, as Grace bit down harder and my nails dug into her hips.

She didn't have to bite me back, but I wanted our bond to be as strong as we could make it.

Her body shattered. So did mine. Still locked inside her, I rolled so we were on our sides, and turned off the plug, both of us shaking. Evan threw a blanket over all three of us.

"You take our alpha's knot so well. I love the eager way you sucked my cock." He kissed her again.

She hummed and leaned in for a kiss.

"Mmmm, you taste like Evan, Boo-Bear. Both of you were so good."

She was so eager, so responsive, so willing. I adored it. *Boo-Bear?* That old nickname sounded so right.

Evan smirked. *Boo-Bear?* he mouthed. *So cute.*

He claimed my mouth with greedy kisses, his body grinding against Grace as I grabbed his ass.

"Mine," I growled. I nuzzled Grace's neck, tracing the bond mark under her breast with my finger. "Mine."

"No, you're both mine. I claim you. You're my husbands now. I'm keeping you." Grace sighed and closed her eyes.

Yes, I liked this development.

"You're ours now, Peaches, and we're yours, now and for always." Evan kissed her temple.

"That we are." *Keep me. Love me forever.*

It would be awhile before my knot deflated enough so I could slip out without hurting her. Her breath slowed as I stroked her hair with one hand and rubbed Evan's back with the other.

"That was amazing," Evan said softly. "I feel little bits of her."

"Thank you." I kissed his forehead. It wasn't strong, but she was there. Once Evan bit her, completing the circle, it would hopefully be stronger.

"For what?" He gazed up at me sleepily.

"Thank you for being able to love her, too." I kissed him, curling my legs around both of them.

"How could I not? Boo-Bear." Evan nuzzled me.

How could *we* not? Yeah, if she had to leave us, we'd be fucked.

Chapter Twenty-Seven

Evan

I extracted myself from the bodies and blankets in Wes' bed. It was early, but I wanted to see everyone before they went hiking. I'd taken another knot–and had Grace's sweet pussy–sometime during the night. While I *loved* Wes' knot, taking it while I was inside Grace brought it to a whole different level.

Grace mumbled, and I kissed her temple. She curled into Wes, who didn't move. I covered them both with a blanket, pulled on a pair of sweats, and went down the backstairs into the kitchen.

Brennan was making coffee. I came up behind him and kissed him.

He kissed me back and made a face. "You need a shower."

"Don't you like peaches in your lemonade?" I teased, liking to see my alpha squirm. "I wanted to see you before you went hiking."

"Oh, I figured you'd be tired after last night." He poured himself a cup of coffee.

But I got a look at his face before he turned.

"It bothers you. I... I'm sorry. I should have discussed it more with you." That was something I hadn't expected. I assumed he'd be okay with me fucking Grace, since I'd been talking about it for days and he said nothing against it.

Jett joined us, dressed for hiking, and, grabbing my waist, gave me a toe-curling kiss.

"What was that for?" I asked, enjoying it very much.

"That aphrodisiac you pumped through the bond all night, Baby. While my husband is always amazing, last night was incredible." Jett grinned and then stole a kiss from Brennan.

While I *would* soothe my alpha, I wanted to tease him a little more first. I didn't just want Grace with me and Wes, I wanted her in this pack. That meant Brennan needed to get used to her. Maybe even like her.

Or fuck her.

Each of my guys gave me something different. They could do the same for her. Spencer could take her to fine restaurants and science shit, then swat her ass while she called him *Daddy.* She could cling to Brennan's back as they went for a long motorcycle ride, then he, Jett, and I could have her in the swing. Jett could teach her to box and they could make spicy food together.

Mmmm. She liked two dicks, how would she like *three*?

When she joined in during my heat, she could have *four*. I was getting some of that when my heat came.

"You know, I'm not sure what I liked better, taking Wes' knot while I fucked Grace, or watching her take his knot as she sucked my dick." I grinned at Jett.

Brennan growled.

I wrapped my arms around him and purred, soothing him, sending love through our bond. "Hey, don't be jealous, Handsome. There's enough of me for everyone. My getting some pussy doesn't make me love you any less. Promise."

The tension in his back went down a notch.

"Do you really not want me to fuck her? You said nothing before. Does me actually doing so change things? It's fine if it does, I just need you to talk to me." I enjoyed being with Grace. But Brennan meant a lot to me, and sometimes feelings changed.

Also, he was the head alpha, the leader of the family. Brennan's opinion mattered. His attitude set the tone for the whole pack. I wanted him to like her.

Jett wrapped his arms around us, and I soaked them up.

"I'm just worried about you getting hurt," Brennan admitted.

"Um, I'm not sure Grace is into that." I shrugged.

"Don't come to bed smelling like her," he warned.

"Thank you, Alpha." I stole another kiss. I could do that. Or not.

"This is why I live at school." Riley rolled her eyes. She was dressed in a hoodie and cargo pants, hiking boots in her hand. "Can we all have dinner together again? Last night was fun." She dropped the boots by the rack, then opened the fridge and rummaged for the juice.

"We're not having a family dinner tonight," Brennan snapped.

Her face fell as she nearly dropped the juice. "Because I'm not family?"

"No, Ri." Brennan let go of me and rushed over to her. "Shit, no." He wrapped her in his arms, coating her in that head alpha energy. "While you annoy the fuck out of me sometimes, this is your pack, your family, and I hope that you don't feel for one second like you're not."

Their relationship was cute. Sure, Riley annoyed him, but so did the other sisters. Slowly, he was getting used to her being around.

He'd even gotten her a dirt bike and learned to play her favorite video game.

"Stop smothering me, you fucking alpha," she retorted. But there was love in her voice, and she didn't squirm. She needed it too. Approval. Care. Acceptance. Love.

Brennan let go of her but put a hand on her shoulder. "You're part of this pack, Ri, promise."

"It's Grace, then. You don't like her." Riley's eyebrows rose.

"I don't trust her. While she might be Wes' mate, she's not part of this pack."

Oh, I didn't like that statement *at all.*

"How long does memory loss last anyway? She should remember more." He grimaced.

"She does, every day, but a lot of it is about Wes," I shrugged. "Concussions *can* cause memory loss. Also, she was given some version of Oxotipoline. The combo can be brutal."

Jett whistled. "Fuck."

"Give her a chance," I pleaded. "You don't have to fuck her, just get to know her."

"Yeah, not fucking her," he snorted.

Yet.

"She's not ready for you." I shook my head. Maybe one day, but not now.

"Ugh." Riley made a face as she poured herself some juice. "Stop talking and feed me, you assholes."

"Fine," Jett laughed. "I'll make some pancakes."

Brennan, Jett, and Riley had left to go hiking. Wes and Grace were still sleeping. Spencer went to play tennis at his club.

I was in my suite, working. I'd read the most recent updates on Rose's case. Her mom had confessed to having a doctor drug Rose, but was begging to be tried here, instead of being remanded to her local court.

The police had called the local Centers and Rose's mom hadn't tried to bring her there. It looked like that was the truth—she'd brought Rose here to have a larger group of alphas to choose from.

Now I was confirming and preparing for my visits this week. These were all routine. When I took Rose to Finchley, I'd also meet with my 'school babies.' There was enough in the budget to have an activity so they could all meet Rose. Maybe pizza and a movie in one of the lounges?

Wes came in, dressed, hair wet. "Spencer called. I've got to go into work for a little bit. Will you hang out with Grace?"

"Sure. Love you." I kissed him. "Text me later. She's still asleep?"

"I think she's going to take a shower. Love you." He pulled me to him.

Kissing me again, he left, and I went to find Grace.

"Grace, are you in there?" I asked, knocking on the open door of her room.

"Hi." Her voice came from someplace.

"Can I come in?" I called.

"Sure."

I went into her room and saw her looking through the dresser drawers. Wearing *my* T-shirt.

Ooh, I liked that. So sexy.

"Thank you. It was you who bought me clothes, right? Well, you and Ri?" Grace held up a crop top.

"Yes. Jett helped. How do you feel?"

"I... I'm a little sore." Her head ducked with embarrassment.

"I'd think so. You took two knots yesterday, you also had my dick *twice*." I came up behind her and wrapped my arms around her.

Grace tipped her head up. "Mmmm, I can't wait to be the filling tonight."

"I love your sense of adventure, but your ass is not ready for my cock." I kissed her, happy she was so enthusiastic. "Do you want me to make you a bubble bath?"

Considering she still smelled of sex, she hadn't had that shower yet. What was her favorite scent? Probably peach.

She nodded. "I'd like that."

"I'll get it started." I gave her another kiss and went into my bathroom. It featured a giant, raised soaking tub that could easily fit three. The shower was also large, with glass doors and several showerheads.

Starting the water, I added some bubble bath, and got out a green bath fizzy that would help ease her sore pussy.

I lit a few candles and got out some clean and fluffy towels for her and put them on the towel-warmer. Maybe I should clear out a drawer in case she wanted to keep things in here. I'd put things for her in Wes' bathroom, but mine was nicer, with things like towel-warmers and good lighting.

Yeah, I'd do that. As the bath filled, I cleaned out a drawer and a corner of the sink. I found a small tray and a basket and put them on the sink so she'd have a place to put things.

When I came back into her room, she was sitting in the window seat, wrapped in a blanket.

"I'm still amazed at how wonderful this room is. You thought of everything," she told me.

I came closer to her. "Feel free to change everything around. Pile pillows wherever. Move the furniture. Be comfortable. Let me know what else you need or want. This is *yours*." I held out a hand to her. "Bath time, then food. Maybe after that we can watch one of my favorite movies."

Since she didn't know any of them, seeing her reaction would be fun.

She put her hand in mine and gave it a squeeze. "Let's take that bath."

Let's? My dick danced at the thought. I'd finish my work later.

I let her lead me into my bathroom, the tub almost full of water and bubbles.

"The corner of the sink with the tray and basket and the drawer under are for you in case you want to keep things in here," I told her. "Given I have a bathtub, I don't mind if you use my bathroom."

Standing on her tip-toes she pulled me down to her and kissed me. "Thank you." She looked at the bath. "That looks amazing."

I unwrapped the bath bomb and tossed it in. "That's going to make you feel better."

She took off her T-shirt and put it on the counter, then climbed in. Bliss coated her face. "This feels amazing, but I need my tub pillow."

"Your tub pillow is coming." Stripping off my pants, I put them next to her shirt and turned out the light. The candles cast a soft glow, making her look like an ethereal sea creature.

I switched on the jets, then climbed in behind her, the warm water soothing as she leaned into me.

A happy noise escaped her lips as my arms wrapped around her and she snuggled into me.

Oh, this was nice. I could see us doing this a lot. Just the two of us and the water. I kissed the top of her head.

Yes, this was perfect, and I wanted a lifetime of this.

Chapter Twenty-Eight

Grace

I sat in the front seat of Wes' truck as we drove into the city so he could go to his important meeting, and I could see Spencer's company.

Today, I actually wore clothes–cute dressy things Evan had chosen for me. There were even earrings and a necklace. It was quite a change after wearing Wes and Evan's shirts and yoga pants, while being a *blanket potato* for the past few days.

"Are you sure you're feeling up for it?" Wes asked again, his laundry scent getting intense for a second.

"It's a tour; I'm not going back to work." I rolled my eyes. All I'd done the past few days was nap, lounge in the window seat of my room, and check in with Mrs. Beekman and Luc from the integration team, and watch movies when I felt up to it. I was feeling better and remembering a little more every day.

"I'm actually hoping it will trigger my memories," I added. Not knowing what happened still made me anxious.

"Okay. Don't push yourself." He squeezed my hand.

I squeezed it back. "While I've loved staying in with you, it's nice to get out."

As we drove, Wes pointed things out like Jett and Lexi's police station and the building Brennan worked in. Then a building that said *Compass BioTek* came into view, and we pulled into an underground garage.

Wes took my hand as we rode the elevator up. He looked nice in a striped button-down and slacks, his hair neatly combed in a way that made me want to mess it up, and a wool pea coat. We entered an understated but not sterile lobby, and he went up to the receptionist.

"Hey, Wes." He grinned. "Lose your badge again?"

I tried not to laugh.

"No. I need a guest pass." Wes nodded to me.

"Oh, is this Dr. Ellington? I have her credentials right here." The receptionist handed me a badge on a lanyard. "Welcome to Compass BioTek."

"Thanks." I put it on and let Wes lead me to an elevator. "Wow. I haven't even started–or been hired."

"Riley has one. That's how she gets in and eats free ice cream in the cafeteria. Did Spencer tell you? She came by yesterday with *Marcos*." He waggled his eyebrows.

"Yes, and then texted him all night while we played video games." I laughed. Riley kept having excuses to stay over at the house. As much as I enjoyed spending time with the guys, it was fun to do things with her–or all of us together.

Like a family.

Wes looked at his phone as we got off. "I'm supposed to leave you with Spencer. I actually have two meetings. My department meeting, then this special meeting. If you get tired, nap in my office."

"Or, I'll get some ice cream and text Ri a picture." I held up my phone, which was *fancy*. Much fancier than anything my world had. Riley had a great time showing me how to use all the features.

Wes laughed. "She'd love that."

Today was the afternoon she did stuff with Evan, which seemed so sweet. I was pretty sure that I stopped having much of a relationship with my brothers once I hit high school.

Wes tipped his forehead to mine. "You'll be okay?"

I let his warmth, his scent swirl around me. "Yes."

Spencer was waiting for us, looking dapper as usual in a dark grey suit with a pocket square that matched his tie. Who even did that? But it was a look. A sexy one.

"My good doctor, I'm so excited to show you my company." Spencer beamed at me.

"Spencer, I'm sorry to bother you, but you are attending on Monday?" an older woman asked, joining us, her accent a little like Spencer's. "Wes, you're back. You must be Grace. Welcome."

"Hi, Mrs. Katsopolis." Wes grinned, then leaned in. "She's known Spence his entire life and has all the good stories. She won't tell me, but maybe she'll tell you."

"Oh, you." She waved him off with her hand. The older woman had kind eyes, but also seemed like she took no nonsense from anyone.

"Grace, perhaps you'd like to accompany me?" Spencer offered. "It's a dinner, for science, and there will be people to talk to that you'd find interesting,"

Oh? The idea of talking about my field with my interdimensional colleagues excited me. Especially now that it was not quite as hard to think.

"It sounds wonderful. Let me ask my assistant." I looked up at Wes and batted my eyelashes. "Am I free on Monday, for science?"

"*Please,* take one for the team and go to *all* the science dinners with Spence," Wes told me. He kissed me on the cheek and gave my hand another squeeze. "I'll see you later."

"Shall we?" Spencer and I got into the elevator. When the doors opened, he led me to an area with restricted signs, swiping his badge.

"Special Projects is the division that I'm most excited to show to you. We have two qubit projects. Ultrafast quantum nano-computers and totally secure communication. While they have separate uses, we also plan on pairing them. Think of the medical possibilities," he told me, eyes alight.

"Oh." Something clicked. "I'd only considered those in the military sense. But yes, the instantaneous ultra-secure communication of medical information could revolutionize so many different treatments."

"You worked for the military?" His voice went quiet.

"A defense contractor, maybe?" I frowned, trying to remember exactly who it was. Both made sense within the context of my memories of security and fences.

"We have some other projects as well. There's a particular one that I think you'd fit well in. It's not biotech, per se, but more of a personal passion," he told me. "Depending on your quantum computing skills. But I'll happily find a home for you here, regardless."

"I appreciate it. The idea of having a job prospect is comforting." If I stayed, I'd need a job. Guilt about all the money Wes had spent ate at me.

This second, I didn't even have money to buy him a birthday present–or do anything. While I knew I was safe with Wes and Evan, not being financially independent here bothered me.

We entered a lab, and Spencer eagerly brought me around, introducing me to everyone. The atmosphere was friendly and full of camaraderie and excitement. Most unlike the bits I remembered from my job back in my world.

As someone showed me their work, it hit me. They were *actually* working on constructing physical prototypes. It wasn't theory here, like in my world. It was *real.*

For a moment all I could do was stare and absorb the amazing scene before me.

Finally, Spencer led me off toward another lab.

"You're *building* quantum nano-computers," I breathed to Spencer, trying to hold off my nerdgasm.

Things I'd only dreamed about proving were *becoming reality here.*

"It's still only a partial theory, but yes, we're trying to build actual working prototypes. Oh." He paused. "You're not that far."

"No. It's all math and simulation, and trying to build computers actually able to run our simulations." Excitement built within me as another memory bubble popped. "That... that's what we were doing. Running simulations, trying to get the math right. We'd mess around and do other things, too. Ah, the simulations you run when bored." I laughed.

"Boredom is the gateway to brilliance," he stated as we went to see their new particle accelerator.

"This is the size of a stove," I breathed as I examined it. "The ones I used were much larger." Miles long. What a marvel. "Is this using particle-charged plasma and lasers?" I'd read about the potential.

"Indeed. If you were working on a quantum computing project, what did you use them for? Or was it another project?" he asked.

"I used them for other things, but we were trying to use a particle accelerator to solve some of our quantum computing issues," I replied, more memories coming to me.

He nodded, and we continued the tour.

He led me to an office that said *Doctor Ellington.* "Now, this is for you. You don't have to work here to use it. But I want you to consider working here–when you're ready, of course."

I chewed on my lower lip. "I might not be ready for what you'd like me to do–for this."

This seemed *amazing,* and I yearned to be here for the revolution these innovations would bring. That's what I liked about Spencer's company. His tech not only helped people, but making them accessible was a major part of their mission. Though the healthcare system seemed a lot better here than in my world.

"My good doctor, of course you're ready," he assured. "I believe that together we can accomplish so many things."

His confidence in me was astounding. What if I disappointed him?

"Now, the project I'm most excited about is our virtual supercollider. It's pure theory right now—an idea with part of a team. I want to build a computer simulator that would eradicate the need for particle accelerators and super colliders for most projects," he told me, leaning against the desk.

"Why? They're not that dangerous." I frowned. That also sounded like an incredible project.

"They can be. At least here. My father and Mrs. Katsopolis' wife were research partners, mapping the fifth and sixth dimensions using qubits. The collider they were using exploded, killing many people and leveling a building. I'd only recently left the lab when it happened," he whispered.

"I'm sorry to hear that." It also explained why, when I'd mentioned qubits, he'd mentioned mapping dimensions.

"It was tragic, and I'm grateful that it didn't cause a black hole–or worse. While I understand the theories, I'm not the scientist my father was. But as I said, the virtual supercollider is only one of many projects we're doing here. I'm confident we'll find the perfect project for you to work on," he assured.

"May I mull everything over, maybe look over some things, so I can see what I could actually be of help with?" I wasn't sure what I could contribute.

"Of course; take your time." His eyes lingered on my face. "You wore the earrings." Spencer smiled. "I was unsure what sort of jewelry you preferred."

"Oh, you chose these? Thank you, I love them."

"They look amazing on you. But then pretty much everything does." His gaze went direct and intense.

My core tightened, and my heart fluttered. *Smooth, you are so smooth.*

I was here for the compliments.

"Thank you." I picked up a lab book filled with complex equations and notes, and paged through it, curious. "What's this?"

"All I have left of my father's time and space research. In case you wish to attempt to return home. Unless you remember your work," he added.

My fingers traced the equations. "Mine was a very different approach. I think." I turned to another page, the question I needed to ask heavy on my heart. "Do I have to go home?"

Was this how he knew so much, such as what neutrons smelled like? What else did he know?

"Honestly, I think it would be best if you stayed. There are rules to interdimensional travel, and I know very little of them," he told me.

"There are?" I put the book down. Anxiety shot through me. What had I done?

I meant that in every way.

He nodded. "Yes. The main one I know is that there's a travel ban. At least from this world to others. I also know that this isn't known information, since in this world interdimensional travel, for most, is just a very plausible theory that never went far because of a horrible explosion the last time someone got close."

It hit me. "Your father's lab."

"Yes. It's not known to most why it happened, or that he and Dr. Katsopolis didn't die in the explosion. They were taken into custody *before* the explosion. Considering they never returned from wherever they were taken, I presume they were punished for crimes they didn't know they'd committed." He sighed.

How awful. I put a hand on his shoulder. "I'm sorry."

"Thank you. This isn't something I've ever mentioned to anyone, not even Mrs. K or Evan. I was afraid of what might happen if they knew what I'd seen," he confessed.

"I understand that." This was a lot to take in.

"It seems unfair to prosecute someone for ignorance, especially in the sense of a scientific breakthrough. Who came for them?" I asked.

"I always thought of them as the *temporal police.* They seemed like your basic black ops government agency," he shrugged. "That morning you smelled a little like them, though it has since dissipated."

Interdimensional travel might be possible. There were consequences and an *agency* that dealt with rule breakers. Shit.

Not to mention that all of this wasn't known to most people.

The pieces fit together. "There's a smell to interdimensional travel."

"Yes. I did a lot of research after my father was taken by the temporal police. At first, with childish hopes of rescuing him and Dr. K from wherever they took them. I gave up on it, since the little I discovered made me realize that some things are best left alone," he told me. "That just because we can do something, doesn't mean that you should. Unfortunately, sometimes you don't know that until you've done it."

"Oh." It was almost painful to have all those hopes of proving my research, of figuring it out, dashed.

Yet if they were a means of coming here, of being with Wes, then they were no longer necessary.

"How old were you, when he was taken?" I asked softly.

"Fourteen." He sighed. "Afterward, my mother and I moved near Evan and I attended high school in Rock Springs. She thinks my father died in the explosion, and that devastated her. I went to university here in Rockland and started a company. Eventually I sold it, helped Evan and his family out after their parents died, developed this company, and joined the pack. That's the story of my life."

"Thank you for sharing. Do we exist in a simple universe of parallel worlds, a multiverse, or something else?" I asked, curiosity bubbling up inside me. "I never found a version of Wes in my world, so I figured we're not in a multiverse. Though there could be a lot of reasons for there not to be a Wes. Still, it's much easier to believe that the universe is infinite and the laws of physics are absolute–and some worlds are similar because there's only so many ways to evolve."

"There is a multiverse. We don't exist within it. I know that much," he replied.

"Oh. That's amazing." I'd always thought of parallel worlds as being like books in my favorite section of the bookstore. While some were quite different, some contained a lot of the same themes, or they shared character names or places. Others might be a lot alike. But in the end, each book was its own story.

While the multiverse was like fanfiction for a specific fandom—exploring the infinite what-ifs and could-have-beens of that individual world.

"I won't stop you from trying to go home, if that's what you wish. But I want you to understand that being able to do it intentionally and reliably, could have consequences. Also, you said that your research was theoretical. It could take some time to recreate what you had and execute it," he added. "I don't have enough of my father's work to be of much immediate help."

"I never even considered that being able to travel interdimensionally would have consequences." If I thought about it, having an agency policing interdimensional travel could make sense.

Reliable interdimensional travel could have many implications. All this made me frown. "I shouldn't go back?"

"Do you want to?" There was no judgment in his voice.

"Not really. I still don't know why or how I got here. Ugh. I want my memories back." I sighed in frustration.

How could I move forward if I couldn't fully remember my past?

He squeezed my hand. "I understand. I'm curious as well. It would mean so much to Evan and Wes if you stayed."

Me, too.

"Will the temporal police come after me?" That was a worry I hadn't thought I'd have. Were they the ones chasing me?

"I don't know. Perhaps it's allowed in your world. Maybe it was an accident. I have no idea," he said. "I suppose only time will tell."

Time was the enemy. I needed to know what I was up against before loving Wes and Evan did irreparable damage to all our hearts.

Even if it was already too late.

Chapter Twenty-Nine

Evan

When I came into the kitchen, Jett and Bren were sitting at the kitchen table, talking and eating cookies while drinking wine. The smell of a delicious dinner hung in the air.

Brennan's eyes fell on the bags in my hands and grimaced. "More things for Grace?"

"Maybe I wanted to buy myself something at the home store." I shrugged. Not a lie.

"No Ri tonight? Cookie?" Jett offered. They were crackly and covered in powdered sugar.

I leaned in for a kiss from each. Dropping the bags on the floor, I swiped one, and bit into the soft chocolaty goodness. Flavor exploded across my tongue. I didn't know what they were, but they were tasty. "Wow."

"I know," Jett replied. "Grace made them."

Brennan shrugged. "They're okay."

"You've eaten five," Jett teased.

"They were there." He shrugged again.

"Ri had an assignment to finish for art class. She'll be here for Wes' party on Saturday. I still don't agree with having a cookout *instead* of the usual birthday dinner," I said. Again. After all, Wes was turning *thirty*. We should be going someplace extra-special.

Brennan made a face. "Wes is happy with it. We saved you food. Do you want me to warm it up for you?"

"Thank you. I'd like that." Dinner with my sister was a while ago.

"Is Grace even feeling up to us having a party here?" Jett asked as Brennan stood up.

"She spent all afternoon talking qubits with Spencer. I think she can handle dinner. Wes and I are going to take her out for her birthday," I told them.

Okay, both Riley and Spencer had mentioned wanting to come. Riley also had a couple of expensive suggestions. But that's what I got for sending her to a school where most of the teenagers had allowances the size of my paycheck.

Jett poured me a glass of wine. "We should do something for her. I need to wrap her present."

"You, too?" Brennan made a face as he brought me my dinner and topped off his wine.

"It's her *birthday*," Jett replied. "Everyone should feel special on their birthday."

"How are things at work?" I dug into my food, not feeling like starting a fight.

We sat and caught up—something I realized we hadn't done in a while. Jett was still on desk duty. Brennan had a property he wanted to snatch up—an old estate outside of town he thought would make a good event venue.

"Wow, you're right. If you do it, Grace and I can get married there," I told Brennan as he showed me some pictures.

"Why? Why do you like her so much?" His brow furrowed, confusion coming through the bond.

"Why do you not?" I countered. "No, think about it. Think beyond her not remembering, her timing being bad, her past with Wes being weird, or what Caroline did. Is there something Wes and I don't see? If there is, I genuinely want to know."

He could be intuitive when his stubbornness didn't blind him.

Brennan crossed his arms over his chest. "She doesn't load the dishwasher right and washes all her clothes on warm. Also, she eats ice cream with a small spoon instead of a big one and holds her mug weird."

"Barbaric," I teased. "Is that all you've got?" I wanted to figure out what his issues were so we could fix it.

"Are the other reasons really not enough? She's hiding something," he insisted. Jett squeezed his shoulder.

She *was* hiding something. When should we tell Brennan and Jett that she was from *another world?*

I put my dishes in the dishwasher and gave them another kiss. "I've got to get some work done. One of my cases is complicated."

"Okay. Spend tonight with us?" Brennan ran his hand down my chest, reminding me of the quickie we'd had this morning.

"Mmmm, twist my arm." I gave him a teasing kiss.

I dropped Riley's stuff off in her room, then went down to the basement and tossed the stuff I'd bought myself in the washer. I picked up the bottle of soap and frowned. This wasn't our usual laundry detergent. While we had de-scenting cleaning products, we didn't use that sort of soap.

Huh. Maybe Riley brought it. Scents should start being more pronounced for her, and they might get overpowering at times. I put it back and found the kind I preferred. Perfect.

Wes and Spencer were in the living room deep in some sort of work conversation, both with their computers out. If Grace also worked there, what would dinner conversations be like?

Giving them a wave, I headed upstairs to look for Grace, with the things I'd bought for her.

One of the double doors of her room was wide open, and I spied her in the window seat, which was crammed full of pillows and blankets. She leaned over a notebook, scribbling furiously, with Wes' tablet beside her, resting on a fuzzy blanket.

Relief filled me at seeing her like this. While she'd made big blanket piles on the bed in the hospital, I'd yet to see her make any sort of nest here. Not on her bed, or the floor, or using the giant beanbag I'd put in Wes' office for her.

A nest was crucial to an omega's emotional and mental wellbeing. They provided comfort and safety. I had a couple throughout the house for me to relax in, filled with soft things covered in scents that comforted me—like those in my pack. I'd even snagged a couple of pillows from Wes' room that smelled like Grace.

Not all gammas made nests—and the urge to make yourself a cozy area or roll up in blankets wasn't only for omegas. But I wanted Grace to feel at home. To me, her creating a little space for herself, even if it wasn't a nest, was a sign that she was feeling safe and comfortable here with us. I'd even been cycling blankets and pillows through Wes' room, then leaving them places for her so she'd have things with our scents if she wanted them.

With everything Grace had been through, I wanted her to have that stability, that comfort.

Feeling unsafe could not only destabilize an omega's mental state, but it could wreak havoc on omega hormones. An omega who felt unsafe might not go into heat, because they sensed it would be dangerous to bring children into the world. A lot of those things still applied to gammas.

It took over a year for my hormones to properly stabilize after Caroline.

I knocked on the open door, peeking in. "Anyone home?"

"Hey, how was shopping?" She looked up and grinned at me.

"Brought you some things. Can I come in?" I held up the bags.

"Of course." I leaned in and gave her a kiss.

"Mmmm, please sir, I want some more." She grabbed the collar of my work polo and dragged me in for another kiss.

There she went, calling me *sir*. Mmmm. My dick strained against my pants. I never felt the urge to top anyone–except her.

I caught equations on the papers. "What are you doing?"

"Trying to recall my parallel world research. It's not going well." She sighed and moved everything to the windowsill. Jett should build her a shelf in the window so she had a place to put things.

"Are you going to try to get home?" I didn't want her to leave.

She scooted over and moved the blankets. "Sit."

"You want me to join you?" I asked. An omega's nest was sacrosanct. Her wanting me to come in with her meant *everything*.

"It's a pile of blankets, not a marriage proposal." She grinned, patting it again.

"Oh, it is, and I accept." I laughed as I squished into the nest with her. She covered us with a blanket that smelled of Wes. Pulling her to me, I hummed as I looked out the window into our landscaped backyard, which was illuminated by subtle lighting. This was exactly what I needed after a long day–a delightful meal, a glass of wine, some cuddles with Grace, and a hard fuck.

"Trying to get home could be long and complicated." She closed her eyes.

"Then stay. Work for Spence. Marry me in a rose garden." I meant every word.

Grace hummed. "That sounds amazing. But I don't think I'm smart enough to work for Spencer. You're so much more advanced here when it comes to qubits–and this simulator? I'm not this good. I want to be part of it, but I'm used to things being pure theory without even the means to prove it."

"Spencer's actually going forward with that? He's been talking about it forever, since–did he tell you why?" I asked.

"He told me about his dad, and even gave me one of his old notebooks to look through," she replied. "But the company is amazing."

Wow, Spencer told her about his dad. He'd been wrecked after the accident, even tried to continue his research for a bit.

"Grace, you're enough. Spence knows how to recognize talent, and he wouldn't have made the offer if he didn't believe in you." I tipped my forehead to hers.

"What would it look like if I stayed?" Her voice went soft as her eyes pleaded with me, asking for reasons to stay.

"This." I gave her a kiss, pouring all my desires into it.

She giggled. "But what about everyone else?"

"Brennan will come around. While he's a stubborn, hardheaded alpha, he can be trained," I grinned. "Speaking of hardheaded alphas, tomorrow night, or even Saturday morning, will you help me make a birthday cake for Wes? I've got his favorite recipe, but it's a little much for me."

Her face lit up. "Is this the recipe for Wes' grandma's lemon sponge? Oh, I've heard about it so much. I'd love to. I... I don't have a present for him."

"Birthday sex is always a good one. I have ideas." It was a good thing this window seat wasn't very big because the need to get handsy was growing. I'd have sex with her in it if she asked. Shit, I'd have sex with her *anywhere*.

She laughed. Oh, I loved that laugh. It was like champagne bubbles popping.

"I meant an actual something." She frowned. "I don't know what would be good—or even have any money."

Which I understood. One thing that had caused me anxiety early on was that I made the least of everyone in the pack—not that Jett made that much more. While packs took care of each other, balancing out the finances so everyone could do something that made them happy, it still made me feel like I wasn't contributing enough. That I wasn't enough.

Something Caroline had capitalized on.

"How about after your doctor's appointment, we pick something out together? You can pay me out of your first paycheck," I suggested, knowing she probably wouldn't accept me just buying it. "Or we could work out a trade—maybe some baking lessons?"

"Ooh, we can work out a trade. I want to see you in nothing but an apron." Her hand smoothed over my chest.

The need to have her consumed me. "I love your little hideaway."

"It's so messy, I don't actually need this many pillows in it." She chewed on her lower lip.

"However many pillows you want is the number you need." I grinned. "If it bugs you and feels messy, reorganize it until it's how you like. We can go to Home Things tomorrow if you want different things or feel like you're missing something. Yes, the saying that if you give an omega adult money they'll buy blankets, pillows, and candles is true."

"I love all the things you've got—and I love this window seat. But I don't want anyone to think I'm messy." She shook her head, frowning slightly.

"It's your *room*, you can be messy if you'd like. That's the great thing about having your own spot. If you're messy and your partner isn't, you can keep your mess in your room. Likewise, if they're messy and you're not, you can retreat to your nice, tidy room," I told her. "You know, a window seat overflowing with pillows isn't messy, it's cozy." Nests came in all forms.

"My mom always said burrows and blanket forts were untidy. Granted, when I was tiny, I liked to make a burrow out of the clean laundry and watch TV in it with my dolls and stuffed animals, so I can understand how that might be an inconvenience." A wistful smile played on her lips.

Clean laundry. Little Grace, long before she ever saw him in her dreams, made nests that smelled like Wes. My hand went to my heart. *Aww.*

"I used to make a fort with the clean sheets over the clothesline," I told her.

"Blanket forts." She sighed happily. "I was so sad the day my mom told me that I was too old for them, even with my younger brothers. Not that she'd ever let them stay up for long–even if they were in *my* room. She took away my dolls and toys for the same reason. Though my dad hid one of them for me. We always had so many fights about my room not being clean enough."

While I was happy she was remembering more, those were some very sad statements. Nesting sometimes appeared as an instinct in very young children, ones too little to test. This wasn't the first time I'd been told by someone that a loved-one thwarted their nest-making at every turn.

"We can make a blanket fort," I offered, wanting to make her happy. "Wherever you want and we can keep it up for as long as you want. We're not too old. Do you want some help arranging things in your room to get them just the way you want? I'm pretty good at it. Also, I brought you some things that Rose and Riley picked out for you," I offered. After all, nesting could take some practice–and everyone had a different approach.

"They did? Did you have fun?" She turned over and tipped her head up to see me.

"Yep. Want to see?" I caught the bag with my foot and brought it over so I didn't have to get out of the nest. "They got you these lights to drape over the canopy on the bed and this pink circle canopy thing. I'm not sure if it's for the window seat or the beanbag chair in Wes' office." I held it up.

"We should hang that up with more lights," she laughed. "I'd like some lights for the window–if that would be okay."

I kissed her nose. "Yes. It's your room. Lights for the window, sure. A canopy for the window–or a curtain that goes across the seat to hide the pillows, we can do that. Or maybe a screen that goes inside the door so you can have your door open but people won't immediately see into your room?"

She nodded. "Those are all such good ideas."

This room was long, so it might need something extra to make it cozy enough for her to feel safe. I should also talk to a contractor about a door between her room and my bathroom.

"We'll get it figured out. Now, where should we start?" If we stayed here any longer, I was going to start making out with her.

Together, Grace and I rearranged everything to her satisfaction, which included stealing a very soft rug from a room we never used and placing the daybed on top of it, hanging the lights, and trying to get all the pillows and blankets to look neat without having to put any in the storage under the window seat.

"What are you doing up here? It sounds like you're dropping things." Brennan stood in the doorway, frowning. "I thought you had work to do."

"I'm procrastinating. Why work when you can decorate?" I replied.

"Oh, I didn't realize it was late. I'm so sorry." Grace's shoulders slumped. "We were moving things around."

Brennan looked around and shook his head. "It looks nice. It's fine."

"I love all the lights," Jett said from behind him.

"I worry that it's still too messy." She frowned as she eyed the window seat.

"If you're happy with it, it's fine. If not, we'll keep rearranging it." I wrapped my arms around her, trying to comfort her.

"Who is *that?*" Jett eyed Mr. Hippo, who had the place of honor on the bed, along with the bear I'd gotten her in the hospital.

"That's Wes' favorite childhood toy." I grinned. "Mr. Hippo."

Jett started laughing. "Mr. Hippo?"

"I think it's sweet, it was the last toy his mom gave him before she left." Her voice went soft.

"I know. He gave it to you?" Brennan's voice was quiet as he crossed his arms over his chest.

She flinched. "Mr. Hippo's an old friend. He's just keeping me company for now."

"That was nice of him. I know Mr. Hippo means a lot to Wes," Brennan said quietly.

"We just wanted to make sure you were okay," Jett said.

"As you should. She's dangerous with a reel of lights." I tried to lighten the mood. "Also, Grace doesn't know the difference between step stools and sitting stools."

"Evan," she laughed, elbowing me.

"I'll come see you after I finish with Grace," I promised Brennan and Jett.

"Sounds good. We were going to watch some TV anyway," Brennan said, as he and Jett left.

Grace turned to the window seat and frowned.

"It'll take time to get it right." I took her hand. "Let me show you something."

I led her into my suite, through my sitting room directly into my bedroom, and then into my walk-in closet, which adjoined my bathroom.

But I didn't lead her that way. Instead, I opened another door, and flipped a switch that turned on a low light. The room was small. A couple of steps led to the raised platform that the bed was on, shelves built into both sides of the walls to act as both tables and places to put my books, candles, and special things. We'd had this built when we moved in.

The mattress took up most of the space and was covered in rich spice-colored blankets—saffron, burgundy, dark green, and matching pillows. Tapestries covered the walls and ceiling. There was a small window with a plant in it, the wooden floor covered with a handmade rug and some floor pillows.

We didn't go in, I just held her hand as we stood in the doorway. I wasn't ready to let her in. But I wanted her to see. To understand.

"I didn't know this was in here," she breathed.

"I don't even let the guys in here very often. This is my most private space, filled with my coziest things and happiest memories. And it's *not neat.* I wanted you to know that if you want to be tidy, go for it, but don't feel as if you have to. If you want something like this or a cute alcove, we could do that."

She leaned into me. "Thank you for sharing."

I pulled her out of the closet and back into my bedroom. I flipped on a lamp, and the room was bathed in an orange-red glow, complementing the saffron and burgundy color scheme. My bed had heaps of blankets and pillows, and it hadn't been made since Brennan messed it up. Clothes were heaped on my window seat. My backpack sat on the chair.

"My bedroom is messy, too. You know who cares? *No one.* Sometimes, I let the guys in here when I feel like it. They don't care either." I pulled her down with me, and we sank into the giant featherbed.

The scent of Brennan from this morning, and Wes from yesterday, twirled around me. Sex toys sat on the nightstand. Brennan's boxers lay on the floor. Okay, Brennan didn't like my mess, but it was also my room—he could simply go back to the orderly room he and Jett had.

She buried her face in the blankets and inhaled. "It smells amazing in here."

The room reeked of sex and my men.

"You know what else smells good? You." I nuzzled her left side, her laugh going straight to my cock, then turning to a groan. I started to perfume, my desire for her consuming me.

"So forward, sir." Her eyes gleamed as she lay there in my bed, back arching slightly.

My cock hardened as her peach scent flared with desire. I climbed over her, so one knee was on each side of her, my crotch hovering above her.

"You're in my bed, so I can be as forward as I like," I growled, pulling up her shirt and attacking her breasts. She wasn't wearing a bra.

A groan escaped her lips. "Please, sir, may I have some more?"

"How could I deny such a sweet request? I love it when you call me *sir*," I murmured, resting on my elbows to give her breasts more attention, my cock rubbing against her through my work pants.

Maybe one day I'd bond with her, too. I yearned to connect and feel her through our own bond, not just Wes'—and I wanted her to bond me in return. Omegas *could* bond with each other, but it wasn't legally binding, like an alpha-omega bond.

Her hips rose as she tried to rub herself against me as I circled her pale pink nipple with my tongue, licking and teasing one, then the other. Her hands tangled in my hair as she made cute little noises as my kisses trailed over her ribs and down her stomach.

"I need you," she keened, trying to get my shirt off, her tiny body still pinned between my thick legs.

Taking off my shirt and pants, she did the same. Grace laid back, completely naked, thighs parted, arms above her head.

"Tasty," I murmured, burying my face between her legs, getting her ready for my cock. She was so wet, her curls tickling my face, as I circled her clit with my tongue. I used it to tell her how amazing she was, lapping up her peachy juices, the cries of her pleasure were sweet music.

Her body shuddered, and I looked up at the blissful look on her face.

"I love it when you come for me. Will you let me try something, Peaches?" I asked her.

Grace's eyes lit up. "Yes, please."

I opened the drawer to get the toy I'd bought and grabbed the lube. "Same rules apply to me, say the safe word and I'll stop."

"What are we trying?" Her voice went curious.

"This." I took her hand and ran it down the soft, wide, neon green, sparkly jelly knot, then helped her glide the sleeve over my lubed-up cock, until it sat at the base, nice and tight, mimicking an alpha's knot. "Want me to knot you?"

"I need you inside me." She lay back on the pillows on my bed.

Getting between her legs, I grabbed her ass cheeks and pulled her to me, moving forward and slowly pushing my dick inside her soaking wet pussy.

"You feel so good," I groaned, covering her with my body as I began to thrust, her hips meeting mine, accompanied by breathy pants.

I didn't push the jelly knot into her, instead, I teased her with it. Desire swirled inside me as I fucked my sweet peach, going deeper and deeper, teasing and stretching her, until she was taking part of the jelly knot with each thrust. Finally, I sank into her, filling her with my cock and the jelly knot; rocking my hips, going slow and deep.

"That feels amazing," she moaned, pulling me to her and attacking me with sweet kisses as her hands roamed my body.

"Right there," I told her as her fingers grazed my nipples, and we continued our rhythm, heat building between us, as I nibbled on her neck, savoring each delicious noise she made when I found all the sweet spots.

I was close, so I increased my pace, moving one of my hands so I could play with her clit.

Her back arched and a little cry ripped from her lips as her legs wrapped around me, bringing me right where she needed as she orgasmed around my cock. I came inside her, wrapping my arms around her, and rolling us onto our sides while our bodies spasmed.

"That was incredible," I whispered, planting a kiss on her forehead, still inside her.

She gave me a satiated smile. "I liked that a lot."

Her praise made me warm inside. I'd never used a jelly knot before.

I threw a blanket over us and purred for her, content, hoping she knew how happy she made me. My guys made me happy, but Grace filled a part of me I didn't even know was missing.

Fortunately, my heart had enough love for all of them.

Chapter Thirty

Grace

"When will I get my memories back?" I asked as I sat in the exam room at the Omega Center. Yesterday's conversation with Spencer about not going home made me want to know, more than ever, *how* and *why* I'd ended up here.

"It's hard to say. It hasn't even been two weeks. But most people get their memories back within a month or two," Dr. Davidson told me. "Now, a concussion plus Oxotipoline, depending on the dose, well, that could be longer, but in both cases, we seldom see permanent memory loss."

"Oh." I needed those memories. What if I'd broken interdimensional law and the temporal police came to drag me away?

"You're still recovering, but there are some things you can do to help. Puzzles and logic games are very good for you, also, eat well, hydrate, rest, and perhaps engage in a hobby," she suggested.

Hobbies. Right. I think I had hobbies. "I play the piano."

There was a piano on the second floor. I'd play every concerto I could recall if it got my memories back.

"Music is wonderful for the memory. After your appointment next week, we'll see if you need to continue wearing the monitor. Watch the strenuous activity. I'm glad you found your alpha, but go easy." She winked.

How? The wrist monitor. Whoops.

She chuckled. "See you next week."

"Thanks."

The doctor left, and I took off the exam gown and put my clothes back on, glad to be done. Wes had dropped off Evan and me, and I'd had a variety of appointments, from talking to Luc from the integration team, to meeting with Mrs. Beekman. Someone had even given me a tour, telling me about all the activities and programs the Center offered, and showed me how to get a Center card for my phone, then took me to a cupboard where I got to choose goodies like bath products. They'd even had lavender, my favorite.

Still, it didn't negate the fact that it could be a long time before I got my memories. Before I could feel at ease in this world. Before I could be sure I had done nothing wrong and no one would take me away like Spencer's dad.

Rounding the corner, I slumped to the floor and cried. While I loved being here with Wes, all week I'd been able to stay wrapped in blankets in the house and avoid the fact that this *wasn't* my world. While similar enough, there was so much that was different–like movies and music.

Or that they were actually *building micro quantum computers to implant in people's bodies for medical treatment.*

All these things indicated that I didn't belong here. But, I not only *couldn't* get back, I shouldn't.

There wasn't much left for me in my world. But was there even a place for me in Wes' family? Evan said there was, but Brennan barely talked to me. It was obvious their routine had been altered because of me.

All this was too much.

While I believed Evan with all my heart, did Wes even want me? Or was it just a fascination? I let the tears fall as all the confusion I'd felt came to the surface.

"There you are." Evan sat next to me and pulled me to him. "Why are you crying?"

I buried my face in his shoulder but said nothing.

"Hey. What's wrong?" He wiped my tears away with his thumb.

"It could be months before I get my memories back." I sniffed.

He held me to him and kissed the top of my head. "We're here, and it's okay. Join me? I want you to meet Rose. I think you have a lot in common."

"She's also not from this world?" My voice went dry.

"You're both members of the shitty mom club."

It didn't bother me that he said that, since he was right. Honestly, her cutting me off when I decided to get my PhD instead of moving home and teaching was the best thing she ever did for me. I had no regrets about not setting things 'right' with her before she died.

"Please tell me you met with a therapist today?" he asked.

"Luc the integration counselor?" I shrugged, not sure if it was the same. "Does Wes even want me here?"

"Peaches, he has spent the last week or so by your side, snuggling you, taking care of you, and learning everything about you, like how to make you squeal." He nibbled my neck, making me mew. "Sure, Wes is a good guy, but even with all that's happening, he wouldn't be doing everything he has if he didn't want to. Maybe I haven't been clear enough, but I want you here, too. I understand that you feel out of place, but please, let us love you."

I gazed into his dark brown eyes. "I suppose."

What he was asking was a lot in the grand scheme of things. But I wanted it.

"Good." He captured my lips with his.

"Hey, no making out in the hallway." Carly in her Center polo gave us a huge smile as she joined us.

Evan grinned. "You're just jealous."

"Kinda." She bit her lower lip and grinned. "Hey, my guy said he can do what you need, based on the specs you sent."

I blinked. "What are we doing?"

"Putting a door between my bathroom and your room. I guess the original floor plan called for it, but when our house was built, the then-owners opted out. Carly's alpha is a contractor. Thanks." He smiled at Carly, then stood and helped me up. "Let's go meet Rose. Maybe she'll make you a bracelet."

Evan led me through a gymnasium. In one corner, some people played a game that looked like volleyball and badminton had a baby. In another area, a group was learning self-defense.

"We should have Jett teach you some stuff," Evan said, waving at a couple of people.

"Jett, not Wes?" I asked.

"Boxing can be fun, but I was thinking more like hand-to-hand combat. Unless you'd rather learn to wrestle, that would be Brennan," he grinned.

"I don't think Brennan wants to wrestle with me," I replied. "Wait, didn't he play rugby with Wes?"

"He wrestled too. Still does for fun," Evan said.

We entered another room, which had a piano in a corner, along with a bunch of tables, a coffee cart, and shelves of games and art supplies.

"Can I play the piano at home?" I asked. "Doc says it might help me remember."

"You play?" His eyes lit up.

"I have for most of my life. Learning complicated pieces was a great way to work out frustrations." Especially sexual ones. The problem with having a dream boyfriend was that we both needed to be *asleep* to hook up.

He gestured to the piano.

I started *Turkish March,* letting my fingers take off across a keyboard that was hopefully the same. I remembered playing the piano. They probably had different pieces here, but that could be fun to learn.

The piano felt the same. Sounded the same. Playing felt *good.* Normal even.

Finishing, I looked over at him. "What do you think?"

"I think you and Katie need to play duets. She likes that fast shit. Brennan plays, too. He likes the stuff that just sounds hard." He grinned back. "Let's go find Rose."

We went over to a small table where a redhead was making a necklace out of tiny beads.

"Rose, this is Grace," Evan introduced. "Grace needs to learn to make those bracelets."

"Hi! I do need a birthday present for Wes," I agreed.

We raided the art supplies and made bracelets, Evan going off to do his thing.

"Thanks for helping choose the clothes and lights for me," I told her as I found the beads for our initials.

"I'm glad you like them. It's fun shopping with Ri," she told me. "I miss my friends."

"I'm sure you do. Do they text you?" I asked her. Did I miss mine? I remembered that my colleagues and I would sometimes do things, like go to the bar for trivia night or have movie marathons.

There were girls from undergrad that I kept up with. I had a good time with some of my classmates when I was getting my PhD. But did I have *friends?*

"Oh yes. One of my friends, who's an omega, is going to see if she can come to the school, too, next year. We're both flyers. Finchley goes all the way through undergrad with amazing acceptance rates to grad programs and even med school!" She looked a bit giddy.

"Oh, I was a flyer for my cheer squad both in high school and college." I didn't really like it. But I was good at it, and it made other people like me–something that was important to my mom. It kept my mom off my back and gave me a reason to leave the house without argument. Also, it helped fund my undergrad and gave me an instant set of friends in college.

A few other teenagers joined us, and I ended up teaching everyone how to make friendship bracelets out of embroidery floss.

Her phone vibrated, but instead of getting an excited look, her face fell.

"Everything okay?" I asked.

"My sister wants me to come home and get a job," she told me. "She won't let up. She thinks waiting to take a mate is stupid, and if I'm going to wait, then I should come home and help."

"Rose, listen to me carefully–*do not set yourself on fire to keep others warm.* I know that there are extraneous circumstances, but it isn't your job. Don't give up your future," I explained, adding another row to my bracelet.

"That's what my stepdad says. To stay and get a good education. But..." her phone went off again, and Rose winced.

"The guilt is hard. But sometimes the best thing to do is focus on yourself. It doesn't make you selfish," I assured her.

Rose looked at her phone. "Oh no. She's here, and she wants to see me."

"You don't have to see her," I replied, as I finished up my bracelet.

"I don't?" She frowned. The war in her eyes tore at my soul.

I shook my head. "Family doesn't mean necessity. It's not your job to take care of your siblings, it's not hers either, and it's unfair for the both of you."

"I'll talk to her." Rose sighed. "Let me clean up."

She started to clean up her stuff, and I helped her.

"Change of plans. Wes is taking you on a date tonight," Evan told me. "We'll get the stuff for the cake, and his present, and hit the home store tomorrow morning."

"Oh, okay. A date? Where are we going? What do I wear?" I'd been looking forward to a trip to the home store, but a date sounded fun.

"It's a surprise," Evan said. "You're fine how you are."

The idea made me warm and tingly inside. "What will you do tonight? I don't want you to be left out."

"I'm going to go for a ride on the back of Brennan's motorcycle." He winked.

"That sounds fun. He has a motorcycle?" Huh. Brennan didn't strike me as the type.

Evan nodded. "He does. Jett and I have them, too. Bren looks amazing on his. So do I."

I looked over at Rose as she put the box of beads on the shelf. "Will she be okay?"

"Eventually. I've seen this a million times. The sibling that's sacrificed themselves gets angry that no one else will. Or the one that's parentified. Or is the scapegoat. Or was the golden child until someone became an omega. There can be a lot of anger and animosity among siblings," he said.

"I get that."

Evan ran his hand through my hair. "Wes will meet you in the front. Have fun. I'm going to get back to Rose."

"Go take care of Rose–and have fun on your date." I checked my phone and saw that he'd just texted. *Here.* With a wave, I went to find Wes.

Chapter Thirty-One

Wes

"Hi, Peaches." I gave Grace a kiss as she climbed into the front seat of my truck.

"Hi. Where are we going?" she asked, a little giddy.

"Surprise. Did everything go okay at the doctor?" I drove toward the urban lake.

She shook her head, defeat on her face. "It could take *months* to get my memories back."

"It's okay." It seemed about right from what I'd read, but I could see that she was upset.

"Is it?" She sniffed.

Reaching over, I squeezed her hand. "I'm right here, what do you need?"

"I don't know. What if I put you in danger? Or if the temporal police come after me? What if I can't make a place for myself here?" Tears pricked her eyes as she gazed at me.

She'd told me yesterday about Spencer telling her that it would be safer not to try to get home. I was all for her staying, but I understood her being shaken by the choice being *taken* from her–her worry that she'd unknowingly done something wrong. Not that I understood how and why Spencer even knew all of that.

"We will deal with everything as it comes. You can fit in here. You already do." I squeezed her hand again.

The bond between us still wasn't very strong. At times like this, I wish I got more than flickers–and that she could feel *me* more than she did. I wanted to soothe that anxiety and show her that we belonged together.

"So, I take this job with Spence, stay with you and Evan, and it'll all... work out?" She frowned. "I still don't think I'm smart enough for what he wants me to do."

"You are. But, if you're not comfortable, then find a different project, or pitch your own. If you don't want to work with Spence, we'll find you another job." It would be easier if she worked for Spencer. Both because I'd feel better with her close by and with her having a fake record.

While she needed a record, it was a little weird that *Evan* of all people had it set up. What work friend had that job at the Center?

She sighed. "I feel like such an impostor."

My heart broke. How could I fix feelings like that?

"Please don't. You're the most genuine person I know." Well, her and Evan, which was probably why they were so delightful together. I squeezed her hand again.

"Thanks, Boo-Bear." She gave me a shy smile.

We drove to the lake under the East Bridge. It was filled with fish, paddleboats, and kayaks. It was surrounded by trees and green space, including picnic and play areas. In the summers they had movies, music, and festivals. Nearby were a couple streets of cute restaurants and little shops.

My dad had often taken my sister and me to this lake to fish on Sunday afternoons, and I'd spent a lot of time in this area with my friends.

"This…" She spun around, eyes on the sky, as we got out of the car. "This is our lake."

"Yes, it is." I got a jacket out of my truck and tossed it to her. "In case you get cold."

"Thanks. It smells like you." She pulled it on as the breeze whipped her hair into her face.

That was the plan. I liked it when she and Evan smelled like me. It settled something primal inside me. But I also loved smelling Evan on her, because that combination of lemons and peaches went straight to my dick.

Also, it seemed like the scent of peach lemonade annoyed Brennan, so I'd bought a bunch of candles and wax melts in that scent and hid them all over the house to be annoying.

"It's always a little breezy at the lake. Here." I took the hairband I'd bought her at lunch and put it in her hair so her bangs didn't whip in her eyes. "Now it won't get in your face."

Grace's face lit up, the tension and worry from the car leaving. "Thank you." She checked her reflection in the car mirror. "Cute."

"Yes, you are." Taking her hand, we went and got our boat. We paddled out onto the lake, waving at the others out on this very pleasant March evening. Grace pulled on the jacket and snuggled into me as the sun set. Tiny lights all over the park and the bridge went on.

"This is beautiful." She leaned her head on my shoulder as we floated across the water.

"It is." The sky was ablaze with color.

Which probably meant we were due for more snow.

"Did anyone get in trouble today?" She grinned.

Me. For not getting something done that I was supposed to. But I wasn't going to tell her that. I didn't want her to feel guilty about my staying home to take care of her. Instead, I told her about my day, and she told me about hers.

"Oh, I almost forgot. I made this for you at the center. Happy Early Birthday." She took a beaded bracelet and put it around my wrist.

The beads were in my favorite colors and said GE♥WL♥EW.

"You made this for me?" It looked like something my sister would have made at camp when we were kids. But I loved it.

Grace leaned in and gave me a kiss. Unlike in our dreams, there were people here, and paddle boat sex would be frowned upon. Not to mention the water was icy. We paddled back to the dock and turned in our boat.

She took my hand, swinging it as we walked through the park. "Where to now?"

"Dinner. It's not fancy, but it's a place my dad always took Lexi and me, usually on Friday payday. It's close enough to walk. I... I hope you'll like it." I gave her a shy and hopeful smile.

She smiled back. "I'm sure I will."

We passed a bunch of kids playing in the play area.

"Do you still want kids? It's okay if you don't. Just curious." I pulled her close as she frowned, wanting to reassure her that whatever her wishes were, they were valid.

"All my life I was told that was what was important—a husband and kids. It's not that I don't. I do want kids eventually. The thing is, I don't know how to be a good mom. I don't want to screw them up." Anxiousness crossed her face.

"If you're ever ready, I think you'd make a great mom." I kissed the anxiousness away. "If that never happens, it's fine. If it does, that's great. I'm okay either way."

Kids would be nice. I had a great dad. But my mom *leaving* and my dad moving us away from our pack to start over, left indelible scars on my soul.

She tipped her head up. "You are?"

"I am." Though Evan *really* wanted kids. Grace and I would have these cute, smart, and artistic kids. Her and Evan? Shit. No one would be able to deny those kids anything.

Jett mentioned liking to have kids in the pack. He'd grown up in a big family. Spencer said he didn't care either way. Brennan grumbled about kids being messy.

Yet, I had this feeling that Brennan would be the dad that would spoil them and let them get away with *everything.*

Grace and I left the park and turned onto a street. Lights decorated the trees and hung across the streets. Couples danced on the sidewalk as musicians played. Kids rode by on bikes. The aroma of delicious foods from all corners of the world tickled our noses. Eastside was a working-class neighborhood, the feel was very different from the area Brennan had moved us to after Caroline, or the fancy townhouse where we'd lived before.

At first, I didn't like it here after my dad, Lexi, and I moved here. My friends weren't there. I missed the pack, not understanding why we'd had to leave them. This city was big. Busy. Different. But somewhere along the way, it had become *home.* I missed this area a lot.

We stopped at a busy, cozy brick restaurant on the corner. People ate both inside and out on the heated garden patio.

"Pizza. You have pizza." Grace gave a happy sigh.

Relief filled me. I'd made a good choice.

"The best pizza in the city." I led her inside, where a familiar woman played host. "Hi Gina, I have a reservation for two under *Wes.*"

She laughed, which made her giant earrings jingle. "Reservations? What are we, a steakhouse? Nah nah, I got you." Gina gave Grace a once-over. "Hey, Hon, if he doesn't treat you right, you let me know. I can be a better boyfriend than him." She flashed me a giant grin.

I grinned back. "Table, Gina."

"You know each other?" Grace laughed.

"Went to middle school together," I replied as Gina led us to a corner patio table. It was her family's restaurant.

"It was like that where I grew up. Couldn't go anywhere without seeing someone you knew–or being seen and having them tell your mom." She rolled her eyes.

We ordered a pizza and enjoyed a pleasant night. Evan was with Brennan, so he was fine. Jett was refereeing fight night at his boxing gym. Spencer had to do stuff for work.

"Do you take Evan here?" She sipped her beer.

The restaurant was busy, mostly with families and groups of teens.

"He doesn't like pizza. Usually, I meet my dad here. He likes to sit inside by the front window." I tried to see my dad a couple of times a month. Lexi was over at his place all the time.

Grace gasped. "Evan doesn't like pizza? Here I thought I might be in love with him."

"If I can find it in my heart to forgive him for that, I think you can, too," I told her. We both laughed.

I paid the bill, and we took a walk, ducking into shops and getting some ice cream. Sure, it had gotten cold while we ate, but I knew how much she liked it.

"Tonight has been perfect." She gave her cone another lick. "I... I don't think I have many friends. Not ones I regularly do things with or talk to. I think I do things with some of my colleagues, but..." She sighed. "From what I remember, everything I went through in high school lost me a lot of the friends that I'd had all my life. Missing high school cheerleading competitions because your parents pulled you out of school to send you to a church-run *wilderness camp* for your *bad behavior* doesn't help your social credibility. That made me put my guard up."

That church-run wilderness camp was where the terrible stuff happened.

"I understand. When we moved here, a lot of the friends I'd grown up with didn't stay in touch. When I made friends and then went to a fancy private high school across town instead of the local one, it made things hard sometimes. Leaving university to join the military. It can be tough."

She nodded and put her arm around me.

"You'll make friends here. I have a couple of people in mind to introduce you to at work," I told her. "If you spend any time at the Omega Center, you're going to end up taking a dance class, joining a book club, or finding a group of friends for spa days."

"The Center has some interesting offerings. You know, I wouldn't mind joining a book club." She finished her cone and threw away her trash.

"My sister and her pack, they're nice people and their omega makes moon cars or something. Go be friends with them. Annoy Brennan and hold wine night in *our* hot tub." I grinned. We loved the 'sister pack.'

"They seem fun."

The moon hung heavy in the sky as someone played a romantic song on the trumpet. Taking her in my arms, I swayed back and forth.

"Wes," she giggled, "what are you doing."

I took her hand and spun her. "Dancing."

An elderly couple held each other in the moonlight. A young couple showed off their steps. A dad twirled his bundled-up child in the air.

The song ended, and I took her hand and kissed it.

"Having fun?" I asked.

"I am. Going on a paddle boat with you, seeing your favorite places, this is everything I could want on a date. Ready to go home–or maybe there's a make-out spot you'd like to show me?" Grace waggled her eyebrows.

"I have ideas. But I'll show you our make-out spot another time." Pulling her to me, I nibbled her neck, making her squeal the way I liked. The older couple gave us a fond look.

My dad was out with Lexi. We could go visit my old bedroom. Maybe take it for a spin. Because the make-out spot we'd go to in our dreams had rules about doing what I'd very much what I'd like to do.

But you know what didn't? My childhood bedroom.

Oh yes. Happy early birthday to me.

We pulled up at my dad's house. It was an older house that had belonged to my dad's grandparents. Him having a place for the three of us to live, along with much of his family being in Rockland, had motivated him to move back here after the divorce.

The house was dark, and I texted my sister.

Me

> **Please keep Dad out for another hour?**

Lexi

> **We're about to see a movie.**

Me

> **Perfect.**

Good. I turned to Grace. "This is where I grew up. Want to see my bedroom?"

"Please." Her shoulders wiggled happily. She got out and looked up at the roof. "Oh, we sat up there sometimes."

I took her hand, and I unlocked the door and led her inside.

"Let me give you a tour." I showed her around the little three-bedroom house. It really hadn't changed much since I'd moved out to go into the military. Lexi had lived here until after she'd graduated from university, gone through the police academy, and moved in with Katie to start their pack.

"I love it," Grace told me as she looked at all the photos on the wall of Lexi, my dad, and me.

There were no pictures of my mom out here. I had some, but I'd put them all away. She hadn't just divorced my dad, she'd left us. It had been a very long time since I'd heard from her. She hadn't even come to the party Evan and I had to celebrate our mating.

"There's Lexi's room." I pointed to the closed door with stickers on it. "Here's mine." I put my hand on the doorknob. Mine had a little sign on it that said *Wes' Room: Keep Out. Lexi, this means you.*

I opened my door.

"It's your room." Her chest shuddered a little as she took it all in.

"Yeah. While we've taken stuff out of our rooms, they're still about the same. Dad said he never felt the need to change them."

"That's nice." Grace's brow furrowed, like she'd remembered something unpleasant and sighed.

I kissed her furrowed brow. She was probably remembering how her mom would take all her things–or that they probably made her room into a workout room or gave it to her brother after she left.

My room was cleaner than she'd usually seen it in my dreams, because the bed was made. But a bunch of my sketchbooks were on my desk, probably from when Lexi was looking through them. Also, there was no Mr. Hippo, since he was on Grace's bed.

I kissed the top of her head. "We spent so much time here when it was too cold for the park. We'd talk. Play games." I waggled my eyebrows. "Study anatomy."

It was here where I'd explained sex to her after she'd been so confused after her biology class. I'd shown her how it worked here. We'd tried out my knot in here.

This was also where we'd bonded. I hadn't just bonded her, she'd bitten me back–on the shoulder, where my military tattoo now was. It just hadn't left a mark. That was another reason to believe that she had been close to being a full omega.

The last time I'd seen her in my dreams had been here, too.

Scooping her up, I tossed her on the bed, like I had so many times in our dreams.

She giggled. "Are you going to cover me with blankets, too?"

"Of course." I took off her shoes.

Like I had when she'd had a bad day and needed cuddles and comfort, I piled all the blankets around her, including the ones in my closet.

"Here." I handed her another one of my stuffed animals to hold since we didn't have Mr. Hippo.

Taking off my own shoes, I climbed in with her and pulled her to me and began to purr.

Memories of all the times I'd done this hit me. It had been one of my favorite things–to be able to comfort and care for her. She'd been so fucking neglected back home, even before the mistreatment really started.

"I remember this." Tears pricked her eyes as she looked up at me.

"I love you so much." I kissed away the tears. "Grace, I'll love you until the end of the universe."

"I love you, too, to the end of the universe. I... I never want to leave you again."

I held her tight to me. "You never have to. Promise."

She was mine, and I'd never let her go. Ever.

Chapter Thirty-Two

Brennan

"What do you think? Pass? It's really run down," my business partner and longtime friend Terrance asked after we finished touring the estate I was considering buying. Terrance was almost as tall as me, but broad, his brown head shaved bald.

"The gardens, though." That's what made this place extra special. But it was more run-down than I'd expected.

"The upkeep will get expensive," he countered. "It's also not very big."

"Some of our properties aren't that large. What about an event venue instead of a boutique hotel?" I threw out, as we walked back toward his car and my motorcycle. As we toured it, Evan's suggestion kept playing in my head.

Even if he wanted to marry *Grace* here. Ugh. I'd gotten pictures of them going to the home store, baking a cake, and decorating the backyard for Wes' party like a happy couple.

Terrance thought for a moment, stroking his dark goatee. "Like for weddings and mating parties?"

"Yes. Along with excellent eighteenths, pack celebrations, awakening parties, and gala dinners. Outdoors in late spring through early fall, indoors the rest of the time, but there might be a few rooms available for the happy couple or whatever," I suggested. "We don't have a property that does this. While it is a little far for a weeknight party, that might appeal to people."

He shrugged. "But we're high-end. How much would we have to invest in it so it would hold up to the brand standards, and could the market bear those costs?"

"True." I'd have someone run the numbers. We dealt only in ultra-luxury or very special hotel properties. I checked my phone. "I should head back. It's Wes' birthday today. They're throwing him a barbecue."

"Um, about Wes. Is he courting someone? Last night, my wife and I were over at the lake under the East Bridge with the twins, and well, he was in the paddle boats with this little blonde who was definitely *not* Evan." Terrance pulled up a picture on his phone.

He showed me a photo of Wes and Grace in a boat at sunset, her head on his shoulder.

"Fuck." Anger welled up in me.

"You didn't know. Sorry." He put his phone away. "It isn't my business, but you know, after Caroline and everything."

Terrance knew Caroline, too. He'd been there for me in the aftermath, just like he'd been there for me so many times in my life.

I didn't know that Wes and Grace had *gone out in public.* Evan and I got back late, and considering the house reeked of popcorn, I figured they'd stayed in.

"That's Grace." I rubbed my forehead. "Hey, do you remember whether Wes had a girlfriend back in high school?" I frowned. That bothered me.

"Um, maybe?" His face scrunched in thought. "He brought dates to dances and stuff. I think. Oh, wait, there was that girl he used to draw pictures of. He said she was his long-distance girlfriend or something. I sort of thought she was made up. Why?"

"Just wondering." Huh.

He rubbed his chin. "Does Evan know about Blondie?"

"They made Wes a fucking birthday cake after buying out the home store," I huffed.

"One omega isn't enough for Wes?" he laughed. Terrance was an alpha, his wife was a beta. We'd been friends since the third grade.

"She's a gamma or some shit like that. Between you and me, she's a fucking headache." This entire week I'd been plagued with Mrs. Beekman calling, or the detectives, or the Department of Dependent Services, or the integration team from the Center. I didn't have time for this. Grace had been in my house for a week, and the cases seemed nowhere near being closed.

"I've got a good private investigator if you need one. She's good, discreet. Give you and your pack peace of mind, if Wes is serious about her," he offered.

"Send me her info?" I wanted to know who Grace actually was and where she came from so that I could send her home. Maybe I could do a gen-scan with some of the blonde hair that was *everywhere*. Yes, I'd find her relatives for her since she couldn't remember them.

Funny how she didn't remember that, but she remembered all sorts of other things about Wes and math and baking.

"Of course. Tell Wes I said *Happy Birthday*. Sorry to miss it, but we're going to dinner with my wife's family." He got into his car and drove off.

Pity he couldn't come. It would be nice to have someone to hide with and avoid Grace.

I sent some emails, including requests to get some numbers run for the property. Contrary to what Terrance said, it might make a suitable venue–or at least a different one–if I could get it on the gala circuit. If I had to attend one more event at the High Tower or the Gladiola, I'd stab someone with a cocktail fork. My phone buzzed.

Katie

The party's started, where are you?

Of course, my sister was at the barbecue. Also, Wes hadn't just invited the sister pack, he'd invited some of our friends. There were *people* at my *house*. Okay, it was his thirtieth birthday, but ugh. Maybe we should have just gone out to dinner.

Me

Trying to buy a property. Be there soon.

Not really.
I anger-texted Wes.

Me

You took Grace out in public last night? You were seen.

Wes

Didn't know I needed permission. Grace is my mate, not my mistress.

He added an emoji of the bird.

When I pulled up to the house on my motorcycle, cars were everywhere. My mother had called me six times. Terrance also texted me the number for the investigator.

"Yes, Mother?" I snipped as I went through the garage.

"Your packmate is having a birthday party and you're *working?*" she scolded.

"I was looking at a property that Evan wants me to buy." I didn't need this either.

"Is the little girl there? Dependent Services is worried. She's a *theta?* When did that happen?" my mother demanded.

I checked the tracking app we used. Yes. Riley was here. Who added Grace? I deleted her.

"She's here. This is about the time that happens." Actually, Riley being a theta made sense. I knew a couple of them. They often ended up in real estate or running casinos or managing properties–careers where they could be independent and make a lot of money.

"I've been told you're refusing required services from the Center. That's unacceptable because this could still go sideways," she told me.

"When can Grace leave, because *I don't want her here.*" I wasn't making my pack do weird counseling to make Grace's life easier.

"Not cooperating draws everything out; you're bringing this on yourself." Her tone rankled.

"I'm a grown-ass person, I have my own pack, you're not the boss of me," I fired back.

"I don't negotiate with toddlers. She'll be here until I say so." My mother ended the call.

Fuck.

I texted the number of the investigator.

"Honey, are you okay?" Jett slipped into the garage.

"Yes, Dear. Just the queen mum giving me shit. No one will miss us if we leave." I pulled him into my arms to ease my frustration.

"Mmmm, tempting. But we *will* be missed. Do you want Katie hunting your ass down? There's beer and steak. Also, a delicious-looking cake," he replied.

"How the fuck is Wes explaining Grace? He took her *out on a date,*" I grumbled. The audacity!

"I think he's mostly like, *hey, this is Grace.* Yeah, I know they went out. He recreated one of their first dates, then took her to his dad's house, to help her remember more things," he replied.

Oh, that made sense. I wanted her to remember everything. Fast. But a warning would be nice.

Riley came into the garage and opened the refrigerator. "Where do you keep the good bourbon?"

"Nowhere you can get to." I locked up the good booze this morning. "Who's asking?"

"No one. I wanted these." She held up an energy drink and a lime soda.

My eyebrows rose. "Did you bring your boyfriend?"

She flipped me off. "Oh, my fuck. He's *not* my boyfriend. And yes, because Grace was helping us study for the math test. Kilroy's here too."

"Of course she's good at math," I grumbled. More friends? Though Kilroy was her friend, they'd met in detention the first week of school.

"Um, she's a *mathematician.*" Riley grabbed my hand. "Fuck, you're grumpy. Let's get you some food before you shit a cactus."

Chapter Thirty-Three

Grace

"He did?" I laughed and took another sip of beer as Wes' dad told me stories about Wes as a kid. He hadn't been at the house last night, so this was my first time meeting him—and unlike Lexi, he didn't know about all the years Wes had dreamed of me.

They had heat lamps going, and the fire pit. It wasn't nearly as cold as it could be, and I wore a flannel of Evan's.

"Oh, the stories I could tell you." His eyes crinkled around the corners as he laughed. "I'm going to get another one of those delightful steaks. Who knew Spencer was such a grilling expert?"

Wes put an arm around me as his dad walked away. "Do you like him?"

"I love him." I leaned into Wes. It had been fun to meet Wes' dad and some of his friends and family. The backyard was full of people laughing, eating, and having a great time.

Music played in the background, since their fancy backyard had a sound system. Also, a giant grill and a bar. Evan and I had blown up balloons and hung streamers. Riley made an enormous banner that said *Happy Birthday, Wes.*

I watched as Evan, Lexi, and a few others played *flying disc,* which was frisbee. Spencer was at the grill, being assisted by Marcos, Riley, and their friend Kilroy, who just wanted to play with fire. They kept chasing each other with flaming sticks. Lena, Lexi's packmate who owned a bar, played bartender.

Even Brennan seemed to have fun as he and Jett sat on a giant wooden swing with their drinks.

This... this was nice.

Katie came over to me. "Hey, Evan says you play piano. Should we play something?"

"Um, sure. I probably don't know anything you do." I'd done a quick search for some popular classical piano pieces, and while some of them sounded close, none of them were the same.

Wes kissed my temple. "Go for it."

"The boys are treating you okay, aren't they?" she asked as we crossed the backyard. "We haven't really had time to talk."

"I adore Evan, and I'd never do anything to hurt him," I blurted.

"Oh, I don't think that at all. I'm not sure anyone that matters does," she told me.

I sighed and looked at Brennan and Jett on the swing.

"Yeah, he doesn't matter." Katie rolled her eyes. She had red hair and eyes that were just like Brennan's. They even had similar builds, though she was a little shorter and slighter.

"He's head alpha, so he sort of does," I muttered, recalling what Luc, the integration counselor, had said about his acceptance being critical.

"All that's a him problem, not a you problem," she replied. "You have a room, right? Do you have what you need? Has Wes taken you out?"

"I have an adorable room and more stuff than I could want. We went on a date last night, it was fun." I grinned. It was so thoughtful.

Katie and I went inside. The cake Evan and I made this morning sat on the table. We'd also gone to the home store, and I'd picked out a lavender candle for myself along with a few other things. Evan and I also stopped at an art supply store, and I got Wes the charcoal set Evan said he wanted, offering to give Evan some baking lessons in return for getting it for me.

"Just checking. Wes can be a little oblivious and complacent. Also, Bren and Wes suck at courting. Spencer's probably amazing at it, though." She gave me a sly look. "What? I see how he looks at you."

He did? Part of me perked up. *Hey, down girl. You already have two guys, and you barely know what to do with them.*

"Spencer? If I accept this job, he'll be my *boss*." I ducked my head, cheeks warming as we went over to the piano in the big open area on the second floor. I hadn't spent much time on this floor.

"And?" She laughed. "It's not uncommon for omegas to work with a mate or packmate. You working with Spencer and Wes wouldn't cause anyone to blink as long as you can actually do the job you're hired for."

Therein lay the problem. I'd looked over several projects, and I didn't feel qualified to join *any* of those teams.

She stretched her fingers. "Do you like to play duets?"

"Absolutely."

Opening the piano bench, she got out some sheet music.

While I didn't know anything she did, for obvious reasons, I was an excellent sight reader.

We played a few things, laughing when one of us messed up. This was fun. Evan, Rami, who was Katie's omega, and Lexi wandered up. It felt so good to play again. The notes tickled all the correct parts of my brain.

Brennan barreled in, anger on his face. "What do you think you're doing?"

"Playing the piano, want to join?" Katie didn't seem taken aback by his anger.

"No. I don't like you playing my fucking piano," Brennan retorted.

"Oh, I didn't realize the piano was yours. I'm sorry," I told him, feeling bad. "But I've been playing since I was little; I'm not going to break it."

"Don't be sorry, this isn't about the piano," Katie told me, brushing him off.

"I don't like people touching my stuff," he growled, eyes flashing with anger.

No. This wasn't about the piano. This was about me.

I couldn't go home. But I wasn't wanted here. I wasn't smart enough. I wasn't anything that counted. Maybe I'd even broken interdimensional law.

"No?" I got up and rubbed my hands all over the piano, even though I could hear my childhood-self getting yelled at for leaving fingerprints.

"Don't be infantile," he snapped.

"Infantile? We both know that this isn't about the piano; but you *don't* like people touching your stuff, do you?" I went over to Evan and rubbed my hands all over him, then kissed him.

I realized what I was doing and broke it off.

Looking up at Evan, my knees trembled with guilt. "I'm so sorry, I didn't mean to use you like that."

"Hey," Evan's voice went soft, as he pulled me to him. "I'm all for you bratting Bren, but don't do it if you can't take the consequences. Peaches, you're *not* ready."

What did that even mean?

"She won't ever be, because there is no place for her in this pack," Brennan retorted. "I don't know what your endgame is, but *you don't belong here.*"

"Bren, she's bonded to your packmate. A bond that *predates* your pack. You don't get to make that choice," Katie corrected.

"No, *you and Mother* don't get to make that choice for my pack." Brennan got in her face, both of them posturing like it might come to blows.

I snapped, "What am I supposed to do, Brennan? As I stated before, I'm not here to wreck anything. I don't want anything from you. I'm not here to steal Wes from Evan or to get your money. You're right, I *don't* belong here. But what if I can't go home? I..." I sagged into Evan's arms. "I don't belong anywhere. I'll never belong. I'll never be good enough."

Self-defeat cascaded down on me, crushing my soul.

"What the fuck, Bren?" Evan held me tight as he ran his fingers through my hair. "I've got you. I'm right here."

"Why are you wearing the flannel I bought Evan?" Brennan growled, as he tugged at the corner of it.

"Really?" Katie goaded.

"Fine." Getting out of Evan's arms, I unbuttoned the flannel, sick of this bullshit.

"Grace, stop." Evan put his hand on mine.

"No. He doesn't want me to wear this shirt." I took it off and threw it at him. "Happy?" I put my hands on my hips and scowled.

"Why is there yelling?" Riley joined us. "Fuckity fuck fuck. Grace, who am I destroying for you?"

"Shit," Katie said. "What happened to her back? Car accident?"

"It's a fucked-up story," Evan said quietly.

Right. My scars. Mortification filled me as I stood there in my sports bra, scars on display. Back in my cheer days I'd always been careful to choose a sports tank that covered them, or I wore a shirt over my sports bra. Our cheer outfits were never usually a problem or I could wear a dance top under it that matched my skintone.

But here I was, in all my glory, back fully on display...

My breath hitched in my chest as I tried not to panic.

Wes ran up the front stairs. "Um, hey, is everything okay?"

"Well, if your bond worked right, you'd know, wouldn't you," Brennan sneered.

"Your bond doesn't work right? Why didn't I know that?" Katie gave him a hard look.

"It's the *concussion.* You can read papers about it. It's a medically documented thing that can happen." Wes bundled me into his arms, pressing my face into his muscular chest. "Hey, I'm right here. What do you need?"

"Things to be right." Tears flooded my eyes, and I buried my face in his shoulder, trying to get comfort from his scent. Our bond wasn't even right. I wasn't from here. I couldn't stay. But I couldn't go.

What was I supposed to do? I'd never be enough. In any world.

"I *will* fuck someone up for you," Riley snarled, hugging my back.

"They're dead." My chest shook.

"I hope you killed them."

"I... I don't know how my mom died. By that point, I'm not sure I even cared." I closed my eyes.

"Her mom." Rami's voice wavered. "Her mom did that?"

"She had an issue with Grace and Wes being together," Lexi said. "Like Evan said, it's a fucked-up story, and that's just the bits I know."

"Who takes issue with Wes? He wouldn't be the alpha I'd worry about," Katie said.

"I think she just hated alphas in general," Wes replied, arms wrapped tight around me. "Strangely enough, her mom also hated advanced math. But, hey, she's gone, Grace. She can't hurt you, and you're here with me and Evan–right where you belong."

He kissed my head, and I felt tiny little flickers of love, as his scent coated me.

Evan wrapped his arms around us, too, adding lemonade. "We're here, and it's going to be okay."

For a moment, I allowed myself to soak this up, to soak up them. It was moments like this where everything felt right. If I could stay on the third floor with them and never venture out, everything would be fine. Like when I was little and would dream of Wes. There in the dreams, with him, life was great.

Then I woke up.

"Let's get you a shirt and then maybe we should go have cake? I can't wait to try it. It looks amazing. Do I even want to know why you're not wearing a shirt?" Wes asked.

Katie turned to her twin. "You need to let this Caroline bullshit go, Bren."

"I'm just trying to protect my pack." The anger left Brennan's voice, but there was no apology in his face or posture.

"You don't need to protect the pack against *Grace*," Wes said.

"I'm sorry, I won't play the piano anymore. I don't want anyone to be mad at each other." Guilt ate at me for causing a scene on Wes' *birthday*.

Brennan looked at me with an intense gaze, and I flinched. Wes growled. So did Katie.

Pine, eucalyptus, and clean laundry flooded the room in an intensity that had me frozen, clinging to Evan as the three alphas faced off.

"Fuck me with a pineapple," Riley breathed.

Rami whined and clung to Lexi.

What was going on? I was a little terrified. Not of anyone specifically, just in general.

"You can play the piano. But clean the fingerprints off it–and learn how to load the dishwasher right." Brennan stalked to his room, slamming the door.

"Bren," Katie yelled.

"Let him have a moment," Evan said.

Katie pulled Rami to her chest, murmuring and stroking his hair.

"How do I load the dishwasher wrong? I wash the big things by hand." I didn't know there was a wrong way to load the dishwasher, unless you were blocking the sprayers or something.

"He's particular about the bowls. Back bowls face front, front bowls face back. According to him, all silverware but knives should go up, not down, in the basket. I didn't realize it bothered him that much." Evan shrugged.

"It's not about the dishwasher. Or the piano. Or even you. It's about Caroline," Katie told me, still holding onto Rami, comforting him. He was slight, his dark hair hung in his brown eyes, dark green shirt bringing out his golden-brown skin.

Rami was the one who worked for the space program and was fascinating to talk to.

"I don't want to cause problems." Guilt ate at me like acid, and I hid my face in Wes's chest.

"You're not." Evan kissed my temple. "I'll meet you downstairs so we can have cake."

"Oh, yes. Let's have some cake. I'm excited to see how it turned out. I can never get it quite the way my grandma did." Lexi stood.

Hopefully, it turned out. It was Evan's first baking lesson.

"For what it's worth, I like it that you're here. I'm going to jump in the pool and rinse off this alpha fuckery." Riley ran back downstairs.

Wes led me upstairs, arm around my waist. "Are you okay? He didn't hurt you, right? Just got bossy and possessive?"

"I didn't mean to ruin your birthday." I felt all weird and uneasy inside, my heart pounding.

"You didn't. It's not ruined. Not one bit." He carried me to his room and dropped me on his bed.

It smelled of him. Of us. With a hint of Evan, who'd crawled in with us in the wee hours to snuggle.

He jumped under the covers with me, crushed me to his chest, and purred. I was plunged into a cozy sea of snuggles, my spine melting, as he held me, murmuring soft words, until my heart stopped pounding and my breath unhitched.

"Better, Peaches? Or do you need more?" He pressed tiny kisses on my face.

I took a deep breath of Wessy goodness, the lungful soothing my frayed soul. "One more cuddle and then we'll have some cake?"

"Sounds good." Wes snuggled me tight, planting little kisses on my jaw, neck and shoulders.

"Cake time, bitches," Riley yelled from someplace.

Reluctantly, I sat up.

"Okay." I looked down at my bra. "Right after I put on a shirt."

Chapter Thirty-Four

Grace

Sandwiched between Wes and Evan, I was cozy and warm in Wes' bed. After many rounds of delicious birthday sex, I should be fast asleep. But something nagged at me. What had I forgotten?

Think. Think. Think.

The piano. I never cleaned the fingerprints off the piano.

Extracting myself from them, I went down to the laundry room in the basement and mixed some gentle soap with warm water in a clean bucket and found a soft cloth. I padded up to the dark second floor. Not wanting to wake anyone, I didn't turn on the light. Instead, I first dusted the piano, then methodically wiped it down and dried it. I put away the bucket and went back to the third floor to return to Wes' bed.

Back to my pile of purrs and muscle.

I stopped in front of my room, the door ajar. A sigh escaped my lips as I surveyed it in the darkness, the only light streaming in through the window. It really was messy, wasn't it?

Taking everything off the window seat and the bed, I took it all down to the laundry room to wash. As I did the laundry, I got my room nice and clean—taking things down, putting things away, washing the windows and scrubbing the floor. I didn't vacuum the rug, because I didn't want to wake everyone, and I couldn't move the bed myself.

The room now smelled nice and bleachy. Everything was in its place. No clutter. No fuss. No one would think I was a slob and get mad.

I made my bed, using only the bare minimum of pillows, making the corners nice and tight. Mr. Hippo, now clean and brushed, sat in the position of honor. One stuffy was allowed. I put the teddy Evan gave me in the wardrobe, giving him a kiss as an apology.

Folding all the now-clean blankets, I put them away in the chest under the window seat, along with all the throw pillows but two, which I put in the window seat. Three?

No. That would be too indulgent. I didn't want anyone to get angry.

I stood back and admired my work. Perfect. Nice and neat. Not even my mother could complain. I yawned as fatigue pressed down on me.

The room was clean, so now I should be clean. After taking a quick shower, with extra soap, in Evan's bathroom so I wouldn't wake anyone by using Wes', I went back to my room and put on a pair of PJs. My hair was wet, but I was too tired to dry it. Flipping off the bedroom light, I sprayed the room one last time with deodorizer, and grabbed Mr. Hippo.

Not wanting to mess up my nice clean room, I crawled under the bed, and went to sleep, curled on the soft rug with Mr. Hippo to keep me company.

Chapter Thirty-Five

Evan

A feeling of *wrongness* tugged at me, and I sat up in Wes' bed, looking around in the darkness. Wes was right there, a big lump in the blankets, but Grace...

Grace wasn't in bed with us. Huh. It was still the middle of the night. Maybe she went to the bathroom? After a couple of moments, she still hadn't come back. I slid out of bed, Wes not moving. That man could sleep through almost anything.

Where was Grace?

She wasn't in his bathroom. Mine, maybe? No, but it seemed like she had recently taken a shower—and used my scent-removing body wash I used sometimes. Odd. Usually, she used my other one, or Wes'.

"Grace?" I called, checking the rest of my suite. My phone was by my bed. No text from her. No Grace.

Maybe she was in her room.

"Grace?" I knocked on the open door, the stench of industrial cleaning products and airborne scent remover hitting me so strongly it made my eyes tear. "Grace?" I flipped on the light. "I'm coming in."

Panic at not seeing–or smelling–her coursed through me. I tried to reach through the bond, but it was still pretty spotty.

I searched the room with my eyes. She wasn't in her bed or the window seat. She had also *completely disassembled her window seat nest.*

My heart pounded as I took in her room.

It was gone. The little round canopy. The lights. All the pillows and blankets. Even the books she'd had on the shelf Jett built her this morning. I opened the window to alleviate the chemical smell of de-scenter. I opened the bottom of the seat, looking for all the blankets and pillows we'd gotten her. The bleachy aroma of scent-removing laundry detergent hit me.

Grace had washed *everything*—and not with the detergent I'd told her to use. No, she'd *sanitized* them with the other stuff I'd found in there, stripping everything of our scents.

The daybed had gotten the same treatment. The gauzy canopy and lights, gone. Only two pillows on the bed. Sheets with perfect military corners–the cozy comforter and fluffy blankets no longer there. Everything smelled of the same detergent. There wasn't even a single blanket on the bed, just sheets.

My throat swelled. She'd taken everything down and eradicated her presence. Then she'd doused the room in de-scenter.

She'd erased herself.

It had just started to look like *her* room. Now, it looked and felt like a guest room.

Worry coursed through me. I thought she was doing okay. Sure, Brennan had unsettled her tonight. But Wes had comforted her, and we'd gotten her to eat cake and have fun again.

The night ended up with the three of us in Wes' bed having great birthday sex.

What had happened? Most importantly, where was Grace?

She wasn't in the wardrobe, or in the place between the bed and the wall—small places scared omegas might hide. Panic shot through me.

"Grace, where are you?" I heard a faint beeping sound. What was that?

Ducking to look under the bed, I spied two bare feet with mauve toenails. Grace was *under* the bed, in some PJs. Not mine or Wes' shirt, but actual PJs that my sister must have chosen. She was asleep on the rug with only Mr. Hippo—no pillow or blanket.

My belly sank.

"Grace." I pulled her out from under the bed, unmoving and lifeless, as panic continued to course through my veins. Something kept beeping.

Her wrist beeped. I checked the monitor. Seizure. Shit. A brief one. The kind we called the doctor in the morning about, not the kind we went to the emergency room for.

She was breathing. But it was shallow. The heartbeat on the monitor was slow. Her temperature was cool, her skin clammy.

Her scent had gone rotten.

Spiral.

Fuck. Fuck. Fuck.

My heart sped. Spirals were the opposite of a heat spike—when hormones rose as an omega's body prepared to go into heat. A spiral was a sign that hormones were drastically dropping—or out of whack.

It could also be dangerous. I should know. It happened to me a couple of times when dealing with Caroline and the aftermath. One of those times was bad enough for me to go to the hospital.

"Peaches, are you okay, can you hear me?" I asked, trying to wade through my panic enough to care for her.

She made a little noise, but she didn't nuzzle me like usual or open her eyes.

What did I do?

Safe. The first thing I needed was to get her feeling safe.

"I've got you. Let's go somewhere more comfortable." I scooped her up and carried her out, making a mental note to get someone to make that door between our rooms *now*. She liked my bathroom better anyway and I didn't care.

We went through my suite and into my bedroom. I grabbed my phone, then brought us through the closet and into my nest, closing the door, and turning on the salt lamp, giving the tiny, cozy room a soft glow.

"I'm going to let you come in here with me until you get nice and warm, okay?" If she didn't feel safe in Wes' bed or her own room, maybe she'd feel safe here with me.

She made a little mewing sound as I tucked her into my messy nest. I took off my shirt and put it on her, removing the bleach-smelling pajamas. Grabbing my phone, I texted Wes.

Me

Grace is spiraling. Need you.

Hopefully, Wes' phone was on—or he'd feel us. I could handle her myself for now, but eventually I'd get her to the point where she'd need him.

After this, we'd both need him.

Drawing her onto my bare chest, I covered her with everything—blankets, pillows, clothes, all things filled with scents that would comfort her and keep warm.

"There you go. You're nice and safe here with me. It's just us. No alphas. You're safe and I'm right here," I whispered, curling around her clammy body, marking her with my scent.

Her heartbeat remained slow, breath shallow. I whispered to her, snuggled her, ran my fingers through her damp hair, and purred, trying to pour all my love into her. I let her know that she was loved and wanted. That I saw her. That I needed her here with us.

Wes didn't come. I texted him again. I didn't want to leave her to get him, but I didn't want to bring her out yet.

"Come on, Peaches, you're going to be okay." I rubbed her back, trying to keep my own panic at bay. While she hadn't gotten worse, she wasn't all better.

"Evan, Evan, are you in here, what's wrong?" someone called. Wes?

"Evan, I'm coming in," Brennan said from my bedroom. A moment later, there was a rap on the door. "Are you in there, what's wrong, what do you need?"

Not Wes. But part of me was happy an alpha had come.

"I don't know." It came out raw and rough. At this moment, I didn't. Where had we failed her?

"Okay. Can I come in?"

"You can open the door and sit in the doorway." I wasn't ready for him to come in, but I wanted, no, needed, to hear his voice.

The door opened, and he sat in the doorway, wearing only briefs.

"Did something happen? Do you want to join Jett and me?" He sounded sleepy, but it was still the middle of the night.

"Grace is spiraling." My voice broke. She *erased* herself. We *failed* her.

"Grace." His voice went sour, his scent bitter. "Grace is in here with you? No wonder it smells gross. Can gammas even spiral?"

"Do you understand what gammas are?" My voice went tart, tired of his attitude.

"They're failed omegas, aren't they?"

"Do you know why they *failed*, versus being a beta with dormant omega traits, or an unawakened omega?" I pushed, needing him to understand.

He made a face. "Genetics?"

"Sometimes. Most times, it's the environment," I told him, still stroking her hair. "At some point the body literally *stops* the process of becoming an omega–usually because of a lack of resources or because something tells them that *it's not safe.* Considering the situations I've seen omegas raised in, can you imagine what must happen for a little body to go *Shit, it's too dangerous to do this* and *halt* a genetic process?"

"Are you saying that if you love her enough, she'll suddenly become an omega?" Sarcasm laced his voice.

I kissed her forehead. No matter what, I still loved her. "I think it's way too late for that."

Sometimes it happened. But from her medical records, it wasn't likely–or could take a long time.

"Oh." He frowned a little.

"The best way to interact with a gamma like her, a *textbook gamma,* is to treat them like an omega but don't expect them to react like them. Do you know why?" I asked, still stroking her hair and snuggling her little body.

He rolled his eyes. "I'm sure you're going to tell me."

"Because their danger response is fucked up. Instead of *fight or flight,* they can get stuck on *random* because their body thinks surprising their attacker is the best choice. So, they do things like slap alphas." Which we needed to be aware of. She wasn't going to act like we'd expect.

"And kiss omegas in front of their alphas," he grumbled.

"That was her being a brat. I'm *here* for bratty Grace." It was also probably a fucked-up danger response, but I felt like baiting him. Would it hurt for him to be nicer to her?

"Are you going to tell me what's wrong?" Annoyance came through the bond.

"She's *spiraling*. Like I used to." I held her tighter, not knowing what else to do. Her heartbeat and breathing were better, but she was still cool and clammy.

"But what does that even mean, we've given her everything, so she–"

"Go look in her fucking room and tell me what you see," I snapped, angry that my words were doing *nothing*. "Then wake Wes' ass up. He's not responding to my texts, and obviously he's so fast asleep he can't feel that something is wrong."

"I felt you, which is why I'm here in the middle of the night. I'm your alpha, tell *me* what you need," he growled.

"You are my alpha, but you're not hers." I pulled her to me protectively.

"Well, of course not," he snapped.

It hit me. It was him. Fuck. On some primal level, she didn't feel safe in the house, even with Wes and me present, because *of him*. He resented her. Brennan rejected her presence. He complained she didn't do things right–which must have triggered a childhood response to her mom berating her for not being tidy.

Which probably led to her midnight cleaning campaign.

"Bren, *go look in her room and tell me what the fuck is wrong.*" My voice shook as anger bubbled inside me. Little Grace probably slept under her bed with no blankets so she wouldn't mess things up and make her mom angry. I'd seen this before in my work.

"You know I hate guessing games. Tell me," he huffed.

"I'm not asking you to guess, you knothead. I'm asking you to *look*." My tone became harsh.

This was what the integration team was supposed to prevent. While she'd met with them several times, they should have met with the entire pack by now.

"Fine." He got up and stalked off.

I rearranged us, getting comfortable.

"That's it, Peaches, you're warm, loved, and safe," I told her. "We're so glad you're here. We love you so much. It's going to be okay."

Oh, that could also be a factor. Culture shock. She wasn't from here, but no one knew that but Wes, Spencer, and me. So many little things must be different for her, and all that could become overwhelming.

While Brennan was a huge part of it, we all fucked up big time, not realizing how many changes she was getting hit with all at once.

We didn't notice how fragile she was inside. How strange it all must be for her.

"I'm sorry, Grace, I'm so sorry, we fucked up. We'll do better," I whispered, guilt filling me. We'd done this. This was our fault. We were given this beautiful soul to care for, and we'd failed her.

"She disassembled her nest and sanitized it. You... you did that once. Right before you ended up in the hospital." Brennan's voice wavered as he stood in the doorway.

"Yep. Because I didn't feel welcome or safe. I didn't feel like there was a space for me in the pack, so I removed my presence," I said softly.

"Oh. What happens when she tells Mrs. Beekman this?"

"This is a major red flag. Mrs. Beekman could remove her." My voice shook, because that would break my heart. "More likely, the integration team will need to do more. I'm pretty disappointed that they haven't done much."

"Remove her? My mother will be livid. We'll just fix it. Put things back up. Maybe she won't notice?"

The callousness of his words made me curl Grace into me tighter, protecting her.

"Do you hear yourself? This isn't about you or your mom or the investigation. This is about *Grace*. About her feeling like she doesn't belong to the point she's made herself sick. There's so much going on with her that you don't know, Bren." I begged him to understand. Being pulled between them hurt me on a fundamental level.

"This is my fault?" he grumbled.

"It's *all* our fault. But a lot of this is on you. You don't have to mate with her, just don't be a dick. Look, she's not after your money. If she and Spencer pull off this simulator, they're going to make a shit-ton," I told him. Well, I was guessing.

"Does Wes actually love her?" Brennan was inside now, and there was no remorse coming through the bond, just annoyance and a little worry.

"He does. But I'm not kidding when I say that she and Wes need some major couples therapy," I replied.

"Do you love her?" Brennan sat on the platform, peering at me, curiosity in his eyes.

"I'm falling for her, hard. So hard." I kissed her forehead again.

"You know what, I'll wake up Wes. Or better yet, just dump her in Wes' bed and come with me." He squeezed my hand. "I'll give you what you need."

Oh, did I need him. I was feeling so unsettled and shaky inside. This had been me once.

But I wasn't going to let Grace endure this alone, like I'd let myself suffer because I felt like I didn't deserve an alpha or pack to make things better.

I let go of his hand and shook my head. "What I need is for you to stop being a dick to her." I gathered her up. "Since you can't do that, we'll leave."

Grace in my arms, I marched right past my alpha toward Wes' room. I needed an alpha *right now*. I think she was feeling safe and warm enough that maybe she did, too.

"Evan, wait," he called.

I turned around. "Don't you see, *we're literally doing to her what Caroline did to me.* She can't go home, Brennan. Wes and I aren't going to give her up, so we're going to have to figure this out. Quick."

"So she says. We don't even know who she actually is." He made a face.

"Stop being a knothead. I'm done with this. She's getting cold." I started walking again.

She snuggled into me. "Mmmm."

Relief flooded my chest. I'd done something right. I could be enough for her.

"We're going to Wes, okay?" I whispered to her.

"You're going to choose her over me?" Brennan's voice flickered between anger and heartbreak.

"I shouldn't have to choose," I snapped. Tears pricked my eyes, and I went into Wes' suite, closing the door.

Wes met me in the doorway to his room, worry on his face and pouring through the bond. "Just saw your texts."

"We need you." I crushed myself into his arms, Grace between us. Desperation flooded me. I needed to feel complete and loved.

"I'm right here. Spiral, like what you did?" His voice went gravely as he held us to him.

"Yeah, I got her temperature up, but we need you." I trembled a little, with need, longing, and desperation. I needed him to soothe my nerves, to reassure me.

"You've got me. *Always.*" He began to purr, filling the room with calming pheromones as the scent of fresh laundry overpowered me, turning every inch of me into jelly, as I melted into him.

"Umpf," Grace muttered. "Mmmm."

Those were good noises.

"Bed, both of you." Wes pushed us into his room and onto the bed, smothering us with his body as he threw lots of blankets over us.

Death by alpha smooshes? *Yes please.*

His chest was up against me, rumbling with his purr, the anxiety and panic I'd felt before floating away until I was content.

Safe. Warm. Loved.

"What happened?" he whispered, his hands running up and down my back, him still practically on top of Grace and me, shielding us with his body, protecting us, loving us.

"I woke up and Grace wasn't here. I found her asleep *under* her bed, with only Mr. Hippo. She'd had a seizure, a little one–and was showing all the signs of a spiral. I... I took her with me into my nest and got her warm, and kept her safe, until..." My chest shook.

Fucking Brennan. He could have fixed everything so easily. He was right there, holding my hand. All he had to do was snuggle us, purr for us, maybe tell her he was sorry. It would have fixed so much.

Instead, he made it worse.

"I'm sorry I didn't wake up or hear my phone," Wes apologized. "Why did you go to your room? Curious."

"It's an omega issue, and I figured that's what she needed. Me and a nice safe space," I confessed. It had seemed like the right thing to do at the time.

"Then it was the right move. I can't think of anyone who'd know better than you what to do in a situation like this." He kissed me. "Thank you. Thank you for taking such good care of her, for loving her. You give her things I can't, and I'm so grateful for that. I... I wonder why she left the bed?"

"I don't know. But she didn't just fall asleep under her bed. First, she disassembled her nest and sanitized everything in her room. We fucked up, Wes. We fucked up so badly. You alphas don't even understand what we've done to her," I sobbed. We were the worst. This was the worst. She'd erased herself because of *us*.

"None of this is your fault," he soothed, stroking my back as he purred.

"It's Bren's—and yours for not shutting his bullshit down before we ever brought her home." Angry tears streamed down my face. I felt awful that she'd had to go through this for us to notice what she truly needed.

"Don't cry, Evs, we'll get ice cream in the morning," Grace mumbled, her face buried in my side. "Promise."

"Mmmm, that sounds great, Peaches." I breathed in lungfuls of her peachiness, which was smelling right again.

"Her mom used to take all her blankets, stuffies, and pillows from her as a punishment for being messy, among other things. When she'd come to me, I'd pile all my blankets on her and let her hold my hippo as I snuggled her. I'll fix this. I'll fix this." He nuzzled the bite mark on my neck with his nose, making me shiver.

"You better. I'm feeling pretty triggered. This is reminding me too much of what I went through with Caroline." I wouldn't wish that on anyone. Especially Grace.

"I didn't even consider *that* parallel. You know, I didn't realize the full extent of Bren's problem until the thing with the piano. Fuck. I'm such a bad mate to the both of you." He nipped my neck.

My cock bucked. Now that I was feeling warm and safe and loved, my body wanted reassurance besides snuggles, purrs, and praise.

"I forgive you, but you *have* to handle this. I can only do so much." As soon as the words left my lips, I felt a million times lighter. "Also, call the integration team and set up the therapy."

"I did, well, for me and Grace. That's what you mean, right? We start this week. The therapist said that she might want you to come in sometimes too–if you're willing. Sorry, I forgot to tell you." He ran little kisses down the length of my jaw.

"No, that's great. You know I'll participate in anything to make this easier for Grace." I stroked her hair. "I was so scared when I found her, and while I should have brought her to you, all I could think of was *me* keeping her safe."

"You were perfect." His hand ran up and down my back, but this was sexy, not soothing. "She's doing better?"

I closed my eyes for a moment to listen for her breathing, then pressed my lips to her no-longer-clammy forehead. "She seems to be sleeping normally now."

"How can I take care of you? My perfect, amazing, omega, what do you need from your alpha?" he murmured, hand resting on my ass.

"I need your cock," I begged. I needed him to rail me hard, fast, and frequently. Good thing I didn't need to be at work until after lunch.

"Done." Grabbing me, he rolled us over and over until we were on the other side of the bed, and he was on top of me, face inches from mine as he pumped the room full of pheromones, making me pant with desire, body on fire.

"What about Grace?" I realized I was naked. I'd only been wearing a shirt before, which I gave to Grace. That meant that I'd carried Grace here stark naked. Oh well.

He climbed off me and tucked the blankets around her, positioning her in the bed's corner. "There. If she wakes, it's not like she's never seen us fucking."

"Good. I need you now." Grabbing my alpha, I tugged on his shirt. "But first, I'm going to need you to take this off."

Chapter Thirty-Six

Grace

"I'm *fine. Stop,*" I groaned. They'd been clingy since the moment I woke up. Right now, Evan and I were *both* on Wes' lap as he tried to feed us breakfast. It was cute for about five minutes, but now I was just annoyed.

"You need to get checked out. Last night, you had a seizure. Evan found you sleeping *under* the bed," Wes insisted as he drank his coffee.

"That's quite embarrassing since I don't think I've done that in years. But that doesn't mean I need the doctor." A therapist, but not the doctor. "We left a message about the seizure, and I have another appointment this week. I. Am. Fine. Stop with the overprotective bullshit." I gave him a little push.

"Wes is an alpha, that's the factory default setting." Jett came up from the basement, looking like he'd been working out. "Has anyone heard from Bren? He left in the middle of the night and won't respond to my texts. Also, he's hiding his location."

"Bren deleted Grace, I added her back in," Evan mumbled.

Wes handed me another piece of bacon. "Eat."

"Fine." I rolled my eyes at him wanting to feed me. The bacon *was* cooked perfectly.

"I have plenty to say to him when he comes back," Wes growled.

"Stop, please." The bacon crumbled in my fist. "I don't want to cause problems between you guys. I'm not here to break up the band."

Jett poured himself a cup of coffee. "Is this about the whole piano thing? You can play the piano. It's Katie that he's pissed at, not you."

"He's been pissed at Katie since they were in the womb." Wes rolled his eyes.

"No. It's me, and I don't know how to fix it other than to leave, but where do I go?" My eyes teared and my chest shook. I didn't want to go. But I didn't want to cause problems.

"Hey, you're not going anywhere. Wes is going to fix this," Evan assured, putting an arm around me. "Jett, go look in her room and tell me what you see."

"*Stop.* I cleaned my room, it's not that big of a deal. It made sense to tidy up since I was already cleaning the piano. Honestly, I don't remember much." I didn't get why it was a big deal. People cleaned their rooms.

"You cleaned the piano in the middle of the night?" Evan frowned over his coffee cup.

"I forgot to clean it earlier. I didn't want to piss off Brennan any more than I do just by breathing." With a sigh, I ate my crumbled bacon.

Jett frowned and went up the backstairs.

Wes handed me another piece of bacon, which I ate, between sips of coffee.

Evan looked at his phone. "Grace, Spencer wants to know if you and I would like a spa day tomorrow. What do you say? Wes has to work and I have tomorrow off."

"Um, okay. That sounds fun. I've never been to a spa," I replied.

Jett came back down, face stormy. "I'm going to beat his ass."

"This isn't a big deal, you possessive fuckers." Exasperation leaked into my voice. "Why are you like this?"

"Someone is speaking my language." Riley came into the kitchen, wearing an olive green long-sleeved romper and combat boots.

"Get the keys to Evan's motorcycle and Wes' wallet, because we're going to go cause some trouble." I extracted myself from Wes' lap, needing to get out of here before I punched someone for being annoying.

"Can you even ride a motorcycle? Not sure your feet will reach." Jett smirked, as he helped himself to bacon and eggs on the stove.

I scratched my nose with my middle finger and turned to Riley. "After my mom cut me off, and took *all* my stuff, I needed a ride, because she also took my truck. One of my classmates sold me his ex's bike cheap. I enjoyed being that math student with the hot pink motorcycle. We even painted equations on it."

More memories that weren't actually useful.

"While I want to fuck some shit up with you, we told Rose that we'd help her with her move." Riley opened the fridge and got out the juice.

"You're going, too? Are you up to it?" Wes frowned as his phone buzzed.

"That's sort of been the plan," I replied. "I'll be fine. We're just moving someone into the dorms."

"I want Grace to see Finchley. You know, if you don't want to work for Spencer, you could always see about a job at Finchley or at Ri's school in the math department," Evan told me.

"I never got my teaching credential. But it's a thought."

Evan checked the time on his phone. "We've got to leave soon, which means Grace and I should put on clothes. Ri, bring your stuff. Do you need to get back to school at a certain time? Is your homework done?"

"Um, yes, it is, since Bren stood me up. We were supposed to ride dirt bikes this morning." Hurt rang in her voice as she kicked the air.

Wes' phone buzzed again. "Spence?" He grimaced. "Yeah, okay. I'll be right in." He set his phone down. "Fuck."

"I'll go with them, it'll be fine. I've met Rose before," Jett offered. "Bren stood me up, too. It'll be okay, Ri."

"Okay." Riley looked anxious.

"I don't know." Wes frowned.

"She'll be *fine*, Wes," Evan soothed. "Jett, you don't have to come."

"I'm fine." I turned to Riley. "For the love of baby Jesus, I'm not sure I can deal with this."

"For the love of baby cheeses? I like cheese," Riley told me. "This is the real reason I live at school. Going from two nosy beta sisters and my beta grandparents, to *three fucking alphas,* a cop, and a social worker? I love them, but they're a lot." She took the last piece of bacon off the table. "Now go put some clothes on, we've got shit to do."

"Is this the last one?" I grabbed a bag off the now-empty bed in Rose's room at the center.

"Yep," Rose told me, hoisting a big tote bag over her shoulder. "Thanks for helping."

"Anytime." I was glad to be out of the house and doing something. To get Wes off my back, I'd gotten a quick checkup at the clinic where they'd run some tests. I'd gotten a shot and told I needed extra snuggles. Okay.

"We'll miss you, stop by and say *hi* anytime," a woman in a pink Center polo told Rose as we walked toward the front.

Evan was waiting for us in the lobby. "All set."

We threw the rest of her stuff in Evan's 4x4, as a car careened into the parking lot. The door opened, and a red-headed woman, younger than me but older than Rose, tumbled out.

"Get in the car," she yelled. "Rose Clarissa Matthews, get in the car right now." She looked tired and stressed, clothes wrinkled, hair a mess.

Something about this immediately struck me as *wrong*. Not just her trying to make Rose get in the car, but *her*.

"Iris, I thought you went home." Rose stepped behind Evan, fear on her face.

"I can't go home without you. I told you that," her voice shook. "Rose, I need to go to work, and *I can't go home without you.*" Desperation flashed in her eyes.

Something was wrong.

"Shit. Dad's an alpha?" Jett whispered, body on alert.

"My uncle's the alpha and head of our family," Rose whispered. "He's the one who's had everyone tell me to come home."

More alpha bullshit. Great.

"Iris, I'm not going home. Both Mom and Ted told me to stay. Evan said the social worker already got you some relief funds and food. Go home, I'll be fine." Rose's voice shook.

"Iris, I'm sorry about the circumstances at home, but you need to leave before security removes you," Evan told her, voice calm and even.

"We don't need charity, we need *you*," Iris insisted. "Now get in." She grabbed Rose's arm and yanked it toward the still-running car.

Rose screamed. Riley grabbed Rose, pulling her back toward us.

"Let go of her now. I'm a police officer," Jett warned, flashing a badge.

"Iris, I get it, things suck at home," I told her, trying to block her from getting to the car. "I'm sure having to pick up the slack while your sister goes to school stings, especially if you've given up your dreams for your family. But the thing is, *you don't have to do that.* You're not the parent."

"My mom is *in jail* because of her, and Ted can't find a job. Who's going to take care of everyone if I don't?" Iris fired back.

"If you *want* to do it, go for it. But if you don't, that's fine. It's not your job to figure out what happens if you leave. You're allowed to have a life, too. Don't let your family weaponize your siblings. Don't resent Rose and the others, resent those who put you in that position," I added, thinking of my brothers and how they'd hated me.

"Grace is telling the truth. Now let her go," Jett ordered.

Iris gripped her tighter. "You don't understand. *I can't.*"

"We have someone who can fix that," Evan soothed. "Let Rose go. Let's go inside and figure this out. I can help you, if you'll let me."

"No." Iris yanked Rose and tried to shove her in the car. Jett jumped on top of her.

"Rose." I ran to her. Riley and I tried to extract her from her sister's grasp as Evan helped Jett.

A bunch of uniformed dudes ran over. They weren't alphas, but big, strong, and took orders. Deltas. The bouncers of this world.

Riley had her arms around Rose, who was sobbing.

Jett turned to Evan. "Do I need to call this in?"

"We'll let security deal with it for now." Evan turned to Rose. "Let's go back inside."

Evan led Rose off some place, leaving Jett, Riley, and me in the main waiting area.

"They're going to have someone fix this, right, because that's shitty," Riley said. "So, she'd been here for days waiting for a chance to abduct Rose?"

"I guess," Jett replied.

"I don't quite understand what happened." I wrapped my arms around myself again–and not just because it was cold today.

"Alpha bark, I'm guessing. Like she literally couldn't go home without Rose," Riley told me.

Alpha bark. Right. I'd seen that in a video. Fucked-up alpha compulsion bullshit.

"I'll smack anyone who tries that on me," I grumbled, still feeling a little violent.

"That's my Grace. We need Jett to teach us some shit." Riley grinned at Jett.

"I'm a little afraid of what will happen if I do." He grinned back.

Riley rolled her eyes. "I need to learn shit for skate smash tryouts. Grace, got any tips? One of my friends set up a clinic for us, and some of us have been practicing when we have a chance, but every bit helps."

"Don't die," I told her. "No, seriously, I never quite figured everything out beyond the basics. I wasn't good, I was there because we needed bodies. One of my professors always said *Have fun, don't die.*"

Riley nodded. "Always good advice."

Evan came back out with Rose, who was now wearing a fluffy hoodie, face tear-stained.

"Rose." Riley ran over and hugged her. "You okay?"

"Yeah. I... am. Am I..."

"You are." I stood and hugged her to me. "You're making the right choice. Remember, don't set yourself on fire to keep others warm."

Riley's eyebrows rose. "Do people actually do that? Because that's some fucked-up shit right there."

"She means it figuratively, not literally," Evan told her. "Let's go. Should we get ice cream first?"

Rose nodded. "Yes, please."

My phone buzzed.

Wes

> **You okay? Evan said someone tried to abduct one of his clients.**

Me

> **I'm okay. Thanks for checking in.**

I meant it. While I was a little annoyed at how big of a deal they made over me this morning, I was also glad to have someone who cared. It had been a long time since someone had smothered me with love. The texts continued.

Wes

> **Do you need anything? Can I take you two out later? Dinner and a movie or something?**

Me

> **Dinner, a movie, and more of what we did last night sounds good to me.**

A casual date with the three of us would be nice.

"You did well back there," Jett said as we got into Evan's car, him and Evan in the front, us in the back.

"Rose, why is it your fault your mom's in jail? You went state's evidence and testified against her or something?" Riley asked.

Rose's head drooped. "She…"

"You don't have to tell me," Riley told her. "It's fine."

"It's not a secret. I'm the beta who got drugged into being an omega so I could mate with a rich pack and save our family. That's why they're mad. It's so hard to find work in our area. We're going to lose our home and have to move in with my uncle, but his family's not doing any better. I… I could help everyone by getting mated to rich alphas, but I didn't." A tear streamed down her face.

I looked at Evan. "They drug random people to change their *biology*?"

That seemed like a scientific marvel, but then they were also building quantum nano-computers here. It was also horrifying if it was against someone's will.

"Um, yeah, it's on the news sometimes." Riley's eyebrows rose.

"It's not random, Grace. Usually, betas are chosen carefully, often screened for markers, since the drugs don't work on all betas. It's also illegal to do what they did to Rose," Evan explained.

"Can't they fix it?" I frowned. "Like an antidote or something? She had no *choice*."

"There is no antidote." Evan shook his head.

"Being an omega isn't going to be that bad, Grace." Rose squeezed my hand. "Now I get some opportunities I wouldn't get otherwise. I'm going to get a great education. I can still be a doctor. One day I'll get a pack of cutie alphas who will spoil me."

"But they took away your choice. *Your mom* took away your choice." My heart broke for her.

"Take a deep breath, Peaches. It's shitty, and I know you relate. Rose's mom, and the doctor, will pay for what they did. We'll take care of Rose, too." Evan rolled the windows down as he drove.

"I'll fuck people up for both of you," Riley added.

Suddenly I wanted Wes, and I had no idea why. So, I texted him.

Me

> Miss you. Work is okay? No one got in trouble?

Wes

> I'm getting it sorted. Miss you, too. People will get in trouble, but not me.

We got ice cream and then drove to a beautiful school that looked straight out of a movie.

"Not bad," Riley nodded. "Some of my friends have siblings here."

My knees sagged as I got out of the car. I felt more emotionally spent than I wanted to admit.

Evan put his arms around me, wrapping me in one of his excellent hugs. "Rose will be okay, we'll make sure of it. Hey, you, me, and Wes are going on a date tonight."

"He told me. That'll be nice." I looked up into his face. "Spencer texted me and wanted to know if I'm going to choose my outfit for the science dinner or if I want him to pick something up."

"You're on science dinner duty? That explains spa day. He has amazing taste, so I'd say choose that if you don't have a specific outfit in mind," he told me as the others got bags out of the back.

"Okay." I texted Spencer back.

"Let's get Rose settled in. Later, we'll get you a tour. I want you to meet one of the science teachers here. She was one of my very first clients." Evan gave me a squeeze.

"Sounds good." I picked up the last bag. "Let's go decorate a dorm room."

Chapter Thirty-Seven

Wes

"Bren, we need to talk." I barged right into his room. His location had been off all yesterday and today, then it had reappeared right as I got off work, showing him home. Alone.

Really, I should go to the spa and give Grace a kiss before she went directly to the science dinner with Spencer tonight. But I had shit to deal with first.

Shit Evan needed me to handle.

Brennan was in the bathroom, in his boxers, shaving. He glared at me. "Fuck off, Wes."

"No. I should have handled this a week ago." I leaned in the doorway.

"You broke pack rules by keeping things from us. I should beat the shit out of you." Brennan glared at me as he continued to shave.

True. But...

"*You* need to work out your shit," I fired back, still angry at the harm his hardheadedness had caused Grace. "Grace joining this pack is inevitable. Unless you want me to leave and put Evan in a shitty position."

"Would you actually do that to Evan?" His voice went warning as his dominance filled the humid bathroom.

"I shouldn't have to. You're head alpha, and your being against her means something, which we saw this weekend," I snapped. I kept picturing Evan carrying her into the bedroom, so still and pale, him worried.

That scent-stripping laundry soap that Grace has used to erase herself with? *Brennan* had brought it into the house so we could get rid of her scent when she left.

"Why are you blocking the integration team from doing their job?" I added.

"We don't need therapy. Our pack doesn't need to integrate, because *we don't need Grace*." He scowled as he put down the razor.

"This is getting old, Bren. I need Evan *and* Grace." I took a step toward him. "How do we fix this? Should I challenge you like they did in the old days? Sit you and Grace down with a counselor to figure this out? Call your mom?"

"Don't you dare," he snapped, turning to face me. Leaning against the sink, his scent went spicy with anger. "It's bad enough that Grace probably tattled and Mrs. Beekman's going to remove her."

Grace didn't actually realize the implications of what had happened. I kept forgetting that she didn't comprehend so many things about this world that we took for granted. Which was half the problem.

"She didn't. Grace isn't out to ruin us, or you. She just wants to belong–and like it or not, she belongs with me and has for a long time," I implored, needing him to relent on this one thing.

"You're taking her on dates. She's getting close to Ri. Evan brought her into his nest," he retorted.

"Evan loves her, too. She's not going to take him from you. I think you'd like her. I'd forgotten that she plays the piano. Grace is becoming part of this family, and I understand this can be scary. But she's not Caroline. If you'd actually have a conversation with her, you'd figure that out. Do you know she even cleaned the piano like you asked her to?" I added.

"What are people going to think?" He scowled.

I gave him a hard look. "We don't owe them any backstory. It's legal. Evan's fine with it. There's no reason to make a big deal about it, because it's not a big deal. Give her a chance, before I'm forced to protect my mates from you."

While I hated to threaten my friend, Evan and Grace came first.

"You aren't going to take Evan from me," he growled.

"Then grow up and get your shit together so I don't have to." I stormed off and went straight to my car, hoping I could still catch Grace and Evan at the spa.

Chapter Thirty-Eight

Spencer

"Spencer, don't you need to leave soon to get Grace?" Mrs. K knocked on my open door. "You're not even dressed."

"My tux is hanging up in my closet," I told her. "I'll only need a moment." Though I did need to get going soon. "The dress was delivered, correct?"

"Yes, the dress, shoes, and jewelry were delivered to the spa where she's getting ready." She smirked. "Is this a *date?*"

I blinked. "I don't know. I haven't been on a date in a very long time."

Mrs. K chuckled and left.

I finished my email and closed my door. Getting changed in my office, I looked at myself in the mirror on my closet door. This wasn't the first time I'd gotten ready for something here.

Oh, I almost forgot. My friend who owned an upscale formal-wear shop, had picked out a tie and a pocket square for me that matched her dress. I'd also chosen her dress at lunch. I changed my tie and added the pocket square. Yes, that was it.

I checked myself again, smoothing my hair. She'd like the dress, right? He didn't have much for her height that wouldn't need hemming. Hopefully she could walk in tall heels.

Nerves coursed through me. Why was I nervous? I'd been to many of these dinners.

No. It wasn't the dinner. It was Grace.

I was anxious about spending time alone with her. I was afraid she wouldn't have fun. My good doctor was this little treasure and I wanted to show her the best of times.

It will be fine. I took a deep breath. Gathering my things, I left.

"Mrs. K, you're still here." I paused at her desk.

"Look at you." She stood. "You match her. It's a date."

"Would it be bad if it was? I don't know how she perceives this?" I frowned.

Mrs. K shook her head, smiling. "It really doesn't matter what you call it as long as you have fun. I'm just teasing."

"Good night, and thank you for all your help on this," I told her. Going down to my car, I texted Grace that I was on my way.

My hands kept shaking as I drove to the spa. I wanted to impress her. I wanted her to be so pleased with the scientific community that she would want to stay here with us.

It wasn't just worry about what could happen to her if she tried to leave, genuinely I wanted her to stay for more reasons than her departure would upset Evan.

You know what, everything would be fine. My good doctor was made for this. She would have an incredible time and meet wonderful people.

I parked at the spa next to Wes' truck. He'd come to get Evan. They were angry at Brennan and not going to the dinner. I understood their anger. The state of her room unnerved me.

Being mad at Brennan wasn't going to fix things. Making sure Grace felt comfortable here, would.

Half the problem was that Jett and Brennan didn't know her origins. But it wasn't my secret to tell and I understood why she was hesitating.

The three of them were in the sumptuous waiting room of the exclusive omega-only spa. This area was the only place alphas were allowed, and several worked on laptops, scrolled on their phones, or talked softly as they waited for their omegas to finish.

"Have fun and don't fall asleep in your soup," Wes said, laughing.

Grace giggled. "It will be fascinating."

It would be.

"Grace." I sucked in a breath at how enchanting she looked in the red dress, her wrap already on. Oh, the jewelry I'd chosen for her looked perfect.

She looked perfect.

She was perfect.

Yes, my good doctor had ensnared my heart and I was happy for it.

"Spencer." She rushed over and gave me a big hug, her peachy scent enveloping me. "We had so much fun today. Thank you."

I looked over at Evan. "You did? I'm so happy."

"This was great, Spence." Evan came over and kissed Grace. "We're going to go. Have fun."

"I will." Grace grinned. Someone had curled and fluffed her hair so it was like a halo; her nails and lipstick matched the dress.

Wes tugged her away. "One last kiss."

"See you later." She waved.

I offered her my arm and she took it.

"I'm so excited. I looked online to see who they were honoring. Oh, I really want to meet Dr. Harlowe and talk to her about her particle cutter," she told me as I helped her into my car.

"That can be arranged," I told her as I got into the driver's seat. Her being excited made me happy.

Is this a date?

I wasn't sure, but I had a feeling that it would be an amazing night.

Chapter Thirty-Nine

Brennan

"I thought Evan was coming with you," my mother commented, joining Jett and me as I brooded in the corner of the ballroom at the High Tower.

Are we done yet? I just gave her a look over my glass of bourbon.

This was one of the most boring venues ever. Sure, it had a marvelous view, but it was stuffy in here with all the people. There wasn't even a balcony.

"Evan sends his regrets," I lied. Evan was pissed at me and refused to come. He and Wes were going on a date instead.

Judging by the way he'd barged into my bathroom, Wes was angry at me, too. Jett was still a little mad, but he stood here with me, making nice with people that wouldn't care about us if we weren't rich.

Spencer had been cool to me but hadn't said anything, so I wasn't sure if he was mad or just preoccupied. With him it could be either.

Ugh. All I was trying to do was protect my pack. Users abounded in this town. Pretty much everyone at this dinner wanted something from my family. Funding. Connections. Approval. We had to be careful.

Why was everyone so mad at me for being cautious?

"Have you hired a housekeeper yet?" My mother wore a glittering emerald dress that complemented her eyes, which were as hard as the ostentatious circle of gems around her neck.

"We don't need a housekeeper," I told her through gritted teeth, raising my glass as someone I didn't recognize waved at me.

"Bren, Dependent Services specifically commented on the cleanliness of the bathrooms," she lectured, eyes narrowing, dragon claw nails tapping on her champagne glass.

"This isn't the place to discuss it." I glared, looking for a reason to get away—or for someone to refill my bourbon. I detested these, and even the recreational Jett had slipped me before the party had done *nothing* to soften the edge.

"Well, you're not answering my calls," she snapped.

"Don't feel bad, he's been ignoring me all day, too." Katie joined us, wearing a glittery pantsuit, Rami on her arm. He wore a suit with a tie and pocket square that matched her outfit.

My mother craned her jeweled neck. "Who's that with Spencer?"

Spencer, in one of his expensive, imported custom tuxes, sailed in, greeting people with his usual poise and charm. He *liked* these things. On his arm was a tiny blonde in a long, red dress. Her short hair was a fluff of curls, and she wore striking jewelry. His tie and pocket square matched her gown, which just *looked* expensive.

"Oh, just look at Grace," Katie breathed. "That dress."

People fixed their gazes on the two of them. Anger rose inside me. No one told me that Grace was coming.

"*That's* Grace. Oh my. She is such a tiny thing. Huh. I didn't realize that she was up to doing things. Is that wise?" my mother remarked.

"I'm sure Spencer will make sure she doesn't exert herself," Jett replied. "I think he brought her to network."

"Is she definitely going to work for Spencer?" Rami glanced around the room. "I might have something for her with the Space Authority. There are also some people I want her to meet."

"I'm sure she'd love to meet people," Jett told Rami.

"I'm happy she's feeling better. All of you are expected at our foundation gala—including her and the little one. But please make sure the girl is dressed appropriately, you know teenagers and their fashion choices." My mother made an exasperated face.

Riley was expected? I'd have to bribe her to go. Shit, I had to bribe *myself* to go. Why did I have to attend these?

We had to bring Grace? Shit.

"Hey, I know Evan is planning some sort of romantic date for Grace's birthday, but are you having a barbecue for her, too? Saturday was so much fun," Katie added. "You should do more of those. You have such a great backyard."

"It was fun. I enjoy talking to Grace," Rami added.

For some reason, my sister hadn't mentioned the piano incident to my mother. Which made me uneasy.

"Given Grace is better, I'll make reservations at Supressa. Or is she more of a Zano person?" My mother got out her phone.

Both were top restaurants that usually had months-long waiting lists. Unless you were my mother.

"Supressa," I said without thinking. "She's new to the city and will love the view. Wait, what? No."

Someone might take pictures. Fuck, someone might take pictures of her and Spencer tonight. They certainly looked picture-perfect together as they made the rounds.

I took out my phone and anger-texted Wes.

"Who's that with Spencer?" My father joined us. He was also an alpha, ex-professional rugby player, and businessman, who headed the foundation with help from my older brother Troy, who was busy dealing with event problems. Something about no chocolate fountain. Whatever.

"That's Wes' mate, Grace," my mother said. "She's a scientist or something."

"Mathematician," Jett corrected.

My father whistled. "She's going to class up the pack."

"Yeah, Spencer probably brought her with him so she can have some intelligent conversations after being alone with Wes all week." Katie laughed, tossing her hair over her shoulder.

"Wes is brilliant, thank you very much. Grace isn't from a society family. She's just pretty," I blurted, sick of their bullshit. Wes *could* have been an engineer, but he *chose* not to.

"Easy, Sport, we're teasing," my father admonished, smoothing his near-black hair out of his blue eyes.

I didn't like their teasing. Never had.

"Oh look, Antonio's here. I'm so glad we were able to get him. I mean, we had to fly him in from where he's filming, even so," my mother said, taking my father's arm.

The actor came in with his alphas, heads in the room riveting. Rami and Katie both gave him appreciative glances. So did Jett. He liked Antonio Caruso's movies. They weren't my favorite, but usually weren't a bad way to spend a few hours. My phone buzzed.

Wes added an emoji of the bird.

"Spencer, over here." My mother waved as Spencer and Grace walked in our direction.

My heart went to my feet, and I texted him back.

Me

Why does no one tell me anything any-more?

Wes

Maybe because we haven't had a family dinner in a while?

Point taken. That was where we updated each other.

"Siobhan, you look radiant," Spencer told her. "May I present Dr. Grace Ellington, Wes' mate. My good doctor, this is Siobhan and Frank Morris–Brennan's parents. Their foundation is sponsoring tonight's science dinner."

"It's so nice to meet you." Grace smiled and gave a little wave, clinging to Spencer's arm.

"I'm glad you're here and feeling better," my mother told her, giving her a head-to-toe once-over, passing judgment. As usual.

"Grace, you look *amazing*." Rami gave her a hug. "I've got people for you to meet."

Grace's face lit up. "I can't wait. Love the pocket square."

"You look great," Jett told her.

Grace turned to me. "Hi, Brennan."

"Grace." What did I even say to her? I could see the anxiety on her face, the burnt smell of her fear among the peaches.

At least she wasn't at our table.

Rami started talking animatedly to Grace.

Spencer came over to me. "Just give her a chance."

Without waiting for a reply, he asked my mother a question.

Spencer *was* annoyed with me. Ugh.

"Excuse us, we have some people to meet before everything starts." Spencer nodded and hauled Grace off to another part of the room.

"Wes has good taste," my father said, eyes still fixed on Grace. "Skittish though. She doesn't like crowds? Or is she still not feeling well?"

At least they took her fear as that, instead of me.

Certainly, she looked the part of a beloved omega in a wealthy pack–pampered and coiffed, bedecked with jewels. In reality, Grace was an alpha-slapping, omega-kissing, beer drinking, little troublemaker.

I never meant to hurt her. All I wanted was for her to leave us alone.

I wanted everyone to leave us alone.

Seeing her room sterile and bleached, the scent of her gone, all the things they'd bought her tucked away, shook me. It catapulted me back to everything that Evan went through with Caroline.

Hurting Grace was the last thing I wanted to do. Something about her was so... fragile, like a delicate little butterfly. But I didn't know how to stop myself.

The idea of someone new joining the pack terrified me. We'd been through so much together. How did we bring someone in after that?

But Wes didn't make idle threats. Also, the law was on his side.

While I could blame Grace all I wanted, the truth was, she wasn't the one tearing the pack apart.

I was.

My eyes followed Grace as Spencer got her a glass of champagne. She laughed at something, glowing, and accepted it, as he introduced her to someone.

She's not ready for you, Evan had told me.

The problem was, I wasn't ready for her.

Chapter Forty

Grace

"Email me and I'll give you a tour and demonstration when you come to town," Dr. Harlowe, the winner of the big science award, told me, holding up her phone.

"That sounds wonderful, thank you. Congratulations again on the award." I held up mine to receive her information. She was with PIIP, a large particle physics research organization. We had a fascinating conversation.

I went to find Spencer. The awards and dinner had finished, but dessert had yet to be served, and people mingled and danced. The food was delicious, the entire evening entertaining and joyous. Not to mention Marcos' papi, the actor, Antonio, had been the host, and led us through a luscious romp of science and whimsy. This wasn't some rubber-chicken, stuffy academic affair.

"Are you enjoying yourself, my good doctor?" Spencer stood at my elbow, a vision in a perfectly fitting tux–his tie and pocket square matching the red of my dress.

"I am. This is wonderful. Thank you for bringing me." I hummed a little. My whole day had been amazing. Wes made me breakfast. Evan and I spent the afternoon at a fancy spa. Now I was here. I felt like a princess. This dress. The shoes. The necklace.

All hail Grace, Princess of Math.

When I'd taken the long, tight, sparkly gown and matching wrap out, I'd been afraid I'd be overdressed. This was a science dinner, not prom. But I fit in perfectly.

Throughout the entire evening, Spencer had been doting and attentive, lavishing me with compliments and introducing me to so many incredible people. Not to mention hearing all the amazing things people were accomplishing across the sciences here was inspiring.

"Dr. Harlowe wants me to come visit and see her particle cutter." I grinned at the thought, hoping that one day I'd have the chance.

"I attend conferences out there, so perhaps you can accompany me. Just think, one day soon you might be speaking at conferences or at dinners like this. There are no limits as to what you can accomplish," he told me, taking my arm, like he'd been doing all night.

My breath hitched as his leather scent washed over me. If he kept saying things like that to me, I was going to accept the job at his company simply because I was going to believe that I could actually do it.

I eyed the couples on the dance floor. The dancing here wasn't what I was used to. It was a cross between ballroom and something from a Regency movie. Different songs had different dances, and everyone seemed to know them. It was exquisite to behold.

"Would you care to dance?" Spencer held out his hand.

"I... I don't know how." I shook my head.

"Follow my lead." His hand remained outstretched.

"Don't hate me if I step on your foot?" I took his hand in mine.

He led me onto the floor in the center of the sumptuously decorated ballroom. "I could never, my good doctor. It's simple counting for this one. *One-two-three-four.*"

We glided across the dance floor, turning and whirling, four-four time, and almost a fox-trot.

I stepped on his foot. My cheeks warmed. "Sorry."

"It's fine, just relax and follow me. Now, leap." He picked me up, turned, and put me down. With one of his hands lingering on my hip as the other hand took mine, we were swept back up in the movements, the music.

After a couple of passes on the floor, I'd mostly figured it out.

"You might not know it at first, but with some basic instruction you can do anything, my good doctor." He beamed as if I'd made a scientific breakthrough.

His words made me breathless. Or perhaps it was the dancing.

When the song finished, he led me over to the well-decorated and fully-appointed beverage table and got me something to drink.

"You looked like you were having fun out there." Jett joined us, getting a drink of his own. His long, dark hair was tied back, but not like he wore it when he went to work. He looked very handsome in his tux.

It had been nice spending time with him yesterday when we'd been moving Rose's things.

Antonio Caruso approached us, looking dapper in a red tux and a black pocket square. He wasn't alone, the rest of Marcos' dads were with him, including the big growly alpha—the one that looked familiar, but I couldn't quite place.

They were all dressed smartly in dark tuxes with red ties. The ex-military looking one with the beard looked like he needed some sunglasses and a big gun.

"I don't mean to be forward, but we have met, haven't we?" Antonio asked me, oozing charm, taking my fingertips and giving the back of my hand the barest of kisses like we were in an old-timey movie.

It was an odd gesture since I hadn't quite figured out handshaking in this world.

Antonio's amber eyes met mine. "I feel like I could never forget someone as breathtaking as you, Bonita. Every time I looked at your table, I nearly forgot my lines."

"We have," I replied, resisting the urge to giggle. "I'm Grace. We met at the movie theater over the weekend. I was with Marcos' friend Riley."

His alphas looked amused, like it wasn't uncommon for him to be silly like this. I motioned Brennan over. He gave me a confused look but joined us.

"Um, these are Marcos' dads," I introduced.

"Oh. It's nice to meet you. I'm Brennan Morris," Brennan said. "This is my husband, Jett Morris."

"I'm Spencer Thanukos. We're part of Riley's family," Spencer added. "Let me introduce you to the one and only Dr. Grace Ellington."

My heart skipped a beat every time he said things like that. Like I was some exceptional person and not some woman who'd barely gotten her PhD and couldn't even remember how she'd ended up in another world.

"Of course." Antonio smiled. "It is so nice to meet Riley's family. I'm Antonio, this is Carl," who was the unassuming one I'd first met as *dad*, "and my alphas, Ivan," the large military looking one, *dado*, "and Darnell," the big growly one, *pops*.

"Thank you so much for helping Marcos study for the math test," Carl added.

I'd talked to him when he'd dropped Marcos off on Saturday at Wes' party.

"Anytime. Marcos is such a wonderful young man," I told them. It had been interesting looking through their textbook.

"Would you honor me with a dance, Grace?" the growly alpha, Darnell, asked.

Was it okay to dance with some random alpha?

"Go dance with Sergeant Hawthorne, he outranks me. I'll dance with you next, promise," Jett told me, giving me a little push.

Sergeant Hawthorn. Of course. From the police station. No wonder he looked familiar. Just out of place, because he'd been in uniform, and I'd had a fresh concussion and had been trying to figure out what was going on.

He didn't touch my hand, but my wrap-covered shoulder, and we went back out to the dance floor, where he put his other hand on my hip. This was a different dance, and we were close to each other. Like before, he smelled relaxing.

"Sergeant, it's nice to see you again. Thank you, for being so kind to me at the station," I said, glad to have finally placed him.

"So, you *are* my Jane Doe. I'd been wondering. Detective Lawson said that they'd found your alpha, and your case had been moved to another detective. Which one is he? I'm guessing Fade is a nickname?" He maneuvered me through the crowd of people, a few nodding and murmuring *Sergeant,* as we whirled by.

"It is. Wes isn't here. But you met him at the theater. He and Evan, Riley's brother, are at home tonight," I replied. Sergeant Hawthorne was an excellent dancer. This was a different type of dance, more akin to a quick waltz, the steps easy to follow if I paid attention.

Sergeant Hawthorne nodded. "You're all right? You got your memories back?"

"Mostly. And I'm fine. Thank you." It was nice that he worried about me, however, his interest also made me nervous because the case was still open. The last thing I needed was for Wes to get in more trouble.

While I was still so curious about how I got to the park, I wasn't sure I wanted the police to figure that out either.

Finishing our dance, we returned to the punch table, where Antonio, Jett, and Ivan discussed boxing, and Spencer and Carl chatted about investments.

The moment they left, Brennan was at my side, expression somewhere between concern and a scowl. "What did he say to you? You had quite the conversation."

"I'm sorry, but I do believe Jett owes me a dance." Grabbing Jett's hand, I pulled him onto the floor. I was having too nice of an evening to deal with Brennan's obstinate bullshit.

Jett seamlessly maneuvered us onto the dance floor. This one was a little more complicated.

"Don't worry, I know all of these. Hazard of being Brennan's permanent date," he assured.

"Sergeant Hawthorne remembered me from when I was brought into the station. He wanted to make sure I was safe, and I assured him I was. That's all," I told Jett as we clapped hands and turned.

"He's a good guy. He was Lexi's first boss. I had no idea he was one of Marcos' dads. Thanks for updating me. Should I return you, or do you want to finish?" Jett spun me.

"We can finish, but after this, I'm going to need a break." Sweat dripped down my back. I'd kept the wrap on all night over my backless dress, to hide my scars.

When the dance finished, Jett returned me to the table. Brennan hovered, a glass in his hand, looking like he wanted to say something.

"Excuse me, I'm going to find the ladies' room." I darted out of the ballroom and down the hall. I used the restroom and took a moment to cool down.

A woman, maybe a little younger than me, was applying her lipstick. She'd been at a nearby table and had been staring at me on and off all evening.

"I don't mean to be weird, but is your dad a chemistry professor at Briar University?" she asked.

"No, he has a hardware store," I replied.

"Oh, okay. It's just that you look a lot like my favorite professor from undergrad." She smiled at me.

Well, at least he was a favorite and not the hated one who tanked everyone's grades.

"Grace, I heard back from the chapter president, and she said there was no issue with considering you for membership. Apparently, there are gammas in other chapters. I'll text you about our next meeting; at least come and check us out?" an omega who was an astrophysicist asked as she washed her hands.

"Thanks, I'd love that." I fished my lipstick out of my purse and touched it up. She and Rami belonged to a professional organization that was all omegas in the sciences. It sounded fun.

I left the bathroom and went back into the ballroom and found Spencer.

Spencer put an arm around my waist. "Shall we get dessert and sit?"

"Please." I liked that gesture as he pulled me close.

The display of desserts was resplendent, filled with flowers and all sorts of tasty morsels. Coffee and desserts in hand, we returned to our table, which was right in front; the only better table was the one with Brennan and his family.

Spencer held out my chair for me, and we sat. His manners were like something out of a fairytale.

"You're enjoying yourself?" he murmured as he took a sip of coffee. "We can leave whenever you wish. I don't want you to overexert yourself on my account."

"I'm getting a little tired, but this has been great, thank you." I tried a little dessert. No, not my style.

"The pleasure is all mine." He picked up a tiny chocolate pastry. "Here, try."

I realized he meant to feed it to me, and I opened my mouth and took a bite. Normally, I'd be embarrassed, but this dinner had shown me public affection, including feeding people bites of things, was perfectly normal here. As well as reiterating that love came in all forms.

The dark chocolate oozed over my tongue and exploded with a hint of orange. I closed my eyes and groaned. "That's amazing."

"They're one of my favorites," he told me, taking a bite of another.

A few people came and chatted with us as we finished dessert, and Brennan's mom made some closing remarks, thanking everyone for coming.

"She's quite formidable, isn't she?" I whispered to Spencer. I'd watched her all evening. Everyone deferred to her.

"She is. Brennan's unhappy when she meddles, and she's been meddling quite a bit lately," he told me.

"Because of me." My head bowed.

Spencer put a finger under my chin and lifted my head. "None of that, my good doctor. I think it's time to leave. Shall we?"

"That sounds great."

Chapter Forty-One

Grace

We said our goodbyes and took the elevator down to the garage. Spencer drove some sort of antique sedan, classy and unique.

"Do you wish to go anywhere else, or are you ready to go home?" He cracked the window.

"As much as I'd like to see how scientists afterparty here, I'm ready to go home... unless you'd like to go someplace," I added, in case he needed to appear somewhere for business.

He shook his head. "No, not tonight. But if you're hungry, I'd like to take you someplace. It's on the way."

"A snack sounds great, thanks," I told him, relaxing into the seat as the car filled with his leather scent, soft music playing.

"How are you settling in? You seemed to be having fun."

"I am. But I'm worried about the temporal police." The thought that I'd done something wrong and they would haul me off terrified me.

"Don't. If they show up, there's nothing we can do. I hope they don't. I... perhaps I shouldn't have told you, but I want to be honest with you." Pain leaked into his voice.

"Thank you. I appreciate it. It's all just a lot." Everything was overwhelming, and even though I'd had fun, tonight only cemented that this was not my world.

"I'm here. So are Wes and Evan. Talk to us, because I don't think we truly understand how everything is different for you. We won't judge you, and I'll attempt to be more cognizant. You're doing fine," he reassured. "Also, gammas are known for being a little unpredictable."

"Okay. But that all means nothing to me." I made a face.

"What do you mean?" He sucked in a breath. "Do they not have gammas in your world? Perhaps they're called something different?"

I shook my head. "We don't have designations at all. No packs or knots or scents or soulmates either."

"You live in a world without designations," he breathed. "That must be an adjustment. I... I don't know much about other worlds, just that they exist."

"It's all the social cues. It's not knowing the references or expectations. People hear *gamma* and have assumptions. To me, it's just a letter in the Greek alphabet," I replied.

"Oh, I see. Culture shock at its finest."

I nodded. "Exactly. When I'm at home with Wes, it's fine. But when I go out in public, I'm terrified. Not to mention, I don't know all the acronyms. If I take the job at your company, I'm going to have to study up."

His hand was very close to my knee. "Of course, I should have thought of that. I'll prepare some information. I want you to feel comfortable, especially if you decide to make your home here permanently."

"I think I will." I gazed out the window at a train speeding past. Public transportation was so much better here.

"I'm so very glad."

"Can you explain why no one shakes my hand?" I'd wondered about that.

"Omegas rarely shake hands, because of scent transfer. While you don't smell exactly like an omega, you do smell like you have a mate, and they're going to extend that courtesy to you, unless you offer," he told me.

"I see." Maybe?

"The sergeant asking you to dance, that could be a little forward, considering you don't know him well, but I am assuming it was police business?" he added as we drove.

I nodded. "He was at the station I was brought into and wanted to make sure I was okay. What about Antonio?"

Spencer laughed. "The actor? He is perceived as being very much the charming, omega flirt and plays that role quite well."

"Ah, I see."

"If you have questions, please, ask me. When Evan told me a little about you, he didn't mention that your world came without designations. It's very curious. Perhaps you have them and just do not label them?" he asked.

"Magic dicks are not a thing where I live, and no one smells so good." I relaxed into my seat, enjoying the way the car smelled.

"I see. Evan told me that you and Wes met in your dreams. While the mind is extraordinary, that seems like a feat, bedtime stories of dream-traveling soulmates aside," he added.

"Bedtime stories of dream-traveling soulmates?" I should look those up. Sometimes I still wondered how Wes and I managed to find each other in the first place. It really wasn't the wedding cake under my pillow.

"My mother used to tell me tales like that. Supposedly, some-times scent matches, soulmates, dream of each other," he told me. "There are several famous romantic books and movies based on the premise. Usually they're not from other worlds."

I sucked in a breath. "Oh. We... we are. I mean, it seems like a cosmic joke to have your soulmate be from another world. Yet here I am? This really is something."

"But you found him. You found him, and you have him. He loves you–and you love him. I know you're afraid, but you have been given a greater gift than you know." A haunted look danced in his eyes.

"You're right." Oh. I bit back the questions. Like *Who were they* and *What happened to them?* The look on his face said that once, he'd loved someone very much.

And lost them.

We pulled into what looked like a drive-in restaurant, bright and colorful, filled with cars and a lot of teenagers. The car settled into a spot, and a girl in fishnets roller-skated up to us.

"Can I take your order?" she asked, snapping her gum.

"Two orders of potato balls, one of each sauce, a lemon-lime soda, and... Grace, what would you like to drink?" he asked me.

I looked at the lit-up menu. "A chocolate whirl?"

Whatever that was. Half the fun of this world was ordering things and seeing if I liked them.

"Perfect." She took his payment and skated off.

I looked around at the servers and the ambiance. This was not where I'd expected him to take me. Besides the car spots, there were tables and benches, filled mostly with teenagers and young couples.

"The best fried potato balls anywhere," Spencer told me.

He pushed a button on the menu, and a small shelf appeared, which he extended through his open car window, pushing his seat back so there was a little table.

"My father used to take me to one of these, back where I grew up in Greece," he told me. "Usually as payment for helping him with something at work."

"I used to love helping my dad in the hardware store." I squeezed his hand.

She brought our food, and Spencer set out the potato balls and all the sauces. I took a sip of my drink. A chocolate whirl tasted like a cross between a milkshake and a slushie.

"Now, taste." He held out a little deep-fried ball.

Closing my eyes, I let him feed me. It was like mashed potatoes in a fried, seasoned coating. "Delicious."

He dipped one in a green sauce. "Try."

We tried all the sauces, as he told me about Evan when he was younger.

"Evan teased Wes about Mr. Hippo, but he had an entire collection of stuffed animal keychains?" I laughed as we finished up and disposed of our garbage.

"That he got out of children's meals. He was obsessed." Spencer laughed as we drove away. "Wes is a good man, and I'm glad he makes you happy. Evan as well. I know it must be so hard for you—and a little scary—to start over completely, but we'll make it work. After meeting so many people and learning more about what projects exist here, do you think you'd like to work for me? Or is Rami going to steal you away?"

Working for the Space Authority was tempting.

"I want to work with you. Honestly, I'd be honored to work for a company doing so much good. But I'm a little unsure what someone like me could contribute. I feel like my PhD doesn't mean the same thing here." I took a sip of my chocolate whirl.

"Grace, if you don't want to work for me because you're not interested, that's fine. But don't do it because you don't think you're good enough. It's an insult to us both." His voice was low and a little growly. "What information do you need to make an informed choice? I'll share *everything* with you."

"What other details could you share about the simulator? I actually find that the most fascinating." The way he said it made my stomach flutter a little—or it could be the deep-fried carbs I'd just ingested.

He gave me a look. "I told you, I'll share everything."

That was almost a purr, and I melted into my seat.

"But you had fun, made connections?" he added. "Everyone seemed delighted with you."

"There would be no harm in joining that omega science organization, right?" It seemed like a good place to make friends and learn more about the science in this world.

"The Daedalus Society? Not at all. Go and make friends, explore, learn. There's a big world out there for you to discover, and I can't wait to see what you think of it. Did you and Evan have a nice time today?"

"The best, thank you for that. I think Evan needed it after everything that's been happening with one of his clients." I felt so bad for Rose. Maybe I should bake her something.

But the spa... it was some sort of omega-only posh paradise. Probably exclusive and stupidly expensive. I'd never experienced anything like it, and would go again in a second.

"The dress; where do I have it cleaned and who do I give it back to? Thank you again, it's beautiful." I readjusted the wrap.

"It's for you to keep. The shoes and jewelry as well. But you kept your wrap on all night, do you not like backless dresses? I should have gotten your preferences."

"I... I have scars on my back, they make people uncomfortable."
I let the wrap down.

He gasped. "I see. Car accident?"

His knuckles tightened on the steering wheel. Spencer's scent
was thick and suffocating, and the windows had been closed since
the drive-through. But I didn't want to open them.

I wanted to drown in it.

"No." I shook my head. "Keep the dress? Spencer, it's too much,
I..." My chest shook a little. He was always so kind to me. Why was
he doing this, other than that Evan cared for me and he cared for
Evan?

"Breathe, my good doctor." His voice went rumbly, setting me
at ease. "In this family, nice clothes to attend functions aren't gifts,
they're necessities. As for the jewelry, I admit, I went overboard,
and didn't truly take your tastes into account. I just saw it and
knew it would look amazing on you."

The necklace was dainty compared to what Brennan's mom was
wearing. It was diamonds and rubies, and the largest part rested
right across my cleavage. The dangly earrings were long and big.
But then none of these were daily wear.

"I love the jewelry. I've never had anything this nice." My voice
went small. It had been a long time since I'd had nice things. I'd
just been trying to get by.

Even when I had, it wasn't like this. My family had been fine, but
not rich by any means–especially with four kids.

"You deserve nice things, my good doctor. In the future, I'll try
to tailor them more to your liking. I do hope that you'll allow for
the occasional item that's flashy. Some of the events that we attend
aren't understated." He smiled as we turned into their neighborhood.

I put my hand on the necklace. He wanted to get me more?

"Too much, too soon?" His voice went rumbly again. "Wes calls me a show-off. But please, let me do this. Wes, Evan, and I all have different ideas of how to spoil you—and you need and deserve all of them."

I kind of enjoyed being spoiled. It wasn't even about the material things. It was the attention. The care. Like Wes getting Mr. Hippo for me. Or taking me to the paddle boats. Evan making sure my favorite ice cream was always in the freezer.

Maybe Spencer didn't ask about my dress preferences, but it was perfect. The only issue was that the shoes were a little uncomfortable, but they *were* stilettos and probably chosen so the dress didn't need to be hemmed. He'd also thought of everything today, even the hair, nails, and makeup.

There were also the little courtesies I got from all of them. Praise, kind words, tasty food. Granted, lap sitting and being fed could get annoying, but it was also nice because that meant I had someone to be annoyed with. That I wasn't lonely and eating ramen out of a mug at ten o'clock at night with only a plant for company.

"Okay." My voice went quiet. "I don't mind bling; I'm just not used to it. But why?" I wasn't even part of their pack.

"Oh, my good doctor, the fact you ask breaks my heart," he said as we pulled into the garage.

My shoulders rounded. "Sorry."

He parked the car and put my chin in his hand and his eyes met mine. "Don't be."

Spencer got out and helped me out of the car, like I was a princess. We went inside, him opening the door for me.

"I do hope you'll accompany me to more of these," he said as we went up the backstairs. "There's so much I attend alone. It would be nice to have someone to talk to about all the projects and technologies."

"That sounds fun. I want to learn everything. It was an incredible experience." Spend more time with him, and meet more scientists? *Yes, please.*

"I can't wait." Spencer brushed my hair with his hand as we stood in front of the piano.

"Grace." Wes, in only a pair of shorts, came barreling down the main stairs and picked me up, twirling me, making me laugh. "How many people fell asleep?" He pretended to nod off.

"It was a very fascinating and festive affair," Spencer told him.

Evan joined us, also only in shorts, smelling of Wes, curry, and sex. He gave me a giant hug, and I rested my head on his shoulder, my arm around Wes' waist.

Wes' fingers traced my necklace and then looked at Spencer. "Are you making a move?"

"When I make a move, you'll know. Tonight was for science." Spencer's eyes danced. They were so beautiful, the brown irises shot with grey.

Taking my hand, Spencer kissed the back of it, his lips soft. He looked up at me, his look growing coy. "Thank you. I can't wait to do this again. Good night, my good doctor. You're a delight."

With a nod, he disappeared into his room and closed the door.

"I'm confused." Frowning, I leaned into my men, not knowing how to feel as so many different emotions bombarded me at once.

"I'm pretty sure he means to court you at some point," Wes said, picking me up, and carrying me up the stairs, princess-style, Evan behind him.

"What does that even mean?" I leaned my head on his shoulder.

Wes put me on the couch in the sunken living room, sitting on one side, Evan jumping to join us, and me in the middle. It wasn't as wide as the one in the downstairs living room, but was deep and comfy.

While I had an armchair, it seemed like I always ended up on the couch with them.

"At some point he might want to be your alpha, too," Evan said.

"Wait, what?" I chewed on my lower lip. He *was* sexy and polite...

Wes planted a kiss on my temple. "Only if you want. He'll back off if you aren't into it–and don't worry about it affecting your job. He's not like that. I'm happy to run interference when and if you're ready."

"That would be okay, for him to be my alpha, too?" I curled into them the best I could in the dress. Part of me was here for it. Go to all the science dinners and conferences.

I was still trying to figure things out with Wes and Evan–and understand this world.

"Only if *you* want. As long as being with him doesn't mean you don't want to be with us, I don't have an issue with it. Spencer's a good man," Wes told me.

"You're not ready yet. Soon, but not yet. You're great for each other. The things you'd do with him differ from what you'd do with us," Evan added, arm around me.

I could see that. "He said all three of you had different ideas of how to spoil me, and I deserved all of them."

"You do." Wes played with my hair. "That necklace simply can't compete with Mr. Hippo, though."

"Nothing can compete with Mr. Hippo. So, it's not weird?" No, I wasn't quite ready for Spencer. But I wasn't against the idea.

"Not at all. The dinner tonight was fun?" Wes asked. "Spence will ask you to do more things, and if you don't like them, tell him so he won't."

"I had fun. I like it here. But I'm still afraid everything will come crashing down. I mean, I even have a fake designation." I sighed, my shoulders rounding with the weight of everything.

"Peaches, we talked about this. Yes, I guessed–and was right. As far as all the tests the doctors have run on you, you're a gamma. Considering everything, especially with what Wes told you about you always being his omega, it makes sense." Evan snuggled me. "Something in your world kept you from being the omega you were meant to be."

"Probably because there are none there. This world is weird." It was hard to admit to myself that I fit as well as I did here.

"But it has us in it." Wes leaned over and kissed me, hand caressing my thigh through the dress' slit.

Brennan came up the stairs, still in his suit. "Evan, I'm home."

"Over here," Evan called.

"Hey." Brennan's face lit up as soon as he saw Evan.

"Hey." Evan's look softened, but he didn't get up off the couch.

"Oh." Brennan looked at Wes and me, face falling.

"He didn't look like he had fun tonight and probably needs a cuddle. I won't be jealous, promise," I whispered, giving Evan's ear a nibble. "Go make up with him."

I knew they were fighting. Because of me.

"If you insist." Evan kissed my cheek. "Fuck her good for me, Wes." He got off the couch.

Wes picked me up, throwing me over his shoulder in a firefighter carry as Evan went over to Brennan.

"Hey, what are you doing?" I laughed as Wes left the sunken living room.

"As beautiful as this dress is on you, I'd like to see what it looks like on my floor." Wes waved. "Night, everyone."

Chapter Forty-Two

Evan

"Hey, Love." Brennan stood close, his pine scent intensifying, jacket off, shirt partially unbuttoned, tie sticking out of his pocket.

But he didn't touch me. I could feel the anguish, the remorse, rolling off the bond.

"I'm still mad at you." Trying to make a mad face, I poked him in the chest, resisting the urge to fall into his arms, and forgive him with no discussion.

A pained look crossed his face. "Please don't be. I'm sorry. I was a huge asshole to you and Grace. This is hard for me. But, I should handle my shit and not take it out on others. I called my therapist."

"Good. I've been texting mine. Obviously both of us still have issues to work through," I said, proud that he'd done it.

"I..." He took a deep breath. "I'll stop blocking the integration team. I didn't want her to integrate, so I didn't see a point in cooperating. But also, I never meant to hurt anyone. I was sort of hoping that if I ignored her, she'd remember her life and go back to where she came from."

I took a step forward, so we were almost touching. "I know. But people still got hurt."

It was hard to get the image of her huddled under the bed out of my head.

"Please, get things going. Our file was flagged because you're dragging your feet, and we don't need that," I told him.

"I know." His head bowed. "How much is her spiral going to affect the case?"

"She never mentioned it when I had her checked out at the clinic yesterday. Grace wasn't raised thinking that she was an omega—or even really knew that she was a gamma—so she doesn't understand a lot of things. But I'm sure the doctor figured out something is up from her hormone levels," I replied.

He rubbed his clean-shaven chin. "That's bad."

"Yep. Look, she loves Wes, and the best place for her is with him, which means she's stuck with *us*. We need to create a space for her in this pack," I admonished, hoping he and I would finally get to a place of understanding.

He took my hands in his, heat spreading through me at the contact. "I'm sorry. I don't want to tear apart the pack. I don't want to lose you. The last thing I'd ever want to do is put you in a place where you have to choose between me and Wes."

"I really don't want to do that." Because I loved them both.

"I'm unsure about this—bringing someone new into the pack. I don't know Grace at all. She's this little wispy, capricious, force of nature, and the unpredictability terrifies me." He exhaled sharply and tipped his forehead to mine, still holding my hands.

"I hear you. Change is scary." That was quite an admission on his part.

"There's also... I can't help but feel like there's something still off about Grace." His brow furrowed.

"Grace's story is complicated, and I'm sure she'll share it with everyone in time," I replied. "She and Wes still have a lot to work out." At some point, we'd have to explain everything to everyone if we were going to make this work.

"What if we bring her in, accept her, and eventually she leaves because they're irreconcilable?" Brennan pushed. "Mates still have issues. Being soulmates doesn't automatically mean a relationship will work."

"Cynical much, Bren?" My eyebrows rose.

But he had a point. Relationships were work. A bite and a bond weren't the magic fix many thought it was.

"You're right, opening your heart to love also means opening your heart to heartbreak," I added.

"I don't want her to break your heart," he murmured.

So much came through the bond—like worry.

Putting my head on his shoulder, I brought our bodies together, wrapping my arms around him, the fabric of his shirt soft against my bare chest. "I don't want her to break my heart either, but that doesn't mean I'm not going to love her. I'm not going to stop loving you. Sure, I enjoy doing things with her—going to the spa was fun. But I'm not going to stop spending time with you and Jett. Promise."

He buried his face in my hair. "I'm going to hold you to that."

"Please do. I don't want to slight anyone inadvertently."

"I missed you tonight." His erection pressed into my leg, his hands running down my bare back.

I looked up so our faces touched, breathless as his alpha pheromones put my cock on high alert. "The night's not over yet."

"We're good?" He pressed his body into me, his hands resting on my ass, as he nibbled on my ear.

"We're good, just try, please. Also, let her know you don't hate her?" My eyes closed, and I ground into him, my need increasing.

He trailed kisses down my neck, his arousal intensifying. "Fine. Now, what do you need?"

Desire consumed me. "You, Alpha. I need you."

He took my hand. "I need you, too. Let's go to bed."

Chapter Forty-Three

Grace

Opening the oven, I checked the cookies. Today was the first day I'd been home alone all day.

It had been nice to have some time to myself. Evan had asked me to watch a bunch of videos and Spencer sent me project information to read over. I'd checked in with Mrs. Beekman, did my assignment for Luc the integration counselor, and then Jett had texted asking me if I'd bake the chocolate crinkle cookies he liked so much.

Still, I'd taken a bubble bath, eaten the takeout Wes had delivered to me as a treat, read one of this world's romance novels while in the window seat, listened to music, and played the piano.

So nice.

The door to the garage opened. A moment later, Jett came into the kitchen, carrying bags of groceries.

"Need me to get the rest from the car?" I asked as I removed the tray of cookies from the oven.

"No, this is it." He set the bags on the counter and looked at what I was doing. "Ooh, cookies?"

"As requested. I'll put the cookies on the racks to cool in a moment. Is the kitchen table a good place?" I had towels and cookie racks all set up.

"Yeah, that's good. If there are any missing, it wasn't me." He laughed as he started taking things out of the bag.

"What cookies? Never saw any," I joked back. "Need help cooking?" It was nice that a lot of the main things in this world were mostly the same, like food, clothes, languages, and traffic lights.

"Bren's my sous chef, but if you could get the dining room table set? It might need to be cleaned off because Ri likes to use it for projects for her art class." Jett got things down from the cupboard.

"Sure. How many for dinner?" I hadn't eaten in the dining room, just in the kitchen or living room.

"Seven. Use the blue plates in the hutch in the dining room and the crystal glasses, but the silverware from here is fine."

Nodding, I got to work. It was a beautiful space that had big open doorways to the living room and the kitchen, with a glittering chandelier poised over an elegant glass-topped table. There were only six chairs. I'd have to find another.

After putting the cookies on racks to cool, I carefully cleaned off all the paints and brushes from the table. Then I found what he asked for in the hutch, along with placemats, napkins, and even napkin holders along with candlesticks. A lot of the things looked brand new.

Delicious smells filled the air, and the murmur of voices drifted in from the kitchen.

Brennan walked into the dining room, holding a chair. He froze when he saw me. "Um, here. We need one more chair."

"Thanks." I folded a napkin to look like a bird and put it on the plate.

"It looks nice. Where did the placemats come from?" He studied my table setting.

"The hutch. I hope it was okay to use them." My belly twitched a little.

"It's fine. They're probably wedding presents we never used and just shoved in there." He placed the chair and stared at me. "I... I'm sorry for getting mad at you. You're right. It wasn't about the piano. I really don't mean to be a dick, Grace. I... I'm just trying to be cautious. Bringing someone into our home, our pack, is a big deal."

Sure, guys like him didn't mean to be dicks, yet they still were. But he had made up with Evan. Also, he had a point–I was living in their house. I was a stranger.

And he'd said he was sorry.

"I'm glad Evan and the guys mean so much to you. It's understandable. You don't know me. But I'm not after your money or power. Promise. I'm totally after Wes, but that's because of his magic dick." My cheeks burned. "I can't believe I said that. Sorry, I've been hanging around Evan too much."

A smile twitched on his lips. "Magic dick?"

"Knots are magic." I shrugged, busying myself with the napkins.

He chuckled. "I see. Um, I suppose you can play the piano."

"Thank you." I folded another. "Back in high school, I used to compete. I know how to treat a nice piano. Promise."

"Oh, did you want to be a pianist?" His look went thoughtful.

I shook my head. "Not really. But I did want to keep my mother happy. I enjoyed it, and I still do, but back in high school that was a driving force. That and stress relief."

"I get that. Um, I should go check the food." He left.

That done, I went upstairs and put on something nicer than Wes' clothes. When I came back down, Riley was in the dining room.

"That's where you sit." Riley pointed to a chair on the far side of the table.

Evan came up behind me and kissed my neck, sending little shivers through me. I tipped my head up. We'd taken a bath together after everyone left, before he went to work. It was fun.

"Finally. Dinner is ready, you assholes," Brennan said to someone in the kitchen.

"You made me dinner? Wow, you do love me," Wes joked.

"Go pour the wine." Brennan sighed.

Wes came in, holding a bottle of wine. He grinned as he looked around the room. "The fam's all here."

"Fuck yeah. Family dinner night." Riley grinned back.

Wes gave Evan and me each a kiss, and Riley a hug, then poured the wine. Brennan and Jett put dishes of delicious-looking food on the table. Spencer came in with serving utensils.

We all sat down, me taking the spot Riley indicated. Brennan was at one end, Jett on one side, Evan on the other. Spencer sat at the far end, with Riley on one side, me on the other. Wes sat in between me and Evan.

They passed around plates of food. There were roasted vegetables, rice, and some sort of tasty marinated steak.

"First order of business, last night's gala queen is Grace. Congrats." Brennan raised his glass to me.

"I think Grace is always going to be gala queen," Jett laughed. "Please, take the honor."

"What does that even mean?" I asked. Everyone was laughing, so it couldn't be too bad.

"The title of gala queen is awarded to whoever in the pack gets the most pictures or mentions after we attend a party. It's a good thing, as long as it's not Bren, he gets grumpy." Evan grinned as he cut his steak.

"I don't like being the center of attention," Brennan muttered, taking a bite of vegetables.

"There are pictures of me?" Horror coated me. I didn't like being photographed.

Brennan's eyebrows rose. "Of course there were. You went with Spence and wore a dress that's now going to be copied."

"Oh." My shoulders drooped. "Sorry."

"Brennan, stop," Spencer scolded. "My good doctor, you did nothing wrong. But yes, if you accompany us to events, you will be photographed. It's a game we play. Usually, I'm the gala queen. There's nothing wrong with being chosen. It's all in good fun."

"Sorry, I... I guess I assumed you were used to things like this." Brennan focused on cutting his meat.

"Speaking of dresses." Brennan took a gulp of wine. "The queen mum is demanding that the entire pack come to the foundation gala. This includes Ri and Grace, and she's reiterated that everyone needs to be dressed appropriately. Evan, can you make sure they have the right clothes?"

"Are you shitting my dick? I didn't sign up for that." Riley made a face.

"I know. I'm so sorry. It's a school night, so I'll pay you double the chore rate with a tip for good behavior. One person of your choosing can leave early to take you back to school. Sounds good?" His look went pleading. "You also get an outfit."

Riley made a show of pondering it. "I guess. We can't exactly not go if your mom has summoned us. Does Grace get paid?"

"No. Grace is Wes' mate. All she gets is an outfit and whatever reward Wes chooses to give her for good behavior." Brennan grinned at Wes.

Wes flipped him off and then kissed me.

What had gotten into Brennan? His behavior was completely opposite from how he'd been the past two weeks. Was this what he was usually like? If so, I could see why Evan and Jett were so into him.

What made him change?

"It will be fine, Ri. I'll dance with you," Spencer offered. "Any other edicts from the queen mum?"

Brennan sighed. "Apparently Dependent Services commented on our bathroom cleanliness. My mother has gotten us a housekeeper. I'm so sorry. She'll be here two days a week. I'm making a list of all the areas we don't want her to clean. Please let me know whether you want her to clean your bathroom."

"Bren, if you're truly unhappy with this, tell your mother *no,*" Jett said. "While I understand her wanting us all at the gala, this isn't her home. We're not her pack. She can't dictate our lives. We'll back you."

I'm glad someone said it.

"It seems weird to fight about someone cleaning the house," he said, focusing on his plate. "I guess we give it a shot, and if it doesn't work for us, we'll stop. It's not like we haven't discussed hiring someone before."

Evan squeezed his shoulder. "That sounds reasonable."

"Oh, Evan, I'm so sorry, but she's derailed your birthday plans for Grace and has made us a reservation at Supressa for Friday." Brennan looked defeated.

Evan paused, fork in the air. "Supressa. Your mother is demanding that we eat at Supressa? I'm okay with edicts like that."

"That's the rotating one, right? I get to come, don't I? I like to eat food," Riley said. "The school dance is Saturday, so I'm available on Friday."

"Yes. While I won't dictate your wardrobe for a birthday dinner, you might want to glance over the dress code so that they let you in," Brennan said. "Grace, I know you were looking forward to a romantic date, but I think you'll like it. The view is spectacular, and Supressa is known for their decor. It's at the top of the hotel the science dinner was at."

Riley grinned at me. "Each Supressa is decorated differently. At my school, eating there is a thing, and people compare which ones they've been to. The one in New York is *fairy* themed. The one here is themed like a European bistro, with trees and fountains and lots of lights. It also *rotates,* and you can see the city. I can't wait. This will be fun."

Jett nodded. "There's one in the Bay Area themed like a Greek temple."

"It sounds amazing," I agreed. A rotating restaurant? That sounded fun.

"We're good company, promise," Spencer added. "They also have delicious mashed potatoes."

Evan nodded. "I can work with that. Don't worry, Peaches, I have a whole romantic weekend planned, and a change in dinner plans isn't disastrous."

"You do?" My heart fluttered. I knew they were planning something. But I hadn't realized that it was more than dinner.

"We'll make it special, even if we're forced to eat at Supressa." Evan laughed.

"I suppose." I actually didn't mind a change in plans, or not picking where I ate on my birthday, or that we were being made to go by Brennan's mom, as long as the food was good and the company decent.

"Last thing. If a guy named Luc from the integration team at the Omega Center calls you, I'd appreciate your cooperation," Brennan added. "Just like I appreciate everyone's cooperation with Mrs. Beekman and Dependent Services. Thank you."

Riley raised her hand. "Is this a paid opportunity?"

"You get paid in ice cream and pizza." Brennan took another sip. Her head lolled back and forth. "Fair."

"How was everyone's day?" Brennan asked, and we went around the table. Spencer and Wes talked about work, and Riley had gotten an *A* on her math test.

"I made cookies for dessert," I offered, wanting to contribute.

"I can't wait," Jett told me, eyes gleaming. "There are none missing, promise. Certainly, I'm not taking any to work."

Riley snorted.

"Please, take some to work," I laughed. "Did anyone get in trouble?" I added.

Riley froze.

"Grace means it figuratively," Wes told her. "It's how she always got answers out of me when we were kids."

Riley relaxed. "Oh, okay. I didn't get detention, but once again, my art teacher failed to understand my artistic brilliance. Kilroy got detention, though."

"Doesn't Kilroy always get detention?" Evan laughed.

"I didn't get in trouble, but my job is sort of the opposite," Jett laughed. "I get paid to get people in trouble."

"I did not get in trouble today nor did anyone make my shit list. Does anyone have anything going on in the next few weeks? Besides the gala and Grace's birthday?" Brennan asked. "I have a quick business trip, but I'll be back late Thursday night. It is calendared. Everyone *please* remember to calendar everything."

"Grace is mine for the weekend. I'm letting Wes come with us," Evan said.

"Good, because Bren's mine. I'm making him go with me to the boxing tournament," Jett teased.

I sat back, watching the byplay.

"On Saturday, I have the school dance. I also have a skate smash clinic," Riley added. "Is the gala anywhere good?"

"No. It's at the Gladiola." Brennan made a face. "My brother always chooses the same three places for all the foundation functions."

Brennan had a *brother?*

"This is why you should buy that venue. Same party, different place," Evan joked.

"I'm running the numbers. While I think people will drive that far for weekend affairs, I don't know about things during the week, which is when most galas and dinners are held," he replied.

"I'm sure you'll figure something out," Evan told him.

"I've got a bunch of meetings this week and next, but I will be where you need me to be when you need me to be there." Spencer patted his lips with the cloth napkin. "Jett, dinner was delicious."

"All I have is a doctor's appointment, where I can hopefully get rid of this," I held up my wrist. "Well, and the billion videos Evan's assigned to me." I grinned at him. There were hours and hours of them.

"Hey, watch the videos or I'm hauling your ass to work with me and making you take actual classes," Evan teased back.

We finished dinner and had coffee and cookies in the living room.

"Those were so good," Jett told me, as he turned on some music.

Riley made a face. "Do we have to practice dancing?"

Jett moved the coffee table and shook his head. "You? No. Grace? Yes."

"Please?" If we were going to elegant dinners, I should learn this world's fancy dancing.

Brennan looked at Jett as he cleared off the cups and plates from the table Jett had just moved. "Teach her the one Rami always makes us do."

"Okay, we'll start with that. There are a few songs that you can do this dance to, but this is the one Rami always wants." He changed the music on the sound system.

Jett took my hand and led me through the dance, breaking it down. It wasn't that difficult, just unfamiliar. Ri followed along, Spencer acting as her partner. Evan and Wes sat on the couch snuggling.

"You know, you could practice, too." Jett rolled his eyes at them as he restarted the music.

"I'm enjoying the view." Wes shrugged.

We ran through the dance a few more times and then a few others, including the one I'd danced with him at the science dinner. Jett was a kind and patient partner, taking care to explain the steps to me. I still wasn't precisely sure what he smelled like, but it smelled nice. He was also good looking and while I did like my tall guys, Jett was a little more of a comfortable height to dance.

Riley was having fun, and Spencer... Mmmm, he was nice to watch. Wes had disappeared. Evan sat there, texting.

"See, you're getting it. They're not that hard," Jett told me.

"Thanks. You're an excellent teacher," I replied.

"This is fun, but I should do homework." Riley looked at Jett. "Will you take me back to school on your motorcycle?"

"My motorcycle? Not my convertible? You're trying to make someone jealous or something?" Jett laughed, pausing the music.

Riley blinked innocently. "What, me?"

Jett looked at Evan. "Is that okay?"

"It's fine. I have drama to solve anyway," Evan replied, still texting.

Riley gave her brother a kiss on the cheek and hugged Spencer, then me, and scampered off.

Spencer looked at me and offered a hand. "Partner change, my good doctor? Just one more. We haven't done my favorite yet."

"Of course." I put my hand in his and felt a little... giddy. Which was silly. But, something about him did it for me, and if in this world I could catch them all...

He changed the music, and then we set off, twirling around the living room floor. No breakdown, just him whispering the steps to me as we moved in three-four time. This was harder than the ones I'd done with Jett, and much more like something out of a Regency movie than the others.

"That's it, you're doing great, my good doctor," he cooed, as we repeated the pattern, my shorter legs trying to keep up.

I gulped at his praise because the way he said it made me believe that I could. Or it could be that his oiled leather scent got stronger with exertion, and that hand on my back...

Down, girl.

But we were only dancing.

Of course, in Regency movies that was where the magic happened.

Evan grinned as Spencer and I made another lap around the room. I ducked my head. *Caught.*

"You are doing so well," Spencer praised as we kept moving. "Last time. You are the most perfect partner, Grace."

"Perfect, hardly." I looked up into his eyes. Something between us sizzled as he picked me up by the waist and spun me around, which was possibly my favorite part of the dance.

Oh boy.

Spencer flashed me a knowing grin, setting me down and not missing a beat. We finished the dance, and he bowed. "Thank you, my good doctor. We'll do this again soon?"

"Please?" I was a bit breathless since this dance practice was the most cardio I'd done since I'd gotten here.

His hand smoothed my hair, his thumb lingering on my face as his eyes met mine. "Oh, I'd love that so much."

For a moment, all thoughts left me.

Spencer kissed the top of my head. "Good night, Grace. Good night, Evan and Wes."

Turning off the music, he left the room.

"He has it so fucking bad." Wes laughed as he picked me up and spun me around.

"It's so funny seeing him down bad for our girl." Evan held out his arms.

Wes tossed me into Evan's arms, and then jumped onto the couch with us, making a big cuddle party.

"Is that okay?" I bit my lower lip as I looked at Wes.

"Of course. I mean, it's Spence." Wes shrugged.

"Mmmm, that's what I need." Evan snuggled into us.

"Will you be seeing Rose tomorrow? I have some cookies for her." I leaned my head on his shoulder.

"That's nice of you. I'm going to see her tomorrow. Her first day at her new school went okay," Evan told me.

"I really feel for her. What happened to her sister?" I curled up on their laps.

"Someone undid the compulsion, and they sent her home. Charges weren't pressed. I'm a little worried about the uncle, but Iris isn't my client, Rose is. This job's hard sometimes." He sighed as he played with my hair.

"Yeah, math doesn't make you cry. Well, sometimes it does, like when you accidentally ruin your friend's research, so you stay late for weeks trying to fix it so they'll stop being pissed at you." I frowned. There was something there, but that memory bubble just wouldn't pop.

"Watch the videos. They're going to help you understand," Evan told me. "I'm trying to make things easier for you, not harder."

"I know. I started Module One. While I'm feeling better, I just can't concentrate for more than an hour." Some of the modules did look interesting.

"Take your time. You're fine."

I nodded. "I also have to finish deciding whether I want to work for Spence. Though I'm not ready to go back to work."

"Work for Spence. That means you get to ride with Wes to and from work–and you have a lunch buddy," he said.

That sounded like a nice perk.

"What got into Brennan? Tonight was... nice," I said softly.

"That's what he's usually like, well, with us. I'm glad he's coming around," Wes pointed out.

"Yeah, he's an asshole, but he's our asshole," Evan added.

"This... this is sort of what I always imagined being an adult would be like." I looked into Wes' eyes.

"We're adults, and this is your life now." Wes kissed me. "Yours, too." He kissed Evan.

This was my life now. That made me so happy.

Chapter Forty-Four

Grace

I woke up with a gasp. Not from a nightmare, like I had sometimes, but from pleasure shooting through me. Someone was licking me, down there, as I slept.

Pulling up the blanket, I saw Wes, under the covers, hands on my thighs, eating me with abandon.

He looked up, face glistening. "Happy birthday, Peaches. Come for me? Breakfast should be soon."

"Ooh, I like this birthday wake-up." I groaned as he flicked my clit with his tongue.

Tangling my hands in his messy hair, I lifted my hips to help get that clever mouth in just the right spot as he brought me closer to my peak.

Two fingers slipped inside and started working me as pleasure built inside.

"Yes, right there, yes," I cried.

His tongue kept moving along my clit, and his fingers pumped faster as an orgasm exploded through my body.

"Wes." I sighed, trying to pull him up onto me. "That was amazing."

Wes grinned up at me, boyishly, head on my bare stomach. "I wrote happy birthday to you with my tongue over and over again."

Well then. *Happy birthday to me.*

"Happy birthday to my bestest girl." Wes blew a raspberry on my belly, making me giggle. "Come here."

Grabbing me, he rolled us so we were nose to nose as he cuddled me, purring for me, the warmth making me feel all cozy inside.

"Do we have time for more?" I asked, wrapping my legs around him.

"Hey, assholes, it's almost time for food," Riley yelled from the other room.

"Someone's making breakfast?" I hadn't expected that.

Wes nuzzled me. "It's your birthday."

I climbed out of the warm bed and pulled on some clothes, as did Wes. As we came down the backstairs into the kitchen, where the smell of bacon greeted me.

Along with Evan and Jett in aprons.

Evan went to the cupboard. "I'll get everyone coffee."

Riley stood there, with the fridge open, pouring champagne into a giant mug. She held it out to me. "For the birthday girl."

Brennan took it from her hand. "It's before lunch. That means you have to put juice in it. Why a mug? We have an entire cabinet of proper glassware."

"Really?" Riley got out the apple juice.

I nodded. "Yep, like how you can have vodka for breakfast if you add tomato juice, hot sauce, and celery."

Jett put bacon on the kitchen table and made a face. "Well, that's one way to get your vegetables."

Spencer came into the kitchen fully dressed in his usual nice suit. Everyone else was in their pajamas.

Evan brought me a cup of coffee. I sat down at the kitchen table. Unlike the dining room, the kitchen table didn't have assigned seats.

Riley placed a giant glass beer mug filled with champagne and apple juice. "What?" she said to Brennan as she squeezed in between Jett and Spencer. "It's from the cabinet with the glasses."

Wes and Evan sat on either side of me.

"Thank you." I took a sip. It wasn't a combination I had before, but not unpleasant. At least I had nothing planned for the day until later when Evan was taking Riley and me dress shopping for the gala.

We had pancakes, bacon, fried potatoes, and scrambled eggs with cheese and vegetables. As we ate, Riley cheerfully regaled us with stories about her and her friends at school, Brennan and Wes chiming in since they'd gone there, too.

"Thank you so much for breakfast," I said to Jett and Evan as we finished. It had been nice of them to do that.

"Now it's time for presents," Jett said as Brennan cleared the table.

"I'm first." Riley plopped a black bag with black sparkly tissue onto my lap.

Nestled in the tissue was a black shirt that had been shredded and studded and turned into a work of art. It said *Rockland Raiders* in silver and purple. Riley's favorite skate smash team.

"Thank you, it's amazing," I told her. "You did this yourself?"

"I did. I also got us tickets to see them play the Capitol Crushers, which is pretty much the best team in the PSSL. Me and you. No boys. It'll be so fun." Riley beamed with pride.

"I'm excited, thank you, wow, that will be so much fun," I exclaimed. We'd watched a game on TV together the other day and it had been fun.

Brennan's eyebrows rose. "You can't go to a sporting event by yourselves."

"Um, I went with my friends a couple of weeks ago. Also, I'm pretty sure Grace is an adult. However, if you overprotective fuck-nuggets want to use your own money to go, fine. I'll let you know where we're sitting." She scratched her nose with her middle finger.

"You did this yourself with your own money? I'm honored. Thank you." Wow, that was quite a purchase for a teenager.

"Pretty sure Ri has more money than most of us," Jett joked. "If you and your boyfriend get serious, you're going to have to go honest, considering his dad is a police sergeant."

Riley scowled. "We're not dating, fuck you very much. Also, my work is for the greater good."

Spencer gave her a sharp look. "We've talked about this. You also made your sisters a promise."

"I'm not doing that, well, mostly. Just stupid shit the rich kids pay me for. When can I get a work permit? Because if you're going to make me an honest woman, then I need an honest paycheck, because my retirement island isn't going to buy itself." Riley leaned back in her chair.

"Sixteen—so, November," Spencer replied. "We're expanding our summer internship program to include high school students. You're welcome to apply. It is paid, but not much. It will get you in the door. We have two sessions. Hopefully one of them doesn't clash with any other plans you've made."

"Ooh, really? I can't wait. Working for you is going to be fun." She bounced in her chair.

"You do know that you'll be working with Wes, right?" Brennan laughed as he rinsed something off in the sink and then loaded it into the dishwasher.

"Fuck, no," Riley scoffed. "No offense, Wes, but I'm going to work with Grace."

"What exactly would a hacker and a mathematician do for a biotech company? Sounds like the start of a joke," Brennan teased, refilling everyone's coffee.

"We could hack reality. No, hear me out. What if the universe was a simulation–and we could hack it? Wouldn't that be *amazing?*" Her eyes danced with delight.

Spencer's face went awash with horror. "Please don't."

"Ri, I'd love to work with you. But let's choose something else. If reality is a simulation, we don't want to piss off the person running it by hacking it," I replied, understanding Spencer's look. If someone governed travel between worlds, someone could do so for reality–and I did *not* want to meet them.

"Spence, Ri is talented, but hacking reality is just a theory, like time travel." Brennan shook his head as he finished pouring coffee refills.

I looked at Brennan. "Did you ever consider that the reason we think it's a theory–and have never met anyone from another time–is because someone is monitoring it? Consider parallel worlds, could you imagine the chaos that could stem from it? Worlds conquering each other for the resources or simply for the hell of it?"

Yeah, I hadn't laid awake at night thinking about the temporal police.

"Whoa, that sounds amazing." Riley did a little dance in her seat again.

"Just because you can do something, doesn't mean you should," Spencer warned. "But why don't you think about a project you and Grace could do together that doesn't threaten the fabric of time and space and send me a proposal?"

"This is way too serious of a conversation for this time of the morning. More presents. This is from me and Bren." Jett dropped a large bag on my lap.

I pulled out a butter-soft black leather motorcycle jacket. "This is beautiful."

"To go with your boots," Jett replied. "There's more."

I pulled out a black motorcycle helmet that had *Peaches* airbrushed on it.

"Thank you, thank you both," I said. That was thoughtful.

"Now, we'll be nice and safe when we steal Evan's bike and go fuck shit up. I have one, too," Riley told me.

"Motorcycle license. We need to get you a motorcycle license, driver's too, since you live here now," Evan said. "I totally forgot that."

"Well, I'm not cleared to drive yet. I didn't even get this off." I made a face, holding up my wrist, which still had the little monitor. "But again, thank you, these are great."

"Oh, there's this." Brennan half-tossed a box at me.

I caught it and unwrapped it. "Wireless headphones, thank you."

"They're for the piano. Spencer seems to resent the piano waking him up at two in the morning." Brennan rolled his eyes. "Button for soundless is on the side of the piano. You can keep them in the bench with mine."

"Thank you. That's so nice." I clutched them to my chest.

He shrugged. "Like I said, we can't interrupt Spencer's beauty sleep."

Spencer shot him a scathing look.

"My turn." Evan handed me a bag. "I hope you like it."

"I'm sure I will." Had *everyone* gotten me a present?

I took out a beautiful messenger bag. "It has equations on it. Thank you."

Leaning over, I gave him a kiss.

"No kissing at the table," Riley scolded, throwing a piece of tissue paper at her brother.

"That's not a house rule," Wes replied. "I'll go next. Here."

He handed me a large, flat, rectangular present.

I undid the wrapping and stared, heart in my throat, tears in my eyes. It was a framed and matted collage of pictures that Wes had drawn. Pictures of me. Of us. Little me. Big me. It looked like most were from his sketchbooks. One was obviously recent—me with my short hair, reading in the window seat.

"Oh, Wes." In the center was a charcoal portrait I'd never seen. "This one... wow."

"It was for an art show. It won a prize." Wes gave me a bashful look.

I gave him a kiss, overwhelmed at the thoughtfulness of the gift. "It's perfect. Thank you so much, these are perfect."

Joy spread through my chest.

"Last, but certainly not least." Spencer withdrew a long velvet box from his suit jacket, leaned over the table and handed it to me, then gave me the barest of kisses on the cheek. "Happy birthday, my good doctor."

Heat spread through my cheeks. "Thank you so much."

"What is it?" Riley crowded over my shoulder.

I opened the velvet box and exhaled sharply. Inside was a gold necklace made up of dainty flowers, a stone winking from the center of each. The flowers got bigger towards the center of the necklace. Matching dainty earrings, a little dangle of three flowers, accompanied it.

Peach blossoms. They were *peach blossoms.*

"It's beautiful, thank you." It was delicate and classic. A touch fancy for every day, but I could wear it on many occasions.

"Peach blossoms, for our peach." Spencer smiled at me.

Something about that smile made my squishy places warm.

Wes cocked his head and gave him a look. "This is how it's going to be?"

"It's her birthday, Wes. I thought that she might like something new to wear to dinner tonight." Spencer met his gaze.

"They're teasing each other," Evan whispered in my ear. "Wes knew about it, because Spence wanted to coordinate with what you were wearing to dinner."

Yesterday, Wes surprised me with a sparkly, emerald green dress for tonight–and had gotten Evan a matching tie.

We finished breakfast, and I offered to clean up–since I didn't have to go to work.

"Thank you." Evan's voice drifted from the backstairs as I grabbed empty cups from the table.

"For what?" Brennan said. "They were headphones. It's not like I got her a bracelet engraved with the opening bars of the third movement of Kirkokov's 4th."

"That is oddly specific." Evan snorted.

"Oh, come on, you know she was the girl at the piano competitions that warmed up with it to intimidate everyone," their voices trailed off as they walked up the stairs.

Huh. I needed to look that one up, though I'd run across Kirkokov's pieces. They were very technical–like Rachmaninoff technical.

Wes came back down, dressed. "Are you sure you don't want me to stay home with you?"

"I'm looking forward to relaxing. No videos to watch for Evan, no check-ins or appointments. Evan is picking me up later for dress shopping. Then we're going out to dinner." I gave him a kiss. "Those pictures are beautiful. Thank you."

I cleaned up, packed Evan a lunch, and then went upstairs to my room. Someone was coming over the weekend to install that door in my room that led to his bathroom. I went into the wardrobe. What did I want to wear today?

Evan knocked on the open door. "Anyone home? Oh, you put the lights back up."

"I like them. Um, I need help putting the canopy up. I... I really don't remember taking everything down, just tidying up." I still felt bad that I'd undone all the work we'd put into my room.

He put an arm around my waist. "I know. Everyone's left–and my first meeting was canceled, so I don't have to leave for two hours."

I leaned into him, rubbing up against him, wanting a little more of what I'd gotten this morning. "Oh dear, however will we amuse ourselves?"

That hour or so Evan and I often had between when everyone else left and when he needed to leave was quickly becoming one of my favorite parts of the day. It wasn't even about sex, sometimes we just had coffee and cuddles.

"I got some new bubble bath," he offered. "Vanilla peach."

"Oh, yes, sir," I laughed as he scooped me up. That sounded nice.

Maybe we could play with the jelly knot.

"Mmmm, I love it when you call me *sir*. Almost as much as those little notes you tuck in with my sandwich." He kissed my nose.

I'd been packing him lunch, since he didn't get free lunch at work like Wes and Spence.

He brought me into the bathroom, where the giant tub was practically overflowing with vanilla-scented bubbles. Gently, he stripped me, and settled me into the tub. Turning the water off, he lit some candles.

"This is perfect. Want to join me?" I leaned back onto the bath pillow.

His eyes sparkled as he flipped off the light, so the bathroom glowed with candlelight. "I thought you'd never ask."

Chapter Forty-Five

Evan

I was finishing up my case notes in the office that I shared with some other advocates when there was a knock on the door.

"Evan?" Claire stood there. "The headmistress at Finchley called; there's been a situation."

My phone had been quiet. "Who with?"

"Rose."

My heart dropped. Sunday's events with Iris aside, she'd been having a good week at her new school. She'd been making friends, getting adjusted to her classes...

"I know you're about to be off for the day, but you're needed there. Her uncle showed up, and the police were called," Claire said. "I'm sorry. Hopefully, it won't take long."

Oh shit. "On it. I'll be right there."

Well, there went dress shopping. If it came down to it, Grace and Riley could go themselves or we could go another day. I was just a little worried about what my sister might choose without guidance, since Grace had no idea what Brennan's mom expected us to wear. Maybe Spencer could take them. I texted him.

Me

> I need a favor. There's been a work emergency. Is there any way that you can take Grace and Riley dress shopping?

Spencer

> Of course. I don't have any more meetings today. Is everything okay?

Me

> Hopefully. I was going to take them to the fancy mall. Thank you so much. See you at dinner.

Spencer

> Always. Please let me know if I can do anything else. Are you okay?

Me

> I'm okay. It's a client. Thank you.

I grabbed my laptop and things, hurried to my car, and drove to Finchley. When I arrived, the police were still there. The gate looked damaged. I parked and found Rose in the headmistress' office, sobbing.

"Rose, are you okay? Did he hurt you?" I rushed over to her.

"Evan." She wrapped her arms around me.

"I'm right here. Now what happened?" I pulled a chair over.

"My uncle showed up. When they wouldn't let him on campus, he tried to drive through the gate. He's been quiet all week, so I thought everything was fine." She looked up at me through tear-stained eyes.

"Nothing is your fault," I told her. We talked a little longer, and I got her calmed down. At least he hadn't hurt her.

Still, he *tried to drive through the gate.* I'd gotten Rose's sister and stepdad connected with social services. They'd received boxes of food and were getting assistance with their bills. What was the problem here?

Especially because it was the *uncle*, not the stepdad, causing all the problems.

"Can I talk to you, Evan?" Headmistress Nikita joined us. Taller than many omegas, there was something about her that made most people pause before crossing her, even if she was a little young for a headmistress.

"Of course." I squeezed Rose's hand. "I'll be back."

I went out into the hall. "Was anyone hurt?"

"No. Thank goodness." She sighed. "I love Rose. She's a dear. But we have rules here, and if her family is going to cause disruptions, we might have a problem."

"Understood, Headmistress. Hopefully this won't happen again," I replied.

"I love having your clients here, and I want to keep Rose safe from whatever horrific things happened at home, but I also can't put the rest of the students in danger," she told me.

Finchley had good security, but that was partially because most of the families sending their omega children here were very wealthy. They were the sort of families that might be concerned about people trying to drive their cars through a closed gate.

"Are the police still here?" I asked.

She nodded. "I'll take you. Rose was already questioned before you got here, but I stayed with her the whole time."

"Thank you," I told her as we went outside and found the officers.

"I'm Evan, I'm Rose's advocate," I introduced myself, since I didn't know these officers. "Can you shed any light on why her uncle wanted her so badly?"

The beta officer shrugged. "Something about needing her at home. People can be assholes. Not sure he was even sober. Detective Esposito will call you."

"Thanks." I went back to the office and found Rose. "Hey, should we go back to your room?"

"Thank you." Rose stood. "Weren't you taking Ri shopping? I hope I didn't ruin anything."

"No, it's fine. Pretty sure Spencer took her and Grace someplace fancy. I keep getting pictures," I replied as I accompanied her back to her dorm. "I've got time. We're not going out to dinner until eight."

"Oh, yes, it's Grace's birthday. Riley told me that you're going to Supressa tonight." Rose smiled. "I heard it's so fancy."

"Me, too. It should be fun." I wasn't sure what I thought about one of my clients being friends with my sister. But it wasn't actually against the rules.

We went back to her room, and she picked up her phone. "Oh, I have pictures, too. I'd forgotten my phone in my room. I was charging it."

She grinned as she flipped through the pictures and showed me one of Riley in a sparkly dress.

"I like that one." Rose showed me another. "So elegant."

It was a jumpsuit with flowy black pants and a lacy white top.

"Very nice." A little understated, even for family, but it could be dressed up.

A picture popped up on my phone. It was Grace, in a silver dress with a giant-ass train.

Tell Grace she looks beautiful, I texted my sister. She looked like a bride. I sat with Rose as she told me about her week.

My phone rang. "This is Evan."

"This is Detective Esposito with the Westside Precinct," a woman spoke. "You're Rose Matthews' advocate?"

"I am. Do you need me down at the station?" I asked, hoping it wouldn't take too long.

"I do, thank you."

With a sigh, I hung up. "Rose, I have to go. But please, text me if you need me. I'll be out of town this weekend, so I might not get right back to you, but I *will* get back to you. If it's urgent, call the Center, okay?"

I texted the pack group chat as I got in my car.

Me

> Work emergency. Spence is with Grace and Ri. I'm leaving Finchley and heading to the Westside Precinct, I'll make dinner on time. Promise.

Good thing I kept extra clothes in Brennan's office. Given we lived in the 'burbs now, it made sense.

I drove to the precinct, greeting the people I knew.

An alpha female detective I didn't know came out. "Evan, I'm Detective Esposito. Come with me."

She led me to a room, where on the other side of the window, sat a man in a cap and a flannel shirt. We weren't alone, either.

"That's Rose's uncle?" I said softly.

"Yes. Rose told me about her... situation, and we accessed her mom's record. It makes me think there's more to this than simple trespassing. It also makes me wonder whose idea it really was to do such a thing to a teenager." She eyed the scene through the window suspiciously. "I wouldn't be surprised if the uncle has debts."

Oh. I sucked in a breath. "No, it wouldn't. Stepdad has been very supportive of Rose staying at school. While Rose's mom was the one who brought her to the Center in the first place, she also has been adamant that Rose not go home. Not stay at school–*not go home.*"

As if they wanted to keep her safe. But from who? The uncle?

"I'll call the precinct in her home area and see what I can find out. Something's not right. You're welcome to listen," Detective Esposito said as another detective went into the room with the uncle.

I checked the time. "I can stay for a little while."

"Hot date?" she joked.

"Taking my girl out for her birthday." *My girl.* It sounded so good to call Grace that.

"Nice, where are you going?" she asked.

"Supressa," I told her.

She whistled. "Nice. Always wanted to go there."

We, and the others, watched the detective question him.

"I'm the head of the family, which means she's under *my* care. Not her mom's, not her stepdad's, *mine,*" the uncle argued. "I have a right to drag her uppity little ass home so she can help support us."

"She's legally a ward of the Omega Center. You have no authority over her," the large male alpha detective told him.

"That's a shit rule. She's needed more at home than chasing some dumb dreams of being a doctor," he sneered.

"Oh yeah? Are you the one who convinced your sister to shoot Rose up with illegal drugs? Your financial situation isn't very good either," the detective pushed.

"I don't know nothing about that," he shrugged. "But everyone pulls their weight, and I need her home. She can't help the family from here."

They went round and round, and eventually the others left, leaving Detective Esposito and I alone in the room. All I got from the uncle was that he wanted her home. Never once did he say anything about her being mated to a pack–and he brushed off those questions. You could almost believe he just needed Rose for childcare and household tasks; maybe to get an after-school job to help with the bills.

Except that her mom drove her *hours* to match her with *better alphas*. There was also the fact that her mom had withdrawn her from school. I told Detective Esposito all my suspicions.

"I've been doing this for a couple of years–and something about this is off," I told her.

"When you add in what her mom did, the incident with her uncle commanding her sister, how far away they are, yeah, something's up. It just might not be my jurisdiction. All we can charge him with right now is trespassing, and we can't hold him for much longer." She made some notes. "I do appreciate your help. I'll work with Headmistress Nikita to help keep Rose safe, and I'll be in touch."

"Thanks." I went to my car and checked the time. I messaged the chat.

Me

Done at the station. Going to Bren's office to get dressed.

Brennan

I'm here. I'll wait for you.

Something wasn't right with Rose's entire situation. Hopefully, the detectives would figure it out before someone else got hurt.

Chapter Forty-Six

Grace

"This isn't the fancy mall," Riley said as Spencer's car cruised through a little neighborhood full of shops that looked high-end.

Evan had texted that there was something going on with Rose he had to deal with and that Spencer was sending a car to get me. I'd met him at work, we'd picked up Riley, and here we were.

My outfit for dinner was also in his trunk.

"No, it's not." Spencer parked and went around to open my door as Riley scrambled out the back.

He led us into an unassuming shop, where an elegant man greeted us. The shop was filled with racks of dresses.

"Spencer, it's been too long," he gushed, accent almost French.

"Andre, it was Monday." Spencer chuckled. "Thank you for taking us on short notice. This is Riley and Grace. This is Andre, it's his shop."

Monday. Had the red dress come from here?

Andre looked us up and down. "Perfect. The racks are here for your approval."

He led us toward the back of the shop, where there was some sort of waiting area with couches. There were also two small racks, filled with outfits.

Spencer went through them, separating out a few things. There weren't just dresses, there were sparkly jumpsuits, sleek pantsuits, even a tux.

We also weren't alone. An older woman browsed a rack in the corner. A couple of girls a little older than Riley were comparing dresses to a fabric swatch.

"I want to wear this." Riley came over holding a short, black, studded number.

"The gala has a dress code—and a theme. This year's is *All that Glitters*," Spencer said, moving to the other rack.

Riley rolled her eyes. "It's *shiny*. Do I even get to pick?"

"Out of the ones I select for you, yes," Spencer replied. "Brennan's mother is... particular."

With a huff, Riley put it back. Spencer loaded a bunch into my arms and Riley's.

Dresses selected, we were moved back into an area with a settee, lots of mirrors and several large dressing rooms.

Riley went into one, and I went into another. We began trying things on. The dresses in my pile were all sleek, beautiful, long dresses with a hint of sparkle, not unlike what I'd worn to the science dinner. Most had high backs or wraps.

I started with a black shimmery one.

"Can you zip me?" Riley called from her dressing room.

"Sure." I left my room and went over to hers. "You look great."

She wore a black and white sleeveless formal romper. I zipped her up. Riley looked at herself in the mirror, then had me take a picture.

We tried on dresses, spinning in the mirror and taking pictures of each other. Occasionally, Riley would go out and get Spencer's opinion—or chat with the girls trying on blue dresses for something called an *excellent eighteenth*. Spencer was back out where the racks had first been, drinking a glass of champagne and answering work emails on his phone.

Andre came back to check on us a few times.

"Nothing is the one, is it?" he finally asked me.

"They're all beautiful," I replied. No, none of them were *the one*.

He nodded. "I have better ones. Ones that fit the dress code, but might be a bit flashy for the queen mum's idea of what family should wear."

"I'd like that. Thank you." It was pretty funny how people referred to Brennan's mom as the *queen mum*. It also explained a hell of a lot.

Andre came back with an armful of dresses. "You try these."

"Thanks." These were puffy, princess-y numbers.

I took out all the low back ones and then tried a blue one first.

"Ooh, that is more like it," Riley breathed when I came out.

I looked in the mirror; it was very Cinderella.

She had on a tux and spun. "I could match the boys. Like?"

"So dapper. You need a hat," I told her, twirling.

"I want a hat." She nodded.

I tried on the rest of the dresses. The yellow one didn't look right. The green one was a little fussy for my taste.

Last was a silver gown, with puffy sleeves and a little train. It had a corset back I couldn't quite lace up. The neckline showed off the girls but wasn't too daring. It showed my scars a little so I threw on the wrap.

I walked out into the dressing area and looked at myself in the mirror. Oh, my God. It was exquisite, with light sparkles in the brocade. *That train.* I looked like I was going to the Met Gala.

"Oh, my dear, you look extraordinary," a woman said as she stood there. "Are you getting married?" She was old enough to be my mother.

"This is for a gala. I think it's too much." The train was massive. How would I navigate in that?

She smiled. "At your age, there's no such thing."

Andre came back and beamed. "Perfect. The train bustles for dancing." He showed me. "We'll have it altered for length."

"Wow." Riley came out in a silver jumpsuit, looking adorable. She took a picture of me. "Evan needs to see you in that."

She went to try more things on, and I just stood there, looking in the mirror.

The older woman came back out, in a demure blue beaded number. "You are precious in that. Which gala is it for?"

"The Morris Foundation. I've never been. I don't know if it's appropriate. All the dresses I've tried are lovely, but this..." I felt like a princess.

"I'm going as well. You'll be fine. I'm Evangeline," she introduced.

"Grace." I swished the skirts. I nodded at her outfit. "That dress is nice."

"It'll do. But you, you will be the delight of the red carpet in that gown. If you don't have a special someone, you will after wearing that." The corners of her eyes crinkled as she smiled. "Do you, because I am happy to make introductions if you don't?"

"I do, two actually." I giggled. I had *two*.

Perhaps there'd be a third at some point. Maybe.

"Lucky them." Her smile widened. "You're so pretty. Are you an actress?"

"A mathematician, actually," I replied.

She nodded. "You work at a university?"

I shook my head, still swishing. "I just moved here, and I'm still looking, but there's a company I'm interested in."

We talked a little longer, and she returned to her dressing room. I just stood there, not wanting to take off the dress.

"Show Spence." Riley pushed me out into the main room. She now wore a black, spangled dress with a handkerchief hemline. "Spence, Grace needs this one."

"Grace." Spencer exhaled sharply, standing.

The look on his face made me want to kiss him. Yeah, I wanted this dress, pretty please.

"Oh, you look exquisite." Spencer kissed my hand, then he looked at Andre.

"It is a little more, but, ah, she's lovely," Andre said.

"He brought me more dresses," I ducked my head a little.

Spencer grabbed my chin gently and moved my head back up, his touch searing me.

"It is appropriate for the gala, though a little beyond what Siobhan likes for family. Still, it's exquisite." His eyes never left mine. "You are exquisite."

My lady parts grew warm. *That praise.*

"Perhaps you show him the blue?" Andre asked.

I tried on the blue dress for Spencer along with my favorite of the ones Spencer had chosen.

"We'll get the silver, if that's what you prefer, but we'll need it altered," Spencer said.

"Wait, I can?" Something about it made me giddy.

"Of course. I can't wait to see Wes and Evan's faces," Spencer told me, reaching out and stroking my hair.

"I want this one." Riley came out in a silver dress with a high-low hemline.

"Ri, it's extraordinary," I breathed. "Now we match."

"I know." She giggled. "I feel so fancy–and it's silver so it goes with the theme."

Spencer nodded. "Go ahead. You'll need the right shoes and earrings."

Andre beamed. "Excellent. I'll get you rung up."

Riley squealed and threw an arm around me. "We are princesses."

I grinned, her excitement was contagious. "Yes, we are."

"Grace, can I ask you a question?" Riley said using liquid eyeliner to give herself cat-eyes.

We were in her dorm room, getting ready. After dress shopping, Spencer had offered to take us some place, but Riley insisted that we get ready in her room. Evan would come and take us to the restaurant.

"Of course." I tried to decide what color eyeshadow to use.

"You love my brother, right?"

I applied a pale shade all over my eyelids. "I do."

While we hadn't said it yet, I did love Evan very much.

She moved to the other eye. "You know, your story doesn't make sense? The whole thing with you and Wes meeting as kids and all that, right?"

"It doesn't, does it?" I put a darker shade in the crease. We'd never really come up with a backstory for me.

"No. Um, you know I know that you didn't have a record?"

I nearly dropped the eyeshadow brush. "You do?"

"Yeah." She got out a tube of mascara. "Even if your mom took you from here when you were seventeen, you'd have a record."

"Maybe I just visited. That's why his dad and sister never met me." I added some highlighter.

She gave me a look. "You went to university. There'd be a record of you someplace, somewhere."

"How do you know I didn't have a record? Did Evan tell you?" I frowned as I added a hint of sparkle.

"Yeah, when he asked me to make you one. What? He and Wes didn't do it themselves. They're not that smart." She added another coat of mascara to her long eyelashes.

"Oh. Evan didn't say it was you. Wow, you're talented." I mulled that over. She was talented enough to create a government record for me? Wow.

"It's a secret. Also, Spencer's right, I promised I wouldn't do shit like that anymore." Riley appraised herself in the mirror.

I took a deep breath, taking a moment to put away the eyeshadow and get out my eyeliner. "What did Evan say about me?"

"That it's not his story to tell." She rolled her eyes.

"Evan, Spence, and Wes know. Do you really want to know? I don't want to hide things from you. But... it's a secret." I started to line my right eye. If anyone would believe me, or at least keep an open mind, it would be her.

"I can keep a secret. But you shouldn't keep secrets from Bren and Jett." She frowned and chose a lipstick.

"I know." I sighed. "We'll tell them soon. We're still figuring everything out. It's weird."

"I'm listening." Riley applied lipstick.

"Do you remember this morning when Spence freaked out over you mentioning hacking the universe?" I lined my other eye.

She nodded. "That was weird."

"I met Wes when I was ten in that park we went to. I was also dreaming. I still don't know how it happened exactly, unless you believe those stories of scent matches dreaming of each other." As I finished my makeup, I gave her an abbreviated story of my interdimensional misadventures.

Riley stared at me when I finished. "Fuck me with a pineapple. You honestly expect me to believe that you came here from a parallel world?"

"But I did. Designations don't exist in my world. Evan calls me a *gamma*, but I'm nothing. I can't even remember how I got here. When I saw Wes, after thinking he was someone I'd made up in my head as a kid, I freaked out. Evan was there," I told her. "When I met Spencer, he just *knew*. Like he looked at me and said, *You don't belong here.*"

"Okay, but what? That's so weird." She fixed her hair.

"I know, and I can explain the math later."

For a moment, she was quiet. "That explains why you don't know much about anything most people do. Are you going to leave then? Once you get your memories back and all that."

I shook my head. "No. Wes is here. Not to mention, my research back home was pure theory–pure, *unproven* theory. It could take decades to figure it out. I'd rather stay."

"This is trippy as fuck. You can't tell people this." She put sparkly powder on her face.

"Yep." I nodded.

Riley put in earrings. "Um, how did you *mate* in your dreams?" Her eyebrows rose. "You're actually mate-bonded and feel each other and shit, right?"

"Yeah. It shows up on a test. I'm not actually sure how it happened. Um, well, I remember the actions, but don't know how it transcended our dreams." But it had.

"Wow," she said, again, getting a dress out of her closet. "This is so weird. What's your world like?"

"Other than no alphas and omegas and packs, it's not that different. We have a New York City. Rockland is called something else. There are so many little differences. Like here, the drinking age is lower, the driving age higher. Our version of skate smash isn't on ice skates. Some of your movies and music are close, but nothing is quite the same. Your technology is more advanced, and your healthcare is so much better," I told her. "Everyone's more accepting, too."

She pondered this. "Okay, so you didn't grow up fundie, you grew up in another fucking world."

"Well, I did sort of grow up fundie. My mom converted to the religion I was raised in, got super into it, and they were pretty conservative."

While religion existed here, and some holidays were widely and secularly celebrated, there seemed to be a *much* greater separation between church and state. But then religious freedom didn't drive the formation of this country or shape its borders.

"I'm glad you're here," Riley added. "Don't get me wrong, the guys are all great, but having you in the house makes it more fun."

"Thank you. I'm glad I'm here, too." My phone beeped, and I checked it. "Your brother's on his way, so I suppose we should get dressed.

She held up a long, black dress. "Will this work?"

"That's beautiful," I told her. It was the sort of dress I'd always wanted for a high school dance and never got.

"Evan got it for me. It's actually for the spring formal tomorrow. But considering how much it cost, I figured I might as well wear it as much as I can," she told me.

I nodded. "A black dress is very useful."

"Really?" She appraised it.

"It's hard to go wrong with a black dress. Do you go to dances in groups or with dates?" I shimmied out of my clothes.

"Both. I'm going with the girls from my floor. But I'm meeting up with Marcos, Kilroy, and Hiro." She pulled on the dress.

"Hiro?" I hadn't heard about him yet. But Kilroy was a handful. His mom was an omega and seemed nice.

"He and Marcos have been friends forever. He's super-smart, like calculus as a freshman, smart," she told me.

Um, she was in pre-calculus as a freshman, which wasn't bad at all.

"We're in the same history and literature class. I'm not sure he likes me," she admitted.

"What makes you think that?" I asked, since teenage boys *were* confusing.

"He doesn't talk much and is sort of... standoffish. I don't know. He just sort of broods, while Marcos is charming and Kilroy makes jokes. Anyhow, the dance will be fun." She turned. "Zip me?"

I zipped her up. The dress was fancy—with a very high slit and sparkles. "Beautiful."

She zipped me up. "You can see your scars a little. Are you okay with that or do you want me to try to cover them with foundation?"

"I... I don't know." I bit my lower lip. "The silver dress... I wore the wrap because you can see them just a little but I love it so much."

Riley nodded. "I figured."

"I think I'll just wear the little wrap I brought?" I'd have to figure this out. It hadn't been much of an issue because I hardly wore fancy dresses.

"Okay. They make special makeup to cover scars. We can get some if you want it sometime, and watch some videos and play around with it," she told me. "Don't feel like you have to cover them up. I only mentioned it because I wasn't sure if you could see your back in my mirror."

I hugged her to me. "Thank you."

"Will you tell me why the fuck someone did that to you? Did you end them yourself? No judgement," she told me as we put on our shoes. "I think someone said it was your *mom?*"

"Today is not the day for that story." I glanced at my phone.

Riley nodded. "I understand."

"Ready, because he's almost here."

Riley nodded. "Absofuckinglutely. I hope the food is as good as they say because I'm *hungry.*"

Chapter Forty-Seven

Wes

Supressa sat at the top of the High Tower hotel, the same building the science dinner had been at. A posh, exclusive restaurant, it *rotated,* offering diners an incredible view of the city, as well as gourmet meals, superb decor, and a chance to see the city's elite.

I was the first to arrive and went to the host station. "The reservation is under Brennan Morris."

The host, wearing a black vest and bow tie, looked up the reservation and then gave me a once-over to make sure I met the dress code. "We need at least half of the party to seat. You're welcome to sit at the bar and wait."

"Sure."

I went to the bar and ordered a whiskey sour, then let the group chat know that I was there as I checked everyone's locations. The bar was crowded with people dressed in top fashion, glittering and laughing as the restaurant slowly spun, the walls nothing but windows, as the sun set over the city.

Twinkling lights decorated the ceiling, making it look like a sky full of stars. There were trees, fountains, boxes of flowers, street signs, and murals that looked like buildings. Even part of the floor looked like sidewalks and a road. The live music was meant to transport everyone to a small, old-timey village somewhere in Europe.

"Hey." Brennan, in one of his usual smart suits, joined me at the bar, then ordered a shot of top-shelf bourbon.

I nodded. "Hey. You alone?"

"Jett's parking. Spence will be here soon. Evan went to get Grace and Ri." He downed his drink and ordered another. "It's been a shitty week."

"Yeah." I turned my glass in my hand.

"Are things going okay?" He looked a little uneasy.

When did things get tense between us?

"How the fuck do you handle *two?*" I blurted.

For a moment he looked startled, then he laughed, a big belly laugh that caused a few other patrons to look at us.

"Two's proving too much for you?" He continued laughing.

"I was thinking more like fairness. Evan tried to draw up a schedule, but it was pretty much him taking Grace to his cabin every weekend that he had off." I took a sip of my drink.

Shit, I shouldn't have mentioned Grace. I waited for Brennan to tense up, shut down, or punch me.

Brennan shook his head. "He keeps sending me pictures of fucking wedding venues."

"You too? I keep getting things like cakes and flowers and buffet tables." Fancy, fussy ones.

He took a sip of bourbon. "It's not so much about turns or schedules or even *fair.* It's about making sure both of them get the love and care they need–which will look different for each of them. Keep your insecurities in check and communication open.

We're alphas, it's our job." His eyebrows rose. "You know, our good friend Luc, the integration counselor, probably has all sorts of resources for you."

"I'm sure he does. I'll ask. Thanks," I added, with only a hint of sarcasm, because it was a good idea.

"I'll be honest, I don't want to deal with the shit I'm going to have to now that she's here. I didn't even know that I still needed to." He took another gulp of his drink.

"Me, too," I agreed. "Evan was like *Go to therapy with Grace, it'll be good for you.* So, I did, without realizing that it would highlight everything I need to work out for myself so that I don't hurt her with it."

My alpha insecurities about not being able to protect her were not for her to deal with.

Grace also desperately needed to talk to someone. But that brought up a whole distinct set of issues. Such as the fact that she was terrified that she'd say the wrong thing or reveal too much.

Brennan raised his glass. "Therapy for everyone."

"Why does Evan send *you* venue pictures?" I took a sip of my drink.

"There's a local property I'm considering buying. He thinks it'll make a good event venue," he replied.

"Would it? You don't have one of those, do you?" The hotels he owned had events–like his wedding.

"Not one that's not also a hotel. It'll take some money to fix up."

"You'll figure it out. You're a genius with this shit," I told him. He'd still been at university when he'd won an old hotel in a card game and turned it into a luxury destination.

"Thanks." He went quiet for a moment, sloshing the bourbon around in the glass. "Evan says he's going to marry Grace there. Is he marrying you, too?"

I finished my drink and signaled for another. "Honestly, I'll do whatever he wants. He can marry just her, us both, or all three of us. I'll marry her, too. I don't care, as long as it makes them happy. Grace and I had talked about a wedding when we were young. Would any of those impact the pack?"

Brennan thought for a moment. "Since you're bonded to both of them, not really. It's an excuse to have a party. Well, there would be legal implications for Evan and Grace marrying each other, but they wouldn't affect the pack overall, and would protect them. You *did* formally register your bond with Grace, right?"

I nodded. "Yep. That and getting a legal agreement with her were Katie's first action items. I also got her on everything at work, added her to my accounts, all that."

"Your accounts?" His eyebrows rose.

"My personal ones. She's my mate, and doesn't have a job, or money of her own." I shrugged.

"She came here *broke?*" He frowned.

I shot him a hard look. "She had a lot of education and no family support."

Apparently, education was ridiculously expensive where she came from.

"Did you see her ribs when she first arrived? She barely had enough to *eat,* and that was with her job," I added. Now she didn't look like a half-starved waif. That haunted look was mostly out of her eyes. She didn't look at my arms like she couldn't remember when she was last hugged. But I did what I could so she wouldn't be touch-starved anymore.

"Oh." Brennan went quiet for a moment. "It's inevitable, isn't it? Her joining the pack. Not now, I mean, we're not ready, and there's still an investigation, and I haven't even finished interviewing pack lawyers, but..."

There was a hint of panic in his voice. But he'd just mentioned her *joining the pack.* That was huge.

"Eventually, yes. Especially if Evan marries her." I'd like to see her brought into the pack at some point, but right now I'd be happy with everyone accepting her presence.

"Who is Evan marrying?" Jett joined us. "Whiskey soda," he told the bartender.

"Grace, apparently." Brennan shrugged. "But we'll still need to vote and talk it over–and *we're not there yet.*"

Jett snorted. "We get to vote on whether Evan can marry Grace? Or are we voting on wedding specifics? I think we should throw them out of an airplane."

"Fuck." I laughed, trying to imagine that.

"For what it's worth, I sorta like her. Wes, what was that byplay between you and Spencer this morning?" Jett sipped his drink.

"Spencer keeps threatening to court her." It was my turn to shrug.

Brennan froze.

"That's going to be fun." Jett chuckled. "Like I said, I sorta like her. She adds something to the house."

Brennan shook his head. "Absolutely not."

"She's already Wes' mate, and if he and Evan don't care, why not? After all, Spencer is an adult. It's been ages since he's been interested in anyone. She's a crap dancer, but catches on fast." Jett shrugged.

Spencer lost his wife over a decade ago. It was understandable. The fact that he was interested in courting Grace meant a lot. He was a good guy, and he and Grace had enough in common to potentially build a strong relationship.

"I just don't understand." Brennan sighed as he toyed with his glass.

"What don't you understand? Grace isn't that mysterious," I retorted, suppressing an eye-roll.

"In a way she is, but that's what I like about her," Spencer said, joining us.

A host followed. "I can show you to your table now. The rest of the party is nearly here?"

I checked my phone to see their location. "They're parking."

"We're here for Grace's birthday," Jett told the host. "She *is* one of those people who doesn't freak out if they sing, right?" He grinned at Brennan.

Brennan didn't like being sung to at restaurants. Did they even sing and bring you cake at a place like *this?* The cake probably wasn't free. This was even nicer than the usual restaurants our pack liked for special occasions.

"She's okay with it. She likes chocolate cake." I was glad Evan had asked her back when we were planning on taking her somewhere else.

The host seated us at a prime spot next to a window. It looked like a giant cafe table and had a lantern in the center. Strings of lights swooped over our heads. Brennan frowned, looking around the very busy restaurant–and the people watching him and Spencer.

"Do you have anything more... private?" Brennan asked the host as we sat down.

"For seven, on a Friday? No. Your server will be here soon." With that, the host left.

Brennan put his head in his hands. "My mother probably asked for this table specifically. It's as if she *wants* us to be photographed."

"She's still trying to make the case that Grace is loved and accepted and we're a happy pack with our shit together," Jett replied.

"I know." He rubbed his forehead. "Spence, thanks for getting the girls dresses. While I love Ri's sense of fashion, my mother won't have that same appreciation."

"It's no problem. They chose lovely selections," Spencer replied.

I frowned. "Grace never sent me pictures."

"Did you specify that you wanted any? Perhaps she wants it to be a surprise. Trust me, it's worth the wait." Spencer's eyes sparkled.

A server, dressed in the same black vest and bow tie, came and took our drink orders.

"Merlot," Spencer ordered as the rest of us got ours refreshed. "I have a picture of Ri, but I didn't get one of Grace." He showed us a picture of Riley in a silver dress. "Grace's dress is also silver, but fluffier."

"Ri looks so grown up," Jett said softly.

"She does," I nodded, remembering how little she was when Evan and I were first dating. "Silver. Should Evan and I match her? I mean, Bren, Evan, and Jett match sometimes for these things. But I don't want to ruin any plans you've made."

"Perhaps we should all match," Spencer suggested. "Considering the theme is *All that Glitters* and I'm pretty sure we all have silver vests and ties."

"Evan, Jett, and I do," Brennan nodded. "Good idea. I hadn't thought that far ahead."

"That works." I didn't have one, but it was easy enough to get.

"United front. Works for me," Jett replied.

"Bren, I still have Riley's pack ring in my safe. She should have it for the gala–and it would probably mean the most if you gave it to her," Spencer said quietly.

Brennan played with his pack ring on his right pinky. "Okay, it's time."

"I know we're not ready for Grace to join us, but Wes, you have some sort of ring for her to wear to stuff, right?" Jett asked. "At the science dinner, I saw *a lot* of alphas looking her up and down and licking their lips when they didn't see a visible bite or engagement or wedding ring, or a pack ring or tattoo, and she really doesn't smell claimed until you're right next to her. But I bet Spencer could choose something better. As I've said before, I think we need to get pack tattoos."

"I have something for her. I picked it up today from getting sized. It's not flashy. She might like one of those for special occasions. This is more for every day. It was my grandmother's." I took it out of my jacket pocket.

Inside the velvet box sat an emerald-cut blue sapphire accented with diamonds in an antique white-gold setting. It wasn't very large, but it was pretty.

"Very tasteful," Spencer agreed, looking at it.

"Oh." The server gasped as she brought our drinks. "Do you need help with something special? Perhaps you'd like to put it in a glass of champagne or on a slice of cake? This is for the birthday girl?"

"It is. I've got this, but thank you," I told her, accepting a fresh drink. A ring in your cake? What if you accidentally ate it?

A moment later, Evan appeared, with Riley on one arm, Grace on the other. Riley wore a long black dress with a high slit and lots of sparkles, and chunky heels.

Grace...

If people hadn't been staring at our table, they were *now.*

Evan was wearing what I always thought of as his *dapper suit,* when he wanted to look dashing—and he wore the green tie I'd gotten him. Which matched the fancy green dress I'd bought for Grace. She wore the peach blossom necklace Spencer had given her along with a sparkly hair clip I hadn't seen, and a cute little wrap.

While Spencer and Grace had looked picture-perfect at the science dinner, tonight Evan and Grace were *breathtaking.*

We all stood. All four of us. Spencer pulled out a chair for Riley, Brennan got Evan's chair, and I got Grace's.

"You look beautiful." I gave Grace a kiss. "Evan, you're so handsome."

"Ri, that dress. That's the one from the mall, right?" Jett raised his glass.

"You're fucking right it is. Don't spill anything on it. It's for the dance tomorrow. Fuck me. Look at that view." Riley got out her phone and took a selfie with the city in the background, then one with the restaurant behind her.

The server came over to us. "Any drinks?"

"I'd like a bottle of cabernet, the older the better," Riley stated.

"No." Brennan shook his head.

"Fine, lime soda." She huffed in annoyance.

"Highball," Evan ordered.

The server looked at Grace. "Would you like our champagne list?"

"Whiskey smash," Grace replied.

"Well, that fits," Jett laughed as the server left. "We're pretty much a whiskey and bourbon house. Except for Spencer and his merlot."

Spencer frowned. "We have wine with dinner all the time."

"I don't mind wine, I just don't know much about it. Look! It's so beautiful," Grace breathed as she looked out the window.

"Not as beautiful as you," Evan teased, snagging her for a kiss.

Nothing was as beautiful as them.

The server came back with the drinks. "Let me tell you about today's specials so you can order."

Chapter Forty-Eight

Grace

I dabbed my lips with a cloth napkin and made a happy noise. This was the best dinner I'd ever eaten. Oh, those mashed potatoes.

It wasn't just course after delightful course, or the live music, or even the rotating view of the city. It was the people I was with, laughing, telling me stories, showing me that the six people at the table with me truly were a family.

Pushing back from the table, I stood. "I'll be right back."

Wes stood. "Do you need air?"

"I need the ladies' room, I'm fine." I waved him off and went to the restroom.

While I was in the stall, others came in, talking as they went into the stalls.

"I can't believe Spencer Thanukos and his whole beautiful pack are here. Oh, be still my ovaries," one woman said.

"Why not? Everyone eats. But yeah, that does add to the view," another giggled. "Brennan Morris is much more my style."

"But Spencer's *single.*"

Spencer had a fan club. But he was smart, rich, single, good-looking, successful, and was part of a powerful pack. Brennan was known in many circles because of his family.

"I'd share, wouldn't you?" she giggled.

"Who are those women, though?" a third one added. "Sisters maybe?"

"No," the first said. "Not that blonde. She was with Spencer at some dinner. Saw pictures. Whore."

Whore? Seriously? My blood boiled as I tried to decide if I should leave the stall or not. All that being told I was a hussy for having a dream boyfriend when I was seventeen made me dislike slut-shaming.

"Jealous?" the second one laughed. "It's not like you're in line for his bite."

Time to leave before they came back *out* of the stalls.

"She doesn't even have a bite, she's probably just arm candy," the third said.

I flushed and went out and washed my hands, glad they hadn't emerged yet.

Another woman walked in, she looked at me, and her lips curved into a sneer. I tried to leave the bathroom, and she blocked me.

"A word of advice. Don't even waste your time with a pack like that," she told me. "They've got what they need; they're not looking for new members. You're a plaything. You're not going to get a bite, or pack membership, you're just going to get hurt."

The other three women came out of their stalls and stared at me.

"You're not even an omega," the first one blurted.

"Um, no. But for the record, I'm not a whore, I'm *mated* to one of them. Just because you can't see a bite or use your nose doesn't mean it's not there." I pushed past the woman, tears pricking my eyes.

What I wanted was to go outside. But we were on the top floor, and there didn't even seem to be a balcony.

"My good doctor, what's wrong?" Spencer stood there, his phone in his hand. "Come here." He pulled me into his arms.

For a moment, I rested my head against his soft suit, inhaling his leathery scent, as he stroked my back. I took a deep breath. *3.14159265359.*

"That's it, just breathe. It's okay, Grace." He rubbed my back as he held me.

Safe. I felt *safe* in his arms.

"Let's get you back to Wes." He took my arm and escorted me back to the table, keeping me close to him, as if shielding me with his body.

"What's wrong," Brennan demanded as I sat back down.

Not Wes. Not Evan. *Brennan.*

I shook my head, taking another deep breath, and leaning into Wes.

"Don't lie, Grace. I know that face. Lies also have smells. What happened?" Brennan pressed.

"Bren, she was in the bathroom," Jett replied.

Lies had *smells?*

Riley shook her head. "Bathroom bitches. Should've gone with you."

"Just women calling me a whore and telling me a pack like yours doesn't need girls like me." My voice was soft as my head hung.

"I'm so sorry. That's a hazard of being seen with a pack like ours. Jealousy." Evan came up behind me.

Wes cupped my face with his hands. "Don't believe them. I need you."

"Me, too." Evan took my hand and kissed it.

"There's so much I don't understand." *You're not even an omega.*

"We want you here. Fuck them." Wes grinned, revealing a dimple. "I have a present for you."

"More presents? I... I don't think I've ever gotten so many presents in my life." I chewed on my lower lip, still a little unnerved by the mean girls.

He took a little box out of his pocket. A little velvet box. My heart pounded.

"This was my grandmother's, and I want you to have it." Wes's eyes glimmered boyishly as he opened the box, revealing a pretty art déco style ring with a blue rectangular stone with little diamonds around it.

Taking the ring out of the box, he slid it on my ring finger, eyes never leaving mine. The heat of his hands searing my skin, going straight to my core. The entire time, Evan held my other hand, staying at my side.

"Wes, it's beautiful, thank you." I admired the sparkle. The whole thing made me wet. How much longer until we go home? I'd like to thank him... properly.

"I love you." He leaned in and kissed me long, and deep.

I clung to him, taking the reassurance I needed that I was wanted. He loved me.

"I love you, too," I whispered, breathless, my face close to him.

"My turn." Evan leaned in and kissed me, then kissed Wes.

"Shouldn't I give you rings? I mean, I did declare that you were both my husbands now." I laughed.

"When we all get married," Evan said. "We'll get matching rings."

"You're getting married?" Riley asked.

For a moment I held my breath. What if Riley didn't approve? Wait. We were getting married? Or was this just Evan being Evan?

I mean, I'd spent a whole lot of time dreaming about marrying Wes...

"Eventually," Evan said. "All three of us. Want to be in it?"

"Fuck yeah. I want to help plan it so it's fun." She shrugged.

"Dance with me?" Wes stood and offered me a hand.

I let him lead me to the dance floor, which surrounded a fountain. It was supposed to feel like a little town square. The dance was like one that I'd danced with Spencer, and Wes held me tight, leading us across the floor to a song in four-four time.

"Thank you for the ring," I told him. "What does it mean here? Where I'm from, if you give a girl a ring like that, the way you did, she'll be expecting a wedding."

"We'll give you a wedding. Evan is completely serious. I'm pretty sure he's already planning it, and it will be amazing. You did say we'd get married one day. Why not make it a three-way."

My heart fluttered in my chest. "That I did. Who can say no to a proposal like that?"

"A mate bond between you two won't be legally recognized, but a wedding would, so you and Evan would have that legal connection," he explained as we swirled around the floor.

"I want to be connected to the both of you," I breathed. "I... I want a wedding with you, like we dreamed of. But now it will be even better because Evan will be with us."

"Love it. I can't wait. As for the ring, it's so stupid and antiquated, but it basically says you're taken. You smell like me, if you're close enough, but you don't have a visible bite," he told me.

"Oh." That flutter turned to a pound. "I'm taken."

"Absolutely." His eyes met mine as he turned on the smolder.

My heart. I melted into him as we continued to dance.

"We can get rings, too. Advertise that we're all taken. Brennan, Jett, and Evan do. They all wear them on their right hands, not their left, because Brennan and Jett are lefties. And well, you wear your ring on whatever finger you want. Evan and I don't have rings, we got tattoos," he told me. "But yeah, let's get rings for the three of us.."

"I think I've seen your matching tattoos a couple of times." I grinned at the thought of him shirtless.

He laughed. "It's a little basic of us, the infinity heart on our chests and all, but I like it."

"Do I get one, too?" It was *cute.*

"A tattoo, you? Scandalous. And hot." He nipped at my ear, sending desire shooting through me.

"May I cut in?" Evan joined us, his chest to my back, as we continued dancing with me in the middle.

"I love you both." I leaned back and snagged Evan's lips.

Riley glided along the floor with Spencer. Brennan and Jett danced, too. We were being watched. But I didn't even look for the ladies from the bathroom. I was having too much fun. The song ended, and we all went back to our seats.

"You're nauseating. But I fucking love you." Riley gave me a hug.

"Love you, too, Ri." I hugged her back.

I wanted to be part of this family–at least that little part of it. And well, if Spencer wanted to join in, I wouldn't mind...

The server came over with our desserts–mine had a candle on it.

"Happy birthday, Grace." Wes planted a kiss on my cheek. Evan did the same from the other side, and my thighs rubbed together with desire.

There was a commotion toward the front of the entrance.

"Where is he? Where the fuck is he? I know he's here," a man yelled.

"Excuse me, but you can't go in there dressed like that–" A server *flew* across the room, landing on a table of diners with a crash. Diners screamed and stood, others got out their phones.

A bearded, rough-looking man, in jeans and a T-shirt ran towards our table. "Reverse the court order," he demanded. "Give me custody of my niece. She should be at home with her family, not at school, getting ideas."

Rose. This was about Rose. This must be the uncle. How did he know where we were?

"Give me custody now, Omega," he ordered.

There was something both icy and oily about the way he said it. Alpha bark. That compulsion thingy alphas had.

"Don't listen to him, Omega," Wes growled, as he tried to move so he was between me and him.

"Correct. You will do no such thing, Omega," Brennan added, doing the same for Evan.

Evan relaxed.

"You need to leave," Spencer said to the uncle, his voice forceful, as he moved Riley behind him.

"I need my niece back." The man withdrew a handgun. "Now, Omega."

No. No one hurt my Evan. Anger boiled inside me. How dare he?

"Grace, under the table." Wes didn't bark but tried to push me. Spencer did the same with Riley.

Standing, I grabbed my chair, ran over, and hit the big guy with it with all the force I could summon. A growl ripped from my chest. He crumpled, gun skittering to the ground.

Take that.

I picked his gun up off the ground and aimed it at him. "Fuck with my omega at your own peril, asshole. Security, this man is trying to wreck my birthday dinner."

Threaten my omega and ruin my perfect night? Hell no.

"I'd do what she said." Jett had a gun out. "Police, you are under arrest."

The man growled and lashed out as a bunch of security surrounded us.

"Let's put the gun down, Grace. I think they have it." Wes said, standing beside me.

"Fine." Satisfied that Jett and security had it under control, and Evan was okay, I took the bullets out of the chamber and put both on the table.

Wes whistled. "You can use a gun."

"My dad taught me to hunt." I shrugged.

"Peaches." Evan wrapped me in his arms. "You saved me."

"I love you." I smashed my mouth against his, reassuring myself that he was real and okay.

He kissed me again, my feet off the floor as he fully supported me. Brennan was right there, eyeing me. "I love you, too."

Spencer got on the phone.

"That was *amazing,*" Riley told me. "Why a chair?"

"You're supposed to hit an active shooter with a chair."

"I'm pretty sure that's not what you're supposed to do." Wes sat down and pulled me onto his lap. "I'm glad you're okay."

"I'm fine. Just protecting our boy. I mean, that's what we do right, protect omegas? Oof, I'm so hungry for some reason." I picked up Wes' half-finished dessert and started eating it.

Wes kissed my temple. "Probably that little burst of speed there. Didn't know gammas could do that. Please don't give me a heart attack. If you're hungry, eat."

The police came and talked to everyone. Jett led that show. Brennan was still holding Evan, Riley, and Spencer nearby.

As everyone gave their statements, I sat on Wes' lap and continued to systematically eat everyone's desserts and finished both Wes' and Evan's drinks–as well as another drink and dessert the server brought me for saving Evan.

A police officer came over to us and scowled at me as I recounted my side of the story. "You hit the gunman with a *chair?*"

"I was protecting our omega." I scraped the last bit of mousse out of the bowl.

"A *chair?*" The officer's eyebrows rose.

"What? That's a thing you do. Oh, his gun's on the table." I frowned at the empty bowl.

"A man with a gun charges your omega, and you think it's a good idea for you, the smallest person at the table, a table *with a police officer,* to hit him with a chair?" The officer stared at me.

"She's a gamma, they're wired weird." Jett joined us. "Anything else, Officer?"

"I'll call you if there is." He studied me. "Let's not hit shooters with chairs."

"Sorry, next time I'll be armed." I scowled at him then turned to Wes. "Wes, I need a thigh holster."

Jett laughed as the officer left.

"How do we un-fuck her danger response? I almost had a heart attack." Brennan looked worried.

"It's not weird," I retorted.

He raked a hand through his hair. "For you. But for everyone else in the room, it was."

"I'm not going to flee or hide or wait for some alpha to protect someone I love when I'm capable of doing it." I scowled at Brennan.

Brennan nodded. "I understand completely. Thank you for protecting Evan. That doesn't mean it was easy to watch."

"No. It wasn't," Wes agreed.

"It was pretty efficient," Jett replied. "You're fast."

Evan pulled me off of Wes' lap and kissed me, rubbing his erection against me. "I'm happy you care that much for me, Peaches. Sorry he tried to ruin your birthday dinner. We've trained for stuff like this at work. But I never expected it to happen–especially outside the workplace."

Warmth spread through me. "You can make it up to me tonight."

"Oh, I will." His hand cupped my ass. Wes came up behind me.

"At least everyone is safe," Spencer said. "I've settled the bill. Should we go home? I think we've outstayed our welcome."

Desire pooled between my thighs, and I looked up at Wes. "Alpha, take us home."

Chapter Forty-Nine

Brennan

I stared at the ceiling of the room Jett and I shared, which was illuminated only by the alarm clock on the nightstand. Sleep escaped me as Jett slept soundly, curled into me. My bond with Evan was quiet. Now. It hadn't been for most of the night.

Evan and I had a long talk, and I think he'd be okay. While I knew he loved his job, every alpha instinct inside me wanted me to demand that he quit and stay where I could see him at all times.

That, of course, wouldn't go over well. Also, I'd never actually do it.

But the alpha in me wanted to.

Before I could physically reassure my omega when we got back home, he'd started doing shots with Grace in the kitchen. She'd eaten a lot of sugar while we were being questioned, and all I could think of was that she burned a shit-ton of energy and needed to replenish it, and, well, it was also probably the shock of a gunman trying to hurt Evan.

Finally, Wes hauled the both of them off to his room, and I'd felt them all go for a *long* time.

Part of me wanted Evan here, under me–not with them. But I'd seen Grace's face. She probably needed him. After all, this was her *birthday.*

Sighing, I changed positions, willing myself to sleep.

Fucking shit. Someone tried to shoot Evan. My Evan.

And Grace stopped him.

Grace. All four-foot-ten of her.

Her doing that had been utterly terrifying. It could have ended badly. I didn't like gammas being unpredictable–especially if it meant putting herself in danger. If something happened to her, Wes and Evan would be gutted.

I still couldn't believe she risked her life like that for my mate. Yet, if something were to happen to Evan, *I* would be gutted.

"Hey, sleep," Jett mumbled, throwing a hand over me.

"We could have lost him." I turned over to stare at his sleepy face. That face that had literally saved my life. More than once.

"We didn't. It's fine. If they didn't have plans, I'd tell you to stay home with him. I could handle the tournament myself. But I'm sure Wes has this. You could always ask to go." He chuckled. His hand caressed my face.

I snorted. "As much as I want to stay close, I'm pretty sure Evan's *romantic birthday trip* is just him fucking her in his cabin all weekend."

"She sort of deserves all the fucking though?" Jett replied.

"I never expected Grace to put herself between Evan and a gun." I'd been ready to pounce when Grace hit the gunman with a fucking chair.

"It was kinda hot. You're right, it could have gone wrong, quickly," Jett agreed.

No. Not hot. Terrifying. Is this what life with her would be like?

I felt longing and sadness through the bond and sat up.

A moment later, I heard the door to the bedroom open. Evan stumbled in, holding a bottle.

"Hey, Love. Come here." I held out my arms.

Jett took the bottle from Evan and put it on the nightstand. I bundled him into my arms.

"Someone tried to shoot me," he sobbed into my shoulder. He reeked of booze and peaches.

"I have you. You're safe. What do you need?" I peppered his face with kisses and sent all the love I could through the bond.

"Knots. Please, Alpha?" His whine cut my heart in half. "I need your knot and Jett's cock."

"Always, Love." I stroked his hair, trying to ignore that he smelled of her.

"Absolutely, Baby. Anything you want." Jett kissed him deep.

Jett was so fucking good with him, and it made me so happy Jett loved him as much as I did. It was Jett who fell first and then convinced me that I should talk to Wes about us courting Evan, and the four of us forming a pack.

"You're safe and with us," I told him, kissing the booze off his lips. "Now, let us show you how much you mean to us."

"Here you go." Jett slid a plate with an omelet on it in front of me.

"Thanks." My belly growled as I began to eat. Spencer was golfing, and Wes, Evan, and Grace had already left to spend the weekend at Evan's cabin.

"Food," Jett yelled. We'd drop Riley off at school on the way to the boxing tournament.

Part of me worried about Wes being alone with both of them, given he'd told me last night he had his hands full with them. I texted Evan again, just to make sure he was okay.

"This is amazing," I said as I continued to gobble it up.

Jett laughed, as he joined me at the table with food of his own. "Hungry? Evan did keep us up half the night."

"Not the worst thing." I took a sip of coffee.

At some point last night, he'd slipped out of bed, then came back again right before dawn. I wasn't about to begrudge my omega anything, especially after last night.

Even if he came to bed smelling like peaches.

"Maybe we should have asked them to stay?" Worry about being away from him ate at me.

Jett took my face in his hands and kissed me. "Yeah, that wouldn't have gone well. Look, he'll be *fine*. They're going to the cabin. We have security cameras. I really only have to fight today. We could go up tomorrow if you're still unsettled and crash their party."

I sighed. "I don't want to ruin Grace's birthday trip. You know we're banned from the restaurant now?"

"Well, that's shitty. The food was extraordinary." He made a face and took a bite.

"I'm just happy that everyone is okay," I added.

"Me too. It was fucking scary. Grace has the omega growl, didn't expect that," Jett told me.

"I think with Grace we should expect the unexpected," I replied. An omega growl was a rare and terrifying noise that could stop an alpha in their tracks and was usually only heard in two situations—an omega defending their children or their mate.

My phone rang. I growled at it.

"She's going to call until you answer." Jett pushed it to me. "Ri, your food is getting cold," he yelled again.

I glared but took the phone as I grabbed my cup and headed to the coffeepot for a refill. "I only have a moment," I snapped, answering it.

"No need for that tone. I wanted to make sure everyone was okay," my mother snapped back.

No. Her publicist needed to know what to say.

"Everyone is fine," I told her, taking my coffee back to my seat.

"It was a... spectacle." Disapproval hung in her voice.

Morris' didn't make spectacles. We only got in the news for good things.

"Well, you're the one who made us go to Supressa," I retorted.

Riley came out in black and green workout gear and lime green sneakers, and went straight to the fridge to pour herself some juice.

"I wasn't expecting Grace to *hit a gunman with a chair.* That's unacceptable. Katie will coach her on proper behavior before the gala," my mother retorted.

"Are you expecting gunmen at the dinner, Mother?" My voice went tart. "Grace was *defending Evan.*"

Riley grabbed her eggs and toast and sat down at the table.

"He has alphas for that. It makes you look bad that there were three alphas and a police officer and she was the one who took him down. She can't do things like that. Why would she even–"

"Mother, do you know *anything* about gammas? They react unexpectedly." I rubbed my forehead.

"Well, it's creating a headache."

Something inside me snapped.

"This is *my* pack. Mine. Not yours. If you're so worried about me reflecting badly on you, then we'll take a pack last name and distance ourselves from you. Honestly, I'd love to stop attending your boring parties and having you interfering all the time. Now I have to go." I ended the call.

"Did you just tell your mom to fuck off?" Riley poured half a bottle of hot sauce on her eggs.

Jett hugged me. "You stood up to your mom. I'm so fucking proud of you."

I stared at my phone as the realization of what I'd said hit me. "Oh, fuck."

What did I just do?

Jett gave me a kiss. "Feel good?"

"I'm going to pay for it." My chest went tight. Siobhan Morris *always* got her way–and she wasn't afraid to resort to underhand-edness.

"No, because if she tries, you're going to follow through. Let's do it. Pack last name, pack tattoos, no more of her parties." Jett wrapped his arms around me. "Spence can keep his last name pro-fessionally. He might even be happy to be our pack representative since he enjoys going to events."

"True." My gut churned at what I'd just done. Not that I truly regretted it.

"You don't need her money or influence. You're tired of her trying to run your pack. So, let's go no contact," Jett added.

"It's not that easy. She can make our lives miserable." I cleared my plate, rinsed it, and put it in the dishwasher, my gut wrenching. My mother *had* made my life miserable more than once to prove a point and Jett knew that.

"So can we. We have hackers and mad scientists." He looked at Riley.

"I'll fuck her up for you," Riley told me.

"We've got your back. Grace can always hit her with a chair," Jett added.

I couldn't help but laugh at the image. "Or slap her."

My phone rang. I ignored it. Maybe I'd accidentally block my mother for the weekend. Jett was right, this time I had the power of the pack behind me.

"Do I get a tattoo? Are we making up a pack name or are we picking someone's last name and going with that?" Riley asked. Both were normal, just like keeping your name if you wanted. Jett had taken my last name, but Evan had kept his.

"When you turn sixteen. Wes designed our crest. It's what's on our rings. Speaking of rings. Here's yours." I fished hers out of my pocket. Spencer had given it to me this morning.

"I get one?" She held it like it contained the secrets of the universe.

Regret at not giving it to her earlier shot through me.

"You're one of us." Jett patted her shoulder.

Riley beamed and put it on, holding out her hand to admire it. "Thanks, fuckers. It even fits."

"We know a few things about you," I told her. Okay, Spencer did that. I glanced at the clock on the kitchen wall. "We've got to go soon. Are you going to be okay on your own this weekend?"

Her eyes rolled. "Um, yeah. I *have* spent a weekend at school before. I've got the skate smash clinic today and the dance tonight. Tomorrow I'm going to Marcos' to do homework and eat food."

"Just checking. Spence will be in town, so call him if you need anything," I added, taking another sip of coffee.

"I know."

"Also, you can come over whenever you want. You don't have to wait until we have things planned," I said.

Riley's expression went amused. "I know. Why do you think I randomly come over sometimes? Jett, what's wrong with your boy?"

"We just want to make sure you know that you're a part of this family, that's all." Jett shrugged.

"Not you, too. Shit, one gunman and everyone becomes a sappy fuck." She polished off her food.

We could have lost Evan. That's why we were being sappy fucks. We'd already almost lost him once.

"You okay? Must have been scary seeing someone come for your brother," Jett added.

"This is why I live at school." Riley stood. "I knew one of you was going to take him down before anything happened to Evan. Just didn't think it would be Grace. She's the shit."

I grimaced. "That's not how you react to an active shooter."

"Okay." Riley snorted and put her dishes in the sink. "Um, you taking me in your PJs? Because we need to go."

Jett grinned. "Fine, I'll go put on some pants. After all, I've got a tournament to win."

Chapter Fifty

Evan

Grace sat sandwiched between us as Wes drove us through the mountains to where my cabin was. Originally, we were going to take my car, but Grace had insisted we take the truck so we could all sit up front together.

For that, I was grateful. The contact of her leg against mine, her head resting on my shoulder, grounded me, keeping me from panicking.

Last night, someone tried to *shoot me*.

The trainings I'd been through at work all involved someone coming after a client or attacking the Center. Nowhere did we go over someone tracking *me* down when I was off the clock.

My heart sped as I thought of Rose's uncle aiming a gun at me. We'd been having a great time, eating, dancing, enjoying each other's company and boom...

It could have ended so differently.

Because it was a hotel and a restaurant, he had no problem getting up to us. He overpowered the staff when he couldn't get in. Detective Esposito apologized for not being able to hold him for longer. Apparently, he'd threatened people at the station and someone who overheard me tell Detective Esposito where we were going for dinner told him.

Wes squeezed my hand, feeling my anxiety through the bond. Grace snuggled further into me.

Grace.

She'd put herself between the gun and me. It made my heart swell a thousand times. It also made me want to swat that little ass until it was red for putting herself in danger and not getting under the damn table.

I handed her my water bottle, and she took a drink and closed her eyes. She was hung over as fuck.

Not that I felt much better. I had trouble sleeping and kept raiding the liquor cabinet and bouncing between Wes' bed and Brennan's, needing reassurance that everyone was okay.

That I was okay.

Which was why Wes was driving, listening to some perky-ass station, sipping on an iced coffee while the two of us cuddled in misery.

My phone buzzed. I'd been texting back and forth with my boss, getting an incident report filed for last night. I'd also been texting with Rose to make sure she was okay.

Brennan was being an annoying alpha fuck and kept checking on me. My phone beeped.

Carly

You okay? Claire told me what happened.

Her mate was coming over later when Spencer was home to make that door so Grace could use my bathroom.

Me

I'm okay. Thanks.

I'd be okay. Because I had my pack, my family. I pressed my lips to Grace's forehead. Her eyes opened, and she smiled, then draped herself over my lap.

"Are you okay driving, Wes? I can take a turn," I offered, despite being content with my Grace-blanket.

"It's not that much longer until we get to town. We can stop at that little cafe and have something to eat. Maybe we can show Grace the town–if that doesn't spoil any of your plans," Wes offered as he navigated the narrow, curvy roads. "You two should eat something."

A glance at the clock on the dashboard told me that we were making good time. "That sounds nice. Want some food, Peaches?"

"Eh." She shrugged.

"After we eat, we can get ice cream," I suggested, because she should eat something. "There's this little place that makes this farm-to-table, locally-sourced, ice cream. It's so good. The labels even tell you the names of the cows the milk is from."

"Okay."

Grace and I dozed until we got to town. I pointed out the lake where we liked to take out the boat, the mountains we skied on, and my favorite shops.

"We're people who snow ski?" Her eyebrows rose.

Wes laughed. "I know, right? We have a boat, too."

Riley sent me a picture of her hand with a pack ring on it. Aww. I knew Spencer had one made for her, and I was glad she finally had it.

"Going boating was common where I grew up. I can even waterski. Never been snow skiing though." Grace leaned over me to look out the window.

I'd never actually heard it called *snow skiing* before.

We pulled into a wooden country restaurant with a big porch. This was our favorite breakfast and lunch spot when we came up here.

The place was done up with all sorts of country decor. The server seated us immediately. It was busy but not crowded, and delightful smells tickled my nose.

I slid into the booth, placing myself next to the wall, and Grace slid in next to me, putting her head on my shoulder. Instead of sitting across from us, Wes joined us on our side. It was a snug fit, but not unpleasant.

"Is this okay?" Wes asked us.

Grace nodded, hooking her arm through Wes', head still on my shoulder. "Yeah. Ugh, why did I drink so much?"

Same reason why she hadn't let go of me this morning.

"Can I get you something to drink?" the server asked, giving Wes an appreciative look as he handed us menus.

"Ginger fizz, please," I replied. I needed something to settle my stomach.

"Coffee," Grace mumbled.

"Iced coffee—and waters for everyone," Wes ordered.

Grace gave him a look but said nothing.

"Where exactly did you learn that you should hit shooters with chairs? That wasn't something we learned at the Center—or in the military," I asked, stroking her hair as the server left.

"It's something they teach teachers in the active shooter unit of the classroom management class. Chair, fire extinguisher, anything within reach. I mean you try to keep them out, but sometimes they get in." Her eyes closed.

"Is that common at schools where you lived? People shooting *children?*" The thought made my heart palpitate.

"Sadly. That's why we run drills." Her head bowed.

"That's fucked up," Wes said softly as the server brought our drinks.

"Yep." Grace added a whole lot of sugar to her coffee.

Wes pushed her water toward her. She gave him a look and took a gulp of coffee. No, she wasn't going to win that one. I took a sip of my ginger fizz.

The server came back. "What are we having today?"

"I'll have a bacon cheeseburger and fries," I ordered. That should do the trick. Grease and carbs.

"Fried chicken," Wes said.

Grace frowned at the menu. "I just don't know... oh." Her eyes lit up. "Biscuits and gravy with a side of bacon."

The server gathered our menus and scurried off.

"I remember that my dad used to make the best biscuits and gravy. Haven't had that in ages," she sighed. Polishing off her coffee, she held up her cup as the server came past.

"I know you loved your dad, but I never understood how he could let your mom be so awful to you. If I had kids, I wouldn't let anyone harm them, let alone my spouse." Wes pushed the cup of water toward her. "Do you know why? Is that something you remember?"

"Yeah." She poked at the ice in the water cup with her straw. "For a long time, I didn't either. After my mom disowned me, he divorced her. Made her and my brothers hate me even more. Anyhow, he apologized to me."

The server put a pot of coffee on the table.

"He did?" Wes asked.

"He did." Grace refilled her mug. "Then he explained why he hadn't stood up for me as much as I wanted him to."

"What was his reason? Because I would have left her when she sent you to camp and gotten your ass out of there," Wes said.

"He tried to get me and wasn't allowed by the camp. He was against all of it. The drugs. The holds. The dumb church doctors. The essential oils. Saying I was *troubled*. But..." Grace chewed on her lower lip as she added sugar to her coffee. "He wasn't my dad. All my life I had no idea that he wasn't my biological father. He's the dad of my brothers, but not me. I was a baby when he met my mom. I guess my mom always pulled the *You're not her real dad, you don't get a say* card. He apologized for not having done more to protect me."

Shit.

Wes pulled her to him. "Wow."

"I had no idea. That's why he was mostly reactive–getting me my blankets back when she was at Bible study, making my favorite foods after we had a nasty fight, cheering me up with dad jokes." Her body shuddered as she sighed.

"Did you ever contact your biological father? Do you remember that?" I asked quietly, scooting closer to her, wanting to soothe her, too.

She shook her head. "My dad didn't know who he was. Asking her meant talking to her. I was too slammed working and going to school, and I just didn't have time for daddy drama on top of everything else I was trying to work through. His identity died with her, and I'm okay with that. My dad is my dad, and I forgave him for not doing more–especially when I found out all the ways he tried and failed to help me."

So much to unpack there. My heart ached for her.

"I'm going to hit the bathroom before our food comes." She crawled over Wes and left the booth.

"I wasn't expecting that," Wes told me, taking a sip of his iced coffee.

"Me neither. *If* you had kids?" I kept my voice quiet, but it bothered me, and I needed to address it. "When did we go back to *if?*"

That hurt. I was in my thirties, and I wanted kids sooner rather than later.

Wes put his arm around me. "I was trying not to spook Grace. She's not ready yet–and she's afraid she won't be a good mom. I also don't want her to think that we only see her value to our all-dude pack in being that she has a baby factory."

"Oh, okay." Relief filled me. "She's just starting her career. I can respect that. Don't worry, I'll reassure her that everything is entirely her choice. I don't think she's gotten to that unit yet."

Wes blinked. "You will?"

"Of course. I've given that talk a million times. Because of that whole ingrained attitude about female omegas being made to give male alphas babies." I rolled my eyes. "Also, she doesn't have to have them. There are other ways."

Which we'd looked into, since while there'd been a couple miracle births in the past couple decades, most male omegas couldn't carry children–me included.

"We will get kids, eventually." Wes squeezed me.

"How? Cabbage patch?" Grace said, frowning as she squeezed between us. "I messed up the kid timeline, didn't I?"

"No. Not one bit. We didn't have a kid timeline," Wes assured her.

"He's right. I want a kid or three. But I want you to know you don't have to carry kids if you don't want to. I'm not sure if *cabbage patch* means adoption but that's what we were looking at. You know, with six adults in the house, you wouldn't have more responsibilities than you want." I took a sip of my drink, putting my arm around her.

"Three?" She looked up at me and shook her head. "I vote for two kids, three-to-four years apart, one boy, one girl."

I laughed. "I don't care how many."

"Wyatt and Hannah." Wes grinned at her.

She nodded. "Absolutely."

"I always liked Greyson and Daisy," I offered, grinning back. They had baby names picked out? My heart melted.

"Ooh, those are nice, too," she nodded.

The server brought our food.

Grace ate a piece of bacon and frowned. "What if I can't have kids? I have wacky cycles and killer cramps. The few days before my period, I'm down for the count. Like crying and throwing up bad. It's awful. It's a good thing they're not every month or I would have trouble holding down a job. The doctors always dismissed me as being dramatic, but from talking to other women, it could mean that I have fertility issues."

"Peaches, it doesn't matter." I cupped her face with my hand and she relaxed under my touch. "Can't. Don't want to. None of that matters. Everything regarding your body is your choice. Promise. At your next appointment, tell your doctor about your cycle troubles. If they can't handle it, they'll refer you to a specialist. My sisters get bad cramps, and there are things doctors can do."

Betas had different cycles than omegas, and we should figure out where Grace fit.

"Thank goodness. I mean, I'd be open to adoption if I can't have kids." She took a bite of biscuit, smothered in white gravy. "This is it."

I stole a bite of her food, letting the flavor burst over my tongue. "Oh, yeah."

Hangover food for the win.

"Yup." She took one of my fries.

"If and when you're ready, you'll make a great mom," I added, kissing her temple. "Just make sure you're on industrial strength birth control until then—and I'll stay on mine. Omega males are um, *potent*." I grinned, glad Wes and I had both gotten implants. "Especially when we're close to or in heat. You can't be too careful."

My heat was coming. Soon. Male omegas were very good at making kids, and that urge to fuck and be fucked became overwhelming during our heats.

At some point, we needed to discuss my upcoming heat with Grace. Usually we came here, to my cabin. Even Spencer, who didn't participate, just hung out, worked remotely, and made food. While Jett, Brennan, Wes, and I had heat sex. For days.

Would Grace be part of it this time? I wanted her to, but she might not be ready.

While what happened in the heat nest stayed in the heat nest, Brennan and Jett might not be ready either.

I may have had a few fantasies about the three of them together.

"Good idea, I'll do that." She polished off her coffee and poured herself some more.

"Please drink some water." Wes pushed her cup toward her. "This isn't the day to have a blood feud with hydration. Evan has plans, and you don't want to feel shitty all day."

"Fine." With a sigh, she took a big drink of water, then went back to making inroads in her food. "I guess having six adults would make it easier to raise kids. Do packs have lots of kids? Six adults and two kids could make for low birth rates if everyone did that."

"It depends. I mean, it was just my mom and dad, and there are four of us kids," I replied, finishing my burger. "Our neighborhood was mostly beta couples and throuples."

"There were tons of kids in the pack I lived in before we moved here. But it wasn't quite like our pack. It was bigger. There were families and couples within the pack," Wes said. "We all lived in this condo complex. We had a pool and a gym. There was always someone around to play with."

I squeezed his hand. Wes always got a little sad when he talked about leaving that pack. It had been hard on him, going from always having people around to it just being him, his dad, and sister. His dad also worked long hours in construction.

"Will Ri be okay with it? I'd be so sad if she weren't." Grace took another one of my fries and then dipped it in Wes' mashed potatoes.

"She will. I love that you get along," I reassured her.

"I love her." Grace beamed and drank some more water. "So, we're getting married at some point? Like all three of us?"

"I'd actually like all three of us—if that's okay?" I looked at Wes, who nodded.

"What are weddings like here?" She took another fry and dipped it in the gravy on her plate.

"Whatever we want," I told her. "Basically, it's a ceremony followed by a party. But it can be big or small, at your house or a fancy hotel. Sometimes they're even elsewhere. Bren and Jett got married at one of Bren's hotels, and we flew there. It was an entire week. But if you own fancy hotels, why not?"

"He owns hotels? For some reason I thought he owned buildings," Grace said.

"His mom does. He has luxury hotels," Wes replied, finishing his chicken. "We could get married at one of them. Or we could take a trip there after. Lots of people go on a trip."

"Wes and I rented a little cabin for two weeks—on this lake, actually." It was really nice. We both had finished with the military. I was about to finish my social work program, and Wes would start his new job with Spencer. I'd been serving a longer term in the military than Wes, but I'd started much earlier, given I was older.

Grace's face lit up. "Where do you want to get married?"

"Brennan might buy this old estate nearby to use as an event venue. It would be nice to get married in a rose garden." As we finished eating, I showed her the pictures that Bren had sent me of the place, along with pictures I'd found of potential ideas for decor, food, and flowers.

"These are perfect," Grace said as she finished her water.

"Can we have a band at the reception? The string stuff is nice. But I want to dance," Wes said.

"Of course," I laughed. "Anything else you want? It's your wedding, too."

"The whiskey fountain you sent me. But let's use a better quality whiskey, because that was pale looking," he added.

It was a champagne fountain.

"Sure." Whiskey fountain, why not?

"Ooh, what about a giant cheese board," Grace added. "One of those fancy ones that takes up an entire table."

"And that thing you showed me with all the candy in the jars," Wes said.

My heart swelled. We were talking about *our wedding*.

We paid our check, and Wes held out a hand to help Grace out of the booth, then me.

"I feel so much better," Grace admitted, leaning into me.

"I'm glad." I put an arm around her. "Let's go for a walk and find that ice cream."

Chapter Fifty-One

Grace

We drove down a tree-lined dirt driveway, snow on the ground. A beautiful blue lake came into view.

"The lake has hot springs in it. It's not a warm lake by any stretch of the imagination, but it keeps it from freezing. We haven't gotten the boat out of winter storage yet, though," Evan told me. "We don't have waterskis, but we have a tube we pull, and one of those inflatable water trampolines."

"That sounds like a ton of fun for summer," I told him.

The air inside the truck was heavy with their scents. I was pretty sure sex was a big part of my romantic birthday weekend plans. I was looking forward to it, especially if they finally let me be the filling.

"This afternoon, I thought it might be fun to go to the snow-tubing park," Evan told me. "Another time we can ski."

"That sounds fun. I'd love to learn to snowboard."

"Ri would love you to snowboard with her," Evan told me.

"Are we catching fish for our dinner?" I asked, trying to get a better view of everything. It was beautiful here, and I could see why they'd chosen this place for their honeymoon.

"We could for lunch tomorrow, as long as you're a better angler than Wes." Evan laughed.

"Hey!" Wes chuckled as a giant wooden house appeared. It was a fancy multi-story wood and brick structure with peaked roofs and balconies.

"That's not a cabin." I poked Evan with my elbow.

"I know. I freaked out when they got it for me. It wasn't that I had an issue with a romantic cabin in the woods. That seemed perfectly reasonable. But this—this is a forest mansion," Evan told me.

"It doesn't have enough bedrooms to be a mansion, well, according to Bren," Wes said.

"They got you a *house*?" What a gift. But then their pack had money.

"It's a custom. As part of the pack agreement, the pack gives the omega assets of their own, in their own name, to prevent financial abuse. A house is pretty common. I just wasn't expecting a house like *that*," he explained.

"Oh, that makes so much sense." I admired the beautiful house. My eyes rested on the corner of the roof. "Is that a turret?"

Evan's lemonade scent got stronger. "Oh, Peaches, I can't wait to show you my turret."

The garage was bigger than the one at the house. It was also full of things like snowmobiles, ski equipment, and fishing gear.

We grabbed our stuff and entered some sort of utility room, where Evan entered a code, then brought me into a big airy kitchen. Snacks covered the counter–and not a bowl of chips and a tray of carrots—there was a fancy display of meats, cheese, fruits, and nuts. A bottle of champagne sat in a silver bucket next to a tray of chocolate-covered strawberries, and an enormous bouquet with a *Happy Birthday* sign in it.

My hand went to my heart. "You did this for me?"

"Happy Birthday, Peaches." Evan kissed me. "Let's put our stuff down, then we can have a snack and go play in the snow."

Ooh, I wanted a snowball fight with my guys.

The dining room looked out onto the lake–as did the airy living room. A deck wrapped around the entire floor, complete with a raised gazebo, and a weird-looking fancy grill.

"This living room." I turned around. It opened onto the second floor. There was even a tucked-away reading nook with a cozy round chair, a shelf of books, and a beautiful view.

"I know. But this is my favorite." He pulled me over to one wall and threw open a curtain, where there was a cozy alcove with a big couch. "There's a TV built into the wall. Riley's room is on this floor. There's an office, too. Downstairs is laundry, storage, a game room, the gym, and a little screened-in patio and backyard."

"This is insane." I twirled around the massive, beautiful house.

"I know," Wes told me. "The gazebo is *heated* for year-round outdoor dining."

We went up the stairs and I was greeted with doors and a view of the living room below.

Evan walked me to a far corner and opened a door. "While you're always welcome in my room, I thought you'd like this one."

A low bed was built *into* the bay window wall, piled with fluffy blankets and pillows and hung with lights and sheer curtains. It would be snug with the three of us. The window held a breath-taking view of the lake. The roof was sloped, and the small room felt cozy.

"Oh, Evan." I wanted to dive into that bed full of blankets and pillows, which for some reason seemed inviting, not messy. The room was also uncluttered—there was literally nothing else in the room.

He wrapped his arms around me. "The closet and drawers are built into the wall. It's not a lot of space, but like I said, you're welcome in my bed anytime. I thought you'd like your own little place. There are even secret bookshelves—look."

Evan brought me over to the bed and showed me how the bookshelves *pulled out of the wall* by the window.

"I..." I fell back into the soft bed. "Oh, my god."

He grinned. "I knew you'd love it. Look, the wall lights look like candles."

I tugged on his hand, and he fell onto the bed with me.

"Do you mean that?" He gave me a heated look as the room filled with the special smell that meant he was extra-aroused.

I hit him with a pillow.

Wes growled from the doorway. "If you two don't get out of there, I'm coming in, and I'm pretty sure we'll spoil Evan's afternoon plans."

"Fine." I rolled out of the bed. "My stuff goes here?"

"Usually. This time, I thought we'd all stay in my room." With a wink, Evan popped out of the bed, and took my hand and led me out of the cute room. He opened another door in the hall. "This is your nearest bathroom."

I went inside the granite bathroom. "There's a waterfall in the bathtub."

"Yep. Spencer's room is through the adjoining door." Evan led us back out. "We've got Bren and Jett's room, then Wes' room. Their bathroom has a sauna."

"Wes has a room? I want to see." I opened the door.

The bed looked like rough-hewn logs, as did the matching furniture. It was done in green plaid. There was a fireplace and a big, fuzzy rug.

"This is cute," I told him.

"It is. But I have more to show you." Evan led me upstairs. There were two more doors. We went to the right. There were more sloping ceilings and a view of the lake. There was a fireplace and a gigantic bed, unfussy, but comfortable, with a wooden headboard and more matching lumberjack furniture, which must be a theme. The area in front of the window was almost alcove-like with a little seating area.

"There's a balcony and a hot tub with a lake view," Evan said as he set our stuff down on the low table.

Wes pulled the two of us down into the big soft bed. His arms wrapped around me and Evan, and for a moment I let their scents and muscles wrap around me as he purred.

"Your house is stunning," I told Evan, relishing in snuggling with my guys.

"It is. I love spending time here," Evan said. "And I hope you do, too."

I gazed out at the lake. From here I could see the dock and a fire-pit. "I could get used to this."

"As much as I joke about rich people and their toys, there are perks," Evan told me.

"Wait until you see the boat." Wes crawled out of bed. "I'll be back." He went through a door that was probably the bathroom.

Evan got a mischievous look on his face. "Come on, I want to show you something."

I followed him out of the room, and we went through the other door. There was a little cozy sitting room with a kitchenette and a giant couch, and an open door that looked like a bathroom. There was also a small staircase. Evan took my hand and led me up the stairs. A small landing had a door, a bench, some cupboards, and hooks with robes on them. He kicked off his shoes, and I did the same.

The door was open, and he led me through. The small room was low-ceilinged--like Evan nearly hit the roof with his head--and light streamed in through a skylight. He pressed a switch, and electric candles lit up everywhere. There was a little window with a seat. My feet sank into the thick, padded carpet. The walls were draped with silky saffron-colored fabric.

"I feel like I'm in a spice box." I leaned into him.

"This is my turret." Again, his look went heated as the room went thick with the scent of his arousal.

"This is a sex turret." I looked around. Most of the room was a sunken area filled with pillows and blankets in the deep colors Evan liked.

"Yep. It's a fuck-nest. I plan on having you here tonight." He nibbled on my neck, and I shivered with pleasure.

Yes, take me in the fuck-nest.

Holding my hand, he jumped into the sunken bed, taking me with him. I buried myself under the pillows, relishing in the sensation as my body trembled in pleasure.

"Peaches, keep doing that and I'll have you right now." Evan's nose touched mine. We were under the covers, and it felt like we were in a blanket fort.

"Do we have time for a quickie?" My thighs rubbed together with desire, warmth seeping through me.

"Don't tempt me. With my heat coming, I'm a horny fuck." Evan hummed and burrowed in with me, holding me close, his hard-on digging into me.

"You're always horny." My head rested on his chest. The tension I'd felt since last night melted away. I was cozy, safe, loved, and with Evan. "It's soon?"

I knew little about heats. Just that they were omega fertile cycles and involved days of non-stop sex.

"In three weeks, while Riley's on spring break. Yeah, that was purposeful. Thank goodness for drugs that help you schedule your heat." His hand stroked my back.

"It's what, four or five times a year? That's a lot of time off–do you ever get to take vacations if you're using all your time off for that?" My eyes closed. I needed to finish the modules.

"I'm a dude, so it's more like two or three a year. But yeah, that's part of why omegas didn't used to work. Now there are supplements that a lot of omegas use to adjust and even shorten their cycles–and suppressants so you don't get them at all. A few long weekends a year are completely doable while holding down a job, especially if you time them to holiday weekends. You can use your health days, too."

"Three weeks, that's soon." My heart thumped a little. Days and days of sex.

"I'm probably going to start humping you more than usual as my hormones ramp up. I might even spike–that's my hormones going into overdrive. Basically, if I'm warm and whine that I need you, text Wes and pay me attention." He smiled.

"So, make love to you and tell you that you're pretty until Wes gets there and then do it again?" I ground against him.

"Absolutely. We can talk about this later, but we all usually come here. Even Spence. He hangs out, makes sure we have snacks and water, and then makes a shit-ton of Greek food when we're done. I..." He cupped my face with his hand. "I want you to be here, too. If you don't want to participate, that's fine. Knowing you're here would be a comfort. You could hang out with Spence, take out the boat, explore. If you do want to take part–even if you just come and go–I'd love that, too."

I thought for a moment. "While it sounds lovely, I think I need to watch those modules so I know what this entails."

"I can watch them with you and answer any questions. You have options. If you're not ready to even just be here with us, I'm pretty sure we can convince Spencer to take you on a trip instead," he offered. "He'll show you a great time."

"I can imagine. Those are all great options. Thank you for being so considerate of my feelings." I kissed him softly. "It would be all your dudes, right?"

If it were just the three of us, it would be an easy decision.

"Yeah—and through most of it they won't be able to leave me for long. I also haven't talked to them about this at all. Mostly, I wanted to see if you were even ready to come with us, because if Spence is whisking you away, we should plan that," he said.

"Not sure I'm ready for a multi-day sex party with *all* your dudes, but let's watch the modules so that I understand and go from there? Hanging out here with Spence could be fun, too." We could play chess, talk science, stargaze...

Make out.

Evan kissed me. "That sounds like a great idea."

I kissed him back, long and deep, my body grinding against his. His scent wrapped around me, as his breath grew raspy, his mouth gliding over my neck.

Wes growled in the doorway. "You two keep looking cute, in nests, *with all your clothes on.*"

"Hi, Babe." Evan waved cheekily. "So, this is my nest. Let's have a snack and go play in the snow."

Chapter Fifty-Two

Grace

"Take that, Boo-Bear." I threw a snowball at Wes and ran away laughing.

"I'm going to get you, my princess peaches." Wes chased after me, pelting me with one.

"Babe, don't throw snowballs at Peaches." Evan threw two snowballs at Wes.

Wes grabbed some snow in his gloved hand, packed it, and threw it at Evan. "I will so, Babe."

We'd spent the afternoon tubing in the snow at the fancy snow play area at the local ski resort. Then we got hot chocolate. We were supposed to be going to the car, but Evan had other ideas when he started a snowball fight.

I jumped onto Wes' back, giggling.

"Save a horse, ride an alpha," I laughed, kicking his sides with my heels.

Wes neighed and galloped through the snow, and I couldn't help but giggle as I clung to his back. An older throuple, hot chocolate in hand, chuckled fondly.

Evan looked at his phone. "Okay, we can head back now."

"Can we?" Wes trotted to his truck.

"Yes." He nodded as we peeled off our gloves and jackets and got in.

We drove back to the cabin and went inside. I looked out the giant glass windows. Tiny lights twinkled on the raised gazebo that was off the dining room.

"That's so pretty," I said, leaning into Evan. "Are there people in the gazebo?"

"Yep. So, cool rich people thing? I can pay someone to cook and set up a romantic dinner for us while we have fun." Evan grinned. He looked at his phone. "Dinner's almost ready. You have time to change but not to shower. This is not a dress-up dinner."

"Sounds amazing. I'm hungry. Oh, this is *your* house, so you can have someone clean the house and set up cheese boards without Brennan objecting," I nodded. I'd wondered where the snacks had come from.

He grinned. "Yep. And have someone fix up your room for you."

We all went into Evan's room and changed out of our snow clothes and into jeans and hoodies.

My phone beeped, and I got a picture of Riley and her friends getting ready for the dance. Earlier I'd gotten pictures of the skate smash clinic. I sent her a picture of me with the water in the background.

Spencer sent pictures of the construction in my room as they made a door from my room to Evan's bathroom.

The three of us went out to the gazebo. In addition to the lights, the table had been set with a tablecloth and flowers, as soft music played. The entire area was nice and warm. We had a magnificent view of the lake.

"This is beautiful," I whispered.

"Evan, you did an amazing job planning this." Wes gave him a kiss. "This entire weekend was planned by him."

I kissed them both. "I'm having so much fun."

The three of us sat down to a romantic dinner as the sun set, followed by marshmallow roasting around the fire-pit by the dock.

I hummed as I licked marshmallow off my fingers. The air had gotten chilly, but I was fine close to the fire. The water lapped softly, and the sounds of night surrounded us. I got more pictures from Riley, this time of the dance itself.

"Everything is so perfect, thank you so much. I know I keep saying it, but I haven't had such a nice birthday in a very long time." I gave them more kisses, trying to show them exactly how grateful I was.

"Mmmm, marshmallows." Wes licked the corner of my mouth. "Missed a spot. I'm glad you like stuff like this. Dinners at fancy restaurants are fun, but this…"

"This is the life." Evan stretched. "Anyone up for the hot tub?"

We put out the fire and went back into the house. Evan and I climbed into the hot tub on the porch. Wes joined us, bringing us beers.

"This is amazing." I leaned into Evan and drank my beer as we looked out into the darkness.

Evan nuzzled my neck. "Will you let me bond with you tonight?"

Yes, please. "That's a thing?"

"It doesn't leave a mark after it heals like an alpha bite, and is not legally binding like with an alpha, but yeah," he nipped at my jaw. "It is. You bonded Wes, remember?"

I bit him, but I didn't realize I was bonding with him like he had me.

"Do I get to bite you back." I nibbled his ear, loving the prospect.

He exhaled sharply. "Yes, please."

"I can't wait to see that," Wes told us, giving us each a kiss.

"I'm both relaxed and turned on." I sighed, feeling Wes' hard cock against me. He rubbed my neck, the heat inside me building.

"Good. Because we're just getting started, if you're not too tired." Evan straddled me, capturing my mouth, his erection pressing against my stomach.

We got out of the hot tub and went inside and showered off. With care, Wes dried us and got us into fluffy robes. I felt deliciously pampered—and beyond ready for some cock. But I didn't want to rush any plans.

The two of them led me out of the room and back to the turret, where we went up the stairs past the sitting room and to the door of Evan's pretty fuck-nest.

"Is this okay, Peaches, if we stay in here for a bit?" Evan went inside the room and flipped a switch that left the room with a soft orangey glow.

"Can we come in, Evan?" Wes asked, picking me up bridal-style, after he hung up his robe.

"Please." A bunch of electric candles were lit on little sconces built into the wall. There were a few things on the window-seat, including some water bottles.

"I'm here for all your birthday plans, as long as I get some more dick." My pussy was wet and aching, ready to be taken long and hard.

Evan went out, then came back in naked, and closed the door partway. He climbed in with us and spread my legs as I lay against Wes' chest.

"Peaches, I need to taste you." Evan lapped at my clit, two fingers thrusting inside me.

A gasp escaped my lips as Wes sucked on my neck. Hands toyed with my nipples. His hardness continued to poke into my back. Waves of sensation coated me as I writhed under their touches.

Evan looked up, face glistening with my juices. "Let us take care of you."

"It tickles." I laughed, as Evan's tongue glided over my clit again. Three fingers entered me, and I squeezed, enjoying the way it felt.

Wes leaned over and caught my nipple with his teeth, making me buck a little, my pelvis arching, wanting *more*.

"There." I gasped, Evan's fingers sending jolts of pleasure through me. Still tonguing me, his fingers gently massaged that little spot, making the jolts continue until he found the magic combination.

An orgasm ripped through my body, as I squealed, hips arching again. "More, please."

Evan continued to strum the spot, making my body come again. Their scents intensified, swirling around me in a heady cocktail. I let it pull me under as another orgasm wrecked me.

Evan licked my pussy in a long, languid motion and purred. "That tastes so good."

Wes crawled out from behind me, gently propping me with pillows, pupils dilated with desire, nose twitching.

"I want some," Wes growled.

"Oh, please, sir, may I have some more." The need for another orgasm consumed me. *So thirsty.*

Evan's fingers found that spot again, as his mouth continued lavishing me with attention.

"Oh my god." I came with an intensity I hadn't before, and I gushed again.

"Fuck." Wes buried his face in my thighs, licking me with fervor, as I cried in pleasure. He stroked Evan's cock.

"Right there," Evan gasped, with a slight whine in his voice. "Alpha."

"That's it," Wes crooned. "Get all nice and worked up for me."

"Oh, yes, yes." I trembled again, this one almost painful.

"That was beautiful," Wes said, stroking Evan's cock with one hand and fondling his balls with another.

Evan's cock was glistening with not just pre-cum but those sticky strands he made when extra aroused. *Slick*, the videos called it. It was basically natural lube. His tasted like lemon candy.

"Time for a taste test." Wes licked the length of Evan's dick, twirling his tongue around it to get a good amount of slick. "Mmmm, Babe, you always taste amazing." With a satisfied look on his face, he leaned over and licked the wetness off Evan's lips.

Wes' scent flared, and my pussy pulsed as my entire body grew warm and I moaned. With one hand he ran his fingers down Evan's cock, the other rolled in my juices. He held both hands to Evan's mouth, and he sucked on one then the other.

A moan escaped Evan's lips. "Fuck."

Wes pushed my thighs apart even further and buried his face deep as if trying to absorb every last bit of my essence.

Evan lavished attention on my breasts, and I reached over to stroke his cock as he groaned. "That feels so good, Peaches."

Wes lightly stroked his swollen cock, his knot already partially inflated. "Get her ready for us? If that's what you still want, Peaches? The both of us at the same time."

Evan got a bottle of lube and pushed up my legs as he liberally lubed my ass with one hand, the other pumping in and out of my pussy.

"Please, oh god, please." It was half-whine, half-plea, as Evan circled my asshole with a finger.

Little zings of pleasure went through me. We'd been working up to this, and I was ready. *Finally.*

"I'm going to knot your pussy so hard while Evan takes your pretty ass. Then I'm going to have him, while he fills whatever hole you want him to," Wes said, still stroking his cock.

"Yes, Alpha," Evan moaned. His mouth sealed over mine before I could respond, as he added another finger, stretching my ass even more.

"This is so beautiful," Wes whispered.

I pressed into Evan's hand, as I surrendered myself to them, his fingers working me into a frenzy. The tension built inside me, and a whine escaped my lips as I got through the bond how much they wanted me—the strongest I'd ever felt them. Hopefully, they could feel how much I wanted them.

"Please," I begged, ready to explode. I wasn't even sure how many fingers were inside me as waves of pleasure crashed down on me.

"Please, what?" Wes's voice was rough as he came back over to us, nuzzling my neck, trailing kisses down my throat that lit my body on fire.

"Cock. I need cock, Alpha. Both preferably," I gasped, ready to be thoroughly dicked by them both.

"Good. On your knees, Peaches." Wes' hand cupped my ass as he kissed Evan.

Getting on my knees, Evan kissed the back of my neck and Wes nibbled on my lower lip. I gasped as Evan's kisses went down my spine, his fingers going back to work on my ass, a third one slipping in.

"Eyes on me. You're doing so well," Wes purred. "You still want this?"

"Yes, Alpha. Please," I pleaded. "I need you both." On so many levels.

Evan's kisses hovered over the small of my back as he withdrew his fingers. "Just gonna lube us both up. I'm all slick for you, but I want you to be comfortable," he murmured as he rubbed more lube on my ass.

Wes nibbled, sucked, and teased my lips and mouth. The tip of Evan's cock pressed against my hole slowly, popping past the tight ring of muscles.

"You feel so good," Evan breathed, as he continued to trail kisses up and down my back.

"You're doing great, both of you," Wes praised, lifting me so my hands were on his shoulders. "Eyes on me, Grace, breathe."

I took a deep breath as Evan eased himself in, inch by inch.

"Shit, that feels good," Evan groaned, teeth grazing my collarbone.

My breath came out in pants as Evan latched onto my throat and started shallow thrusts.

"Perfect," Wes murmured, hands over mine as he kissed me again and again.

Evan's breath was against my ear as his strokes got deeper and deeper. I moaned as he stretched me and filled me up, Wes' face filled with desire as he gave us kisses, strokes, and encouraging murmurs as I rose to another peak.

"Ready for it all?" Evan whispered.

I nodded.

Evan pushed, until I felt bursting with omega cock, his balls nestled against my ass. "Oh, Peaches. You're good?"

I exhaled. "I feel so full."

"Just wait." Evan groaned, "Alpha, I want you inside her."

Wes nipped my earlobe. "You want my knot, Peaches? Do you want me to stuff that sweet pussy full as Evan rides your ass?"

"Please, Alpha," I keened, as Evan held me tight against him, my pussy aching for attention. "Fill me up until I explode."

Wes growled as he grabbed my hips, lifting me up, my hands gripping onto his shoulders. Evan stayed close to me as his hand helped guide Wes' cock, glistening with pre-cum, into my needy hole. Gently, slowly, almost agonizingly, Wes lowered me down the length of his dick.

The pressure and stretch of having both holes filled simultaneously made me cry out in pleasure. Evan held me tightly to his chest, murmuring in my ear as he kissed and licked my earlobe.

"Oh, Peaches." Wes sighed, keeping the pressure on my hips firm and steady but gentle, until he was inside me up to his knot, which was now fully inflated.

For a moment we sat there, arms around each other as I adjusted to both of them being inside me.

"Are you okay?" Wes nuzzled my cheek with his.

"Good, just full." The warmth of them in me, of being able to share this with them at the same time, moved through me, replacing the blood in my veins, and filling me full of love.

Evan groaned. "Wes, I feel you. Fuuuuck, I didn't know I'd feel you, too."

Wes touched his forehead to mine as they slowly started moving, one going out as the other pushed in.

"Oh god, that's it." I moaned, looking down to watch Wes' swollen length pump in and out of me.

"I know." Evan sighed, sucking on my neck, our bodies rocking. "I'm so close, Alpha."

"Me, too," I hissed, as they brought me spiraling closer and closer to my peak. "I need all of you, Wes. Knot me, Alpha."

"Please," Evan keened. "I want to know what it feels like when your knot locks inside her."

Wes growled, lifting me up, then plunging me down his cock, this time moving past his knot, lightly but firmly pressing me down until his knot popped inside my channel, filling me even fuller.

My body exploded as I shuddered against their cocks with a fervor that was almost violent.

"Wes, Evan, oh my god," I cried, as the orgasm seized me, holding onto Wes with all my might, that knot of nerves and muscle keeping him locked inside me.

"I'm going to come," Evan murmured. "Bite me, right here. Hard enough to draw blood." He moved my head toward his shoulder.

It was a little awkward with him behind me. Still, my teeth clamped down on his shoulder, as he came inside me, filling my ass with his cum. Another orgasm crashed down on me.

Wes peppered my face with gentle kisses as he rocked into me, knot pulsing. He held me tight to him as he moved. Aftershock after aftershock coursed through me. Both of them murmured to me, Evan staying seated inside me, as Wes continued, the very top of his knot hitting against my clit deliciously as I ground down on it.

I flexed my ass muscles, wanting Evan to move again.

"Mmmm, I can go again. I can feel him, feel the both of you, so good," Evan murmured, licking my neck.

"Take him again, sweet peach." Wes' lips locked with Evan's as their dual rhythm started again, sinking then retreating over and over.

The weight of his knot, the feeling of his pelvis rocking against my clit, pushed me toward another orgasm. Light flashed before my eyes as I felt almost overwhelmed by their thick and heady scents washing over me, the feelings I got from the bond, the pleasure coursing through me threatening to drag me under.

"Give in. If we shatter, he'll catch us," Evan whispered, pressing in deep, making my muscles flutter against the thick length.

My body trembled as bursts of pleasure made me fly higher and higher. I pushed into Wes, letting them thrust and pound until the heat inside me exploded, body bowing. My pussy and ass muscles shuddered hard with pleasure. I shattered into a million pieces, letting the tingling sensation and their love utterly and totally consume me.

"Evan, I feel you moving. Oh, Peaches." Wes groaned, burying his face in my neck, as he came inside me, his knot growing and pulsing slightly with his release.

"I'm going to come," Evan said. "Let me bite *you* now."

"Oh, please."

He leaned around me as his teeth clamped down on my shoulder, the stinging turning to pleasure. Heat filled me as he spasmed, his cum dripping down my leg as Wes' knot kept his inside me.

The three of us rocked in each other's arms until we collapsed in a pile in the nest. Wes' knot caused my body to tremble with little mini shocks as he moved and shifted us, Evan still inside me, into a comfortable position.

"Is everyone okay? That was amazing," Wes said, trying to get his arms around both of us. His purr rumbled through his chest, making me relax into their arms like the satiated puddle I was.

"Once again, I'm boneless." I sighed, feeling so content and happy. *Mine.* They were mine.

"Me, too." Evan purred as well. Both purrs wrapped around me like the blanket Wes threw on top of us.

"I enjoy being the filling," I murmured.

"Feeling Wes *in you?* Fuuuuck," Evan whispered as he licked where he marked me. "But Alpha, I want that knot as soon as you're able."

"It's yours," Wes assured, continuing to purr for us. "I love the two of you so much."

"I love you, too." He kissed me. Slipping out of me, he positioned himself at my back, arms draped over me and Wes.

"Best birthday present. I love you both until the end of the universe," I told them, kissing Evan's mark, then Wes.

"To the end of the universe," Wes agreed.

I cuddled them close, so satisfied, so content, so warmed by their purrs and the feelings of love and happiness coming through the bond that I wasn't entirely sure where I ended and where they began.

And I couldn't be happier for it.

Chapter Fifty-Three

Wes

"Let me go. I thought we were friends–" Grace shrieked, wrestling me from sleep as she thrashed in the dark nest.

"Grace, hey, it's okay. I'm right here. It's just a nightmare. You're okay." I covered her naked body with mine, pulling a blanket over us, trying to comfort her with my presence.

Evan, who'd been hugging my back, sat up. "What's wrong?"

"Nightmare. You're okay. I'm right here." I peppered her face with little kisses.

"Grace gets nightmares?" He frowned, getting closer to us.

"Sometimes. Usually it's not when you're in bed with us," I admitted. "She doesn't remember what they're about, either. I think it's whatever happened that ended with her coming to us."

Evan ran his fingers through her hair. "You didn't think to tell me that she gets nightmares when we're not all together?"

A touch of hurt shot through the bond.

I shrugged as she relaxed under our touch. "I didn't want you to feel obligated to sleep with us every night. You should spend time with Bren and Jett. We're okay."

He made a face. "You should still tell me. I... I didn't even feel them. Maybe I'll feel her better now. I wish my mark would stay like yours."

"It'll scar eventually if you keep doing it in the same place. You can always have it tattooed." I yawned. We'd been up late, and had a number of rounds, since both of them were knot-greedy. Which I didn't have a problem with. After all, I was here to make them happy.

Brennan also kept texting. But whatever. It wasn't a big deal. Also, I sort of got it.

"I'm trying to sleep," Grace muttered.

"Sorry, you had another nightmare," I said, finding a bottle of water, taking a sip and passing it on to her.

She took a sip. "Oh."

"Do you want to move downstairs? Maybe take a shower?" It had grown warm and stuffy, almost stifling. We were all a little sticky.

The nest was great for fucking, and fine for dozing between rounds, but not comfortable for actual sleeping.

"I feel sort of gross. What time is it?" Grace nodded.

Evan took the bottle from her, downed it, got up and found his phone. "Four."

"Why don't we shower off and go back to sleep in a clean bed." I rolled off Grace and picked her up, getting a little whiff of that scent she'd made when she gushed all over Evan. It wasn't quite omega perfume, but it was definitely *eau d'fuck me alpha,* and that made me hard.

I made sure the bedroom curtains were closed to keep the room nice and dark so we could sleep in. Evan's plans for today were more relaxed, and we didn't have to be back in Rockland at any particular time. Though we all had work tomorrow.

We piled into Evan's shower and washed, everyone a little too tired to get frisky. After we got out and dried off, Grace put on one of my shirts and crawled into bed.

"Clean sheets, clean me, mmmm," she hummed.

I climbed in with her, pulling her to me, burying my face in her damp hair. While part of me liked it when she reeked of me, with my cum dried to the inside of her thighs, I could understand the sentiment.

Evan got in on the other side of me, naked, completing our pile. He turned off the bedside lamp, and I purred for them, letting them know how happy they made me, and how much I loved them.

I drifted off to sleep. When I woke up, light illuminated the cracks between the curtains and the window, and streamed in through the bathroom door, which had been left open. Giving a little stretch, I looked at the clock on the nightstand; it was after ten.

My belly rumbled. Breakfast was definitely on the agenda. We had some chores to do. I might as well get started while they slept a little longer.

Carefully, I tried to extract myself from between Grace and Evan. Grace immediately rolled into Evan, seeking his warmth.

"Where are you going?" Evan mumbled, cuddling Grace.

"I'm going to start the laundry. Then I'll make breakfast. I don't know about you, but I'm starving," I whispered, looking for boxers and a shirt in my bag.

His eyes closed. "I'll help soon. I'm just going to cuddle her a little longer."

Yep, I'd worn them out. I left a filled water bottle on the nightstand, then went up to the turret. The scents of us and sex hung heavily in the air, the sheets rumpled. Turning on the fan and air filter, I gathered up an armful of sheets and blankets and brought them down to the laundry room and got a load going.

I went into the kitchen and turned on the coffeepot. It took multiple trips to get everything down, and by then the aroma of coffee filled the quiet kitchen.

Pouring myself a cup, I took it out on the porch and spent a moment sipping it, enjoying the view. I was a lucky man to be able to enjoy this, with the loves of my life upstairs.

Finishing my coffee, I went inside and looked at what was in the fridge. I set out some bacon, eggs, and vegetables on the counter and then went back upstairs.

Evan was sound asleep, curled on the bed. But Grace wasn't there. I peeked through the open door and saw her lounging in the bubble-filled tub, eyes closed.

"Hey, do you want me to bring you some coffee?" I asked softly, coming in. She looked delicious. The idea of stripping off my clothes to join in the tub tempted me.

Grace groaned. "Coffee in the bathtub? Yes, please. Sorry, I'm sore, and Evan had the foresight to bring those magic green bath fizzies."

"You look cute in the tub. I was thinking of making a bacon and veggie scramble for breakfast? Unless you wanted pancakes?" I offered.

"Coffee and bacon, please." She looked out the window at the lake. "So beautiful."

I looked her right in the eye. "Yep, beautiful."

She tipped her head up for a kiss. I captured her lips and went back downstairs to get her coffee. I got one for each of them and returned to the bedroom.

"Brought you coffee, Babe." Placing Evan's on the nightstand, I gave him a kiss.

Evan smiled. "Thanks, Babe."

"Eggs and bacon for breakfast or pancakes?" I asked.

"Either sounds fantastic." He got up on his elbows. "Where's Grace?"

I held up Grace's mug. "Princess Peaches gets coffee in the tub."

She beamed as soon as I came in. "Thank you."

"You're welcome." I handed her the mug. She took a sip and made a happy noise.

Grace held up the mug. "This is perfect. I'll be down in a bit. Anything else on the agenda today that you know of?"

"I think today was meant to be relaxed—a leisurely breakfast on the patio. Maybe a nice walk or some fishing on the dock. Or even cuddling and watching a movie while eating popcorn." The little cuddle alcove in the living room was one of my favorite spots.

She nodded as she sipped her coffee. "Those sound amazing."

I gave her a kiss, then went back downstairs to start breakfast, making more coffee, moving the platter of treats onto the patio table, and getting everything set.

Evan came downstairs first, wearing only shorts, as I was frying bacon.

"Nothing is sexier than an alpha cooking." Evan put his arm around my waist and hummed.

"Careful. You're not wearing a shirt, and frying bacon shirtless is not recommended," I warned, giving him a quick kiss.

"Grace will be down shortly. Spencer sent me a picture of the new door from her room to the bathroom. I also got the full dance report from Riley," he said. "And fifty million texts from Brennan. I assured him that we were fine. Jett won his match, too."

"Glad everything is okay back home. Last night." I inhaled and grinned. "Mmmm. You touched her just right last night. That taste, that smell..." I growled, lining a plate with a paper towel to put the bacon on, remembering the scents she made. My mouth watered at the thought.

"I know. Close but not quite. It makes me wonder, though, about her world. Are there basically a whole lot of omegas who have no idea what they are because something is missing to trigger that biology? Or maybe omegas from her world don't need knots so they don't stand out?" Evan frowned as he got juice from the fridge.

I thought for a moment. "Maybe."

"It could be a good thing parallel world travel isn't a thing, because could you imagine a world being invaded for their omegas—or her world invading ours for our alphas?" Evan added.

"That's a scary thought. Also, resources. Or land. Or using another world as a prison colony. Or conquering a new world because you messed up the old one." I used tongs to take the bacon out of the pan.

"That's why Spencer doesn't want me to try to go home. I… I don't want to." Grace padded into the kitchen, wearing one of those T-shirt dresses she favored. Something about pockets, not that I understood why pockets were so exciting.

"Because you're going to steal our alphas and take them back to your knotless world?" Evan filled the juice glasses.

"Remember when Riley joked about hacking the universe and we were like *Yeah, no, let's not piss off whoever's in charge?* Spence believes that parallel world travel is regulated and that me intentionally figuring out how to return home could garner their attention, and we might not want that." Grace snuggled into me and stole some bacon. "He's afraid that they'll come after me because I shouldn't be here."

"Why does he even know these things?"

Evan nodded. "That's a very Spencer thought. I'm so glad you want to stay here. After all, we have knots here."

"And tasty-smelling people." Grace pressed her nose into Evan's side and giggled. "Why are we talking about parallel worlds?"

"We were actually talking about your biology in the context of your world. It reinforces my previous theory about your world having designations to some extent but not necessarily in the full way they do here," I said as I chopped vegetables for the scramble.

"Oh." Grace stole another piece of bacon, then grabbed a tomato and began chopping.

Evan chopped a pepper. "I'm curious how you'd react to alpha rut pheromones. For me, I get all relaxed and buzzy, and my body is like, *Take me, Alpha, I'm yours.*"

"Oh. That could be fun to try. It felt so good when you ate me with such... fervor." She chuckled.

I stole a kiss. "I can get a little overzealous. But my alpha instincts wouldn't actually let me hurt you, one *ow* or whimper and I'd be making it better."

"Next thing you know, I'm going to actually find this world's Grace, right?" She grinned. "She's just called something else."

"No one can come close to you, Peaches." I kissed the top of her head. I was pretty sure that there was no other version of her here, or anywhere else. She was one of a kind.

Evan pressed a kiss to her temple. "Exactly."

Chapter Fifty-Four

Spencer

"Do you want to do anything special next?" I asked Riley. We were at Andre's dress shop, doing a fitting. She'd just finished, and now it was Grace's turn.

I worried about Riley. While she said she was fine, she'd seen someone try to shoot her brother, which was a lot.

Riley scowled. "I'm fine. I'll talk about it with my therapist if I need to. Like I told the other overprotective assholes, I knew one of you would take out the shooter, and the fact that it was Grace makes me love her more. Also, yes, I'm fine with her mating my brother and marrying him—well, as long as they let me make sure it's fun. Which she will because she loves me."

Grace did care for Riley, which made things so much easier. I concurred with Jett and Brennan—seeing Grace take down the shooter was terrifying. But unlike them, I wasn't surprised that Evan had mated her during their romantic weekend. He had mentioned it. Several times.

I looked over to where Andre was overseeing alterations on Grace's dress.

"Would you be okay if I courted her?" I was already putting plans into place.

Riley's shoulders shimmied. "You fucking bet your dick I am. But please get her something cool like a motorcycle for a courting gift."

Actually, I was planning a trip to take her to see the particle cutter. But that was a thought...

"Ooh, you like her," Riley sang.

"There's something there. I feel it when we dance, when we talk about science, when she passes me the salt at dinner." I gazed back over at her in that poufy silver dress, and she waved.

Riley snorted. "Okay, Sappy McSapPants. But seriously, I'm happy for you."

"Your voice is important. If things are happening too fast, if your needs aren't being met, please speak up," I added. Riley wasn't less important because Grace was in our lives.

"Oh, my fuck." Her eyes rolled. "You know what? I think I need to go to the movies and the fancy pizza arcade."

"Perfect. Are we bringing Grace or is it just us? Either is fine," I assured her.

Riley pondered this for a moment. "We can bring her. I want to see her play the dance game with you. If you want to invite everyone else to join us at the pizza arcade, that's fine. But I want just us three at the movies."

"That sounds fun." I pulled up the theater schedule on my phone. Riley chose a movie for us, and I booked the tickets.

I texted the chat I had with the guys.

Me

I'm taking Grace and Riley to the movies and then to the fancy pizza arcade. You are welcome to join us for a pizza dinner.

Evan

If I didn't have a staff meeting, I'd join you at the movies. The arcade sounds fun.

Wes

Oh, so this is your important meeting?

I sent a picture of Grace on a pedestal in front of the big mirrors and one of Riley.

Me

No, this was my big meeting.

Not that my taking them to their fitting was a secret.

Evan

Very important.

Wes

Shit, she's beautiful.

Brennan

The pizza arcade? It's very noisy.

Jett

You know Riley loves that place.

I added when we'd be there and the movie information. Finished, Grace came over to us. "All done."

"Spence is taking us to the movies and the fancy pizza arcade. I think the boys are joining us for pizza," Riley said as she got her things.

Grace beamed. "Sounds good to me."

The movie finished, and Riley looked over at me and smirked. Grace had fallen asleep on me halfway through.

I loved every moment. Her small body fit perfectly into mine.

"The movie's over, my good doctor." I shook her gently.

Her eyes flew open. "I fell asleep? I'm so embarrassed."

"You didn't snore. It's fine." Riley waved it off, hopping up out of her seat.

Grace sat up and realized she'd been asleep *on* me. "Oh, I–"

I cupped her face in my hands. "Don't be sorry. I *adored* being your pillow."

"Okay." Her voice went small.

"You can sleep on me anytime," I added. It was the first time we had really cuddled, and I yearned for more.

Grace gulped. "Okay."

Riley snorted. "What's the point of having giant dudes around if you don't use them as pillows? Now come on, we have prizes to win and pizza to eat."

Standing, I offered my hand to Grace. She put hers in mine and smiled shyly as she stood. Her hand stayed in mine as we left the theatre and went across the plaza to the pizza arcade.

"We'll order food, play games until the food comes, eat, then play more games," Riley told us as we entered what I personally thought of as *overstimulation paradise.*

Everywhere you looked there were bright lights, games that flashed and made noise, children running and screaming, adults watching the sports ball, and people drinking beer.

Grace's face said it all. Yes. That was why Brennan didn't like it here.

I pulled Grace into me. "Everyone's coming. I'm pretty sure that if it gets to be too much that someone will take you home. We come here for Riley, not because we like it. The wine list leaved something to be desired, but the pizza is wood-fired, and apparently they have a lot of nice beers."

She nodded, tucking herself into me.

"You are so fucking cute together," Riley told me as we found a table big enough for all seven of us.

"Is that okay..." Her scent went a little sour.

"Please, feel free to date all of them. You'd look hot on the back of Brennan's motorcycle." Using the tablet attached to the table, she proceeded to order enough food for an army.

Grace bit her lower lip. "I don't think that would happen."

Yes, I should get myself one, then *I* could take her on rides. Mmmm. What would she look like as we rode through Greece or Italy at sunset?

Riley pushed the tablet toward us. "I'm happy you mated Evan, and that you make Spence happy. Approve."

"Thank you, that means everything." Grace looked at the tablet and ordered a beer and some onion rings.

I ordered everyone's usual drinks, as well as mine, and some additional food items, taking everyone's likes into account.

"Game time. Yes, we're playing the dance game." Riley dragged us over to the dance game.

There were two platforms and a game screen. The moves flashed on the screen, and the players moved on their platforms to match as music played. Score was kept, and fun was had by all.

"Spence and I will show you how it's done. Then you can try it with him. He's bad at it," Riley added.

Opening the app on her phone, she swiped it on the game console to pay for our turn.

"If you insist," I told her, getting onto one of the platforms.

"Oh, I do." She grinned as she chose the song and level.

Grace peered at the screen. "I've played something like this."

Huh, I suppose she might have.

The music played, and I followed the movements on the screen, making just enough mistakes so she'd win, without her thinking I was letting her win. It was good exercise, especially since I didn't play tennis after work today.

The lights blinked around her platform, marking Riley as the winner. We then played again. Grace stood watching us, grinning.

Or rather, she was watching me.

Riley won again. Bowing, she hopped off. "Your turn."

"Okay. Warning, I have done zero cardio lately other than Jett's living room dance practice." She got onto the platform.

"I'll choose an easy one." Riley paid for another game and selected a beginner song.

The game started, this time I didn't hold back–but I didn't show off. Grace, however, knew *exactly* what she was doing. It was difficult to focus on the movements flashing on the screen so I could replicate them, and not her lithe form.

Or the pure joy on her face.

Oh, my heart. The song ended, and the lights declared her the winner.

"Yay, you won." Riley gave her a hug. "Well done, Spence. I knew you'd get the hang of this game, eventually. More?"

Grace smiled at me, joy still in her eyes. "That was fun, but I've got my cardio for the day. Does this place have the game where you roll balls into holes?"

Riley laughed. "Um, what? I don't think so? But let's play the blaster game."

She dragged us to the other side of the arcade.

"You're very good at that game—and you hold back with Riley." Grace smiled at me again.

Something about those smiles and her blue eyes sparked long-forgotten joy in my soul.

"Shhh. I don't hold back that much. She's good," I whispered back.

We played a shooting game that gave you points to use at the arcade shop. A game which Grace excelled at.

"Wow. If your job with Spence doesn't work out, maybe you should join the academy." Jett stood there, holding an iced coffee.

Grace laughed. "Do I even meet the height requirement?"

"For your designation, maybe?" He rested his arm on her head, and she laughed again.

"Ooh, how many points did you get?" Evan bounded over, still in his Center polo.

"She won," Riley told him.

Evan kissed her. "You did, great job." His eyes lit up as he saw the iced coffee in Jett's hand. "Is that for me?"

I was so happy Evan had found such good people to love him. All of them were great guys—even Brennan.

Jett leaned in and kissed him. "You know it is."

Evan took the coffee. "Thanks. Can I join in? Did we order food? I'm so hungry."

I glanced at my phone. "The appetizers will be here shortly. The drinks are on the table."

"Found mine. Or what I hoped was mine." Brennan held up a bourbon. "If it's not, it's mine now, sorry. Oh, fuck, who got that score?"

"Grace. I'd love to see her and Lexi at the range," Jett said, arm still around Evan.

"Yeah? That sounds fun." Wes came over holding a beer and gave her a kiss.

"Why don't we all play a round together," Riley suggested.

"Perfect, then the food should be here," I replied

We all took a seat, and I used the app to pay for all our games. The countdown went off, and music played as the targets moved, and we shot as many as we could before the timer went off.

The targets stopped, and the scoreboard lit up. Grace had won, again, but Jett was only a couple of points off.

"Well played," Jett told her.

She gave Brennan a look. "I can contribute to protecting the pack."

"Noted." Brennan nodded.

"Protect me, Peaches." Evan scooped her off the stool and clutched her to his chest, planting a kiss on her forehead.

"Wow, Grace, you have so many points. We'll play more after dinner, and you can win something cute for Evan as a bonding gift," Riley said as she led us back to our table.

"I love that idea. I'll play a few more games after dinner and win something for you, too," Evan said as he carried her through the arcade.

"That sounds fun," she said as he set her in a chair.

She grabbed a beer and took a long drink, lips wrapped around the bottle's neck in the most tantalizing way.

The server brought out a bunch of appetizers. Probably enough for most people to have for dinner if we didn't have a teenager who regularly consumed her weight in chips, and a bunch of alphas.

"Ooh, who ordered onion rings for me?" Brennan's face lit up as he took one.

"I ordered them, but I'll share." Grace took one.

Brennan nodded. "Thank you for being a good sharer, Grace."

She smirked. "Likewise."

We went around the table and talked about our days, not unlike family dinner. Riley also filled us in on who'd gotten detention. As we finished our appetizers, the server brought the pizzas and refreshed our drinks. She also brought some chicken wings and fries for Evan.

"You're right, this is good pizza." Grace took another bite.

"You have cheese on your face." Wes leaned in and licked it off.

"No licking at the table." Riley dipped her pizza in sauce.

Jett shook his head. "Not a rule." Leaning over, he licked Evan.

Brennan licked Jett's cheek.

Jett waggled his eyebrows. "You mean that, Honey?"

"Oh, I do, Dear." Brennan kissed him.

Riley covered her eyes. "I'm trying to eat here."

I chuckled. "You're the one who said that they could join us."

We finished our pizza, and Riley dragged Evan and Grace off toward the arcade games. Jett and Brennan went to play darts.

"This is fun," Wes said, eyes on Grace as Evan taught her to play a racing game.

"Indeed."

Wes went to play games with them, and I paid the bill. Then I checked my email and did a few things, content that everyone was having a good time.

Now Grace was playing pool with Brennan, Jett, and Wes, while Evan and Riley were fighting aliens.

"You are a cheater." Brennan scowled at Grace.

"I... I must play by different rules. I'm sorry." Her head hung. Grace's scent soured, and my fists clenched.

Wes pulled Grace to him. "Hey, easy, Bren. We didn't tell her what rules we played by. They're probably different where she's from. Just tell her what she did that broke a rule, and we'll redo it. Easy peasy."

"I wasn't trying to cheat." She sniffed.

Oh. No, I'm sure she wasn't.

"Okay, you're right. That's how I got my ass kicked on a business trip." Brennan's look went wry. "Sorry, Grace."

"I mean, if you want to play dirty, I can teach you the game I used to play in grad school when I needed food money." Grace grinned.

The look on their faces said it all. Brennan might still have his reservations, but she was one of us. The idea of her hustling pool so she had enough to eat broke us.

Brennan also shot a look at Wes that clearly said *She's your mate, where the fuck were you while she struggled to have enough to eat? You should have been taking care of her.*

At some point, we were going to need to explain Grace to him.

"We'll play dirty another night," Jett soothed, getting between Wes and Brennan. "Let's finish our game so you can go buy an overpriced toy for Evan with all your game points."

They finished their game, and she, and Riley went off to pick something out.

"Did you have fun at the movies?" Evan asked me.

"She fell asleep on me." I grinned.

Evan bumped me with his side. "Lucky fucker."

"This is okay, me and her?" I said softly. "I don't want to encroach."

He hugged me. "I'm happy for you, my friend."

"That means everything."

"Evan, look what I got you." Grace ran over and got down on one knee. "Will you be mine?" She held out a blinking ring.

"Peaches, I already am." He held out his hand, and she slid it on. "This is for you. I crown you Princess Peaches." Evan placed a crown on her hair.

"I love it." She giggled and leaned in for a kiss.

Riley came back over to us. "While this has been fun, bitches, I have school tomorrow. Who's taking me back to the dorms?"

"I will," I volunteered. Grace could go back with them.

Riley said her goodbyes and followed me down to my car.

"Did you have fun?" I asked as she hooked her phone up to my stereo and played something.

"Yes. We should do this more often," she told me.

I nodded. It was nice to see everyone having fun together like a pack. "Yes, I think we should."

Chapter Fifty-Five

Jett

My phone beeped as I pulled into the garage of the house. For a Tuesday, work had been especially busy.

A text from Cam, my co-worker at the station, lit up my phone.

Cam

> **Can you teach my 7 pm class at the gym? Please?**

Why couldn't she have asked earlier? I got out of the car and looked at the group chat. Evan and Wes were working late, and Spencer was taking Riley to get new skate smash gear for the upcoming tryouts.

I texted Brennan as I went inside the quiet house.

Me

> **Working late? They need me to teach a class at the gym.**

As I walked up the stairs, I heard Volkov's *Sonata in D* being played on the piano. Was Brennan home? That was one of his go-to *I hate the world* pieces. When I got to the second floor, a little blonde was hunched over the piano, pounding out the notes of the dark and powerful piece.

They both liked Volkov. Huh. They had more in common than they wanted to admit. While a lot of things didn't add up when it came to Grace, I still liked her.

It was also obvious that she was thriving here with Wes and Evan. It could be because Wes was her *mate.* But affection, regular meals, cuddles, and kind words probably had a lot to do with it.

He texted me back.

Brennan

Go for it. I'm trying to close on the estate so Evan can get married in a fucking rose garden.

Wow. He was going ahead and trying to buy the estate so Evan could marry Grace there? But Brennan would give Evan pretty much anything. It was also nice that he was coming around to the fact that Grace wasn't going anywhere. Grace and Evan *mated* during their romantic weekend. While Evan had talked to us about wanting to bond her, we didn't realize he'd do it so soon.

Brennan was a little miffed about it, because the investigations weren't even closed yet. But he'd shut those feelings down as soon as he saw how it hurt Evan. I texted Cam back.

Me

Sure.

Might as well. I felt like I always owed her for something, anyway. It wasn't my favorite, and she knew it. It wasn't because it was a ladies' class. We had some bad bitches at my gym, and I was happy to work with them. It was because it was a boxerobics class to pop music.

Pop music was also not my thing.

Grace looked over when she finished playing. "How'd it sound? Sucky? It felt sucky. This piece is difficult."

"You play it faster than Bren, but it sounded fine," I replied. Classical music wasn't my thing either.

Maybe Brennan could eventually put his issues aside and take Grace to classical music concerts. Someone should appreciate them, and not just go to be in the dark with Brennan for a few hours.

A thought struck me. "How are you feeling? I have to teach a class at my boxing gym. Do you want to come with me?"

I should find out what she could do and teach her some things. Especially after seeing her whack a shooter with a chair.

"Can we take the motorcycles?" Her eyes lit up. "I'm cleared for exercise. Also, after playing the dance game, I realized I should probably add more cardio back into my life."

"We have a gym in the basement, and you can use it whenever you want. I'll take you on my motorcycle. You don't have a license. Evan's motorcycle is way too high for you. Your toes won't touch the ground. But, you can try mine later, and show me what you can do, so we can get you signed up for the test," I told her.

Her head lolled from side to side. "Fair. When do we leave? What do I wear?"

"Wear whatever you want to exercise in, and sneakers. You can wear Riley's gloves. You can bring your stuff and change there. We should leave soon." I went into my room to get my stuff.

Our living room doubled as Brennan's office, which is why I often watched TV with Evan in his room. That and no one else would watch cheesy foreign subtitled action movies with me.

Would Grace like them? She liked regular action movies.

I got my boxing bag out of the closet and made sure Riley's gloves were in there. I should take them both regularly. Riley picked up fast and would do well if we put some time and effort into her training.

Going back downstairs, I put my bag on the table, filled up a water bottle for each of us, and got myself a snack. Grace came downstairs in jeans, one of Evan's shirts, and her leather jacket. She had her helmet in one hand and a bag in the other.

"Ready? We can grab food after class," I told her. Would she like my usual places?

Grace nodded. We put on our shoes and went into the garage. She immediately went to Evan's bike, which stood next to mine. Brennan took his to work nearly every day because he didn't like cars. I usually drove my convertible.

"This is beautiful," she sighed.

"What did you have back at university?" Probably a scooter. I grabbed my helmet.

"A little pink street bike. Nothing exciting, but it got me where I needed to go," she replied, pulling on her helmet.

We got on, and she wrapped her arms around my waist, nice and close. The only girl who had ever been on the back of my bike was Riley.

Taking off, we went back into the city, to an old warehouse that had been converted into a boxing gym.

We went inside, and I waved at the owner, who was at the front desk.

"Jett, great job at the tournament. I didn't think I'd see you tonight," Marti said. She was an older beta, tough as nails, and ran this place with her husband. I'd been going here since I was at the police academy—which was pre-Brennan. A lot of us were in law enforcement. It was a no-alpha gym, and nearly everyone was a beta.

"Cam convinced me to teach her 7 pm." I shrugged.

"Who's this?" Marti looked appreciatively at Grace, who stood there, taking in what lay beyond the glass separating the reception area from the rest of the gym–there were several rings and open workout areas.

"This is Grace. She's Evan's," I told her.

"You should train her for Omega League," she replied.

Hmmm. Maybe? I unlocked the door with my handprint and let us into the main gym.

"I'm Evan's?" Grace said softly, staying close to me.

"You are." From the moment Evan told me we were bringing a strange girl home–and she *let* him–I knew. It was in the way she curled into him on the couch. How she trusted him even before she remembered her own name.

It was adorable to see my omega dote on someone that way–and to see her melt for him.

"She doesn't know Wes, but she's met Evan many times. He even comes with me sometimes. Change in the locker room and use any empty locker," I told her.

I changed and got my gloves and hers along with our water bottles and waited for her.

Grace came out a few moments later in some leggings and a T-shirt that had a formula on it. She plopped down. "How much of an ass-kicking am I going to get?"

"It's an easy class. You might even enjoy it. Do you usually do any sports or classes or anything? Well, besides skate smash?" I took her back to the classroom, where a few ladies were already stretching out.

She frowned. "I'm pretty sure that I haven't been very active since I finished my PhD. I don't like running for fun. Hmmm, I think I like cardio-boxing."

"Noted." I handed her a water bottle. "This is for you. Warm up, everyone should arrive soon."

"Ooh, are you teaching tonight, Jett?" one of the regulars asked. Her wife often refereed at my tournaments.

"Yep. Cam can't make it so you're stuck with me." I stretched out, watching Grace, noting how she moved. She was graceful–dance background, probably. Most omegas studied shit like ballet, cheerleading, and ice skating.

The room filled up. I cued up Cam's playlist and taught the class, correcting everyone's form when needed. While this was obviously new to Grace, she followed instructions and took feedback well. She also looked like she was having fun. By the end, it was clear she was tired.

"Good night, everyone." I waved.

Grace laid down on the floor like a starfish. "Oh, my god. Good cardio, but that kicked my ass. I'm going to feel that tomorrow."

She started stretching her legs, still lying on the floor.

"Stretch, drink water. Did you like it?" I did a few stretches myself.

"I did. It was fun." She grinned. "Do you teach this often?"

"Not really." Often enough so that I knew the moves. "Go change, and then we'll eat. Do you feel like anything in particular?" I gave her a hand up. I was hungry, and well, I should get to know her a little better.

"You know, I could go for a big bowl of spicy noodles. Are there any good noodle shops around here?" Grace chewed on her lower lip as we left the classroom.

"I know a great place. It's a hole in the wall though," I told her, wondering if it was a good idea to take her there without one of the alphas. A couple of women in class were licking their lips as she walked past, and they were betas.

We changed, and she eyed my motorcycle as we came back out.

"The parking lot is big, can I give it a go?" she asked.

"Be careful and don't go fast." I watched as she got on. It was a little tall for her. Grace took a moment to familiarize herself then she took off around the parking lot.

Finally, she came back. "How'd I do?"

"That was great." Better than I expected. "Should we go eat?" I'd have to talk to Evan about getting one better suited to her size.

We got on and I took her to the outdoor market, toward the area with strings of small family-run restaurants. The best food was here, not at places like Supressa. Her reaction would tell me a lot about her.

After parking, I brought her inside. The place was small, with a few booths, a bar, and blaring music, and a patio with lights and more tables.

The owner waved and told me in Mandarin to choose a table. I grabbed a menu.

"Reminds me of a place we always ate at when I was getting my PhD," she said.

"Cheap and tasty? I found this place when I came out here for university," I told her. We sat down at one of the round metal tables, and I handed her the menu since I knew what I wanted.

"Pretty much. You're not from here?" she asked, shrugging off her jacket and hanging it from the chair.

"Came here to be pre-med at Rock Tech. Ended up being a cop." I grinned. Spencer had attended there, too.

"Your parents were okay with that?" Hurt flashed in her eyes.

"Yeah, my parents were supportive–both of my career choice and me staying here." Okay, one of my moms was a little sour about it at first, but she got over it.

"How many parents? Two? Four? Nine?"

"Nine?" I laughed. "Three dads, two moms. I also have six brothers–no sisters."

"Wow, and I thought three was a lot." She grinned.

"Oh, it is–most of them are alphas." I rolled my eyes. "I have a shit-ton of aunties and cousins. My omega grandma is the matriarch. We all lived close. There were always people everywhere. One reason I don't mind having Ri around is that I miss a houseful of chaotic teenagers."

She laughed. "I hope you see them a lot. That sounds great."

"It is, and I go back as much as I can. My moms *love* Evan. Stuff him full of dumplings," I laughed.

"Mmmm, that sounds delicious. Can we check out the market sometime?" Her gaze went beyond the restaurant's little plant fence.

"Absolutely." I'd bring her back when Brennan was with us.

Grace was *cute* if tiny blonde girls were your thing. Usually, big dudes were my thing. Caroline didn't do it for me, which was one of the many conflicts we'd had when she'd lived with us. But after seeing Grace's tight little ass shake in class...

Yeah, I could be convinced.

An older server came over. She was one of the owner's mates.

"What are you drinking?" she asked in Mandarin, giving Grace a once-over.

"Beer, please," Grace replied in Mandarin.

I stared at her. So did the server.

"Sorry, my accent is bad," she continued in Mandarin, head ducking.

"I understand you fine, what kind?" she replied.

"Whatever you have is fine," Grace told her.

I ordered beer for the both of us. "Did you grow up on the West Coast, too? Because the guys all learned French and Spanish in school out here."

She shook her head. "I'm pretty sure my doctoral cohort was mostly from China. I probably speak a weird dialect. Um, I think I learned Spanish in school, but I'm bad at it. Do you learn Chinese at school there?"

"Yeah, Mandarin or Russian, and Spanish, but we speak Mandarin at home. Some schools around where I grew up also taught indigenous languages." I eyed her. "You're remembering more? That's great."

Where exactly did she grow up again? Maybe she was home-schooled?

Grace shrugged. "I remember a lot more. But not anything important, like how I ended up on the park bench or a lot about my work. My love of tipsy karaoke isn't vital."

I leaned in as the server brought our beers. "I love karaoke. Do you need to reach out to your brothers, let them know you're okay?"

"We haven't talked in years. I don't think they care." Grace squinted at the menu, and we ordered.

How sad. Had they seen her on the news? Her hitting the shooter with a chair had gone viral. Four siblings, six cousins, all of my parents, and nine aunties, had realized that was my pack and texted me, worried. Not that you got a really clear view of her face. But still...

"You did really well in class. Are you a dancer?" I asked.

"When I was a kid. I did dance, cheer, and tumbling. You know, that stuff." She shrugged.

Called it.

"Any martial arts? I can teach you more than boxing. You mentioned cardio boxing?" I took a sip of beer.

"I... I remember that I took a bunch of self-defense classes." She looked away, toying with her beer. "Just the kind offered at my college. I couldn't afford to go anywhere else, so I took the basic classes over and over."

"Great. Like what they teach omegas?" Which could be lethal. It was designed for small omega bodies back when omega kidnappings were a very frequent occurrence. It also made a good basis for other disciplines.

"Like the type they teach women so you don't get attacked by sketchy dudes. It all depended on the teacher." She looked away again and got that uncomfortable look on her face she sometimes had when talking about personal things.

The server brought our noodles. She also only brought chopsticks. Grace thanked her and opened the packet, digging in, though she held her chopsticks weirdly.

"How did you and Brennan meet?" Grace asked.

I frowned, unsure if Brennan would want me to tell her, since it was very personal. "That's a story for another day."

"That good?" She grinned. "How about when you met Evan?"

"They're not too spicy, are they?" I asked.

"Not spicy enough." Grace added a lot of chili sauce.

"Brennan and I had a destination wedding at one of his resorts. Because why not, right? His longtime friend Wes was coming. I'd met him a couple of times, military, clean cut, good at team sports, you know the type." I grinned at her.

She grinned back. "Right, he played rugby in high school."

"Bren was on the team with him. So, Wes was bringing his boyfriend, Evan, to the wedding. We hadn't met him yet and were curious since they'd met in the military." I took a drink of beer. "What we didn't know is that Wes' boyfriend was an omega–and that they were actually *mates* who'd recently bonded. They show up for the pre-party, and *shit*. I did not know they made omegas that big." I chuckled, remembering that night.

Grace laughed. "Evan is a *big* dude."

"Oh, I do like me a big dude. There was also something about him. Throughout the entire week of festivities, we kept finding reasons to talk to him." Really, it was shameless of me to flirt with him like that. Wes not punching me and Brennan attempting to flirt, too, only cemented that we could all be something together.

"I can imagine. Evan walked into the room at the Center, gave me a hug, and... it's so stupid, but I felt like everything might be okay." She smiled.

"Never thought I'd meet my omega at my wedding," I laughed. "We thought we'd see if we'd work as a pack–and we did. Evan introduced us to Spencer, and everything fell into place. Now, here we are."

My phone buzzed.

Evan

> **You're out to eat with my girl?**

"Evan's jealous. We should send him a picture." I sent him a picture of us with our beer and noodles along with a text.

Me

> **You can't always be with her. Want your usual?**

"Hey." Brennan stood there, holding his helmet, still dressed for work. A few people gave him appreciative looks.

I was so lucky.

"These are so good." Grace pointed to her almost empty bowl with her chopsticks.

"Hey, Honey." I tugged him down for a kiss. "Want anything?"

He was frowning at Grace. "Why are you always wearing Evan's clothes?"

What sort of question was that? She always wore his clothes for the same reason Evan always stole our stuff. It smelled right.

"Fine." Frowning, Grace tugged off the shirt, so she was only in her sports bra, and threw it at him. Then she froze. Her chest shook, and her peach scent took on the burnt tang of fear.

"It's okay." Brennan's voice went quiet, his expression softening, as he put out some soothing pheromones. "Grace, I wasn't asking you to take it off. I was just surprised. I'd think you'd like Wes' stuff better. Here."

With a tenderness I hadn't seen him show her before, he took the shirt and put it back on her–but not before I saw the angry, raised scars crisscrossing her back.

Shit.

"I like his fashion sense." She sniffed, ducking her head.

"Which is fair," I pointed out. Wes tended not to care about his clothes, while Evan could be a snappy dresser when he wanted.

Brennan moved my stuff off the chair next to me and sat down. "You don't need to be ashamed of your scars."

"I'm not, just aware that they bother others." Her shoulders rounded as she put her jacket back on and pulled it around herself.

Sure. We should work on her confidence.

The server came over and looked at Brennan and asked in English, "Are you eating?"

"I'd like a pot of tea and number three with pork," he said.

I also ordered Evan's noodles to go.

Brennan looked at Grace's bowl and shook his head. "That just looks spicy."

"I'm going to find the restroom." Grace left and went inside.

"Was she in a car accident?" I asked him softly, polishing off my beer. That's how Brennan got his scars.

Brennan shook his head. "It's how they made her forget that Wes was real."

I sucked in air sharply through my teeth. "That's fucked up. How is that even legal?"

"It probably isn't." His look turned grim.

The server brought a pot of tea and cups for everyone. Brennan poured all of us tea, putting one at Grace's empty place.

"Remember how I had someone investigate her?" His voice was quiet as he looked into his cup.

"Oh right, I'd forgotten you'd done that? What did you find?" I frowned, because we'd been having a good night. Yesterday at the pizza arcade was fun, too.

"Her record has been altered–and apparently has the fingerprints of something called the Omega Protection Program all over it. At first I was angry, because I knew she was hiding something. Then the investigator explained what it was and why I should leave it alone or ask Grace directly. I didn't even know such a thing existed." He took a sip, looking pensive.

"Oh. I don't know much about it, other than it's similar to witness protection. They're usually getting omegas out of fucked up situations. It would explain the holes in her stories, the inconsistencies, and why things feel weird. It might even explain why Wes couldn't find her. That's been bothering me," I said quietly, thinking over the ramifications.

"Could be. My guess, based on the few things I know about her, is that maybe when her family disowned her, things went sideways and she ended up in the program?" He turned the cup around in his hands. "I don't know. But it would explain a lot."

"Yeah, and her mom's death caused her to come out of it, thinking she was safe. For all we know, her concussion and being on the run had nothing to do with her research, and everything to do with her family. Those scars." I shook my head.

Brennan nodded. "Can you imagine someone hurting you so badly you thought your *mate* was a dream?"

I winced at the thought. "That sounds awful."

"Grace and Evan seem to love each other, as do her and Wes. At the very least, I should try. For them. As long as we continue to have no fear of her being a danger to the pack, of course." He took a sip of tea.

"Sounds good to me." I finished my noodles. I mean, she was bonded to Wes *and* Evan. Spencer looked at her like he wanted to gobble her up.

Yeah, Grace wasn't going anywhere.

Brennan took a bite of noodles and made a face. "Ooh, I forgot to ask for negative spicy."

"Did you close on the estate?" I asked.

"Pending the final inspection. Terrance thinks it's a mistake," he added. "That an event venue won't add to the brand portfolio and it won't be profitable."

"But you don't think it's a mistake—and that's what's important," I told him.

While his business partner was good at the details, he wasn't the visionary my husband was.

I looked towards the restaurant. Where was she? "Hey, she was playing Volkov when I came home."

"Probably not as good as me." He smirked.

I shrugged. Like I would know. "It was fast. We should bring her to concerts."

"It's still hard, having someone strange in my house. Not knowing much about her—and now not being sure if I should even ask, given how much she's been through. Also, what danger could she bring to us?" he huffed.

"True. I worry about who might be after her. Should we up our security?" I asked. We had alarms and cameras, but we were due for a security audit.

"I'll leave that to you and Wes." He frowned and looked around. "Where did she go? She's been gone awhile."

It was a little amusing watching Brennan try to protect us from Grace, while his alpha instincts clearly wanted to protect her, too.

She came out holding a bowl to her chest, a smug look on her face as she sat down.

"What is that?" Brennan eyed the bowl.

"Fried ice cream." Her eyes danced. "Want some?"

Brennan looked skeptical.

"Please." I took a bite, the batter was hot and crispy, the inside cool and creamy, the chocolate sauce adding contrast.

He shook his head. "I'm not really into sweets."

Grace dug into her dessert. She pushed the bowl back to him. "Sure you don't want a bite?"

"Ooh, I want another." I opened my mouth, and she fed me one.

"I guess." Frowning, he took a small bite. His head cocked. "Huh. I like the outside."

"You would," I laughed.

We finished up and I paid. We weren't charged for the ice cream.

"Come back soon," one of the young servers waved at Grace.

"Can I drive home?" she asked me, holding Evan's order, as we walked to my bike.

"When we get closer to home," I climbed on. "Could you even get home from here?"

"Probably not. I should review the road rules here." She pulled on her helmet and got on behind me, holding tight, like she belonged here.

While I wasn't sure Grace belonged in my bed, she belonged with our pack. I just hoped that her past didn't catch up to her and break everyone's hearts.

Chapter Fifty-Six

Evan

I lay on the swing reading a book by the porch light, under a blanket. Wes had therapy tonight and after a good railing and ice cream, was now swimming himself senseless in our heated pool.

And I had a delivery of extra spicy noodles coming—perfect after a long day of work. There was still paperwork to wrap up regarding Rose's uncle. He'd been charged for both what had happened at the school and the restaurant. However, he'd apparently been released on bail, and I had a nagging feeling that it wasn't over.

My phone buzzed.

Jett

> **Come outside in a minute**

What? I checked the location app. Grace, Jett, *and* Brennan were almost here. Had Brennan gone with them to the noodle place? I hoped so. I wanted them to be friends.

Giving a brief stretch, I peeled myself off the porch swing and headed out through the garage. I opened the garage and stood there in my bare feet. The evening was pleasant, cool but not cold. A moment later I heard Jett and Brennan's motorcycles come down the street. Jett's motorcycle pulled into the driveway and stopped, the driver using their tippy toes to balance. Brennan, with Jett behind him, joined.

Grace took off her helmet and grinned. "Hey there, good looking, going my way?"

Jett let her drive! My cock strained against my shorts.

"How'd I do?" Grace struggled to put the kickstand down and get off, and I rushed to help her.

"Great. Make your test appointment, and we'll work our way through the exam book." Jett hopped off and handed me a bag. "Hey, Hot Stuff, I got you some noodles." He leaned in for a kiss.

Brennan led his bike into the garage. "Grace, you can't use Jett's bike to take the test."

"Why not?" Hurt tinged her voice as she followed Brennan. "I know how to ride. Promise."

"Safety, Grace. They won't let you take the test on something that's too big for you," he explained. "I'm not even sure you should practice on it."

"It's a little big, but they all are." She shrugged. "We had to cut down the seat on mine."

"I agree. I'll talk to Wes, see if we can get something smaller for you," I said. Her on a bike was hot, but we needed to be safe.

"Wait to schedule the test because we might have to order something special," Brennan added. "No one has any issues with it, as long as you're safe. Taking Jett's bike anywhere that's not just around the neighborhood isn't. How's that even comfortable?"

"Nothing is my size. I've been dealing with that my entire life." She thought for a moment. "Can I have a sidecar for Wes?"

I laughed at the image. "I love that idea."

Grace wrapped her arms around me, pressing her face into my chest, her little ass wiggling in happiness. She smelled like Jett and hot sauce. Yum. She also looked adorable in her jacket and boots, holding her helmet, and wearing my shirt.

Brennan snorted. "Wes in a sidecar. I'd pay to see that."

Jett closed the garage. "I want a beer. Anyone else?"

Grace grinned and said something I didn't understand as we went into the kitchen and took off our shoes.

"She speaks Mandarin?" Brennan grabbed two bottles of beer from the fridge and handed one to Jett. He opened Grace's and handed it to her. "Evan?"

"I could use a cocktail if you're offering." I waggled my eyebrows, snagging a deep kiss from him. The tiniest wisps of Grace clung to him.

Grace looked around. "Where's Wes?"

Brennan went to the bar cart and mixed me a drink.

"Swimming." I sat down at the kitchen table and opened my noodles. "Fuck yeah. Wait, you know Mandarin?"

"She made friends with the staff, and they gave her free ice cream at the noodle shop." Jett laughed, opening his beer, and plopping down at the table with me.

"I don't know that much." Grace stood in the window looking out at the pool, the backyard lit up by the lights.

Brennan put down a coaster and my drink, then grinned at Grace. "How about if we go dive-bomb him? It'll be cold when you get out, but the pool itself is warm."

"I could do that." She put her beer down. "I'll change."

Brennan put her beer on a coaster. "Let's just jump in with our clothes on. Though Evan might not want his shirt in the pool."

Grace ducked her head and chewed on her lower lip.

"I'm okay if you wear my shirt in the pool," I told her, getting a hint of her anxiety through the bond. It was just a T-shirt.

Brennan got very close but didn't actually put an arm around her. "We're at home. It's okay. I'll take my shirt off, too."

He took off his sports coat and neatly hung it on the back of a chair. Brennan also removed his pants, so he stood there in a button down and boxers.

Brennan unbuttoned his shirt and hung it on the chair with everything else.

Taking a deep breath, Grace removed my shirt, standing there in black leggings and a matching sports bra.

My cock got *very* excited. Jett hooked his leg with mine, eyes dancing with desire. I had no idea what was happening, but I was all for a show with my dinner.

Brennan smiled at her. "See, that wasn't so hard. If I choose not to wear a shirt, no one fucking cares–and if they do, well, I don't give a fuck."

He took off his undershirt, carefully putting it with the rest of his clothes. Pale scars laced his back.

Oh. That's where this was going.

Something must have happened.

Grace's face filled with pain. "Your mom didn't do that to you, right?"

"No, Grace. She can be a bitch but she's never physically hurt me." His look softened. "It was a car accident. Years ago."

It was how he and Jett had met. Jett was first on the scene and had gone with him to the hospital. Katie had been driving, and sometimes, I wondered if that was part of their issues. It certainly was the reason why Brennan didn't like riding in cars and took his motorcycle whenever he could.

"Let's go annoy Wes." Brennan gave Jett and me each a kiss.

He took Grace's hand and led her out the sliding glass doors onto the back porch.

Grace tagged Brennan and set off running for the pool, Brennan chasing after her.

"What was in those noodles?" I asked, watching as they dove into the pool, laughing and interrupting Wes' workout.

"I think he's warming up to her." Jett took a long drink of beer.

"I'm here for that." I watched Grace jump onto Wes' back. "Also, I'm here for him putting his dick in her." My cock twitched at the thought of Grace pleading for Bren's knot.

"One thing at a time. She's not really his type. But I'd watch that," Jett replied.

I took a sip of my cocktail. "Right? You can't blame me for fantasizing. Did you have fun?"

"I did. But now I'm so fucking curious what lady ass feels like," Jett admitted quietly.

"I can only speak to that lady ass, but hot damn." I took another drink, remembering the weekend. "No one told me that when two people fuck a girl at the same time, you can feel the other dick *through* her. When Wes was knotting her pussy with me in her ass? Mind blowing." I readjusted my cock as it tried to escape my pants.

Jett exhaled sharply. "Shit."

"Maybe one day you'll get to try a side-by-side comparison." I grinned.

Jett spat out his beer. "Evan."

"What?" I grinned. "I told you, I have fantasies. You know that she has *three holes*, right?"

"Remind me to make you tell me that in great detail." He gave me a smoldering look.

"Yes, sir." My eyebrows waggled. I was all for her being the filling between me and Jett. He'd be sweet with her if I asked him to.

"*Please* be safe when you play with her. Ask me all the questions, okay? I hear you two sometimes," he added.

Oh. Did he now? It wasn't like that, but I could see what that might sound like to him.

"I am. And I will." It was nice to know that I could go to Jett for advice about her.

"Okay, I wanted to check in." He nodded.

"Thanks. When I joke about wanting her to like my men, I mean you, too. Please, have a hobby together—or more." I grinned. They'd look hot together.

"Marti wants me to train her for the Omega League," he laughed.

"I'd love to watch that. You took her to Cam's class?"

"I taught Cam's class." He rolled his eyes.

"You love Cam's class." Him teaching was hot. "Who suggested the noodle place? Not that I mind, I always have room for noodles." I finished them.

"She did. Ordered a number seventeen and added half a bottle of chili sauce to it. She also likes karaoke. We should bring her with us." Jett grinned.

"Oh, yes, we should. I guess I should study Mandarin seriously so you three can't talk about me behind my back?" I teased. Brennan made sure he was fluent in every language he needed for business, since his hotels were all over the place.

"Absolutely. After Wes orders her a motorcycle, we should change the order to add a sidecar–if they make Wes-sized sidecars for Grace-sized motorcycles," he added.

"Actually, a Riley-sized sidecar would be fun. For when they get sick of alphas and want to go fuck shit up." I laughed. I'd been trying to get Wes to ride a motorcycle for ages. He didn't even want to ride with me.

Grace shrieked as Wes put her on his shoulders, and they splashed Brennan. Seeing her with both my alphas warmed my heart–and other things that were already inflamed.

"Thanks for getting me noodles. They were delicious. Should we go join them in the pool?" I stood and threw away the empty box.

"Anytime." Jett kicked back his chair. "Let's go. We can't let them have all the fun."

"Race you." Taking my clothes off as I ran outside, I cannon-balled into the pool in only my briefs.

Jett, in boxer briefs, jumped in after.

"Evan." Grace hopped on my back and started splashing Wes.

"I'm going to get you for that." Wes tackled her off me and tickled her.

"No, I'm going to get you." Brennan splashed them back.

Oh, my heart. Between this and last night, I felt like maybe we actually had a chance at being a family with Grace.

Chapter Fifty-Seven

Grace

"I've got to finish something for work, but then we can watch a movie with Evan?" Wes asked as we finished up the dishes.

It was our night to clean up after family dinner, which had basically been another prep for tomorrow's Morris Foundation Gala.

"Yeah, if Jett doesn't make me have more dancing lessons." I laughed. Oh, how I loved dancing lessons, especially when Spencer joined in.

I put away the clean pans. Wes took care of the things too high for me to put away without standing on the counter.

"I want to talk to Spencer, anyway," I added.

Wes effortlessly placed a bowl in the top cabinet. "Are you taking the job?"

"I think I'm ready to accept. I... I should go back to work soon, right?" Most of my life I'd been working, given my dad had a hardware store, and we all helped. Now that I was feeling better, not working seemed weird.

His arms circled my waist. "*If* you want to and feel up to it. If you want to stay home for a while, that's fine. You not working isn't breaking the budget. There's a lot to assimilate."

True. A lot of what I'd been looking up online this week was practical, so I wouldn't make a fool of myself.

"Seriously. In case you haven't noticed, we're not hurting for money," he added.

"You do have a lovely home, and nice cars. But you also have five people with incomes." I shrugged.

Wes laughed. "True. Some of them have giant incomes."

I leaned into him. "Honestly, I'm excited. Spencer's company is doing some really incredible things."

"They are. We can drive in and have lunch together. I think you'll like it there. What project are you going to take?" he asked.

Wes had heard all about my options as I'd tried to figure out where and if I'd fit.

"The simulator project." I still wasn't sure if I could do it, but I didn't feel comfortable joining one of the in-progress projects.

"It'll be great." Wes kissed me.

As I went upstairs, music serenaded me. Brennan had his eyes closed as he played something dark and forceful on the piano. I slipped through the living area and went to Spencer's suite of rooms.

I hadn't spent much time here, but it was the same setup as Wes'. The door was open, and I ducked my head in. "Spencer?"

"In here," he called from another room.

I slipped in. Spencer's living room was elegant and understated, much like him, with overstuffed brown leather couches and chairs, and shelves full of books.

"Do you have a moment?" I stood in the office doorway. Wood-paneled and full of dark wood furniture and more books, it felt almost like we should be smoking cigars and having brandy after dinner.

Spencer sat in a burgundy leather chair behind a large wooden desk, working on his laptop. He wore a T-shirt and chinos, instead of a suit, feet bare, but still looked dashing and debonair.

Spencer smiled, his glasses slipping down his straight nose, his arm going out slightly. "Let me finish this email, and I'm all yours."

Without thinking, I slid onto his lap like I would Wes. My hand went to my mouth as I realized what I'd done. "I'm sorry, I don't mean to be weird–"

Why had I done that? It was one thing to lean on him when watching something, it was another to sit on his lap when he was at his desk.

His arm tightened around me just enough to let me know he wanted me to stay without restraining me.

Spencer's breath brushed my ear as his voice went low and growly, "Darling, if this is where you need to be, then this is where you belong."

My breath caught at the endearment as he shifted me so I was curled into him, and balanced on the chair, but his hands were free to type. It felt... nice. Comfortable.

"Perfect. May I call you that? Darling?" Spencer murmured. "I don't know how you feel about endearments. Perhaps we will try a few out?"

"I like it." *Darling.* It made me feel treasured, special, in a different way than I did when with Wes. I wasn't really used to calling people sweet things, other than occasionally using the silly nickname I had for Wes from when we were kids, but I noticed that I *really* liked being called them.

I rested my head on his chest, the shirt soft under my cheek.

"You call me *good doctor.*" I gazed up at him.

"It's a descriptor, not an endearment. But I don't have to use it, if you don't like it," he added, stroking my hair at the nape of my neck.

"I don't mind. It sounds distinguished." I relaxed into him. This felt so nice.

"Good. Everything is *always* open to negotiation. The last thing I want is for you to be uncomfortable." His weight shifted as he went back to typing his email.

I looked up at him as he worked, my head still on his chest. He was devastatingly handsome. He was also kind and thoughtful. But in very different ways than Wes or Evan.

"You're staring," he murmured, still typing.

"I didn't know you wore glasses." They added to his whole distinguished gentleman look. Okay, they were *slutty little glasses.* But still...

"Sometimes." He continued typing.

My mind wandered as Spencer's hard cock jutted into me. What would it be like to have sex with Spencer? To be bent over that wooden desk and taken from behind. Or crawl under the desk and suck his cock as he worked.

Hey, thirsty girl, this is not a romance novel–and we're not there yet.

True. But a girl could fantasize, right?

His lips grazed the top of my head. "Nearly done."

Was this what Evan meant when he talked about getting different things from his guys? Wes and Evan wouldn't blink if I asked for either of those things, but the idea of doing them with Spencer sent a very different thrill through my body. It seemed more right with him, just as sex in the bathtub felt more right with Evan.

Finally, he closed his laptop, and turned his attention to me.

"All done, Dearest. My attention is all yours. Thank you for being so patient. You were perfect," he crooned, his hand once again playing with my hair.

Dearest. I liked that one, too. I also enjoyed him calling me *perfect.* It did something to me after a childhood of never doing anything right.

"I've been going through what you sent me, trying to figure everything out. Not just the different options, but figuring out what this world's advancements are, where my knowledge might be deficient, or if I know things that aren't common here." I lounged comfortably in his lap, even though I should sit up for such an important business conversation.

"My good doctor, are you telling me that you're accepting the job?" Spencer beamed.

"I think I am. I'd like to be on the simulator project, if it's still an option. I don't know if I can do it, but I want to give it a try." Leaning into him, I let his leathery scent curl around me.

"I'm beyond pleased that you chose that project. The delightful thing is that we don't know if it can be done. I'll get everything completed on my end so you can start when you feel ready. No rush. Now we have to figure out who else we need to round out the team, perhaps do a little scouting," he told me, one arm around me.

"I heard from Dr. Harlowe, who once again invited me to see her particle cutter. Maybe we can find someone at PIIP?" I looked up into his beautiful eyes and grinned.

Spencer chuckled. "That would be a good place to start. I'm so glad you're going to join the team. When do you want to start? Again, no rush."

"I'm not sure. The doctor said I can go back to work when I feel ready. I still need breaks right now, when I'm concentrating hard." Which was part of why my progress on Evan's videos had been slow.

He nodded, hand trailing down my neck. "We have no timeline. Perhaps we start with a few days a week in the office and a few days at home. I have other small projects for you as well, as does the head of special projects."

"Yeah?" I perked. "Like helping with the high school internship program? That sounds fun."

"Indeed. I'll let them know that you're interested," he assured as he traced my collarbone. "Anything else troubling you?"

"My degree is fake here. I'm worried I'm going to mess up, say the wrong thing or something, and everyone will think I'm a fraud or know that things aren't quite right. Wes says it'll be fine, but there's so many little differences." I buried my face in his chest, worry consuming me.

His hand stroked my hair in a soothing gesture. "I believe in you. It will take a little time to get adjusted. You're right, we should figure out a long-term solution to your university not existing here, but I know that you can do this. There are so many great things that we will accomplish together."

There he went, once again, believing in me so much that it made me want to believe in myself.

"You belong here, with us, but I understand that every day you find so many little things to remind you of this world's differences. I'm always here if you want to talk," he added.

I belonged here. With them. Each day, it felt like I fit in a little more.

"Thank you." Hearing someone other than Wes and Evan say it made me feel better. Like I wasn't imagining it. It helped me to feel as if staying here was actually the best choice—and not just because I feared the temporal police and enjoyed being dicked down on the regular.

We talked a little longer, mostly about minor differences I'd found in the field, and how special projects operated.

"I'll take you to whatever conferences you'd like," he told me. "It will be nice to have someone to go with."

"There's so much to learn. Not to mention a whole lot to see," I replied.

"There's so much I want to show you." His voice went low again, and the vibrations from his chest sizzled through me.

The urge to kiss him grew. We hadn't really discussed our relationship, we just talked, played chess, and cuddled. He'd mentioned wanting to teach me tennis so that we could play doubles.

I tilted my head up, wondering what would happen if I closed the space between our faces. Obviously, he felt something for me. What did his lips taste like?

"Do you want a kiss, Darling?" Spencer leaned in and kissed me.

My breath hitched in my chest, and I kissed him back, his leather scent surrounding me.

"More," I breathed.

His arms tightened around me, and his kiss deepened.

"Hey, Spence?" Evan walked in. "Oh, fuck that's hot."

Spencer's arms tightened slightly, as if letting me know that it was okay to stay.

"Hi, Evan," Spencer said.

"Don't mind me." Evan laughed.

"Good." Spencer kissed me again, his hand tangling in my hair.

Arousal and love pulsed through my bond with Evan.

Finally, Spencer broke off the kiss and turned to Evan. "Grace has accepted the job."

"That's great. I just wanted to ask about tomorrow?" Evan winked at me.

"It's all settled. We'll pick them up there and then head to the gala together," Spencer replied.

I continued to lounge on Spencer's lap, feeling cozy. "This is about getting ready for tomorrow? Thanks for that."

Riley and I were going to a spa after she finished school for the day. I'd be happy getting ready here. But it was fun being spoiled.

"I figured that you and Riley might like some time together." Spencer smiled.

"It'll be fun." Okay, I was nervous about the gala tomorrow.

"Wes is ready for movie night when you are," Evan told me.

Oh. Right. Movie night.

"Go on. You know where to find me." Spencer gave me another kiss.

"I'm excited to be a member of your team." I slid off his lap and kissed him on the cheek.

Spencer gave my hand a squeeze, sending little tingles through me. "As am I. I can't wait to see what we accomplish together."

"Let's make popcorn." Evan put his arm around my waist, and we left Spencer's rooms. "That was adorable."

We walked downstairs to the kitchen.

"It just... happened. I..." My chest shook a little, worrying about what he might think.

"Grace." Evan planted a kiss on my temple. "In this house, there's no need to feel bashful about needing a cuddle or a kiss or a fuck. You and Spence are cute together. It's been so long since..."

"There was someone, wasn't there." My voice was soft as I got out some popcorn.

He nodded as he took the popper out of the cabinet. "Yeah. When she died... it... it wrecked him. For a moment there, I was afraid I'd lose him, too. While he's had some relationships since then, it's never been serious. The fact that he's even considering courting you makes me so happy."

"Wow." I got out a bowl and put it under the popper, trying to wrap my head around it. "How long ago?"

"It was right before my parents died."

"So young." My hand went to my heart as he started the popper.

"Yep. He's my dear friend, my packmate, and I want him to find happiness again. That it's with you?" He grinned and opened the fridge. "Amazing."

"There's a lot to like about Spencer." I rummaged in the cabinet for candy as the popcorn popped. I wanted a relationship with him. However, I was happy to bide my time, especially after finding out that he'd lost the love of his life.

"There is. Wes is fine with it–as he's said. They just like to banter, since Spence is basically our older brother. I introduced them very early on." Evan laughed as he got out butter and some drinks.

"Yeah?"

"I also told Spencer about Wes the day I met him. That evening I called up Spence and was like *I met this alpha today, and I think he's the one. His name might be Wes.* I wasn't even an omega yet, I still thought I was a beta."

"Which would be why you introduced them to each other early. You wanted Spence's opinion before you got too serious?" I got the salt down.

"Yes. I needed a second opinion, because I didn't chase alphas. But Wes, hot damn." Evan grinned. "Fortunately, Spencer agreed–and they got along. It would be difficult for me to be with someone who didn't get on with Spence. Or Riley, for that matter. I'm glad they love you."

"I'm happy that they love me, too. I love them all." What would it be like to do more than kiss Spencer?

Evan kissed my neck, and his lips brushed across my ear. "What was *that?*"

I ducked my head and lowered my voice. "Is it weird that I want to kiss Spence? I mean I have you and Wes."

He pinned me to him. "No. *Stop.* I already have Wes, Brennan, *and* Jett, and I want to kiss you. All the time. Also, you taking the job is a good thing."

"I'll still make your lunch. I enjoy making it."

"Please. Like I said before, the notes are my favorite part." He grinned.

"I aim to please." I took the butter and put it in a bowl so that I could melt it in the microwave.

His eyebrows waggled. "Yeah? Promise?"

I laughed. "I wouldn't have it any other way."

Chapter Fifty-Eight

Wes

"Will you *stop?*" Evan put a hand over Brennan's to keep him from making the window of the limo go up and down. Again. Something he'd been doing for most of the ride from the house to wherever it was Riley and Grace were at.

"Sorry." Brennan pulled Evan close. Evan put his head on Brennan's shoulder.

Brennan didn't like cars–even big limos. But his mom insisted that we arrive at her gala in a limo. Now, the car reeked of his agitation.

I pulled a bottle of bourbon from the bar. "Shots? One or two to take the edge off?"

The queen mum wouldn't be amused if we arrived drunk. But I didn't like doing these completely sober, either.

"Please." Brennan nodded, still clutching Evan like he was a buoy.

I poured everyone a drink.

"To this being quick and painless." Brennan raised his and knocked it back.

"Hey, can we talk about something?" Evan asked, drinking his up.

"Of course." Brennan frowned, as he held out his glass for me to pour him another.

I frowned too, because I got a hint of anxiety through the bond.

"My heat is coming in two weeks. We're still going to the cabin, right?" Evan inquired.

"Yep. Got my time off locked in." I nodded, pouring myself another, too. We were going for the whole week, though his heat would only be a couple of days. Riley had a spring break trip with her sisters.

"I've got my time off, too," Jett said, putting his empty glass with Evan's.

Brennan's frown deepened. "Of course. Did something fall through with Ri going with your sisters?"

"Noooo." Evan shook his head.

"What about Grace? We're not leaving her at the house, are we?" Jett's head tilted.

"That's what I wanted to talk about," Evan said, the anxiety still riding strong.

"She doesn't have to come if you don't want her to. We'll send her to the sister pack. They like her," Brennan quickly said, arm still tightly around Evan.

"But she can come if I want her to?" Evan perked.

"Should I take her somewhere for part or all of the week?" Spencer offered, looking up from his phone. "There's so many things I'd like to show her. I can arrange to have food sent."

"That's a good idea." Brennan nodded.

"But I want her to be there." Evan's lower lip jutted out in a slight pout, his scent going sour.

"I know you do. I want her there, too. But is she ready for that?"
I asked. I'd been thinking about that a lot.

"Maybe? We've been talking about it–but it's also as much all of
your decision as hers," Evan said.

Jett's head cocked as a strand of black hair escaped his pony-
tail and fell in his eyes. "How do heat pheromones–and rut
pheromones–affect gammas? While they make me feel high, they
don't knock me over the head and compel me to fuck for days
without food and water."

"I worry about that, too," I admitted. "I don't actually know."

"Your bond is still weak," Brennan pointed out. "She probably
won't get the onslaught of feelings like Jett does."

I grimaced at the mention of the bond. Everyone, including Luc,
Mrs. Beekman, and our couples' therapist, were still making me
feel shitty about it not being strong. At least it looked like the police
investigation was wrapping up. The Center would still keep an eye
on us for a while. Even Evan seemed to have a stronger bond with
her than me.

Evan whined, and I squeezed his hand. Brennan held him
tighter.

"It's not a *no*, it's a concern for her comfort," Brennan soothed,
giving him a kiss. "I'm guessing you want her there, in the nest with
us, not just hanging out with Spencer."

Evan sighed, nuzzling him. "I'd be okay with that if it's all we can
agree on. But I'd like her with us at least part of the time."

"She's that important to you, isn't she?" Brennan looked
thoughtful.

"Of course she is. I bonded with her–and *we* feel each other."
Evan glared. He looked at me. "You still want her there, right?"

"Of course I do. I only worry that she isn't ready." It was an
orgy. In the fog of pheromones, the usual lines blurred, which was
where the joke about not talking about what happened in the heat

nest came from. While we regretted nothing, there was also a huge amount of trust built up between the four of us, which enabled us to give in and have a certain degree of vulnerability.

We could choose to hold ourselves back. But I'd also understand if Brennan and Jett weren't ready for her to be there either.

"I'm okay with it," Jett said. "But I think we shouldn't bring her in until after at least the first round, since that can get intense. We should let her know that she can come and go as she pleases without offering any reason or feeling any guilt. It's going to overwhelm her, and while I'll do what I can to buffer, I can get pretty affected in the thick of it."

"You'd be okay with her there?" Brennan peered at him.

"Um, yeah. I'm a little curious." Jett shot Evan a look, who replied with a coy smile.

Huh.

Brennan looked out the window. "We've just never…"

"I know, that's why we're talking about it," Evan replied. "We might not be ready for pussy at our sex party, and I understand that."

Caroline hadn't participated in Evan's heats—and he hadn't taken part in hers. Which had caused tension. They hadn't synced either, which usually happened in two-omega packs.

"Jett's plan seems like it could work. Spencer, she could hang out with you, right? When she needs a break?" I asked. My biology would compel me to stay with Evan.

Spencer seemed very engrossed in his phone. He looked up. "Of course. I enjoy spending time with her."

He always seemed on the periphery of the pack, so it would be nice for him to be drawn in a little more. And, well, I knew all about their kiss and her falling asleep on him in the movie theatre.

"Though..." Spencer looked at Brennan. "I don't know what it is like for mate pairs like them, but you should be prepared if her biology compels her to be with him the same way yours does."

"True. I didn't think of that. Yeah, if we keep her out, but she's crying at the door for me, I'd let her in, just like I would for you," Evan said.

"Fuck, when you put it that way..." I raked my hair with my hand. Right. They were mated. She could very well be as compelled to be with him as we were.

"Bren? I know you aren't besties yet, but..." Evan gave him a pleading look.

Brennan rubbed his chin. "Can I give this some thought? While it's your heat, and I want to make you happy, this isn't an easy thing for me. Though Spencer made a good point."

"Please. I see the effort you're making, and I appreciate it." Evan leaned in and gave him a kiss.

"I didn't even correct her when she, once again, played Volkov too fast." Brennan looked pleased with himself.

"Same menu as usual?" Spencer asked, still on his phone. He usually made the post-heat feast.

"Please?" Evan batted his eyelashes.

"Of course. I'll get the boat out of storage if the weather is nice." He went back to his phone.

"Okay, so I'll talk to Grace, and Brennan will think about it," Evan confirmed.

"While we're discussing things, I want to clarify that I like Grace and I fully intend to formally court her." Spencer's eyes met mine as he put down his phone.

"Please, take her to all the science things and galas and stuff. She had *fun* with you at the last one," I replied. Yeah, she could people so we didn't have to.

"What if I do more than science things?" Spencer prodded. "What if I teach her tennis or golf? Perhaps whisk her off to places she's never been? I can't wait to hold her hand and walk along the beach in the moonlight. Do you think she'd like to scuba dive with me?"

"The beach?" I'd sort of wanted to take her to the beach first. Because she hadn't been *here*.

"Doesn't she like the beach?" He frowned.

"I was planning a beach trip for the pack during the summer," Evan replied.

"No. I..." I stopped. It sounded silly to say it out loud.

"Oh, I see. Does this mean I shouldn't take her to the annual PIIP Symposium? I got us added since it's invitation-only. She wanted to tour PIIP and see the particle cutter," Spencer said. "We want to do some investigating for our project now that she's formally joining the team."

I thought for a moment. Wow, a romantic trip to an exclusive science convention. That sly dog. "That sounds like something she'd love."

"Pretty sure that's just a meh ocean. We'll take her to a better one," Evan said.

Spencer tapped on his phone. "I will refrain from taking her to good oceans until you do, but anywhere else is okay?"

"That's fair," I replied. "Please, teach her all the boring sports." I grinned at Spencer. "Seriously though. She loves dancing with you and Jett in the living room."

"Grace catches on fast." Jett nodded.

Brennan looked out the window. Evan put his head back on his shoulder. Jett reached over and squeezed Brennan's hand.

"Brennan, do you wish for me to wait?" Spencer asked. "I'm not trying to push things. I just haven't felt this way about someone in a long time."

Brennan shook his head. "This is a me problem, not a her problem. I'm happy that you're at a point where you want to pursue her. But, once again, we're not ready for her to join the pack yet. At the very least from a purely legal standpoint, even without the investigations. Though we now have a lawyer who isn't Katie."

"I appreciate you trying," I told him. "She's been loading the dishwasher the way you like."

"True. She still holds her mug weirdly."

"Such random things to be bothered about." Evan rolled his eyes. "Spence, treat my girl like a princess, okay?"

A smile danced on Spencer's lips. "It will be my privilege."

Chapter Fifty-Nine

Grace

"Is Marcos going to be there tonight?" I asked, as Riley and I got our hair done at a fancy place. We'd already finished nails and makeup.

"Marcos?" Riley frowned at her phone.

"Well, I saw his dads at the last one. If he were going to this one, it might be more fun for you. You could hide under a table with a tray of canapes and talk about people," I said. "Just a thought."

Riley wasn't looking forward to this.

She laughed, tapping on her phone. "Love it. Did you ever do that?"

"Not at galas but other things, with my best friend. Usually it was a tray of taco dip." Thinking of her, of the way she betrayed me, still hurt all these years later.

"Pretty sure there will be no taco dip. I hope they don't make me go to lots of these." Riley frowned at her phone. "Marcos won't be there. But Hiro will be there with his parents. I don't think he'll hide under a table with me, but it could be okay."

"Yeah?" I remembered what she said about not thinking he liked her.

"Yeah. It turns out he's this reserved and serious guy with resting broody face," she said. "At the dance he was kind to me, and we studied for the literature test together. I can see now why he and Marcos are friends."

"I'm glad he's a nice guy."

"I'm trying to get him to apply to the Compass BioTek internship program with me," she added. "Is it okay if I give Kilroy your info so his mom can text you?"

"Sure." I'd met her when she dropped Kilroy off for Wes' birthday party.

We finished getting ready.

I looked at my phone. "They're almost here."

"How do I look?" Riley smoothed the fabric of her silver gown with her hands. Her hair was down and wavy. She looked fantastic.

"Amazing." I maneuvered my dress. I felt so special in it. Not to mention the way Spencer looked at me sealed the deal. "Should I put up the train so I can move?"

"No. Not until they take your picture on the staircase," Riley told me. "The front of the Gladiola has this enormous staircase and at fancy parties they take pictures of everyone going in, and it's a thing to have your dress trail down the staircase. Look."

She showed me pictures of beautiful women in cascading dresses, smiling as they walked up a staircase–like at the Met Gala.

We went out into the lobby. Riley giggled as we passed a mirror. "We look like princesses. Let's send Rose a picture."

"We do," I agreed as we took one on her phone. I felt like a princess. I even had clear heels. When Andre altered the dress, he'd made it so it helped hide my scars, and Riley covered the rest with makeup, so that I didn't have to use a wrap if I didn't want to.

"Remember, don't let the bathroom bitches get to you," Riley told me. "You have an alpha–and my brother. And maybe a Spencer?"

"True." I smiled as a limo pulled up. I'd never been in a limo, let alone one so big.

The door opened, and Wes got out. He wore a black tux with a silver vest and tie. Since Riley and I were both in silver, all the guys were matching, which was sweet. Riley got in.

"Grace." Wes' jaw went slack. He kissed my hand.

"We need to go." Brennan's head appeared.

"Will all this dress fit?" I tried to gather it up.

"You can always sit on my lap." Wes helped me and the voluminous dress into the limo. There was a lot of dress.

"My good doctor," Spencer breathed. "You look exquisite. As do you, Riley."

"We're hot and we know it," Riley agreed as we drove off.

"You look great," Evan agreed. "But Grace, how am I supposed to undo all those laces on the back of your dress?"

I grinned. "I'm sure you'll figure it out."

"Scissors," Jett grinned.

"Noooo," I laughed. "No scissors."

Brennan stared at me.

I looked down. "Too much boobage? I needed something that wasn't backless, and that seemed to be the tradeoff."

Brennan gave Spencer a look. "Really?"

"She looks ravishing–and it's perfectly acceptable for the gala." There was a bite in Spencer's tone.

My cheeks warmed. Spencer thought I looked *ravishing?* That went straight to my pussy.

"Is there something wrong with my dress?" I squirmed.

"Um, no." Riley rolled her eyes. "I showed you all those pictures. If anything, your dress is a little plain."

Brennan shook his head. "There's nothing wrong with it. My mother doesn't like family wearing dresses with trains."

"Hopefully, this means that we won't get invited to the next one. We talked about this, Bren. It's not your mom's pack," Jett said. "United front. Let's take a stand against tyranny."

"Maybe Spencer should walk you up the stairs so I can watch you from behind." Wes grinned, eyeing me.

Brennan shot him an annoyed look. "Wes, we've gone over the entry plan. Though now I'm thinking that you and Grace should be last so no one steps on the train. Yes. Evan, Jett, and I are first, followed by Spencer and Riley, and Wes and Grace taking up the rear. We stop and pose on the landing as a pack, then go to the top. Don't stop or answer questions going up the stairs other than the landing and the top—we're family, not guests. Once we're at the top, we wait for our group, take *one* picture together, then go into the Gladiola, where we'll take more photos. Again, no questions. Best manners because someone is always watching. Mingle, but keep talk light, no politics or anything controversial, Ri, *do you understand*?"

"Fine." Riley made a face.

"Also, as tempting as it is to get drunk at these things, please resist. I'm saying this mostly for my own benefit," he added, raking a hand through his dark hair.

"It'll be fine, Grace," Wes told me. "It's a party for charity. Aside from being bored to death, what can go wrong?"

The limo pulled up in front of an elegant building with columns and a large staircase in front that felt more like a museum than a hotel. A red carpet lined the stairs, as did reporters with cameras and microphones. Spectators watched from behind red ropes.

I looked out the window of the limo as Katie got out, offering Rami her arm. Lexi followed along with the rest of their pack. They went up the staircase in pairs and trios, and our limo moved to the front position.

Brennan took a deep breath. "Here we go."

He got out first and offered a hand to both Jett and Evan. Spencer got out next, and people called his name from the crowd. He helped Riley out. Brennan took Jett and Evan's arms and went to the foot of the staircase, waiting for Katie's pack to finish their ascent.

Wes helped me out of the limo, and I froze at all the people watching as Riley helped maneuver my dress out of the limo and onto the sidewalk.

"Breathe." Wes' breath was warm on my cheek as he whispered in my ear. I pulled my wrap closer since it was a little chilly.

Spencer squeezed my hand, then took Riley's arm, whispering something in her ear, as he led her to the foot of the staircase where Jett, Evan, and Brennan had started to walk up.

Arm in arm, Wes and I walked down the red carpet to the foot of the stairs as I tried to ignore the people taking pictures.

"You've got this," Wes whispered. "You're the most beautiful woman here–and I think this dress will look even better on my floor than the red one."

I laughed as we made our way up the stairs. "It will definitely take up more space."

We joined the others on the landing, took a photo, and then started back up in the same order.

When we got to the top, we took a picture in front of a sign advertising the foundation. We all went inside the hotel, where we went up another staircase, and took another photo. Then we were ushered over to another sign, this one accented with flowers and greenery. Siobhan and Frank Morris were waiting for us, along with a guy who looked like Brennan.

"You made it." Siobhan's smile didn't reach her eyes as she surveyed our attire. She nodded at Riley's but frowned a little at mine.

"We wouldn't miss it, Mother, Father." Brennan's teeth were gritted. "Troy, another great party as usual."

"Yes, well, a lot of work went into it. Not that you'd understand, little brother." Troy's look was politely scathing.

Right. Brennan's brother, who ran the foundation.

"Grace. Riley. Oh, you two really do class up the pack," Frank told us.

Riley struck a pose. "I aim to please."

"Why don't you go mingle," Siobhan told us, in a clear dismissal, as more people arrived.

We checked in at a table and entered an open area where there was a bar, servers with canapes, Katie's pack, and some other people. Soft music played. The mood wasn't as festive as at the science dinner.

"Grace." Rami, in a black tux with silver accents, rushed over to me. He looked me up and down. "Girl."

"Careful, she's mine." Evan laughed, putting an arm around me.

"You're coming to the meeting on Wednesday, right?" Rami asked, pulling me over to the side as Brennan dragged Jett and Evan off to the bar and Lexi cornered Wes.

"I can't wait." I was going to try out a meeting of the Daedalus Society. Hopefully, it was a nice group of people. I'd like to make some friends.

"That dress," Rami added, looking me up and down appreciatively.

"I know. I took a video. It's incredible," Riley said, joining us.

"No one's wearing anything like it." I bit my lower lip. The women here were wearing things more like what I'd worn to the science dinner.

"That's because this is all family right now. Troy's family, Liam's pack, the cousins who either work for Siobhan or are on the foundation board. The guests will be dressed more like you," Rami told me. "Have you met Troy and Liam?"

"I think I just met Troy. He's Brennan's brother and runs the foundation with Brennan's dad?" I'd seen him at the science dinner.

"Yes, and Liam is the eldest brother. He helps Siobhan with the company. Katie, of course, is legal counsel for both," Rami replied.

"Which means Brennan's the only one that doesn't work for the family," I finished. He had *two* brothers?

The three of us gossiped in the corner as other people trickled in.

Katie joined us. "Rami, time to mingle. Grace, Ri, you both look amazing."

She hauled him off, and I didn't see Wes, Evan, or Spencer.

"Hiro's here. Come meet him." Riley dragged me back off into the fray. More people had arrived, and I saw fancier dresses.

We stopped in front of a lanky young Asian teenager in a tux, dark hair in his brown eyes. With him were an older teenager, a man and two women. They were in all black, the only nod to the *all that glitters* theme was the ostentatious jewelry that the women wore.

"Hiro." Riley grinned. "Kenta."

"Riley. These are my parents. I go to school with Riley." Hiro didn't quite grin, but he looked happy to see her, dark eyes dancing.

"Councilman Nakamura," the man introduced. He was a tall alpha. His suit looked very fancy. "These are my mates, Yui and Sara."

"Hi, I'm Grace." I gave a wave. I was pretty sure the smaller one was an omega. The other might be an alpha. I wasn't the best at figuring things out by scent yet, and there was a lot going on in the room.

The older teenager, Kenta, grinned. "The one with the chair."

Councilman Nakamura gave us a look.

My cheeks warmed. "Perhaps."

"I'm Yui, it's so nice to meet you. I haven't seen you at the parent guild meetings," the smaller one said. Her features were dainty, her black dress classically stunning, and her earrings made my ears ache. Two silvery bite marks peaked out from the collar of her dress.

"Councilman, there you are," an alpha with an accent said.

"Excuse me," Councilman Nakamura said, leaving us.

Hiro, Kenta, and Riley were talking animatedly about something that had happened at school. Sara watched over Yui.

Yui took a phone out of her tiny purse. "Let me get your information. Do you have a committee? I'm getting together the carnival committee for the next school year. It's never too early to start planning."

I gave her my number, and she went off to join her mates. Yeah, I knew this kind of mom, and saying *no* wouldn't get me anywhere.

Wes put an arm around my waist. "Who was that?"

"The mom of one of Riley's friends. I think I just joined the carnival committee." I frowned, hoping it was okay.

"That's perfect. I love the carnival," Wes assured. "Where's Riley?"

"With two boys from school." I saw them going off into the crowd.

Wes and I got a drink and tried some canapes. While I got several compliments on my dress, it kept getting stepped on.

"I'm going to go try to hike this dress up." I headed toward the bathroom. Frowning in the mirror, I tried to bustle the train.

"Here, let me help." Evangeline, the woman from the dress shop, appeared. "You look stunning. Grace, right?"

"Yes, and thank you," I told her, happy for the help.

She quickly helped me use the tiny hooks sewn into the fabric to hook up the train.

"Thank you so much for helping," I said.

"You must meet my daughter. She moved away to be with her pack as well. I love it when she visits. They are outstanding men. Established. Mature. Wealthy. Respected. Everything a mother could want for her baby girl," she bragged.

"How nice for her," I replied.

We went back out into the foyer, which was still full of people and music. Hopefully, dinner would be soon. I looked for Wes, but I didn't see him. I spied Evan, Brennan, and Jett, looking very bored as a bunch of alphas talked at them.

"This is my daughter Cari and her pack. Cari, this is Grace, she's new to town. I met her at the dress shop." Evangeline beamed at a svelte brunette omega. Her dress was pink, ruffled, and stunning. It might be hiding a baby bump–it could also be the light.

"It's so nice to meet you," Cari simpered, wearing even more jewelry than Yui. She seemed like the popular girls in high school who pretended to be my friend until I truly needed them.

"It's nice to meet you. You're here alone?" one of her large alphas told me, voice accented.

"I'm here with my mates." I still didn't see Wes, though Spencer was speaking with a few people I recognized from the science dinner.

"Grace is a mathematician, she just moved here to be with her mate," Evangeline added.

"What sort? Actuary?" an alpha that smelled of copper asked, his arm firmly around Cari's waist. He wore a bunch of large rings and an expensive watch and had a Southern accent.

"The theoretical kind. I work mainly with qubits," I replied, still searching the crowd for Wes.

"Oh. That sort. Do you work for Redstone or the Space Authority?" the first alpha asked.

"Compass BioTek, actually."

"Oh no, you don't want to work there," Cari told me. "Surely your mates can find something better? Or Rolf, maybe you know? Rolf knows so many people. I'm in real estate development, so I can't help you. But if you're newly mated, you should come and see my latest property. It's a vacation share, the classy kind. Just think, a chance to go on a special vacation every year with your mates, without having to be bothered with the upkeep of an additional home." She dug a little card out of her purse and handed it to me.

"Oh, thank you." I glanced at it and tucked it into my purse. Timeshare. I was in another world, and I was being sold a timeshare. She probably knew of some life-changing essential oils, too.

"Here, you should have something to eat," the copper-scented alpha said, taking something off the tray and handing it to Cari.

"Do you need anything else to drink?" another asked.

"I'm fine, thank you." She looked up, smiling.

"Is Compass BioTek really a terrible place to work?" I frowned.

Cari shrugged. "You could do better. Your mate is in real estate, finance?"

"Cybersecurity." I wasn't sure I liked these people and kept hoping to see Wes or Riley so I could escape without being rude.

The first alpha nodded. "Very nice. The Center matched you long-distance?"

"I've actually known him for a long time, it's quite the story."

"I do love a good love story. With my pack, it was love at first sniff. Even before I met them in person, I knew they were perfect. You met your alpha in the wild then? You saw him and just–knew? Like a love story?" Cari gushed, her head tilting so I got a good view of her bite marks.

"I first met him when I was ten. It is a bit like a love story," I agreed.

It seemed like plenty of omegas met their alphas 'in the wild' so I wasn't sure why she was gushing. But then again, what did I know?

"If he's here, we might know him," Cari pried.

I kept looking but didn't see anyone I knew. "Maybe. His name's Wes Lawson."

"You liar." Her voice and expression were playful, but her eyes weren't.

"No, that's his name. Maybe we know different ones." I frowned.

"Hardly. I've known Wes since I was at the university, and I know his mate–and you, my dear, aren't it. Oh, did you sneak in? I won't tell. Are you trying to meet rich alphas? I can help you find much better ones than the likes of him." She laughed, but it was tight and fake.

"You know what? I should find him. Nice to meet you." I hustled off, despite it feeling rude. This seemed weird.

Cari grabbed my wrist, her pink nails digging into my gloved wrist, stopping me. "You shouldn't lie about things like that."

I frowned at her touching me. "Why would I lie about Wes being my mate? People do have more than one."

"Wes would never take another." There was a hard edge in her voice.

Arms wrapped around my waist and the scent of laundry enveloped me.

"Grace, there you are. Evangeline, Caroline, you're here. I see that you've met my mate." Wes sounded less than pleased to see them.

"Wes." Cari's posture changed, and she practically melted into her mate as if he could make her invisible.

"They've opened the doors for dinner, let's go find our table." Wes guided me out of there before Cari could say anything.

"I don't know what just happened," I whispered, as he steered me to some open doors.

"That's Caroline. Brennan's ex. Fuck. We had no idea that she was coming. Brennan's going to be livid." With his hand in mine, we made our way through the ballroom.

"Shit." *That* was Caroline. The one who tried to replace Evan. The one who hurt Brennan. The one who thought revenge porn and robbery was the answer.

"Yep." His expression went grim as we found Brennan, Jett, and Evan sitting at a round table festooned with flowers and sparkles.

Brennan frowned. "What's wrong?"

"Caroline's here. She cornered Grace," Wes explained.

"Fuck." Brennan growled.

"It'll be okay." Evan put an arm around him.

"Incoming," Jett muttered.

"Boys, it's been so long," Caroline fake-gushed, three alphas now at her back, her mom nowhere in sight.

"Caroline," Brennan grunted. Everyone else glared at her.

"Evan." Her look took on one of concern as she leaned in and lowered her voice. "I'm so sorry to hear what Wes did to you. Do you need me to call the Center for you? You have rights, you know."

"I'm not sure what's happening," Rolf said to the one that smelled like copper.

"Thanks for your concern, but the integration team has it under control. We're good. All Wes did was to bring some peaches into our life." Evan gave me a kiss.

"Caroline, I think you should take your seat." Brennan's voice was firm.

"You actually let someone else in your pack, Bren?" Caroline frowned, arms wrapped around her stomach.

"Let's go find our seats, Dear. You've been standing too long," the copper-scented one drawled, putting his arm around her as if trying to herd her away.

Caroline's expression was halfway between upset and furious as her alphas led her to another table.

"We're leaving." Brennan shot up from his seat, expression angry.

"I'm okay with that." Riley appeared, holding half a pie.

Brennan's eyebrows rose. "Where did–you know, I don't want to know. Let's go." He waved Spencer over. "Spence, you can stay if you want, but we're going."

"Sit down." Siobhan strode over, a fierce look on her face.

Brennan shook his head. "You can't actually expect–"

"They're big donors, and you not sitting down could cost us not just that gift but others. Now, I'd hate to cut all those scholarships Evan gives out because we didn't get enough funds," she whispered-scolded.

"You knew." Hurt tinged his voice.

"You're making a scene. Sit," she hissed, then sailed off.

Brennan put a hand to his face.

What a bitch. Threatening to take scholarships away from kids. Not telling her son his ex was attending.

"We can still leave. We'll find another way to fund the scholarships," Evan whispered.

"Yeah, we'll start our own foundation or something," Jett added.

"Siobhan has a point about appearances and donors. Sometimes you have to be nice to people you hate," Spencer said. "But you also have a good reason to leave. It's your call. I'll support you either way."

"I will totally protest tyranny by leaving," Wes said.

"Me, too. Not telling you she was coming was a dick move," I told him, feeling bad that his mom was such a bitch.

"Please, let's go," Riley replied.

Troy joined us, expression hard. "Sit down before you ruin everything. People are staring."

People weren't staring. They were coming in and finding their tables. Okay, Caroline was glaring at us. Scratching my nose with my middle finger was tempting–though Riley already had that covered.

Brennan rubbed his forehead. "We might as well sit and eat. It's not like they're at our table. Now we have a reason to leave as soon as we can."

"Are you sure?" Jett prodded. "We have your back. We could end this."

Brennan's shoulders slumped as he sat back down at the table as Troy left. "Causing a scandal at the gala will hurt those who rely on the foundation's funding."

"Do you need me to hit your mom with a chair?" I offered.

"Fuck, no." Brennan shook his head and lowered his voice. "She has good reflexes. You might have to push her off a balcony."

Laughter bubbled out of my mouth as I took a seat between Wes and Spencer. Riley was between Spencer and Evan. Brennan between Evan and Jett.

"That's that bitch from the mall, right?" Riley asked, eating her pie with a plastic spork.

"Unfortunately. Why didn't anyone tell me?" Brennan pinched the bridge of his nose.

"You look amazing," Spencer whispered, getting very close to me.

I ducked my head. "Thanks."

"Did she hurt you or upset you?" Concern tinged his scent.

"Not enough for you to worry," I assured. "We can dance together tonight, right?"

He beamed. "My good doctor, it would be my pleasure."

Katie came over, Rami on her arm. "Hey, I just saw Caroline. I had no idea that she and her pack were coming. I wanted to give you a heads up so you can cut out after the program."

"Too late." Brennan sighed. "But thanks."

Rami got a sly look on his face. "I wonder if the band takes requests."

Mischief glinted in Evan's eyes. "Oh? You're sly. You know, Grace knows that one."

"Please be cautious. My mother will forgive you two for a lot, but it only goes so far, especially in public," Brennan warned.

Rami went over to the band. Katie shook her head, trying not to laugh.

"Does Caroline have a song she hates, and he's requesting it? I'm here for that level of petty," Riley said, taking a picture of the almost empty pie tin.

"Me too," Katie grinned. "She used to pay bands not to play it. It's also one of Rami's favorites. Ri, why do you have a pie?"

Riley smirked. "The question is, why don't you?"

Music started, and Evan offered me his hand. "Grace?"

Evan led me out onto the dance floor. Rami joined us with a woman with dark skin and hair, who was heart-stoppingly beautiful and wore a white sparkly dress.

"That's Nevin, she's Liam's omega. Liam's a dick, but she's nice." Evan whispered as we glided across the floor.

"She's an amazing dancer," I replied, watching her effortless movements.

"Nevin used to dance professionally," he replied. "ooh, Caroline doesn't look happy."

Caroline had a sour look on her face. Brennan's parents stood near the corner of the floor, but they looked amused, not upset.

Jett joined us on the dance floor with another woman I didn't know. Her dress was black, her light brown hair was short. Everything about her was understated but perfect–and probably expensive.

"Troy's wife. She's also a dick, like Troy, and, like Troy, works for the foundation. But we're having fun teasing the alphas right now. It's what we usually do, dance with their mates, then we give them back," Evan whispered as he continued to twirl me across the floor. This dance was fun, he'd taught it to me the other day in the living room.

Troy, a man that I presumed was Liam, along with Katie and Brennan, all stood near the edge of the dance floor, watching their spouses dance–amused. Rami winked at Katie and led Nevin toward them. He twirled Nevin into her alpha's arms and took Katie's hand. They went back out onto the dance floor. Troy cut in on Jett and took his wife's hand. Brennan and Jett came over to us.

"Grace, will you dance with me?" Brennan offered me his hand, as Evan and Jett took off across the floor.

"I endorse this political statement," I whispered, as we danced past Caroline, who looked livid for a woman who was supposed to be happy with her rich mates.

"I'm not trying to use you, I wanted to make sure you were okay," he added. "She wasn't mean to you? Or hurt you?"

"No. I didn't know who she was. Her mom helped me with the train of my dress in the bathroom. I met her at the dress shop. She wanted me to meet her daughter and called her *Cari*. I didn't know; I wasn't trying to start anything," I murmured.

Brennan was an excellent dancer, possibly better than Spencer. Evan gave me a saucy wink as we danced by.

He grimaced. "I know. I'm angry my mother hid that she was coming."

"That's shitty." I saw Brennan's parents take the floor, along with a few other people that could be cousins. "Was this dance planned?"

"Yes and no. It's not uncommon for us to open with a family dance during dessert. It's also not uncommon for Rami to drag everyone up beforehand," he told me. "Your dress is beautiful, Grace. You'll probably end up gala queen again, especially if they got a good shot of you on the staircase."

"That wasn't my intention." I watched my feet as we danced.

"I know. But I'd rather it be you than me." He smiled.

The song ended, and we returned to our seats, where someone had set the first course.

"Beautiful." Wes gave me a kiss as I sat.

Frank and Siobhan went up to the bandstand, along with someone I didn't know. The music stopped, and they welcomed everyone, and introduced the other person, who seemed to be the host, like Antonio had been at the science dinner.

We ate our salad while they talked. When the talking stopped, Wes stood.

"Drinks?" Wes asked.

"I'll go with you, because I need another." Brennan joined him.

They took orders and left, as the servers took our empty plates and others brought around the entrees.

Riley gave Spencer a pleading look. "Can we go now?"

"Let's hijack a limo and get ice cream?" I suggested.

"All in favor." Evan laughed, raising a hand as our meals were served.

"Why do Grace and Evan have different dinners?" Riley eyed the plates that were brought out.

Everyone else had salmon and a slice of prime rib with potatoes and asparagus. Evan and I had a tiny bacon-wrapped steak, a lobster tail, roasted root vegetables, and mushroom spinach risotto.

"We're special." Evan grinned. "I'll trade if you'd rather have mine."

"Ooh. I want this." Riley speared his lobster tail with her fork and put it on her plate.

"I had a different dinner at the science dinner, too." Huh. I'd thought that they'd run out, and I'd gotten a substitution plate.

"It's an older custom, giving the omegas a special dinner," Spencer replied.

"Oh." I frowned at my dinner. "I... I'll trade."

Jett gave me a curious look. "No one's ever given you a special dinner before?"

Wes joined us, setting down drinks for me, Spencer, and him. "What's wrong?"

"Grace is concerned because we get lobster and you don't," Evan teased.

"Oh, right." Wes put an arm around me. "It's a thing they do sometimes. Eat your dinner. Unless you want me to feed you?" His eyebrows waggled.

I laughed. "It's fine."

"Here, try." Spencer held out a fork full of salmon and fed me. "Delicious."

Brennan brought drinks for him, Jett, and Evan. We ate dinner, then I slipped out to go to the bathroom before the main program started. The ballroom was warm, and I needed some air. Riley came with me.

"Do you want to leave? You seem so unhappy," a male voice said, from some place in the lobby.

"You have us, and our children. There is no need to be upset. They don't deserve you anyway," another added.

"I know. I'm so happy to have you and our babies. It just hurts to see those who rejected me with someone else," Caroline sniffed.

I saw them in a corner and hoped she wouldn't see me.

"Rejected? Not the story I heard," Riley muttered as we entered the bathroom.

"Me, neither," I replied.

They weren't there when we went to return to the ballroom. Good. I hoped they'd left. But Hiro was there. Marcos was, too.

"I'll be right there," Riley grinned. "Marcos decided to crash the party."

"Hi, Marcos. Hey, I'm going to get some air." I went out onto a tiny balcony off the foyer and leaned on the rail. There was a set of stairs going down to the gardens below.

"You're Wes' *mate*," Caroline said from behind me. "I don't understand."

I sighed, still leaning against the rail. "Go back to your pack, Caroline."

"How could you move in on an omega's alpha?" There was a bite in her words.

"I promise, I'd never hurt Evan." *Unlike you.* It was funny that she was spouting concern for Evan when she'd tried to poach his pack. I turned to face her, mostly because her being behind me, when I couldn't move forward, made me nervous.

Not that my back being to the rail was any better.

"But you? How could they let someone like *you* into their pack? I'm still surprised they even did. Brennan's a control freak. You're not even pretty. And math?" she scoffed.

"I like math. Now excuse me, I should get back." I tried to move, hoping she'd let me, but she didn't. My heart thudded in my chest. I didn't like being trapped, and I didn't think her motives were pure. Given she looked pregnant, I didn't want to punch her.

Though if anyone needed punched in the tits, it was her.

"How did you even meet him?" she huffed.

"Caroline, please, I'd like to return to the dinner. Won't your alphas be missing you?" I turned my body so my back was to the stairs instead of the edge of the balcony.

Where *were* her alphas?

"You're after their money, aren't you," she demanded, stepping toward me, trying to get me back up against the rail of the balcony.

"No." I sidestepped her, slipping out. She was still between me and the door to the inside, but the staircase was now free. "I should go." Without waiting, I took off for the stairs, heart thudding.

"Yes, you should," she sneered.

"Grace, are you out here?" Riley called.

I tripped and took a tumble down the stairs as a scream ripped from my throat.

Chapter Sixty

Brennan

Caroline was here. Fuck. What was even worse was that my family *knew*–and the only person who thought to warn me was Katie.

Dessert was being served. We still had the family dance and the main program, and then we could leave.

Seeing my ex brought up so many emotions, and not the ones I expected. I sort of pitied her new pack. But, she'd gotten what she wanted–wealthy alphas.

I also pitied *her*, because she didn't seem happy either. If she were happy, she'd be flaunting her pack and belly, not taunting Evan.

But Caroline could be one petty bitch when she wanted.

"Grace." Wes shot up out of his chair, expression stricken.

Evan stood up at about the same time. "Something's wrong."

Frowning, I looked around the ballroom, as fear shot through my bond with Evan. "Caroline's not in her seat."

Wes was already halfway to the door, with Evan behind him. I joined them. I was not letting Evan face her without me.

Troy stopped us. "The program's going to start."

"It's Grace, get out of my way," Wes growled, ready to elbow him.

"Fine." He stepped aside. "But not you," my brother added to me.

"If you had told me that Caroline was coming, none of this would have happened. If something happens to Grace, so help me." I pushed my older brother aside, aware that people were watching. Fuck them.

We ran out into the foyer, where the reception had been earlier.

"GRACE," Wes yelled, clutching his chest. "I think she's this way."

"What the fuck did you do, you bitchnozzle? Hiro, call emergency. Marcos, you know first aid, right? Grace!" Riley screamed from some place I couldn't see.

I saw two of Caroline's alphas run through a doorway that led to a balcony—the same direction as Riley's scream.

"Get away from my mate," a male alpha growled at her.

"That bitch fucking pushed her. Grace did nothing to her," Riley yelled back even as the alpha towered over her.

Two of Caroline's alphas and Caroline were crowded onto a small balcony. Riley stood toe to toe with Caroline.

Where was Grace?

"Step away from the teenager," I growled. Protecting their mate was no excuse to intimidate a child.

"Grace." Evan darted down the stairs, fear continuing to roll through the bond.

"What the fuck did you do?" Wes took a step toward Caroline, scent spicy with anger.

"We were just talking and whoops." One hand went to her mouth, the other was wrapped around her belly. "Your mate's clumsy."

"Grace, hey, stay with me," Evan said from the staircase. "Jett, Jett, I need your help."

"I'm right here." Jett slipped past me and ran down the stairs. "Don't move her."

Wes' face contorted in anger as he lunged. "You *bitch*-"

I grabbed him before he committed a crime–or her alphas made a move. "Don't touch her," I growled. "Riley, go help Evan. Now."

"Don't threaten my omega," the one that smelled like copper warned, moving in front of her.

"She hurt Grace. Grace has done nothing to you." Wes strained against my grasp.

"She did not," he snapped back.

"Stop it right now, Wes. Control yourself," I growled quietly. The law wouldn't be on our side, even if she weren't pregnant.

Caroline shrugged, tucked behind her two alphas. "We were *talking*. It's not my fault she can't walk in heels."

"Pretty sure that's not what happened, oh, and he got here after me," Riley called.

The alpha bristled. "My mate would never."

"Spencer, get Lexi and Katie for me, please?" I asked, smelling him behind me, positioning myself in the doorway to block Caroline's exit.

"I'm right here," Katie said from behind me.

"I'll get Lexi," Spencer said.

"Emergency's coming," one of the teen boys said, now sitting on the top stair with a crying Riley, the other joining him.

I could feel the panic from Evan, the concern from Jett, as Wes went to Evan and Jett.

"This is all a misunderstanding. Cari wouldn't push anyone. Now she isn't feeling well. We're taking her back to the hotel," Rolf said.

"You're going to stay right there until we figure out what happened," Katie said, helping me block the doorway. "Caroline, what the fuck? Grace is Wes', not Bren's."

Caroline rolled her eyes. "Why would I hurt her? I told you, she's clumsy."

"Hmm, I wonder. You're a petty bitch who can't get over the fact that Brennan didn't choose you. So, over and over, you've made him pay for it. You were the one who dumped him, remember? What, you expected him to give up everything and travel with you? Chase you across Europe and declare his love?" Katie fired back, expression contorting into a sneer.

Hurt filled Caroline's face as her tulip scent soured. One of her alphas growled.

I gave her an incredulous look.

"You *wanted* to travel. You said that you didn't want to be tied down after you got your degree." So, I went to graduate school, built up my business, and went on with my life.

"She wanted you to chase her. You didn't. Then you found Jett," Katie said. "I'm guessing that she came to your wedding intending to fix the biggest mistake of her life. Only instead, you met Evan, ruining all her plans for a happy reunion."

"You replaced me," Caroline spat, clinging to her alphas.

I frowned, confused. "You said that you didn't want me. I thought you were my match, and you rejected *me*. Even when I offered to wait, you didn't want me to. So, I let you go like you asked. I didn't set out to find Jett–or Evan. It just happened. When you came back from your travels, I gave you a job, and let you into our lives. I even thought that there could be a place for you in our pack."

Anger filled her eyes as I stared at her.

"That was all fake? Some grand plan to ruin my life because I let you do what you asked?" I blinked. What? I couldn't wrap my head around all of this.

"I just needed a few years to travel–and I came back and you were getting *married*. I'm worth so much more than some beta and an overgrown oaf of an omega." Her eyes teared, and the alpha, who smelled of copper, put his arms around her.

"You don't need them, they don't know your worth. Don't worry. You have us," Rolf soothed.

"Don't call my mates names. Cari, you told me not to wait." I was perplexed. I'd done exactly what she asked, and it made her *mad?*

Katie cackled. "Your plan backfired, you manipulative cow."

"Stop telling lies about my mate," the copper-scented alpha growled.

In many ways, I was glad that I hadn't mated her straight out of university like I'd wanted. I loved Jett. If he hadn't been such a stubborn asshole after my accident, I...

No. I wasn't going to think about that very dark time, other than it had brought me Jett.

And Evan? While Caroline, on the surface, was the quintessential omega we were taught that an alpha should want to be with, Evan was everything I needed.

"Katie, Bren, you're needed in the ballroom, *now*," Troy hissed from behind me.

"We should go," the copper-scented alpha said. "Excuse us. Our mate is tired."

"Troy, if you're not here to help, go fuck yourself." I turned to Caroline. "I was willing to share everything I built with you–my pack, my business, my mates. You could have been part of it, but you chose to hurt those I love."

Which I realized almost too late.

"I don't know what happened, but our mate is happy now, and I don't appreciate whatever this is you're doing," Rolf grumbled. "Let us pass."

I focused on Caroline; the anger threatening to explode inside me. "Happy? If she was happy she wouldn't be causing trouble right now. You put my omega in the hospital. Twice. You stole massive amounts of money from the pack. Tried to destroy my business. Threatened my pack to the point that I had to get a restraining order against you—and let's not forget the sex tape. All for what–you wanted me for yourself, and if you couldn't have me, no one could?"

It seemed so petty.

"Of course I did, dumbass." She scowled.

"You did?" Rolf looked at her.

"He rejected me, so I ruined him." She shrugged.

His head went from side to side. "Oh. Good job."

Good job? Fucking shit, she really did find mates perfect for her.

"I don't even know what I saw in you." I shook my head. Wow, I'd wasted so much time and energy on her.

Rolf growled at me. "It's your loss."

Sure. They might be her match but she still didn't seem happy.

"Emergency is here. They came in through the garden." Evan buried his head in my shoulder as his pain and sorrow barreled through me.

Spencer was on the stairs with Riley and the teenagers. Troy seemed to have disappeared. Good riddance.

"We're leaving," the copper-scented alpha said.

"Hold on, we need some statements," the officers told him.

"You called the *police?* It was an *accident.* How could you?" Caroline shrieked, tulip scent growing spicy with anger.

"There is no need to question my mate," Rolf snapped.

"Bren, Evan," Spencer called.

I turned my back on her, taking Evan's arm and going over to Spencer. The officers could handle Caroline.

"We're needed. They're taking Grace to the hospital," Spencer said, helping Riley stand and putting an arm around her. Her anise scent was salty with sadness.

The taller boy gave Riley a hug. "We'll get your homework if you're not at school tomorrow, okay."

"Yeah, text us if you need us," the other added.

I think that was Marcos, the one who'd been over to the house. Riley nodded, makeup smeared.

We went down the stairs, where the paramedics were wheeling Grace out of the garden, Wes holding her hand, a stricken look on his face, laundry scent no longer fresh, but sour.

Jett joined us. "Wes is going with Grace. Spencer already called for our limo so it can take us to the hospital. Do I even want to know what happened?"

"All I care about is that Grace is okay." My heart thudded in my chest as Evan clung to me, terrified, scent sour, as we crossed the garden and went into the lobby of the hotel.

"Brennan, where are you going? Emergency is here? What's going on?" My mother strode across the lobby looking *pissed*.

"Caroline pushed Grace down the stairs. Something that wouldn't have happened if you had *told me* that she was coming. Grace is being taken to the hospital." I stood firm, putting myself between her and the rest of my pack.

"Wes has it handled, get to the ballroom. It's not over." Her hands went to her hips.

I shrugged and strode toward the doors of the lobby, where I could see a limo pulling up at the bottom of the stairs as the ambulance took off. People were watching along with the press that wasn't allowed inside.

She stormed over toward me when she noticed that I hadn't followed. "You'd abandon your family? You know how important this dinner is."

"My pack is my family, and they need me more than you do. We'll be at the hospital. I'll let you know how she is," I replied as everyone left the lobby.

Spencer turned and looked at me. "Coming?"

"Absolutely." Without looking back, I exited with my pack.

Riley, Evan, Jett, Spencer, and I got into the limo, and I closed the door, ignoring my mother, who was running down the stairs.

"Let's go," I told the driver.

The weight of a thousand planets lifted off my shoulders as the Hotel Gladiola faded into the distance.

"Oh, I'm going to pay for that. But there's no other choice." I rubbed my temples.

Evan put his head on my shoulder. "Damn straight. I can't even figure out why she *wouldn't* want us to go to the hospital. She's the one who has us playing *happy pack* in public."

"The timing doesn't suit her, since *happy family* is more important than *happy pack*. It's all about image. Well, that and control. I'm so tired of it." Being forced to go to these dinners. Her dictating *everything*.

I was done.

Jett squeezed my shoulder. "This is a long time in coming. We have your back."

"If she cuts the funding for the scholarships, we'll figure it out," Evan said. "I like the idea of starting our own foundation."

"Me, too. I think we should go forward with it, regardless." Spencer rolled down the window since the limo was filled with concern.

"Thanks. I'm so glad I have you." My pack. My everything.

We got to Mercy Hospital and found Wes pacing the waiting room.

"I will fuck shit up if she's not okay," Riley grumbled.

I hugged Riley to me. *Same.*

People were looking at us, but we were all still in our finery.

A doctor finally joined us. "Wes Lawson?"

"That's me." Wes stood.

"She sprained her wrist and fractured a couple of bones in her foot. Everything else is fine, though we'd like to keep her overnight for observation," she told us.

"Can we see her?" Evan asked.

"Of course. Follow me." The doctor led us through the emergency room to where Grace was.

"You're here." Grace's face lit up, and she sat on the bed, still in her silver gown.

Wes, Evan, and Spencer were immediately at her side. Riley texted someone.

"Of course we are," Wes told her.

"Did that bitch push me? I can't remember." Grace made a face. She had a fabric splint on her wrist. A removable walking cast on her foot peeked out from under her dress.

"I didn't see it but I think she did," Riley told her.

It wouldn't surprise me. My phone rang. My mother. I ignored it. Jett put his arm around my waist. Grace was going to be okay. Thank goodness.

Chapter Sixty-One

Grace

"Hey, did you have fun?" Rami asked me as we left the Daedalus Society meeting. The omega science association met regularly at a beautiful library.

"It was great, thank you so much for encouraging me to join," I told him. His friends were nice.

It was very interesting that it was named after Daedalus. In my world, he was an inventor from Greek mythology. But in this world, he also had a soft spot for omegas and would teach them, going as far as helping some of them hide as betas so they could pursue their dreams.

Katie was waiting on a bench, along with many other alphas. She got off the phone. "Hi, how did it go?"

"Great as usual." Rami melted into her arms.

She looked around. "Please tell me that you're not here alone."

"Spencer's getting me. He had a late meeting." Honestly, I was glad for the break. I'd only been in the hospital overnight, but the guys had been smothering me. Sadly, we couldn't prove that Caroline pushed me.

It wouldn't surprise me if she did.

"I'm right here, Katie." Spencer walked in looking debonair, phone in his hand. "Sorry, my good doctor. My meeting went long."

"It's fine." Giddiness bubbled up inside me. While we hadn't kissed again, he'd been very attentive, bringing me treats, playing games with me, making me a cheat sheet of terms so that I'd feel more comfortable when I started work.

He offered his arm, and I took it.

"Goodnight! Thanks again for introducing me to everyone." I waved, and we left.

"Do you want to go home or would you like to do something?" Spencer asked as we left the library and went onto the street.

"More potato balls?" I asked, recalling our post-science dinner snack.

"I was thinking more like a drink at a rooftop bar? Selfishly, I wanted to spend a little time with you alone. Wes and Evan have been plastered to your side since you got out of the hospital." His look went wistful.

"That sounds great. It's nice just to be out and about. Even if this boot is clunky." I kicked out my foot, showing off my glamorous removable walking cast. The wrist splint wasn't much better.

My phone buzzed.

Wes

How was it?

Me

Fine. Do you need me to rush back? Spencer wants to take me out.

I wanted to check, just in case someone had planned something special. Yesterday, Riley had come over with bubble tea and a new video game.

Wes

Have fun. Love you.

Me

Love you, too.

We walked down the street to a hotel and took the elevator all the way up to the roof. The air was crisp still, but heat lamps and little lights greeted us as people chatted at small tables or around fireplaces. There was a long bar with more lights. It was both cozy and sophisticated.

Spencer led me to a small fire pit. We took a seat together on a free couch.

"Is this okay?" he asked me, getting close.

"Perfect." My heart skipped a beat. Was this a *date?*

We ordered drinks. A merlot for him, a whiskey smash for me.

He leaned in and kissed my cheek. "Hi, Darling."

"Hi, Spencer." I leaned my head on his shoulder, the action feeling *right.* "Is this okay?"

"Perfect." He put an arm around me. "How did the meeting actually go?"

I sighed. "Some people were nice–like all of Rami's friends. But some of them were weird. Is it because I'm not an omega?"

"Did you tell them you work for me? That could be part of it," he replied as the server brought our drinks.

"You do great work, so why would people be weird?" I took a sip of the drink, grateful for the warmth of the fire–and him.

"It's not our biotech, it's the work we're doing with qubits. Some people think that we should stay in our lane. The thing is,

I have the money to fund such projects, and they fill a need. Why should I not?" He took a sip of wine.

Everything made sense.

"Oh, okay. I mean one of the things I love about your company is that Special Projects is basically a mad scientist incubator. The people who were most standoffish were talking about the symposium PIIP is having. It sounds nice, because then I could see Dr. Harlowe's particle cutter. But when I asked about it, I got snapped at, and told it was exclusive." It felt pretty unprofessional considering the Daedalus Society was supposed to be about omegas in science supporting each other.

"That is mean, but unfortunately not everyone is nice. I'm sorry they were like that." He squeezed my knee. "You wish to go?"

"It would be fun. But there's always next time." I took another drink, then swirled it in the glass so that it caught the light.

"What if I told you I got us on the list?" His look went hesitant.

I perked. "You did?"

"It was supposed to be a surprise. Mrs. K is finishing our travel arrangements. We already have people going from Compass BioTek. I simply asked if we could be added. The conference hotel is full, but I found someplace better for us to stay. I know that you wanted to see the particle cutter. I hope I didn't overstep." His brow furrowed with worry.

"Overstep? Spencer, it's perfect. Thank you." I leaned in and kissed him.

"Now you can arrange for your tour." He beamed.

"This is an amazing surprise." I got to go? It was going to be fascinating, not to mention the people I'd meet.

"I like you, Grace, and I intend to court you. You're all right with that when I do?" He took my hand in his, the warmth searing right through me in all the right ways. His eyes met mine and didn't leave as he brought my hand to his mouth and he kissed the back of it.

"Spence."

"We're going to have so much fun, Darling." His eyes gleamed, and he told me more about the symposium and the plans he'd made as we finished our drinks.

"Do you want another?" the server asked.

"I'm fine, are you?" He looked at me.

"I'm fine, thanks."

Spencer settled the bill, then stood and offered me his arm. "Are you hungry? I'll warn you, I was told not to feed you much because someone is planning on ice cream sundaes."

I laughed. "They are? I knew they'd do something. No, this was perfect, thank you."

"No, you're perfect." He led me to his car, and we drove home.

On the way, he told me some of the topics that my future co-workers would be presenting on and the topics he was excited to hear about at the symposium.

"I'll send everything to you so that you can see what you're interested in," he told me.

"I can't wait." It was perfect.

"This is only the first of many trips. I want to show you so many things. I want to teach you tennis and golf, and take you scuba diving," he told me as he drove down our street.

"Please. They all sound fun."

We pulled into the driveway. He got out and rushed around to my door to open it and help me out.

When we entered the kitchen, Wes and Evan, both shirtless, were putting out ice cream and toppings on the table.

"Perfect timing." Wes kissed me. "Science club was fun?"

"Rami introduced me to nice people." I kissed Wes, then turned to Spencer. "Thank you."

Spencer leaned in and kissed me on the cheek. "The pleasure is all mine, my good doctor. Goodnight, everyone."

With a wave, he went up the backstairs.

Evan got a giddy look on his face as he grabbed the ice cream scoop. "So? Where did he take you?"

"A rooftop bar. We just had a drink and talked. That's okay, right?" I grabbed a bowl and looked for the container of cookie dough.

"Always." Wes gave me a reassuring kiss. "If anything is too fast or weird, let me know. I will run interference."

"Thank you." I put some ice cream in my bowl.

"Are you two courting now? What did he give you?" Evan put chocolate ice cream in his bowl.

"We're not yet, but he said he'd like to." I added chocolate syrup.

Wes' arms slid around my waist. "I knew it was coming. He mentioned it to us the night of the dinner."

"I got a gift, though." I added sprinkles. "He's taking me to the PIIP symposium, and I can see the particle cutter. It's fun and thoughtful. Um, I hope he checked the calendar, so it doesn't interfere with anything?"

"He did. This is the exclusive science fair on the beach, right??" Wes put vanilla in his bowl.

I nodded. "I'm excited."

"Good. Please, have fun traveling with him." Wes added chocolate, caramel, and nuts. "While I'll take you anywhere you want to go on vacation, I'd rather stay home than travel for business. He'd make a great partner for conferences and when you start giving speeches and things. I mean, I'll go if you want, but he'll go and enjoy himself because he's that guy who finds everything interesting, and you can take him anywhere, and he'll blend in."

"That sounds good." Relief that he wasn't jealous flowed through me. I eyed him. "Me give speeches?"

"You will one day." Evan kissed my cheek. "Let's go upstairs."

We took our ice cream up to our living room on the third floor, and squished together on the couch and watched an episode of Evan's favorite show, which they'd been trying to catch me up on.

After we finished, Evan gathered our bowls and gave us each a kiss. "Good night. I'm going to let you have this human pillow to yourself, and I'm going to go snuggle the other ones."

"Thanks. Have fun. Good night." I snuggled further into Wes.

"Mmmm. I love this. Are you doing okay? I wanted to check in with you. I feel like I don't do that enough." Wes kissed my forehead.

"I'm okay. Promise. Will you take me to your beach one day? The one you went to with your sister? Oh, I was so jealous you'd get to go every year." Cozy and full of ice cream, I leaned my head on his shoulder.

"That sounds like a great idea. I want to show you anything that you'd like to see. You're my everything, and I love you." He kissed me long and deep.

"You're my everything, too." Finally, I had everything I wanted–including a place where I fit. Who would have thought I belonged in another world?

Chapter Sixty-Two

Spencer

"Like I told the other alphas in your pack, I'm hesitant to let Grace remain in your care, considering how chaotic you are. She needs stability, not upheaval." Mrs. Beekman scowled at me from the other side of my desk as she lectured me in my office at Compass BioTek.

"I understand, Mrs. Beekman. Normally there isn't this much excitement," I assured. The last thing that Grace needed was to be separated from us.

Perhaps I may not have claimed her yet, but the idea of her being taken away made me want to punch someone.

"At least her injuries weren't more serious," she chastised. "A fall down the stairs like that could have been devastating. Why was she even alone? You're not being careful enough with her. The only reason she hasn't been removed yet is that she's insistent that she stays with you."

It could have been so much worse. Still, seeing Grace lying crumpled on the stairs haunted me. I could still hear Riley's sobs, and smell Evan's fear.

"You're right. Wes is still adjusting, because her needs differ from Evan's. I assure you, I will personally ensure that Grace gets the attention and care she deserves." Which I was putting into action tonight.

While I should let Wes and Evan have a little more time, after nearly losing her, I didn't want to wait any longer. Life was too short, too fragile, too fleeting.

"Good." Mrs. Beekman nodded. "It's imperative that you all continue working with the integration team. Also, she's not alpha-sized and military-trained. She needs to be better protected."

"You're correct." I nodded. There was no other answer if we wanted to keep her.

"I'm glad you're so reasonable. Thank you for meeting with me." Mrs. Beekman smiled and stood.

After I showed her out, I went back into my office and returned to work.

"Spencer?" Deb knocked on the door. She was the director of Special Projects, and I'd known the alpha for some time.

"Come in."

"When is Dr. Ellington going to start? Considering how long you've had that office set up for her?" Deb came in, closed my door, and sat, looking serious as usual, in her crisp blazer, her short, graying, hair no-nonsense.

"In two weeks." After Evan's heat. The paperwork for Grace to start had been finished. I was looking forward both to truly getting this project started, and to her being part of my company.

"Who is she? I can't find any of her papers or examples of her work–or where she was last employed." Deb frowned a little. "I trust you, and I liked her when you brought her on a tour, but technically this is my department."

"You're right. Apologies. She's very talented but hasn't been given the chances she deserves. I'll be forthright, she's mated to my packmate, Wes, over in cybersecurity. Grace might seem an unconventional hire, but I assure you that she's going to do such great things with us." I needed to finish getting her background situated and had a few more favors to call in.

Deb thought for a moment. "I trust you–you've got an eye for talent. You have a new packmate? Congratulations. I know Wes. It seems like he's always scolding Margie's department for one thing or another."

"Thank you." I talked little about my pack at work. Not because I wasn't proud, but because I liked to keep my personal life private.

I added, "That's why everything is taking so long. She relocated to be with us and is still settling in. Our pack is going away for a week, so I figured it would be better for her to formally start after that. However, I don't see why she couldn't come in before that to meet with you."

"Perfect. I'll set up some time with her next week." Deb stood. "Have a great weekend."

Deb left, and I tried to finish up my work so I could make it home in time for family dinner.

Mrs. K came in. "Everything is set for the symposium. Grace is going to have such a wonderful time." Her look went a little wistful, since she used to travel with her wife to such things.

"Thank you. I'm looking forward to it." While it would be interesting, it was mostly because I'd get her all to myself. I loved the others in my pack, but Evan could be quite possessive.

"The flowers are here for you to take home. The delivery is also set to arrive this evening. Interesting choice for a courting gift," she added from the doorway.

"Oh, it's just the beginning." I smiled. Grace's injuries put a hitch in some of my plans. Of course, she couldn't use this gift yet either, but considering Wes hadn't gotten one for her, I thought it would be a good choice.

Ribbing Wes was always an enjoyable pastime.

Mrs. K beamed at me. "I know you loved Elaris. You always will. But I'm happy that you've found Grace."

"Me, too." It was time. "Thank you for your help. Do you have weekend plans?"

"The grandchildren are coming to visit. Don't stay too late." With a wave, she closed my door.

While I didn't plan on staying long, I'd get done faster if people stopped bothering me.

I entered the kitchen, holding the flowers. Delicious smells greeted me, and I waved at Jett and Riley as they cooked.

Upstairs, I heard laughing. Brennan and Grace sat at the piano. Her wrist was in her lap, and it looked like she was using her good hand to play one part of the piece, and Brennan was trying to play the other. I think they were playing Kirkokov's 4th.

"Bravo," I praised them when they stopped. That was one way to play the piano.

"Yes, we're off to the concert hall." Grace looked over at me and gave me a huge smile.

Oh, how I loved those sunshine smiles.

Coming over to the piano, I handed her the flowers with a little flourish.

"For me?" She clutched the flowers, eyes almost tearing.

"Yes, Darling. I have something special coming for you later." I put a hand on her shoulder.

"You do?" Grace beamed as she leaned into my touch.

I couldn't wait to spend more time with her. To see what she liked and didn't.

"Everything is set for the PIIP symposium," I added.

"I'm so excited." Her eyes lit up with delight as she wrapped her arms around me. "I've already emailed Dr. Harlowe so I can get to see the particle cutter while we're there."

"This is it then?" Wes appeared, eyeing the flowers.

"He got me flowers." Grace held them out. "Will you put them in water for me so Bren and I can finish playing? Please."

"Of course. It's almost time to eat, so finish up." Stealing a kiss, Wes took the flowers and went downstairs.

I got changed, and the seven of us sat down for dinner in the dining room, with the flowers I gave Grace in the center of the table.

Brennan reported that the police had closed the investigation against us as a pack. Grace was excited about her new job. Evan was planning a summer vacation for the pack. Inspections on Brennan's new project were going well.

The queen mum wasn't happy with us. So far, the only fallout was that we were no longer invited to the next one of her functions and Katie was being pulled as our forced-upon legal counsel.

More would be coming, surely.

As we finished dinner, my phone beeped. Perfect timing.

"Grace, Darling?" I asked. "Would you please come outside with me? Your present is here."

"Of course." She stood, eyes alight with curiosity.

Riley perked and gave me a sly look. "You got Grace a present? What *kind* of present."

I took her hand and planted a kiss on the back of it. "Grace, I would very much like to court you. While I have many things planned for us, I thought I'd start with this. Even if you have to wait a bit to use it."

"Spencer." Her voice went breathy as I led her out to the driveway.

"Spencer Thanukos?" the delivery driver asked.

"That's me." I signed for it, and he took the motorcycle off the truck.

"This is for me? This is so beautiful. I've never had anything so nice." Grace ran her hand over the handlebars of the omega-sized green and black motorcycle, complete with a detachable sidecar.

Relief at her liking it sluiced over me. While I'd seen the types she'd been looking at with Evan, this wasn't exactly those. I'd chosen this particular model for the safety rating.

"The sidecar is for Wes?" Riley teased, joining Grace.

"I won't fit in that." Wes joined us, eyeing the sidecar.

"I was thinking it might be more for you, Ri. Something about you two running off and causing mischief?" I grinned at Riley. The sidecar was a custom addition, but I had a feeling it would be a good choice. It would be beneficial for the two of them to spend time together.

Riley gave me a fist bump. "I like the way you think."

Wes scowled at me. "This is how it's going to be?"

I wrapped my arms around Grace, knowing he spoke with annoyance, not anger, and smirked at him. "Something about snoozers and losers?"

"You did not," Jett said as he came out with Brennan. He immediately went to the motorcycle and inspected it, pointing things out to both Grace and Riley.

"She's a little beauty. How did you even get one of these? The waiting list is huge, and I didn't know they even made them in omega-size." Brennan stood with me and Wes.

"I have connections." Money talked. I ordered a matching one for myself, though it hadn't arrived yet.

"That's adorable. And small. I'm surprised a sidecar even fits." Evan put an arm around Wes.

A very limited number of companies made omega-sized motorcycles. Most alphas just had their omegas ride with them.

Jett looked over at me. "This is perfect for her. After her wrist and foot heal, of course."

Which was why Wes and Evan hadn't gotten one for her yet. But again, snoozers, losers. This was, after all, something *she* wanted.

I came up behind her, breathing in her peachy scent. "Do you like it?"

"Spencer, it's perfect." She leaned up to kiss me.

I leaned down to take the offered kiss. My lips brushed hers, and she hungrily met mine. Her arms wrapped around me, and I deepened the kiss, a moan escaping her lips. I broke it off before I tossed her over my shoulder and brought her up to my room.

Not tonight. But I'd take more kisses. Certainly, I'd enjoy the game as long as she did.

"I'm so glad you like it." I gave her a softer, gentler kiss, pleased that I had made the right choice.

"Hurry up and heal so we can take this everywhere. I'm so excited." Riley bounced around.

"You accept my gift?" I added.

She looked up at me with her big blue-grey eyes. "I accept."

"Perfect." I ran my fingers through her hair. "So perfect."

This was going to be fun. I couldn't wait.

Chapter Sixty-Three

Grace

"All packed?" Evan squeezed my hand as we drove through the familiar streets to the house, the radio playing softly.

"I think so." I'd gone with Evan to the Center for another check-up to make sure my wrist and foot were healing right. That and to talk with the doctor about Evan's heat, my nervousness, and what to expect if I ended up participating.

I'd gone away with reassurance, information, and a little treasure chest of things, including those green fizzies that made your squishy parts feel better.

Tomorrow, after Riley went to the airport, the pack would head up to Evan's cabin.

"We're going to have a great time. Jett's got a hike planned. We'll go out on the boat, and we'll roast marshmallows. I'm sure Spencer has some things planned for you and him, and remember, you can join us *anytime*. If you do, you can leave at *any time*. If you don't join us, *it's fine*," he added.

That's what I was most nervous about, because even after watching the modules on heat and a whole lot of heat porn this past week, I didn't truly know what to expect.

But overall, I was pretty excited.

"Spence will give you all the sex, anyway." Evan grinned at me and waggled his eyebrows.

I smacked his arm lightly. "Evan."

"Sleep with him already, I know you want to." He laughed.

Oh, I did. I planned on it. We hadn't actually slept together yet. There had been lots of kissing and cuddling since he'd given me the motorcycle last week.

"I sort of like this whole proper gentleman old-fashioned taking-his-sweet-time thing he's doing." My head ducked as I grinned, wondering what it would be like to slide down on his knot.

"Stop with the lust. Or I'm going to toss you in the back seat." Evan play-shoved me as he turned the corner.

"Sorry, not sorry." I stuck out my tongue at him.

Evan, Wes, and I had been feeling each other more and more. It was reassuring, not intrusive. Teasing Evan with sexy feelings was half the fun.

We went into the house. In the kitchen, Jett, Riley, and Brennan were making dinner. Which was an adorable sight.

My family. This was *my family.*

And I couldn't be happier.

"You're all packed and set?" Evan put his arm around Riley's waist. She was going off to the Pacific Northwest, where her oldest sister was dean of a school. Their other sister, who was in nursing school, was joining them and they had a lot of fun things planned.

"Yep. All packed." She looked at her phone. "Wow. Look at Rose go. This is part of the dance team's routine for the talent show."

I watched the clip where Rose did a complex combination into an aerial flip, and another of a perfect arabesque.

"She's so good. Is this something we can go to? We should support her." Especially because she took the whole thing with her uncle trying to break into her school–and shoot Evan–hard. None of this was her fault, and I hoped it was all resolved soon.

"We can," Evan told me. "The Finchley talent show is always a good time."

"Evan, please set the table," Jett asked as he went to the fridge.

"Grace, Kari Jaroff is going to be performing a night of Volkov for charity at the Performing Arts Center next month. Would you like to attend with me?" Brennan asked, giving my arm a light touch. "You know, so you can hear how it's played properly." He grinned.

"I'd love that. It sounds fun." I had no idea who the performer was, but why not? It was nice of him to think of me.

I went upstairs. Before I could reach the third floor, arms wrapped around my waist, and I leaned into Spencer.

"Hi." I tilted my head up, inhaling his leather goodness. Yeah, I was going to hit that sometime this week.

He planted a light kiss on my nose. "Deb is very impressed with you."

"I'm so glad." I'd been nervous about meeting with the head of special projects.

"I'm looking forward to this coming week." He pressed me to him, and I melted into his arms.

"Me, too." I leaned up to kiss him again. "I'm going to put my bag away." And trade out the big, clunky removable walking cast for the smaller one I wore around the house.

In my room, I traded out the cast, then went over the list of what I needed for the week one last time. Evan and Wes had gotten me a couple of new things for the trip–and I'd gotten new clothes for my job. I couldn't wait to use the math messenger bag Evan had gotten me for my birthday.

Wes stood in the doorway. "I'm so happy that you're coming with us."

Lots of love and reassurance came through the bond. I went over to him and threw myself into his arms, careful of my braced wrist.

"Wes, I'm nervous." I closed my eyes and grounded myself in his heartbeat. "At the same time, I appreciate how far we've all come."

I was also very curious and had let Evan tell me some of his fantasies.

The one where I was the filling between him and Jett seemed doable. Especially if we were all high on pheromones.

"If you end up deciding to wait until it's almost done, that's fine, too. Your entertaining Evan means I might be able to sneak away for a shower." Wes kissed the top of my head.

He went to move, but I wrapped my arms around him. Ever since my fall, I had wanted to be held. All the time.

"I've got you." Wes held me tight, sending out reassurance through the bond.

"Okay." I snuggled into him.

"We all have you. Even though I'll be upstairs during his heat, I've still got you. If you need me, find me. It will end with you being fucked, but you're probably finding me for that, anyway." He gave me a heated look.

Yeah, I'd been needing that, too.

"Do you need a little something now?" he whispered.

"I think I do."

Wes closed the door and picked me up like a princess and laid me down on the daybed. Slowly, he took off the clothes I'd just put on.

Stripping off his clothes, he jumped on top of me. Giggles escaped my lips as he covered my naked body with kisses, getting all my ticklish spots.

He licked my pussy and growled a little. "Sorry, I'm famished."

With a grin, he pushed my legs open further and feasted on me, getting all the right spots with his tongue.

"Wes." I tangled my hands in his hair.

Two fingers slid inside me and pumped as he continued to tease me with his tongue.

"I'm going to come," I breathed. He flicked my clit with his tongue and my body exploded.

Wes cuddled me to him. "Mmmm, I love that–and I love you, Peaches."

"I love you, too. Do we have time to make love before dinner?" I rubbed my legs together.

"No, you do not." Evan stood in the doorway between my room and his, well, our, bathroom. "Fuck her after dinner. It's time to eat."

"O-kay." I kissed Wes again and put my clothes back on.

"Maybe I'll join you." Evan kissed me.

Wes took my hand, and we went downstairs and all sat around the table together. Tonight's dinner was some sort of saucy chicken dish, mashed potatoes, and roast vegetables.

Riley bubbled over, excited about seeing her sisters and all the fun things they had planned for their spring break trip.

"Guess what? The estate is mine. Renovations are going to start soon." Brennan took a sip of his drink.

"I can't wait to see it." Evan leaned over and kissed him. "Summer vacation is booked."

"I'm excited to learn to scuba." Riley took a bite of potatoes.

"Me, too," I agreed. It was something that always sounded interesting, but I'd never had the opportunity to learn.

"Also..." Brennan got an intense look on his face. "Once we talked about a pack last name. I was wondering if that was something we still wanted to consider. Obviously, no one would have to take it, but I..."

A huge grin spread across Jett's face. "Honey, I'm so proud of you. You're ready to do this and tell your mom to screw it?"

"This would be a pack decision, since there might be fallout. We won't vote yet, but I want everyone to think about it. Also, we could have a pack name or a last name without going nuclear on my mother–and vice versa," Brennan said as he took another bite of chicken.

"Can our last name have *fuck* in it?" Riley stuffed an entire roll in her mouth.

Brennan's eyebrows rose. "Probably not, but I'm open to suggestions."

"I think it's time," Spencer agreed, taking a sip of wine.

"I'm all for it," Wes said as Evan gave Brennan a kiss.

A knock on the front door made Brennan frown.

"Three guesses that it's Mrs. Beekman coming for a surprise inspection before we leave." Jett rolled his eyes.

"Mrs. Beekman's just doing her job. Well and thoroughly," Evan replied.

I took my phone out of my pocket to see if there'd been a message, but there was nothing other than a note to enjoy my week away and that we'd meet again when I got back. Huh. I put it back in my pocket.

"I'll get it." Spencer stood and left the dining room.

"Make sure everything gets on the family calendar," Brennan directed. "Grace, that includes anything for your work. Riley, that includes all of your summer plans."

"Grace." Spencer stood in the doorway, distress on his face. His voice broke. "Grace."

My heart fell at his expression. "What's wrong?"

Spencer's arms wrapped around me as he buried his face in my hair. "Grace."

"Who are you and why are you in my house?" Brennan growled as an unfamiliar scent entered the room.

"Do you have to take her? I promise, she did nothing wrong." Spencer's voice was panicked.

My belly dropped. *No. No. No.* Not now. There's only one thing it could be. Tears pricked my eyes as I clung to Spencer.

"Dr. Ellington, it's time to go," the male voice said.

They found me. I really had done something wrong, and the temporal police had come for me. Fear sliced through me.

"What do you mean you have to take her?" Riley's voice rose. "She didn't do anything wrong, you moron."

I kissed Spencer. Pulled myself away, I kissed Wes, savoring the feel of his tongue, the taste of his lips, blood roaring in my ears.

While I knew this was a possibility, I hadn't expected it to happen so soon. Or at all.

"Grace, what's happening?" Wes frowned, worry coming through the bond.

"Do I have to? It was an accident, I'm sorry, I..." My voice shook.

This was when I died. They were going to take me away and kill me. Just like Spencer's dad.

"Dr. Ellington, we need to go. Please don't make this difficult." The agent was nondescript, but very stern, and wearing a black suit—exactly what you'd expect from some secret interdimensional agency.

"I love you. I'll love you until the end of the universe." Tears pricked my eyes as I kissed Wes again, the last kiss I'd ever get from him. Trying to memorize his face, his touch, before I left him forever.

At least I got this time with him. At least I now know he's real.

I went over to Evan as I squished my face to his, grateful I'd gotten to know him as well. "I love you, too." Biting my lower lip,

I looked at everyone. "I love you all so much." The tears streamed down my face.

Never would I see them again. But it was worth it. Finding Wes. Meeting the rest of the pack. Being part of their family even though it was only for a short time.

"Will someone tell me what is going on? Who are you? You can't just come in and take her." Brennan stepped menacingly toward the unnamed agent.

"I assure you, I can and will. Dr. Ellington, we must go. Please don't be difficult." His voice, and expression, weren't mean. But they weren't kind either.

"I'll love you to the end of the universe, too. But what's happening?" Wes grabbed my hand.

"Wes, you need to let her go." Spencer's voice went firm. "I'll explain later."

I started to sob as I followed him to the door. There was no point in resisting.

"She isn't even wearing shoes. Fuck." Riley ran after us. "Let her stay."

He was already opening the door. I put on a sandal from the rack by the door. Slipping under his arm, Riley tried to block his path. There was probably no time to get my other cast, or my purse.

"I'm sorry, but we need to go." He sidestepped her.

"Don't take her away," Riley begged, hugging me.

"You need to go inside. It is for the better," I told her, giving her a hug. "I knew this could happen. I love you, too, Ri."

"Ri, please come inside," Spencer told her from the doorway.

Evan hugged me. "I love you."

Riley continued to rant at him as Spencer brought her inside.

"Jett... Bren... I'm so sorry." I didn't know what else to say.

"We must go," the agent told me, taking my arm and dragging me toward a waiting black car not quite like anything I'd seen.

"Please let me stay, I did nothing wrong," I sobbed as he opened the car door and pushed me in the front seat. A whine escaped my lips. "I'm sorry. I don't even remember, I'm so sorry. Let me go."

Something pricked my neck, and he shut the door, climbed into the front seat and drove off. My hand went to my neck. "Ow."

"Grace." Wes ran after the car.

I tried to open the door, and it was locked.

"Let me go. I'm happy here. I won't do anything, I promise," I pounded on the window. Wes' face, the emotions through the bond, they all broke my heart.

All of them were becoming something I hadn't had in a long time. A family.

The agent's hand shot out in front of me as he opened the glove compartment. Taking out a small bottle, he shoved it into my hand. "Drink this, it will help. Hold on."

He pushed the center of the steering wheel, and for a moment all the breath left my body, and it felt as if I was on a rollercoaster, plunging down a steep drop.

The bottom fell out of my stomach as everything outside my window streaked for a moment, then turned back to the city.

But this wasn't anywhere I'd been before. The car drove quickly, making sharp turns. All I could do was to try not to vomit.

"I'm sorry, but we have no time," he said as we squealed to a stop. "Come on."

He vaulted out of the car and opened my door.

"Here." The man put a hat on my head and shoved sunglasses on my face, dragging me out of the car. "You need to drink that. It will help," he said as he pushed me into an elevator, which was dark and janky.

"What's happening? Who are you? I..." My chest shook, but I opened the bottle and chugged the contents. It was sweet, like the fake fruit juice we used to drink at vacation bible school.

The door opened, and he dragged me out into a hall, which felt sterile, like we were in a police station. Which we probably were.

Vertigo struck me as my head exploded with pain. He had my arm in a vice grip and didn't stop moving.

"It's going to be fine," he said as I whimpered, my vision going black.

"There she is. Finally. Where were you hiding her?" another voice said, heels clicking on the floor. Their scent was overwhelming, like a department store perfume counter.

The pain hurt too much to open my eyes, but we were still moving, and the feeling like I was going to be sick didn't subside. I took a deep breath. *3.14159265359.*

"Doesn't matter," he snapped. "Don't trust anyone. Don't mention where you were," he murmured in my ear.

"She's not even prepped. I need to hear her statement first. What is she wearing?" she added, clearly unamused.

"We've got to bring her now or they're going to call it," he retorted.

The vertigo and blackness passed as we came to a halt. I opened my eyes as we stood in front of guarded, double doors. Blood roared in my ears as my knees went weak. Was this where I was going to be tried? Did I get a lawyer? What was wrong with my dress? *79323846264*

"She'll be fine." He turned to the guard. "Let us in."

The doors opened. It was clearly some sort of courtroom, though sterile and surreal, like from a futuristic movie.

The man, Weigmier, put his hand on the small of my back, pushing me into the room, as he took the hat and glasses he'd had me wearing.

What was going on? I took a deep breath. *3383279502.*

"Just be truthful and tell them everything you remember," he murmured, giving me another little push.

It was as if a switch went on in my head, and everything became illuminated with a blinding intensity.

"Yes, sir." My voice shook as I trembled, looking at the stern judge who beckoned me to what was most likely the stand. There were a lot of people.

Including some that looked familiar–and seemed *very* unhappy with me.

My head buzzed and my heart thumped so hard I thought it might leap out of my chest.

I sucked in another deep breath, completely losing track as to what place of Pi I was on. Because I remembered.

I remembered everything.

...to be continued in Dream Mates (Into the Parallel Omegaverse, Book Two)

Glossary of Select Terms

<u>Designations</u>

Alpha: Larger, faster, and with better senses, they make up about a quarter of the population. Their barks and pheromones can influence people. Male alphas have knots, female alphas have locks. Their scent holds a distinctive note that marks them as alpha. Female alphas can carry children.

Beta: They make up over half of the population and are your average ordinary people. Like the other designations, they can have kids, join or form packs, and an alpha can mate with them. They don't have knots and can't bond people, just accept them.

Gamma: Medical designation for a specific type of 'failed' omegas. While sometimes a genetic switch is thrown, halting development, most of the time it is environmental. Something is so dangerous in their environment that the body declares it unsafe to become an omega and halts a genetic process. These are called *textbook* gammas. Gammas can have many omega traits, but it varies from person to person, and is often proportional to how close they were to becoming an omega. Gammas rarely respond to barks, pheromones, or danger the way omegas do. Common causes of gammas are war, famine, extreme poverty, and asshole parents, and not as common as they used to be.

Delta: They have a lot of alpha characteristics–especially in regard to size, speed, and senses. They make excellent soldiers and security. They're rarer than the 'big three' designations (alpha/beta/omega) but much more common than any of the rarer designations.

Digamma: Essentially, Digammas are 'failed' alphas. Something is so dangerous in their environment that the body declares it unsafe to become an alpha and halts a genetic process. Exceedingly rare to the point where not much is known about them.

Zeta: Sometimes a genetic anomaly creates a designation that is a cross between an alpha and omega, some of them can even switch between the two. Like gammas, each zeta is a little different. Incredibly rare and coveted.

Kappa: The life of the party, they're usually adrenaline junkies with poor decision-making skills. They're an extremely rare designation because they've almost chaosed themselves out of existence.

Theta: Thetas tend to be misanthropic loners who like to amass wealth. While they do mate and form packs, they often aren't with alphas as they don't like to be told what to do. They wanted to be needed but don't like to be smothered. They're closer to alphas than betas. A rare designation.

Iota: A rare designation, Iotas don't have scents, they also can't smell other scents and don't respond to barks or pheromones. This can be dangerous because they can't catch the scent-cues other designations can. Because they can't be barked or influenced, some iotas think they're better than other designations. They're closer to betas genetically.

Omicron: Omicrons are charming and charismatic, but are conceited and don't think the rules apply to them. They want to take over the world and fix it, and aren't afraid to use violence, which has caused this designation, which is an alpha mutation, to be declared illegal. While they often can pass as alphas, because of their size, strength, and speed, and that they smell enough like an alpha, they lack knots/locks. Often, they test as alphas when young.

Rho: Medical designation for a feral alpha.

Sigma: Often loners with anger issues, they tend to commit crimes to punish people. They don't want to be part of the system, and generally think it's bullshit. Even though it's an extremely rare designation, and an alpha mutation, they're illegal. While they often can pass as alphas, because of their size, strength, and speed, and that they smell enough like an alpha, they lack knots/locks. Often, they test as alphas when young.

Tau: Medical designation referring to someone who lost their bonded scent match, also known as *soulbroke* and *shadow*.

Phi: A rare super-mutation of alpha and illegal. While they can be a loner like sigmas, they can also be fun like kappas, and even charismatic like an omicron. They can become violent and aggressive. Unlike the others, they can more easily hide among alphas, because males have a bulb that can pass as a slightly-deformed knot and their smell is often undistinguishable. Commonly, they test as alphas when young and have the size/strength/speed of an alpha. It is thought that Phis were created for battle long ago and it went horribly terribly wrong.

Omega: One of the three main designations, omegas are usually smaller than the other designations and tend to be nurturers and caregivers. They're the most physically compatible with alphas, so they're often sought after as mates, even though they make up less than ten percent of the population. They can and do partner with other designations. Omegas have the same rights as everyone else. They have an extra element to their scent that marks them as such. They can create and accept bonds, though they don't leave a mark behind. Omega males are very good at making children.

Other Terms

Alpha-Blockers: A type of medication that dulls alpha senses and instincts. It's most commonly prescribed to violent alphas, young alphas who aren't in full control, and criminals. There's a huge stigma on them, so many who should take them, don't.

Awakened/Blossomed: When someone fully comes into their designation after puberty.

Bond Test: A government test used to detect an alpha-omega bond.

Designation: The term used to indicate someone's specific genetic dynamic. The three main designations are alpha, beta, and omega. Other designations exist, including ones that are considered illegal.

Equalist: Someone who believes that designations should not be used so that could be on equal terms.

Fundie/Fundamental: Someone who believed that packs are about population control and the stripping of rights by the government. They think that every alpha has the right to their own omega, even though it is statistically impossible. They often keep to themselves and usually don't take part in government services or programs or go to hospitals.

Heat: An omegas fertile cycle, which results in wanting sexual attention and satisfaction from their alphas and partners. Female omegas often have four to five heats a year; male omegas have two or three. Heats can last from a couple of days to a week.

Heat Spike: A quick rise in hormones, often right before a heat, that result in temporary heat-like symptoms.

Heat Suppressants: A type of medication some omegas take so that they don't go into heat. Heat suppressants are completely legal, though prolonged use can have side effects.

Mate Bond: The connection that forms when certain designations bite another in a certain way where proteins are released into their bloodstream creating a chemical reaction. Some bonds, like alpha-omega, have legal implications. Not all designations can make or accept bonds.

Mega-push: A street drug that can 'push' certain betas over to being an omega and often used in human trafficking. A legal version is available but highly regulated.

Omega Center: Omega Centers offer services ranging from healthcare and pack matching, to education and housing. Omegas don't have to register with the Center, but once registered can use their services, including having an advocate–an assigned social worker that guides them through the process and helps them understand all their options.

Oxotipoline/Eazy-E: A sedative commonly used in human trafficking. The designer version, Eazy-E, is sometimes used by sexual predators.

Prick-Test: A simple blood test used to test for the three main designations–alpha, beta, and omega. All children are tested in middle school. The test is mostly accurate, but not always. It doesn't test for rare or illegal designations.

Scent-Blockers: A type of medication omegas take to blend in/function in society. These range from light scent-blockers that simply dull an omega's distinctive scent to heavy duty ones that lock down both omega scent and instincts, enabling them to hide as a beta. All are completely legal but can be hard for hidden omegas to get. Prolonged use, especially of the heavy-duty blockers, can make them lose their effectiveness and/or cause health issues.

Scent-Match/Soulmate: That perfect match between two people—usually an alpha and omega. They usually know it by smell. Scent-matches are rare and plenty of people have happy and long relationships without being scent-matches. Sometimes scent-matches dream of each other, but that's mostly in books and movies. A scent match can be 'lopsided' when it is not alpha/omega, usually where one becomes an alpha/omega and the other stays a beta. A 'deadmatch' occurs when a couple would have been a scent match if they had been an alpha and an omega but instead both stayed betas.

Shadow: A term for someone who has lost their bonded scent match, also called *soulbroke*. The medical term is *Tau*.

Spiral: Dangerous drop in omega hormones which can result in unconsciousness, irrational behavior, and/or hospitalization. Often a trauma response.

Trevadol: A commonly prescribed anti-depressant. One side effect is that it can mess with the basic prick-test. This isn't considered much of an issue because this drug is for adults, and once the prick-test is given in middle school it isn't usually given again without reason. Some hidden omegas take the drug solely as a precaution because of that specific side effect,

Ultra-bullet: Super-fast train that can turn an hours-long drive into moments.

Un-Bonding: The chemical process of dissolving a mate bond. It's governed by an extensive legal process to make sure that it is not abused.

About Jane Handler

Jane Handler is the author of why choose omegaverse romance, including the HockeyVerse series. A hopeless romantic, Jane grew up reading romance and often got them taken away by her teachers for reading during class. Now she writes why choose, romance. When not writing, she's camping, eating sushi, doing laundry, or binge watching TV.